MY FIRST
TWO THOUSAND YEARS

MY FIRST
TWO THOUSAND YEARS

THE AUTOBIOGRAPHY OF
THE WANDERING JEW

GEORGE SYLVESTER VIERECK

AND PAUL ELDRIDGE

SHERIDAN HOUSE

This edition published 2001 by
Sheridan House Inc.
145 Palisade Street
Dobbs Ferry, NY 10522

Library of Congress Cataloging-in-Publication Data

Viereck, George Sylvester, 1884-1962.
     My first two thousand years: the autobiography of the
     wandering Jew / George Sylvester Viereck and Paul Eldridge.
          p.cm
ISBN 978-1-57409-128-1 (pbk : alk. paper)
  1. Wandering Jew—Fiction. 2. Reincarnation—Fiction.
3. Compulsive behavior—Fiction. I. Eldridge, Paul, 1888- II. Title.

PS3543.I32 M89 2001
813'.52—dc21
                                             00-066182

Printed in the United States of America

ISBN 978-1-57409-128-1

TO
GRETCHEN
AND
SYLVETTE

CONTENTS

PROLOGUE: MOUNT ATHOS

THE AUTOBIOGRAPHY OF MR. ISAAC LAQUEDEM

xi

EPILOGUE: MOUNT ATHOS

PROLOGUE
MOUNT ATHOS

I

THE SEVEN PLOVERS

THE sun hurled spears of fire at the golden cross crowning the marble peak of Mount Athos.

Suddenly the flaming glory was darkened by the shadows of seven black-breasted plovers hovering for a moment, as if in deliberation, over the ivy-crowned tower of the monastery, and vanishing with a shrill cry.

"What an unearthly sound!" exclaimed Aubrey Lowell.

"Their screams," remarked his companion, a German of colossal stature, "echo the sounds of the battle-fields over which they have flown."

"It is incomprehensible to me by what subterranean channels the Holy Fathers keep in touch with the outside world, in times such as these," Aubrey remarked.

"Not many months ago," Professor Bassermann replied, dropping his voice to a whisper, "a mutiny against the Government broke out on a Russian warship. Eluding the Grand Fleet, at least thirty of the officers and the men landed, no one knows where. A little later thirty newcomers, holy hermits, no doubt, sought refuge in one of the monasteries."

"I presume," Aubrey said, "the Holy Fathers were not pleased by this invasion."

"The Holy Fathers," Professor Bassermann continued, "are desperately afraid of being drawn into a political controversy, and are in mortal terror of the long arm of the Czar, and of the Kaiser. It is fortunate that our diplomatic friend in Constantinople secured an introduction to Father Ambrose for us. In such perilous times every traveler is subject to suspicion and may be denied an asylum. Fate was in an ironical mood when she tempted us to go globe-trotting during a World War. Who knows how long we may be compelled to wait here, until we receive our visa!"

"Meanwhile," Aubrey said, "we can probe the mysteries of the place. I am sure every shrine has its secrets. In every fold of the altar cloth rustles a century. Even in the sunshine, the ghosts of past generations seem to wander about."

"You are in a mood for fantasy, my friend," replied the other.

"In a spot where for twelve centuries men's minds have dwelt upon the eternal, everything seems to glow with hidden significance. Here all things are possible."

Their ears caught the rustling of wings overhead. Once more a shadow flitted over the landscape.

"What is that?" asked Basil Bassermann.

"Plovers—seven plovers. This is the second time they have flown over the belfry."

"You counted them?"

"Yes, and I counted seven," Aubrey remarked. "The very atmosphere admits of no other number."

"Superstition is a form of atavism to which all minds are subject. Even my blood," Professor Bassermann conceded somewhat ponderously, "feels the dust of ages rising from all these ancient objects."

"What a confession for the foremost scientist of Harvard!" Aubrey taunted the old professor. "You know," he added after a pause, knitting his brow to recapture a thought, "I have studied the history of superstition a little. There is an ancient story about seven plovers. The seven soldiers who assisted at the crucifixion were transformed into plovers, doomed to circle the sky forever."

"Perhaps it means that we shall never get our visa," Professor Bassermann remarked with a wry face. "Are your sacred fowls harbingers of evil? Our old peasants always say that plovers prophesy rain."

"They foretell something. What it is, however, has for the moment escaped me."

He nervously passed his hand through his hair.

"We are both tired and overwrought from travel," Professor Bassermann interjected. "There is a tension in the air which affects even me. Surely of all places this must be the very hotbed of superstition. By the way, do you know that Father Ambrose, as soon as he divests himself of his stole, is a remarkable psychologist? Most of the monks here are crude and ignorant, but he has studied the library of Mount Athos, the oldest in the world, and is acquainted with the history of mental science from Aristotle to Freud. You will probably find that many of your ideas are in sympathy with his. He is a mystic."

"What is a mystic, Professor?"

"You're half a mystic. A part of your brain is open to the lantern of knowledge, but there are dark alleys in those gray convolutions that shut themselves stubbornly to facts."

"To facts, perhaps, not to truth."

"Truth is based on facts, Aubrey. There can be no valid truth outside of human experience."

"I," Aubrey replied, "seek a reconciliation between the miraculous and science, between the revealed and the unrevealed mysteries."

"*Ignoramus, Ignorabimus,*" Professor Bassermann sighed. "We know not, and we shall not know. We can cut up a body or dissect a nerve, but the vital essence eludes us forever. Yet very likely your seven fowls presage some mysterious visitor or some startling event. While we are chatting aimlessly, the belligerents are upsetting the map of Europe."

"The peak on which we are standing has seen many revolutions of the wheel of fate. If only," Aubrey remarked dreamily, "the rock could speak, what marvelous tales it could unfold! Inanimate stones would be more eloquent than the camera, if we only knew the secret that loosens their tongues."

"Meanwhile we must depend upon annals written by man," Bassermann drily insisted.

"Man could tell more than the stone if he were able to release the race memory that survives in the primordial cell. Forever dividing, but never perishing, it is his nearest approach to immortality."

"I am afraid, my dear Aubrey, that is a task that even your master Freud would hardly dare undertake. But we don't need psychoanalysis to tell us that all religions and superstitions from remotest antiquity merge in this remarkable promontory."

Professor Bassermann pointed to the left, his firm stumpy fingers revealing his grasp on reality. "There lies the plain of Troy, where the wrath of Achilles shook the tents of the Greeks. This soil has drunk the blood of Patroclus and the tears of Priam. These clouds have beheld the face of Helen. And here," pointing to the right, "Mount Olympus rises defiantly into the air."

"How wonderful!" the younger man exclaimed. "If we stray through the orchard, we may come unawares upon some god in exile. Perhaps the pagan gods profess Christianity. Perhaps they dwell in one of the twenty monasteries, bending knee in the daytime to the ritual of the Greek Church. But at night, when no one can spy upon them, they throw the monk's gown from their lovely bodies and celebrate again the Eleusinian mysteries."

"What a pretty fancy! You should be a poet, not a neurologist. We have by no means exhausted the history of this unique place. Down below, there are still traces of a ship canal built by Xerxes. To the Greeks this promontory was known as Acte."

"And over there?"

Aubrey pointed to a high mountain grown with tall, somber trees.

Both were too much engrossed in their conversation to notice the approach of Father Ambrose. They were startled when a deep melodious voice, giving to the English something of the honied inflexion of Homer's heroes, replied: "That is the mountain where Christ was tempted."

Father Ambrose crossed himself in the Greek fashion from rignt to left as he uttered the holy name. A few white locks saved from the shears crowned his fine head with an aureole of silver.

Professor Bassermann eyed the old monk curiously, making some mental notes for his next book on the psychology of faith. His own immense head loomed like a dome consecrated to some skeptical deity. His eyes probed, but not unkindly, men's brains like the little lanterns with which a surgeon illuminates the cavities of the body. Hair, once blond, still struggled to exist. Mental concentration had devastated his scalp as the tonsure had robbed Father Ambrose.

Almost boyish in contrast with his two companions, Aubrey Lowell, lithe-limbed, keen, reluctant locks brushed back, still stared at the legendary mountain top where Jesus wrestled with himself. Over his blue eyes, penetrant, analytical though they were, spread the mist of a dream.

"By the way, Father Ambrose," Professor Bassermann questioned, "what is your version of the story of the seven plovers? What is it that they foretell?"

Father Ambrose did not answer. In spite of the balmy weather, he drew his garments closer to his body. He shuddered and made the sign of the cross.

In a trice, without warning, the face of nature grew sullen. Black, angry mouths, the clouds swallowed up the sun. The air was dense with suppressed excitement. The wind howled through the long corridors and sobbed and whispered in the secret recesses of the cells. The chime of the Vesper bell flowed out into the infinite. The silver notes of the holy chant wrestled with the storm like ministering angels with Satan. At last the imps of Storm lay vanquished. The hurricane paused in its course to do reverence to God.

Suddenly, however, a terrific clap of thunder smote the sky. The holy chime of the bell broke off with a shrill dissonance. Demons seemed to people the belfry. Rain came down like a cataract. Flashes of lightning chased one another like battling fiery dragons. The bells jangled hideously out of tune. Unearthly noises, like a satanic parody of the holy sound that marks the elevation of the host, alarmed the ears of the horrified monks. It was as if a High Priest had suddenly gone mad in the midst of a sacred ceremony and interspersed the Lord's Prayer with unspeakable blasphemies.

Trembling but resolute, Father Ambrose seized a crucifix. In phalanx, as if for battle, the brethren followed him. Solemn, with gleaming eyes and trembling nostrils, the militant army of God swept up steep stairs mumbling the ritual of the Exorcism. Infected somewhat by the general hysteria, Aubrey followed. Professor Bassermann alone measured the situation with critical calm.

In the steeple the army paused. Father Ambrose stepped forward. "In the name of the Father, the Son and the Holy Ghost!" The monks crossed themselves. "If the spirits of the damned have entered, I bid them depart into the air whence they have come. He that has bound the Devil, shall He not vanquish his breed?"

Another thunder-clap. The bell resounded hoarsely like laughter from beyond the tomb.

"Courage, brethren!" the monk cried, seizing a candle with one hand and holding the cross like a sword with the other. The others followed behind him. In the flickering light, shadows swayed to and fro. From every corner of the attic, a demon seemed to grin. The darkness was haunted by a thousand malevolent voices. Aubrey's teeth chattered. His heart galloped against his ribs.

Again Father Ambrose raised his voice:

"In the thrice blessed name of Jesus Christ our Lord, I bid thee get hence, Satan! But if thou art the soul of a sinner roaming the earth without rest, know thou that there is peace for thee also in the infinite mercy of God and of his Mother the Blessed Virgin. But whoever thou art, depart and return not to vex pious souls!"

The Holy Prior continued to challenge the Evil One, and the holy fathers chanted the ancient hymns of the Church. The infernal artillery in the skies surrendered at last. The hoarse laughter in the belfry died in a sob.

The sun aureoled the sky once more. But the ancient bell of Saint Athanasius that had tolled the glory of Heaven for a thousand years was cracked. Never again would its voice resound in praise of the Father, the Son and the Holy Ghost.

In the blinding glare of the lightning and the final crash of the thunder-clap, unnoticed by anyone, a stranger had entered the monastery.

MR. ISAAC LAQUEDEM

TOWARD six o'clock the evening repast was served in a large rectangular hall. The stained glass of the large windows, wrought by monkish craftsmen, glorified the martyrs of the church. The table, made of precious oriental wood, was carved with the scene of the Last Supper. In the corners of the room images from the book of the Apocalypse grinned and stared ferociously at the diners. The walls were overdecorated in the manner of the later Greek artists, save one, at the head of the table. Upon it hung in severe simplicity, an immense black cross with the image of the Crucified, ghastly in its unredeemed whiteness. Every line of the body and of the head articulated nobility and sorrow.

Preceded by Father Ambrose, sixty monks filed into the hall, taking their accustomed seats at the table. Their step was light, their voices pitched to joy. The excitement of the afternoon was followed by the inevitable reaction. They were glad to be alive, glad to have thwarted the Evil One in the belfry.

Professor Bassermann and Aubrey Lowell occupied the seats of honor at the side of Father Ambrose. The former, calm, critical, undisturbed by the occurrences of the day, made additional mental memoranda for a new essay on religious hysteria, to be inscribed upon the cylinders of his dictograph which accompanied him on his journeys. Aubrey's nerves, however, were still atingle. Father Ambrose had informed him of a new arrival, a traveler from afar, who had also sought refuge in the monastery from the uncertainties of the World War, bringing excellent credentials from the prime ministers of several Balkan states and from Russia.

The newcomer was expected for the evening meal. He did not appear, however, until after the first course had been served.

Aubrey raised a goblet of precious Byzantine glass inlaid with gold, but his arm became paralyzed in mid air. He gazed aghast at the crucifix. Blood, redder than his wine, streamed from the five wounds of the Crucified! He looked at the monks. He expected to

15

hear an outburst of wailing and chanting and a rush to the altar, but neither Father Ambrose nor any of the brethren noticed the miracle. Their attention was engrossed in the sacrament of eating the delicate viands that were spread before them in the glittering plates of ancient design.

Aubrey touched nervously Professor Bassermann's elbow. The Professor followed the direction of his friend's eyes, but before he had adjusted his extraordinarily thick, heavy-rimmed spectacles, the blood had ceased to flow. The limbs of the Crucified gleamed white and ghastly as before.

Aubrey explained in a few words what he had seen. The Professor shook his head disapprovingly. He was not, however, totally disinterested. Aubrey's delusion—for he could not conceive it as anything else—presented a problem that arrested his mind for the moment. At the same time, he was disgruntled because he knew by unpleasant experience that mental exertion at meals interfered with metabolism. He looked around. His eyes fell upon the window behind him. The last rays of the setting sun, like long red needles, bent in the vain endeavor to pierce the pane.

"My dear friend, the sun is a sadist in his playful moods. His rays reopened the wounds of the Crucified!"

"So you think it was merely an optical illusion?" Aubrey exclaimed. "How fortunate that you were not a guest at the wedding feast of Canaan. One word from you would have changed the wine back into water!"

"I agree with you," the Professor replied. "An experienced hypnotist is not easily amenable to suggestion. Had I been one of the disciples, I should have seriously handicapped Christianity."

"But you *were* one of the disciples," said a pleasant voice, with just a touch of mockery, "and your name was Saint Thomas."

A tall young man, evidently a gentleman of leisure, with black hair neatly parted and large melancholy eyes, seated himself at the table.

"Mr. Laquedem," Father Ambrose introduced the stranger to his American guests.

"Pardon me," the newcomer remarked, "I could not help overhearing part of your conversation. You remind me of two figures in a painting of the Last Supper by a celebrated Russian. You, Professor, resemble his conception of Saint Thomas, whereas your friend suggests John the favorite disciple."

Suddenly, the oldest of the monks placed his hand upon his heart and screamed as if someone had stabbed him. His companions splashed wine over his face, rubbed his temples, fanned him. It was not easy to revive him. "It seemed," he whispered, "that I saw our Saviour nailed to the Cross a second time."

When quiet was restored, Aubrey and Bassermann studied the newcomer. Mr. Laquedem was a man of uncertain age. At the first glance, one would have taken him for thirty, but on closer scrutiny, one discovered lines incompatible with youth. The name was Semitic, but there was little of the Hebrew in his caste of countenance. Certain traces suggested the Spaniard; others, so Professor Bassermann insinuated, the Russian. His quick nervous movements, his voice when raised by excitement, little mannerisms almost too trifling to be noticed, seemed more Oriental than European. In certain moments, in certain moods, he was positively Assyrian. The secrets of Egypt seemed to slumber in his long lashes. His eyes changing color with his moods, were baffling. Now they flashed like the glint of a sword, now softening, they seemed to swim with tears like eyes of one who had seen the fall of Jerusalem.

"What is your country?" Professor Bassermann asked.

"You speak English like a native," interjected Aubrey.

"I am something of a linguist," the other smiled.

"You are a Russian, are you not?" Bassermann again insisted.

"Call me—a Cosmopolitan."

Isaac Laquedem toyed with the conversation. He tossed it like a ball into the air and caught it again unexpectedly with the skill of a juggler. He displayed a marvelous knowledge of out-of-the-way subjects. He spoke with such confidence of obscure authors and half forgotten periods of history that Aubrey, who listened fascinated, suspected him of being an imaginative and delightful liar rather than an erudite.

III

PROFESSOR BASSERMANN SUSPECTS

AFTER the repast, Father Ambrose invited the guests into his study, a room lighted with ancient candles in curious holders of bronze and precious wood. The tables were littered with yellow-tinted tomes in many languages. Parchments from Egypt brushed against the most recent treatises from the medical bookshops of Paris. The monk was acquainted with the revolutionary theories of the explorers of the unconscious,—Freud, Adler, and Jung.

Isaac Laquedem had retired to his room, but his valet, a young Japanese, brought with the compliments of his master, Russian cigarettes wrapped in silk, with the imperial initials.

"A brand manufactured especially for the Czar!" Professor Bassermann explained.

Aubrey lit one of the flavored cigarettes of the stranger. Curious Eastern visions rose out of the poppied smoke that curled in fantastic pillars, and colored his remarks to Bassermann and Father Ambrose.

The Japanese was patiently awaiting further orders. It was not clear whether the youth understood one word of the conversation. For a moment, an intolerably superior smile lit the wrinkles of his odd oriental mouth, but when Aubrey looked again, he saw merely a responsive servant. With a kind nod, Father Ambrose dismissed him, but Professor Bassermann, whose suspicions of the stranger had by no means been allayed, asked him whether he had traveled much with his master.

"Yes, sir," the valet grinned.

"Have you just come from St. Petersburg?"

"Yes, sir," the grin broadening to his ears.

"Do you like traveling?"

"Yes, sir."

"How old are you?"

"Yes, sir," very meekly.

Professor Bassermann suspected the lad was shamming. He asked other questions timing mentally the promptness of the response.. The Oriental, eluding the scholar's cunning psychological traps, withdrew respectfully, walking with his back toward the door. His step was noiseless, almost that of a cat. The three scholars were still discussing the valet, when Isaac Laquedem reappeared in a velvet smoking jacket. His eyes, a little cynical, a little sad, but shining with an almost uncanny luster, took in the situation.

"Kotikokura is very useful to me," he remarked nonchalantly. "I picked him up in the East some years ago."

"Does he speak English?" Professor Bassermann fired the question off like a shot.

"Perfectly."

Bassermann looked eloquently at Aubrey. Isaac Laquedem caught his glance.

"Like all Orientals, Kotikokura has learned the wisdom of silence. He notices everything. He has a marvelous memory, but he never reveals himself even to me. Even I do not know what slumbers in the sub-caverns of his mind."

"It is easy enough," Aubrey remarked, "to rob the brain of its secrets. Psychoanalysis is the key that unlocks the uttermost portals."

"I have read a library of psychoanalytic literature," Father Ambrose remarked, "but its practical application is not clear to me."

Aubrey Lowell explained Freud's theories and his technique. Laquedem listened with grave attention. "Every century or so," he remarked, "a new idea is discovered. To follow backward every thread in the tangled skein of one's existence, to detect the little flaws that mar the woof, must be a fascinating experience!"

"The unconscious mind," Aubrey added, "never forgets. The circumspect navigator sounding its secrets will find treasures as well as monsters in its mysterious depths. Every brain is a scroll scrawled over many times, but it is possible by patient analysis to decipher much, if not everything, that has gone before."

"Unless the tablet itself is destroyed, human ingenuity can extricate the meaning of the original record, irrespective of subsequent interlineations," Professor Bassermann remarked.

"Yes," Aubrey continued, inhaling the smoke of his cigarette voluptuously, "I believe that it is even possible to establish memory reaching beyond the confines of the life of the individual. What are instincts, but inherited race memories?"

"It is perfectly true," remarked Professor Bassermann, "that each organism carries within itself the history of its kind from the beginning of all life. But to attempt to conjure up the past stored in the memory cells smacks more of hocus-pocus than of science."

"Have you ever experimented in this direction?" Father Ambrose remarked.

"No," Aubrey replied, "psychoanalysis demands intense concentration. A perfect analysis, according to orthodox Freudians, requires three years. Even a preliminary sounding of the subconscious takes several months. Besides, the subject must be thoroughly in sympathy with the experiment."

"Time is heavy on your hands here," Father Ambrose added. "It will be weeks—maybe months—before you receive your visa. I am most anxious to be present at such an investigation. Even a preliminary study would be a fascinating experience. But where could we obtain a subject for the experiment?"

He unconsciously gazed at the stranger. Professor Bassermann caught the direction of his glance. He whistled softly to himself and then, as if seized by a sudden idea, he remarked: "Perhaps Mr. Laquedem would be willing to reveal his secrets to three stern priests of science?" His distrust of the stranger was evident in his words.

Isaac Laquedem smiled. "Professor Bassermann with the penetration of his remarkable mind has read my thoughts, for I was just about to volunteer my services."

IV

PROBERS OF THE SOUL

THE next morning at ten o'clock, Father Ambrose and Aubrey, assisted by Professor Bassermann, completed the preparations for their experiment. The library, always somber, was artificially darkened.

Chairs were so placed that the subject would gaze directly into the eyes of his questioner. Aubrey, Bassermann, and Father Ambrose were not concealed, for that would have distracted Isaac Laquedem's attention, but they were so placed as not to intrude themselves upon his field of vision.

Immediately facing Laquedem's chair, Professor Bassermann placed his traveling dictograph which, more precise than a stenographer, was to record every word that would escape the lips of the subject as well as every question of the scientific inquisition. On the table, near his chair, the Professor placed a chronometer that would register mechanically the time elapsing between question and answer. By this simple expedient, it would become evident if Laquedem was answering the questions in a straightforward manner or if he shammed. The least hesitation would be recorded instantly by a little curve.

Professor Bassermann also placed before him a gauge with a rubber tube to measure the pressure of the blood. Any emotion that conceals itself from the scrutiny of the closest observer is recorded in the pressure of the blood as it pounds from the heart to the brain. The terror that neither blanches nor reddens the cheek, the remembered lust, the mental strain recalled, but unuttered, appear in the lines of the psychologist's chart.

All these devices of science Professor Bassermann and Aubrey explained to Father Ambrose who, being familiar with the theory underlying the various laws, found it no difficult matter to appreciate the cunning of each delicate mechanism.

Isaac Laquedem appeared preceded by Kotikokura who carried

a box of cigars for his master with the same air of importance, as if he had been a court chamberlain bearing the crown jewels of a king. Laquedem was dressed in black. He was wearing his velvet smoking jacket which caressed his figure snugly. His hair, not brushed back as on previous occasions, betrayed a propensity toward curliness.

Kotikokura, an exaggerated imitation of his employer, affected the extreme London style of the period antedating the World War, trousers encircling tightly legs which to Aubrey remotely suggested something furtive and simian. His white vest and the rolled lapels of his coat served as an admirable frame for his yellow head. The cravat harmonized exquisitely with sleeve kerchief and socks. His manners were perfect and his carriage was modeled on that of Isaac Laquedem. He was a yellow caricature of his master.

At a word from Laquedem, the valet left. He was gone before one realized that the door had closed behind him. For a moment Aubrey had the weird impression that Kotikokura had crept out of the room on all fours.

Laquedem calmly lit a cigarette. He seated himself on one of the chairs sinking deeply into the velvet cushions and puffed little spirals of smoke to the ceiling.

Professor Bassermann commanded: "Relax! Relax entirely!"

"Are you going to hypnotize me?" Laquedem asked.

"No, I merely want to ease your mind. Imagine that you are going to sleep. Don't resist my questions. Answer spontaneously and say whatever comes into your head."

"But isn't that hypnotism?"

"No. You will presently fall into a state of repose resembling sleep; you will give me, so to speak, the key to your soul. I shall unlock door after door until I open the gate of the unconscious. But first, we must lull to sleep the inhibitions which are posted like sentries at the threshold of the conscious mind. No thought escapes unchallenged by them. Upon every shadow that leaves the caverns of the nether brain, they fasten a mask, to protect it from recognition before it can merge into consciousness."

He spoke slowly, monotonously, all the while gazing steadfastly into the calm eyes of Isaac Laquedem.

Professor Bassermann had hypnotized many people. It was his claim that every person was susceptible to hypnosis. But the quiet smile that quivered about the lips of the stranger rasped his sensitiveness. It had been his original intention to lull Laquedem into a mild state of semi-consciousness, but he now strained every nerve to impose his will upon the subject.

The Professor's face twitched with exertion. Beads of cold perspiration appeared on his spacious forehead. Several minutes passed in this mental duel. The tension between the two minds was tangible in the room. It seemed to creep up and down the ornate pillars. It sank into the carpet, it laid its hold upon everyone present.

Laquedem never moved. His pupils plunged like a knife into the eyes of Professor Bassermann. The latter, overcome by a sudden faintness, held his hand to his head. He resolutely shut his eyes and turned away. Another minute and the great psychologist would have been hypnotized by his subject!

To hide his confusion, Professor Bassermann lit one of Laquedem's cigars. Laquedem smiled.

"Don't you remember, Professor, that we met almost like this before?"

"I recall no such meeting."

"Oh, yes. It was in England."

"Indeed?"

"At Oxford."

"I was there only once as a student."

"Oh, no, no. It was long before that. In the year sixteen hundred and—" He snapped his fingers impatiently. "I forget the year."

Was the stranger dreaming? Perhaps he was after all in a semi-hypnotic condition. Professor Bassermann examined the pupils. They were clear. There was no sign of suspended consciousness.

"What do you mean?" he asked.

The stranger shrugged his shoulders. Father Ambrose looked at him with startled eyes.

"I think he is shamming," Bassermann softly whispered to Aubrey.

"No, I think there is a certain antipathy between him and you that breaks the thought current. Let me try."

He did not attempt to put Laquedem to sleep with his unaided eyes, but used a glittering ring, a strange device showing a serpent, the symbol of infinity and of knowledge.

Perhaps the struggle with Bassermann had exhausted Laquedem's power of resistance; perhaps the caressive stroke of Aubrey's fingers against his temples overcame his resistance. Laquedem's lids trembled, then a gentle haze veiled the flame of his vision. His breath came heavily like that of a sleeper, his pulse beat against the wrist with subdued regularity. The cigarette fell from his hands, burning a hole in the carpet. His hands dropped. The pupils were still visible through the half-closed lids.

Isaac Laquedem was asleep.

At that moment, a little yellow head peered into the room. Kotikokura was on guard, to see that no harm befell his master. A glance at the group seemed to reassure him and he disappeared again, unseen, with the stealthiness of one who has lived for a long time in the jungle. Only Laquedem's left hand stirred slightly for a moment. It was as though an invisible message of assurance had passed from him to his yellow valet.

When Aubrey gently began his invasion into the mind of Isaac Laquedem, Kotikokura sat in the cell appointed for him, softly chattering to himself. Then he fetched a safety razor with a gold handle and began to shave not only his face, but his arms and his wrists which were disfigured by an ungainly growth of stubborn hair.

Professor Bassermann felt Laquedem's pulse. "He is asleep," he said.

Father Ambrose touched Laquedem's forehead making, by habit, the sign of the cross. The sleeper reacted violently. A groan rose to his lips. He clutched his hands convulsively. But a few strokes from Aubrey recomposed his trembling nerves.

Isaac Laquedem was no longer asleep. Aubrey made no attempt to prolong the hypnotic spell. Hovering in a state between waking and sleeping, peculiar to psychoanalysis, Laquedem's thoughts, like flights of birds, darting hither and thither, could alight where they pleased.

Nevertheless, he replied alertly to every question put to him by Aubrey. He also replied, though less quickly, to questions put to him by the others. A curious relief betrayed itself in his features, as slowly drawn out of the depth of memory, his story unfolded itself before the astounded ears of the three men.

THE AUTOBIOGRAPHY OF MR. ISAAC LAQUEDEM

I

I WITNESS THE TRIAL OF JESUS—MADAME PILATE'S
RECEPTIONS—I QUARREL WITH JOHN

THE day set for the trial of Jesus was mild and cool. I dressed myself carefully in my new uniform of a Roman Captain, an honor unique for a Hebrew boy.

The streets were crowded with pedestrians and riders on donkeys. The Jews in constant fear of persecution or oppression, grasped any occasion, however insignificant, of making merry or at least of vociferating. It was this, and not the fact that a matter of colossal importance was about to take place, that brought large multitudes to the Court. The same need for excitement and noise made them shout afterwards: "Crucify him! Crucify him!"

The people entertained no hatred for Jesus. They had seen many erratic prophets. Peculiar claims to divinity or royalty rather amused than angered them. But this was a rare privilege,—to see a prophet taken seriously by the priests, and actually brought to trial.

The Courtroom was already filled. I recognized a few officers who invited me to join them, but I preferred to remain alone in a corner. Two young men near me were talking in Latin, and changed immediately to Hebrew, taking me for a Roman, no doubt. They were tall, thin, wore short beards, and their dress was a compromise between the Roman toga and the Hebrew kaftan.

"Whatever," remarked the older of the two, "our love for our country may be, we must acknowledge that Jerusalem produces no artists."

"If only," replied the other, "our ancestors had accepted the Golden Calf in place of the tablets. . . ."

"Yes, we should have had artists instead of priests, for we certainly do not lack ability."

"The priests are a plague, but I prefer them to the reformers. I prefer them because they are corrupt. Beauty may grow on the soil of corruption even as the rose feeds on ordure. But reformers, being obstinate, ignorant boors, are always at war with Beauty.

27

Did you ever hear the fellow whom the priests are dragging before the Governor?"

"Yes, on two occasions."

"What does he say?"

"He hides the poverty of his thought under a cloak of parables. A paradox conceals his lack of logic. 'Love your enemy!' he says. What lack of pride! How typical of slaves! Strength and hate are brothers. Indeed, it is more important to hate than to love indiscriminately. Jesus of Nazareth speaks as a slave preaching to slaves!"

"Why do they take him seriously? If he is crucified, he may become a source of danger. Some poet may write a song about him, embellishing his philosophy and his ancestry."

"He calls himself the Son of God . . ."

"I should like to go away from Jerusalem to Athens or Rome——"

"So should I."

"Any place indeed, where one does not meet so many sons of God."

Pilate entered, followed by two Roman officers. He seated himself upon the judgment seat and breathed heavily for several moments. He was becoming too stout and tired rapidly. The Jews glanced furtively at him. They had heard all sorts of fantastic stories about his cruelties and his orgies. The Romans, however, looked at him smilingly. A few of the officers nodded.

Procla, the wife of Pilate, came in unnoticed, and hid behind a pillar near her husband. She was slim and tall. Her eyebrows, several shades darker than her hair, contrasted vividly with her pale face. Her lips were always red, her hands moved restlessly.

"Bring in the prisoner," Pilate commanded.

Jesus was brought in by a soldier. He was dressed in tatters and on his head he wore a withered wreath. The populace hissed. Some called out: "King! King!" An old woman spat. Jesus showed no emotion. His blue eyes were fixed beyond Pilate.

"Silence!" Pilate ordered.

"What is this man's guilt?" he asked of the High Priest, a stout individual, gaudily dressed.

"He blasphemes against our faith."

"Words, words, vague words! Is he guilty of any concrete transgression against the law?"

"He calls himself king, Pilate."

"He speaks in metaphors," Pilate yawned, bored. "I do not find him guilty."

"He is guilty! He is guilty!" shouted the populace.

"You hear it, Pilate," the High Priest added. "He is guilty. It is the truth."

"Truth? What is truth?" Pilate asked, addressing Jesus.

"Everyone that is of the truth heareth my voice," answered Jesus gently.

"He blasphemes again. Blasphemer! Traitor!" shouted the people.

"You hear it, Pilate?"

The air was becoming insufferable. Pilate was feeling drowsy. He longed to be back at the palace, drink cool wine, and read the new edition of Ovid's Ars Amatoria, which amused him greatly.

"Ye have a custom that I should release unto you one at the Passover; will ye therefore that I release unto you the king of the Jews?"

"No, not this man! Barabbas!" shouted a thousand voices. "Crucify him, crucify him!"

Pilate turned his head for a moment and saw Procla. "Ah, my dear, you see it is not possible. I would gladly save him for one of your philosophic receptions, but the rabble, my love——" He made a gesture of despair. Pilate's wife did not answer. She made an indefinite motion.

"Take him!" Pilate commanded, and turning to a soldier, "Bring me some perfumed water that I may wash my hands and face."

"Saviour! Save yourself! Try a miracle! King, look to your crown!"

The people were frantic with joy. They laughed, shouted, parodied the words of Jesus. " 'Everyone who heareth my voice——' "

"Who heareth his voice?"

"Where are your chariots, King?"

A cross was dragged through the crowd, and laid upon the back of Jesus. He accepted the burden with the same meekness and unconcern with which he had accepted the judgment.

I pushed through the crowd, and shouted at him, "If you are man, raise your cross and smite them."

Jesus answered without looking at me, "Love your enemies!"

"Love! Love! It is more important to hate," I answered, remembering the conversation of the young men.

The people pressed in front and back of Jesus. The soldiers made a passage-way with their elbows, swearing at the top of their voices. Jesus stumbled under the weight of his cross.

"Why do you hanker for martyrdom if your back is too weak

for a wooden cross?" I asked. Somehow I felt his humiliation was my humiliation. It made all Jewry contemptible. My thwarted pity turned to mockery. I was not mocking Jesus alone. I was mocking myself. I was mocking all Judea.

Jesus, paying no attention to his tormentors, flashed a look of anger at me, which struck me like a blow. To regain my composure, I continued, "You are a slave, preaching a slave-creed to slaves!"

"Your crown is falling, King!" several shouted. The wreath fell. Someone raised it, and was about to replace it tauntingly upon the head of Jesus, but it crumbled in his hands.

Many laughed, slapping their thighs.

Procla motioned to me. "Cartaphilus, I must see you this evening."

I nodded.

The rabble followed Jesus for a little while, jeering and throwing pebbles and refuse at him, but gradually growing weary, began to disperse. Something prompted me to continue. I walked leisurely at a distance, watching the shadow of Jesus and the cross, changing positions and sizes and mingling with each other.

Suddenly from a nearby alley, John emerged, frail, slim, almost boyish, his tawny head disheveled.

"They are taking him! They are taking him!" he cried.

"Well, it's of his own volition. He deliberately courted disaster."

"They are taking him," he whimpered.

I placed my hands upon his shoulders, and looked into his eyes. Their blue was clouded; they seemed almost black. He stared at me uncomprehendingly. "John, wake up, don't you know who I am?"

"They will crucify him!"

"Others have died before him, even gods. But still the world goes on. What is he to you?"

John looked at me, bewildered.

"Have you forgotten our ancient friendship, John?"

"They are taking him to the Place of Skulls!"

"John, answer me," I almost shouted, "is Cartaphilus nothing to you any more?"

"They will crucify him!" He buried his face in his hands. His curls overflowed both. Their trembling betrayed his intense agitation.

"What is Jesus to you? Why have you given your heart to him?" I asked bitterly. "You have forgotten Cartaphilus."

He did not answer.

"John, we have been together since childhood. Hardly a day passed without our seeing each other. We discovered sex together.

We discovered love together. We discovered Woman together. Arm in arm we walked, discussing philosophy, declaiming poetry, laughing at the foibles and stupidities of mankind. Our lives mingled like two rivers, each giving magnitude to the other. Our thoughts intertwined like the roots of two trees. How can you leave me so utterly?"

He did not answer.

"And for what reason? For whom?"

"Jesus is the Son of God."

"The Son of God? He is a carpenter, and a carpenter's son. You know that, John."

He looked at me. In his eyes was the meekness of Jesus. I was furious. "You are even imitating his slavish look. We prided ourselves in being freemen. We despised the humility of our people. Have you forgotten that also?"

He looked at me again, and without uttering a word, walked back to the city.

II

MY MISTRESS MARY MAGDALENE—THE EYES OF JESUS
—JESUS PUTS A SPELL ON ME—I AM THE SOLE WIT-
NESS OF THE CRUCIFIXION—THE EXECUTIONER'S
DITTY

At the turning of the road which marks the limits of Jerusalem, a
woman heavily veiled knelt before Jesus, kissing his feet and hands,
and sobbing bitterly. The soldier and the executioner, believing her
to be his mother, waited a while in patience, but noticing that she
seemed reluctant to release their prisoner, they ordered: "Come on,
Jew! We have no time to lose."

They dragged the woman away, and continued their walk. The
woman remained with her face in the dust. Curious to know who it
was, I approached her, and placed my hand gently upon her head.
"Come, come, you must not despair so. And, after all, is it not of
his own free will that he carries the cross?"

She did not budge, but her sobbing subsided.

She raised her head. Her hair splashed over her shoulders like a
fountain of gold.

Before she uncovered her face I knew it was Mary.

I lifted her. I tried to embrace her, but she repelled me. "You,
too? You, too! Mary, be reasonable! John has left me. Now you!
Half of my life has vanished with John . . . and now, you! How
shall I survive this? How shall a man live, whose heart has been
crushed like iron upon an anvil?"

"Believe in Him."

"Believe in him? Who is he?"

"The Son of God."

"You love him, Mary! He has taken you and John from me!"

"Believe in Him, Cartaphilus, and in Heaven we shall be together."

I laughed bitterly. "How he has perverted your minds with his
diabolical nonsense!"

"It is the truth."

32

"Love me now, and never mind what will happen in Heaven."

"I love you, Isaac."

Ordinarily my Jewish name irritated me; but now it sounded sweet and familiar. I opened my arms gently, as if to embrace her.

"No, no! You do not understand. I love you, but never again that way — —" She looked at me as John and Jesus looked.

"Oh!" I shouted. "He has poisoned you all. He has made slaves of you!"

"Believe in him, Cartaphilus, and you will be so happy!"

"Mary, have you forgotten how happy we were? Have you forgotten the days? Have you forgotten the nights?"

She did not answer, gazing blankly into the distance.

"Mary—my love!"

She remained silent.

"My first, my incomparable love! Mary! What can existence mean to me now? You were dearer and more precious to me than the very breath of my nostrils. My life was ecstasy. I had found the perfect friendship of John, and—you! I was happy beyond all mortals! I dreamed of a love untouched by jealousy, cruelty, selfishness. I dreamed of a Paradise infinitely more beautiful than Eden. And now—both of you are bewitched by this pseudo-prophet!"

"Cartaphilus!" she admonished. "He is the Son of God!"

I disregarded her remark.

"If at least you loved a man, I could either smother my jealousy or slay my rival! It is not Jesus you love, but the dream of a madman—a ghost!"

"Cartaphilus!"

I remained silent for a while.

"Mary, believe in him, if you will—but remain with me!"

"He who believes in Him, must leave all things behind him and follow."

"He is a demon, Mary! Such selfishness is not human!"

" 'Everyone that is of the truth, heareth my voice!' "

"You are possessed!"

She looked at me meekly. It was a meekness that stung me to the quick, the meekness of John, the meekness of Jesus.

I could not bear her eyes. I rushed away. Her golden head disappeared in the distance. I hurried to catch up with the sorry procession.

Jesus dragged his feet slowly. The cross, toppling to one side, beat lightly against his side. Suddenly he fell. I bent to lift him. He looked at me, but beckoned to one of the soldiers, saying in faulty Latin: "Help me, Roman!"

I was white with anger. Jesus staggered to his feet. Tauntingly I muttered: "Where are your followers? Where is your father in Heaven, you fool? All have forsaken you. Go on! Go faster! Go to your self-chosen doom!"

Jesus turned around and looked at me. All meekness had vanished from his face, now ablaze with anger. "I will go, but thou shalt tarry until I return."

His voice struck my ears like a hammer. His eyes were two long spears tipped with fire, hurled against my head. The earth quaked underneath me. My face burned as if enveloped by flames.

"I will go, but thou shalt tarry until I return!" Did he repeat the words, or was it an echo that mocked me?

I walked on, breathing heavily as if I had been climbing a mountain.

"What did you say?" I touched his arm. He would not answer.

"What did he say?" I inquired of one of the men.

"I don't know, Captain."

"He merely grumbled," another added.

But I had heard distinctly what he said.

"He is raving!" I shouted. "He is raving!"

The soldiers laughed.

We reached the Place of Skulls. The soldier that accompanied the executioner left, and the executioner set to work immediately. I seated myself on a rock, and watched, unobserved.

The stroke of the hammer against the nail which was to pierce the right palm was light. Nevertheless, the pain must have been intense, for Jesus pulled his hand from which a long thread of blood was streaming to the ground, out of the large, bony hand of the executioner. The latter, annoyed, struck his fingers a sharp blow, and crushed them.

Jesus shivered.

The right hand firmly fixed, the Roman turned to the left side of the cross. He placed the nail against the palm and struck one powerful blow, which united the hand to the wood.

Jesus swooned.

I was on the point of swooning myself, but bit my lip until it bled.

The executioner did his work quietly and deftly. Only from time to time his breath lengthened into a low whistle of a Greek love song which had been in vogue at Rome some years previously. Pilate used to whistle it after several glasses of wine. The long nails for the feet were crooked. He straightened them out on a stone, beating lightly with his hammer against their humped backs. A few drops of the trickling blood touched his sandals, and he rubbed his feet in the dust.

Two Roman soldiers approached as he was delivering his last strokes, more for the sake of finishing the accompaniment to the air he was whistling than for the need of fastening the body to the wood.

"He will never fall off, friend,—of that you may rest assured," said one of the soldiers. The three men laughed.

He rubbed his hands with sand, and asked one of his friends to pour water over them out of an earthen jug. When he was ready, the three men walked a few steps away from the cross and turning their backs to it, seated themselves on the ground. The executioner filled three cups with a very dark wine, which he took out of a small ditch, where he had hidden it, to keep it cool.

Jesus moaned, "Water, water!" many times in Hebrew and in Latin.

I wished to go away, but could not. Something riveted me to the spot.

The three men were playing dice while emptying their cups in one or two gulps. The rare passers-by turned their heads away and spat. It was an evil omen to see a crucified man.

The sun was setting directly in front of Jesus—a large red sun, like a scarlet wound in the bosom of a doomed divinity. Two butterflies, one gray, one white, chased each other in endless circles, until they struck his beard.

Frightened, they dashed suddenly out of sight.

The executioner swore loudly. He was losing steadily. He even accused his friends of using loaded dice.

Jesus moaned.

The executioner lost his last piece of silver, and cursed all the gods of Israel and in particular the man on the cross. He knew he would be unlucky by the way he missed the first stroke of the hammer against the rascal's right palm.

"You were a stoic once. Don't be overwrought over a trifle. To-morrow your luck will be different. The gods are moody."

"I sell the garments of that Jew for two pieces of silver."

"They are not worth it," answered one, "I have seen them. They are cheap wool."

"I'll take them," said the other.

The sun vanished suddenly behind the horizon as though it had slipped out of the hand of an absent-minded god. The air grew immediately chilly, and several large clouds rolled together on the peak of the hills. A thin, mangy dog stopped a moment in his endless wanderings, lapped a few drops of the blood at the foot of the cross, sniffed the sand, and ran on.

Jesus turned slowly, painfully, his head from the right to the left shoulder, as though it had become a thing of stone. Tears trickled down his face and became entangled in his beard.

He mumbled something. "My God, my God, why hast Thou forsaken me?"

The hopelessness of his voice pierced my heart. More than ever I resented the folly and the futility of his sacrifice. Not God, but he himself had deliberately chosen the cross, a cross too heavy for his back.

One of the soldiers sang an obscene parody on a sentimental song, which made the other splurt out the mouthful of wine he had been trying to swallow while laughing. The dice became wet. The executioner wiped them, swearing. In the distance a cow mooed. Another cow answered. The echo of the shepherd's call rolled a few times and died away. A crow, a worm in its beak, dashed by, flapping its wings noisily.

Jesus moaned, "Water, water!"

The executioner lost his last coin. He was too angry to drink a toast.

"It is all due to that Hebrew. His moaning upset me and made my hand tremble." Running to the cross, he shouted, "What the devil are you groaning about?"

"Water. Water."

"You shall get water, you shall!" And filling to the brim a wine cup, he placed it to the lips of Jesus, saying, "Drink, Hebrew, drink!" Jesus sipped a few drops, his body shrank, and he dropped his head upon his left shoulder.

"What did you give him to drink?" asked one of the soldiers.

"Some strong vinegar, which I was taking home, to pickle cucumbers."

The soldier laughed. The other said, "I believe it killed him."

"He does look as if he were dead."

"Pierce him with your sword and we'll see."

One of the soldiers drew his sword and pierced Jesus below the ribs. A stream of blood and water rushed out. Jesus shivered for a few moments, then remained still.

"He is dead now," said the soldier, while examining the garments he had won. "What rags!"

"Come along to Jerusalem," said the other. "We haven't won your money to hoard it. Come!"

The executioner was reluctant. The soldier whispered something in his ear. He smiled.

Remembering my appointment with Pilate's wife I arose, shook myself violently, and walked to the palace.

III

I PHILANDER WITH PILATE'S WIFE—PILATE'S CAST OFF MISTRESS—LYDIA PUTS ME TO BED

PROCLA welcomed me as cordially as usual, although I noticed an absent-mindedness in her manner, the reason for which I suspected too well.

"You're late, Cartaphilus."

"The noise and the stench of the rabble made me sick. I rested awhile."

She stared at me. Did she guess that I was lying?

"The Jews are very noisy, are they not, Cartaphilus?"

"Very."

"And yet you can be deliciously silent."

"I have but few of the characteristics of the Jews. I hardly look like one." I hoped Procla would agree with me, for I longed to be taken for a Roman. I often looked in a silver mirror—the gift of an Egyptian courtesan—imagining myself the possessor of a Roman nose!

Procla smiled and tapped my cheek. "No, no, my dear, you are a Jew, and look like one, and that is the reason I care for you. The Jews have a strange fascination for me. What nation has such eyes . . . like . . . like . . . the poor fellow's who was condemned to the cross today?"

"I hate his eyes!"

"Yes, yes, they are eyes which one may love or hate passionately . . . but which one never forgets."

I did not answer.

"You were his friend, were you not?"

"I knew him as a boy. He was just like everybody else. I thought he would become a good carpenter."

"As you were a good cobbler!" She laughed a little.

"My father was a cobbler. I merely helped him on occasions. I never learned the trade. My mind was elsewhere, and my hands were not fashioned for menial labor."

38

"Of course. And what made the carpenter turn to religion?"

"Religion is a species of mania—a desire to escape from reality. He was a Jew and a carpenter; he wished to be neither."

Procla sighed and fanned herself lazily. "Come nearer me, Cartaphilus."

I approached her, and taking her hand, small as a girl's, in mine, I said "I love you."

"I know."

I kissed her.

"I am very sad tonight. Your love will dispel my sadness."

"Is Mary Magdalene fickle?" she asked, smiling.

"Mary?"

"Of course. Does not everyone know that——?"

"Mary is dead!" I exclaimed.

"Is it possible?"

"Worse than dead!"

"Oh! She has left you?"

"She was a fever that seized my heart for a season. Now that I am myself again I am utterly yours."

She smiled. "Dear boy, you should know by this time that I am faithful to Pilate."

"You inflame me, Procla; you madden me . . . and then you push me away."

"Gently, however, you must acknowledge."

"Yes, very gently."

"Let me see your eyes, Cartaphilus." She took my head between her hands. "You may be right, after all. Perhaps you are not a Hebrew. There is more pride and hatred in your eyes than . . . in his."

I stood up. "Please do not speak of his eyes any more!"

She burst out laughing. "You are jealous, Cartaphilus, jealous of a corpse on a cross!"

I would have dashed out of the room, but Pilate entered, jovial as ever, and a little unsteady on his feet. "Oh, my young friend, Cartaphilus!"

"What a magnificent poet Ovid is, my dear!" He addressed his wife. "And how he knows love. You must read the book, and you too, Cartaphilus. But you don't seem to be over-cheerful tonight. Has he fallen in love with you, my dear?"

"He has been in love with me always."

"Ha, ha, ha! He, he, he!"

"Please . . . I beg you . . ."

"Come, come, don't be angry, Cartaphilus—Much-Beloved. You're the only Hebrew I care for,—but then you are not really a Hebrew, are you? You look and act like a Roman. Who knows who your real father was? Ha, ha, ha! Maybe a Roman Officer!"

I was not entirely displeased by this insinuation.

"We were speaking about the Jew you condemned to the cross this morning, dear, and his eyes. . . ." Procla interjected.

"You know how I hate to think of state matters at home. So let us not— —"

"He had such eyes as I have never seen. Cartaphilus hates them, but I — —"

The Governor waved his hand.

"By the way, Cartaphilus, I have a gift for you. Ha, ha! a magnificent gift. Will you excuse us for a few moments, my dear? I want to give my friend— —"

I saluted, and followed Pilate, who was laughing uninterruptedly. He led me into his private library in a remote wing of the palace. The two torches which lit the room were wavering, making curious patterns. Like a tree, I thought.

"A magnificent gift, I assure you."

I thought it would be a sword or a piece of statuary. He knew my passion for these two objects. Instead, however, he pointed to a couch in the farthest angle of the room. Upon it reclined a woman.

She was a Greek, slim and athletic. She wore her brown hair tied in a knot. Her small firm breasts, trembling like doves, bespoke passion. Her face was illuminated by a smile, but there was tragedy in her eyes. The smile emphasized the somberness that slept in their depths.

"Lydia, come here." She approached us. I remembered having seen her once in the country home of the governor. "Cartaphilus— the Much-Beloved—your new lover."

"I regret giving her to you," he added, "but one must not be selfish . . . and I am near fifty. Lydia has afforded me more pleasure than any other woman, excepting Procla. Procla is incomparable. . ."

He slapped my back.

I wondered if the compliment to his wife was intended to tantalize me. However, Lydia was young and pretty, and the pride of being the Governor's successor thrilled me. I bowed and thanked him profusely.

"But does Lydia accept me?" I asked suddenly.

"She has chosen you herself. And now take her away. I must keep my wife company. She is lonesome tonight."

I took Lydia to my villa. We spent a few hours carousing and love-making. My tension relaxed, I fell asleep on her bosom. I dreamt that Jesus was coming toward me. On either side of him, and keeping him by the hand, were John and Mary. They were talking and laughing, and seemed very happy. They looked at me, without recognizing me, and passed on. I called after them. "John! John!" "Mary! Mary!" They walked on. I knew that if I called Jesus, they would stop. But I refused to do so, preferring to see them turn a corner, and disappear.

I awoke. A feeling of great loneliness overwhelmed me. Lydia was snoring—daintily, but unmistakably. Her mouth was half open. Her teeth looked like tiny chisels. I dressed myself and walked out. It was still dark. I breathed deeply, hoping to overcome my drowsiness and my headache. The streets were empty, except for a soldier or some laborer. I remembered the dream too vividly, and as if to run away from it, I took very long strides. I am certain I had no intention to go to the Place of Skulls. On the contrary, it was what I desired to avoid most. Was it a kind of somnambulism that led me to the cross? I walked so fast, my head bent, that I nearly struck the feet of Jesus before I became aware of my whereabouts. I stopped short as if suddenly imprisoned.

It was dawn. A flock of crows turned in wide circles about the head of the crucified one. Enormous flies with bellies and wings the color of mother-of-pearl were devouring the black wounds, buzzing like jews' harps. One alighted on the sharp tip of the nose, and remained motionless, as if meditating, or in profound amazement. An old woman passing by, muttered a prayer.

Like a disk thrown by a clever athlete, the sun turned about itself, seeming motionless. Cocks, vainglorious and ridiculous prophets, crowed their ancient illusion.

I was seized with nausea. I shivered like a man in fever. Was it simply a physical disgust, was it sorrow, was it something for which the human tongue had fashioned no word? Suddenly, as if prompted by an extraneous power, I raised my arms and shouted to the dead man, "I hate you!"

"Thou must tarry until I return," answered the voice, and the words reverberated for a long while. I was stunned. Who was it that spoke? It was no illusion, I was certain of that! I heard the words as distinctly as if someone had spoken them into my very ear. "I hate you!" I repeated.

"Thou must tarry until I return."

I fled. I was afraid I was becoming mad. When I reached home, Lydia opened her eyes. "Come back to bed, Cartaphilus," she whispered.

"I am ill, Lydia. My head aches."

She rose, undressed me, and helped me to bed.

IV

BAD DREAMS—I RECOVER—JERUSALEM IS NORMAL—
THE MADNESS OF JOHN—MARY AND THE RAGA-
MUFFINS

I was in bed for several days, almost steadily asleep. I saw in my
dreams the court scene, the crucifixion, John, Mary, Pilate's wife—
but in the most grotesque arrangements. My head was like a vast
merry-go-'round.

On the morning of the third day, I awoke, with a jerk. My headache had disappeared. I was very hungry. Lydia was overjoyed.
She kissed me innumerable times, told me how anxious she was
about me, what strange things I was talking of in my sleep.

"What did I say?" I asked.

"Oh, so many things. You seemed to be afraid of someone's eyes.
You shouted, 'Away, away!' oh, I don't know how many times.
Then you cried, 'Crucify him! Crucify him! I hate him!' But the
worst time, when I was really scared, was when you got off the bed,
your eyes closed, and began to sob, 'I will not tarry. I will not tarry.'
But I knew it would soon pass. I once saw Pilate in a worse condition than this. The Phoenician wine has queer powers. You must
promise not to drink so much of it, Cartaphilus."

It seemed to me that I was hearing my mother's voice. She used
to admonish me in the same gentle manner. I threw my arms around
her neck.

Lydia was happy.

"You must be hungry, and I am chattering here. I shall prepare
a dinner fit for my lover."

I knew that Lydia was my only salvation. I was already thirty
years old, had seen and read many things, and I realized that happiness was largely an effortless and spontaneous consolation.

I took a walk in the city. Jerusalem was normal. I looked into the
faces of the people. They seemed supremely unconscious that an
event of importance had taken place two days previously.

I reached the gate of the Temple. John was leaning against it.

43

"Isaac— —"

My blood rushed to my head, but I made believe I did not hear him.

"Isaac— —"

I turned around. "My name is Cartaphilus."

"As you will. Cartaphilus—the Much-Beloved—He has risen!"

"What do you mean?"

"Jesus has risen from the dead. They have buried him, but He has risen."

"No man has ever risen from the dead."

"Cartaphilus—Isaac Laquedem—Isaac aforetime—believe me— He has risen!"

"You are raving."

"I am not raving. I saw Him, and they who will not see Him now, will see Him . . . who knows when? Believe me. . . Look now, before it is too late."

"John, come back to your friend. Let him take care of you, make your career, make you happy. . ."

He looked at me very sadly. "I am waiting for the Master. It is to Him I shall go . . . and as for you . . . Isaac . . . You must tarry until He comes again."

He sighed. His eyes filled with tears, and he turned his head.

"You are stark mad!" I shouted, and walked off. It was the intolerable phrase that I wished above all to crush within my memory. How did he know about it? Did the whole city ring with its echo? Was it a trick of the Nazarene's followers to repeat the same words again and again to frighten the people into belief?

Refusing to be cowed, I began to whistle, but I soon realized that it was the song the executioner had whistled. My mouth became acid. I decided to go to the garrison, and listen to the ribald jests of my companions. Anything to forget.

On the way, I saw a number of fishermen whom I recognized as the intimate followers of Jesus. Among them was Mary, badly dressed, and her hair in disorder. She was talking haranguing them.

"Mary," I said, "how can you associate with those ragamuffins?"

"He has risen, Cartaphilus! He has risen!"

"Both John and you are mad. His eyes have maddened you."

"He has risen from his tomb and will be with us again this evening."

"If he has risen from his tomb, it was you and your friends yonder that have taken him away and buried him elsewhere."

She stared at me.

"The dead are dead forever."

"Don't you understand, my dear, that you must see Him again tonight, and believe in Him, or else you must tarry——"

"You, too? You too speak of my tarrying? He has poisoned you with his nonsense! He has turned the heads of all of you."

"Cartaphilus, you loved me even as I loved you. Our love was beautiful. For the sake of that love, join us! Be among those who are saved!"

She looked at me, but her eyes were the eyes of Jesus.

"Go away!" I shouted furiously to hide a strange uneasiness. "Go back to your ragamuffins!"

V

PRINCESS SALOME YAWNS—THE PARABLE OF THE QUEEN BEE—I ANOINT MYSELF WITH PERFUME—THE PRINCESS COMMANDS—THE MASKED PARAMOUR

THE Governor summoned me to appear at once. Princess Salome, stepdaughter of the late King Herod, famous for her beauty and for strange amorous adventures, had arrived in Jerusalem.

"You shall be her guard of honor, Cartaphilus," he said, "you speak not only Latin and Hebrew, but the one language that like a spear, pierces the armor of the mightiest princess."

The Governor sat in an arm-chair, his right foot hugely bandaged. "I cannot tell whether the gods are merely playful, Cartaphilus, or take delight in nothing as much as in torturing man."

Pilate's wife entered. She had become thinner, and as she smiled, the edges of her eyes massed into tiny hills of wrinkles.

The left wing of the palace was reserved for the Princess Salome and her suite. I appointed a company of soldiers, in charge of a young lieutenant to guard the gate, while, according to the arrangements made by the Governor, I awaited Salome and her orders in the immense hall which faced the artificial lake in whose waters gold and silver fish glistened like jewels.

Lydia was a little uneasy, and made me promise to beware the lures of the Princess, of whom she had heard the cruelest stories.

"Am I not a Roman soldier, my dear?"

"No soldier is a match for woman, Cartaphilus," she answered very seriously.

Her jealousy did not displease me. I promised her eternal love, and made sport of the wiles of all other women. But as the door of the bed-chamber opened slowly, my heart beat with an unaccustomed violence, and I forgot completely both Lydia and my martial valor.

Salome remained standing upon the threshold—a luminous figure —a sun motionless upon the peak of a mountain.

I saluted. "I am Captain Cartaphilus. The Governor has done me the great honor of appointing me guard of honor to Her Highness, Princess Salome."

She nodded. Her mouth opened slightly, allowing an instant's glow of her teeth—diamonds breaking through a rose. The glitter of her eyes and her burnished hair merged with the green and scarlet jewels studding the coronet. She walked to the throne in the center of the hall. Her steps were tiny and measured in the manner of Egyptian ladies, and the gems of her slippers made aureoles about her feet. Her bare arms covered with bracelets the shapes of crocodiles, balanced slowly and rhythmically. Her breasts, full-blown, were encased in two golden bowls, the centers of which were surmounted by large rubies.

I stood at attention.

"Are the roads in Jerusalem safe for chariots, Captain?"

"There are several roads, Princess, expressly built for them."

"That is well. It is my desire to ride in a chariot today."

I lingered, hoping that Salome would deign to speak of other matters, but she remained silent, playing with a piece of jade the shape of a tortoise, which hung as a pendant from her gold necklace. The jade was green, but her eyes were greener still. They were like a sea of green fire.

Delicately, but unmistakably, Princess Salome yawned.

I was piqued. Instinctively rather than consciously, I decided to avenge myself.

I saluted, and left.

Pilate had told me that Salome was well-read and conversed brilliantly, but while we rode in the chariot, I tried in vain to engage her to speak. I quoted philosophy, recited poetry and invented epigrams. She smiled vaguely, asked what the distance was from Jerusalem to Nazareth, the size of the Roman army of occupation, the names of the principal rivers of Palestine.

She evidently considered me a bore and yet even in the most exclusive circles of the Roman society, I had the reputation of a wit and a man more than usually attractive to women. What had she discovered in me that made her snub me?

I yearned to hate her, to mock her, but the slightest touch of her robe, thrilled me with unendurable desire.

I accompanied the Princess to the various places of interest in Jerusalem and the surrounding towns. She listened condescendingly to my remarks on the history, the poetry, the legends.

We walked along the shore of the lake. The sun, about to set, lay wearily over the water, which the fish ripped silently from time to time like sharp knives.

Salome bent over the orchids and lilies, caressing their pistils and hard petals. A bee buried itself into a flower, and emerged soon, his wings gilded with pollen.

The Princess sighed.

"How fortunate are these creatures of the air!" I remarked, "unhindered in their love and in their search for beauty!"

I expected as usually, a vague smile or an imperceptible nod of the head, but the Princess deigned to speak.

"Fortunate indeed . . . these flowers which receive a varied and mingled love from distant fields, carried gracefully upon the glittering backs of the bee and the butterfly! They are spared the indignity, the imposition of a particular male."

Her voice had a slight tremor like Mary's.

"Do not these flowers yearn perhaps for the exclusive and intense caress of one particular individual?" I asked.

Salome replied: "It may be that their petals open with a greater joy to the caresses of a particular individual, whose wooing is subtle and exquisite like a zephyr that stirs the wings of a bee."

"Cannot a man's touch be as subtle and as exquisite, Princess?"

"Man is clumsy. His conceit makes his touch heavy and coarse."

Did she direct the remarks to me? Had I been clumsy and conceited?

"Man does not possess the subtle means of conquering an exquisite love," she continued.

"What are the subtle means of conquering an exquisite love, Your Highness?"

She did not answer my question.

"Ah, to be indeed . . . like the bee . . . to soar . . . high . . . high . . . to be pursued by a thousand lovers . . . to be finally conquered by one whose wings, powerful and indefatigable, touch tremblingly those of the Queen!"

"Oh, the incomparable joy of pursuing the Queen!" I exclaimed.

"Alas, for the conqueror, Captain . . . for he may not live beyond love's moment! The Queen demands his sacrifice!"

"What joy would life hold for him after love's moment?"

The Princess looked at me, her eyes half-closed.

My knees ached to bend, and my tongue to utter: 'Sacrifice me, O Princess!' I restrained myself. 'Not yet, Cartaphilus! The bee that soars to the dizzy heights of the Queen must be more delicate and more subtle!'

I anointed myself with rare Egyptian perfumes. My curls glistened from the delicate oils. I covered my arms and fingers with jewels and donned a new uniform, the gift of Pilate. The scabbard of my sword was of heavy gold, the hilt encrusted with lapis-lazuli.

I dismissed the lieutenant, remaining on guard myself. I walked up and down the great hall, thinking of a subtle and beautiful manner of attack. From time to time, I glanced at myself in the large Corinthian mirror. I was young and handsome!

'Man is clumsy and his conceit makes his touch heavy and coarse.'

'Yes, Princess, but even the bee must possess the conceit of his ability to fly high . . . high . . . until his wings touch the tips of the Queen's wings. Strength is conscious of itself.'

The door opened, and a very tall and powerful man, whose face was veiled, entered, accompanied on either side by a lady-in-waiting of the Princess. I stopped them. One of the women placed her forefinger to her lips, whispering: "The Princess commands."

They broke the wide reflection of the moon which flooded the room, and entered into the royal bedchamber.

Who was this man? What was the meaning of this intrusion? My plans were crushed under his feet, as a delicate vase under the paws of an elephant.

Meanwhile, the women walked in and out of the room, carrying delicacies, wines, spices, perfumes. To my inquiries, they whispered mysteriously: "The Princess commands."

Someone played upon the harp a sensuous, languorous melody, and another danced.

The feet that stamped upon the floor, trod upon my heart.

Who was this man? What mighty prince? What youth of unconquerable beauty? I looked at myself in the mirror and saw a face, ugly and commonplace, crowned with an enormously Jewish nose.

'Cartaphilus, you were vain indeed to believe yourself the glorious king who conquers the Queen! You are but an insignificant captain, a shoemaker's son, a Jew!'

The entire night the revelry continued, alternating between laughter and music and dancing, and vague amorous whispers and groans which I could hear as I pressed my ear against the door.

Again and again I was on the point of dashing into the room.

of shouting epithets of abomination and of piercing to the hilt of my sword the body of Salome.

The rays of the sun, like long fingers, caressed the powerful legs of the royal throne. I looked in the mirror. A haggard, drawn face stared back at me. Even my wildest debauches had never left me so completely bedraggled.

The door of the royal bedchamber opened cautiously. Was it Salome? Had she come to atone for her intolerable cruelty? Had everything been merely a nightmare and an illusion? Was she ready for the nuptial flight, for the honeymoon in the clouds?

The tall man, who had entered the previous evening, appeared upon the threshold. Was this an illusion indeed? Was he the magnificent prince, the chosen one of Salome,—a Nubian, black as charcoal, heavy-featured, and colossally muscled like a giant bull!

I drew my sword. "Halt!" I commanded. A woman in back of him, placed her forefinger to her lips: "The Princess commands."

I replaced the sword into the scabbard, and motioned to him to pursue his way.

"What subtle means have conquered an exquisite love, O Princess?" I asked aloud.

It seemed to me I heard some one laugh.

"Daughter of Night and of Evil!" I shouted, and rushed out.

VI

MY FIRST MARRIAGE—PROCLA ASKS A QUESTION—THE DESPERATION OF LYDIA—THE CURIOUS HETAERA— I CONSULT A LEECH

LYDIA was a mother to me—a young and desirable mother. She was a slave to my whims. I married her. I tried to persuade myself that it was merely gratitude, although I knew very well that such a sentiment was foreign to me. What I really wished was to force myself by an outward symbol to lead a normal existence. I wished to be able to say to myself: 'Cartaphilus, forget—forget whatever preceded Lydia, forget John, forget Mary, forget the eyes of Jesus and forget Salome."

I wanted children to rediscover myself in them. fresh and pure. I wished to drown the voice that tormented my nerves, with their laughter and noises. But the years passed, and no children came. Lydia, fearing that it was her fault, prayed in the various temples, took drugs, fasted, consulted oracles.

I felt the need of ceaseless occupation. I engaged in many business ventures, in most of which, by dint of hard work, I succeeded. I became wealthy. I lived in luxury, and for some years, at any rate, I was considered one of the principal citizens of Jerusalem. To Romans I was a Roman. The Jews, except in the most orthodox circles, were grateful, because unlike others who had forsaken the fold, I did not persecute them.

John and Mary had vanished. My inquiries and searches were all futile. The followers of Jesus were not numerous enough to attract attention, and they remained unmolested.

Pilate returned to Rome. He had grown old, and bored even with Ovid and with his wife. Whether he really committed suicide afterward, as the rumor had it, or not, I cannot tell. At any rate, I never saw him again. Procla kissed me good-bye.

"Cartaphilus, what is the secret of your youth?"

"My wife's cooking. She is without equal." I laughed.

"You jest. This is your habit now with me. Is it because I am

51

getting old? With old ladies one jests; with young ones one sighs. You used to love me once, Cartaphilus."

"I love you still, Procla."

"How can you? I look like your grandmother."

"You are beautiful."

"There is nothing more pathetic—and more futile—than being beautiful, but old. I would rather be very homely, and young. What makes you so youthful, Cartaphilus? Is it a racial characteristic? Romans who lead so gay a life would be bald and stout like poor Pilate, and complain, like him, of rheumatism . . . but you . . . you have not changed one particle all these years. . . . What is your secret . . . ?"

"You exaggerate my youth, I am sure; and moreover, you exaggerate your age."

She sighed. "Farewell, Cartaphilus. It is no longer in my power to persuade men. Farewell."

This was the first time that any one mentioned to me the suspicion that I possessed the secret of youth. Like a brazen drum the words: 'Thou shalt tarry until I return' re-echoed in my ears. Had Jesus, by some curious magic, some incomprehensible trick, stopped the flow of sand in the hour-glass for me? Was my body secure from the assaults of age?

I had strangled my own suspicions. Suddenly, however, it was borne upon me that the words of Jesus or some other thing had wrought in me a curious transformation that made me different from other men. For the first time I seriously reconsidered the strange spell he had pronounced upon me.

Was it true? Was I really to linger on and on, see friends and things I cherished die and crumble away? Was I to stare into infinity, seeking for him, at whom I shouted 'I hate you!'? My youth prolonged into eternity seemed to me a much greater catastrophe than the wrinkles of Pilate's wife which a few years would erase forever.

"Lydia, my dear, it seems to me that my hair is getting gray at the temples. Look!" I wished to see if she, too, was aware of my predicament.

"Let me see. Let me see," she said, excitedly. In her eyes, less lustrous than of yore, I saw a great delight. She ruffled my hair, and looked very closely. "No, not even one gray thread." She burst into sobs.

"What's the trouble, my dear?"

"Nothing."

I did not want to press the matter, fearing that I would have to explain too much, perhaps. The next day, she took an overdose of a drug, prescribed for her by the physician, for some intestinal derangement. For three days she was in agony. Her head seemed to have shrunk to half its size. Her body assumed the contours of a skeleton. She looked at me wistfully.

"It was the only way out," she said.

"No, you did a terrible thing. You have hurt me beyond words."

She shook her head. "I have noticed for a long while how my hands grated on your skin, and my lips brought nothing but a chill. You are young. I am old. This was what you meant the other day when you asked me to look at your hair. I understood."

I was stunned. "No, no, my dear, it was not that. It was not that! I hoped that I too— —"

Her convulsions became more and more violent. The physician could prescribe no antidotes. More painful even than her approaching death, was her misunderstanding of my motive. I had really killed her—unwillingly!

On my return from her funeral, Aurelia, the most beautiful courtesan in Jerusalem accosted me. King Herod himself had paid for her embrace one thousand talents in gold.

"Cartaphilus, spend the night with me!"

My first impulse was to upbraid the insolent woman, but I felt so lonesome, a sorrow so deep gnawed me, that I could not wrench my arm from her grasp.

Fatigued by her caresses, I fell asleep profoundly. When I awoke, she asked me, smiling: "Cartaphilus, where is the place?"

"What place?"

"I have searched your body everywhere with my lips. . ."

"Your lips pleased me."

I was always gallant.

"I am glad of that. But I have not discovered it. . ."

"What do you mean?"

"The prick of the needle where you insert the magic potion that gives you undying youth. I have loved much. I have shared the couch of many. I have known the loves of old men from whose touch the skin shrinks as from a reptile. I know that you must be sixty, but you have the skin of a boy, the muscles of a gladiator, the insatiable endurance of youth. I have given you joy when you were most distressed. I can give you tenfold, a hundredfold greater joy, Cartaphilus. I know the love secrets and the love potions of fifty nations. I know," she whispered, "the secret of unendurable pleasure indefinitely prolonged. . . . All my knowledge will be yours, if only— —"

"What?"

"If only you will let me share your secret."

I pushed her away from me.

"Cartaphilus!" Her delicate breasts trembled. "Make me your wife, and let me partake of the elixir. I have been all women to all men. I shall be all women to you alone."

"You are raving, woman! The heavy wine has gone to your head. Let me sleep."

Her face grew livid with rage. "You fool! You really believe that I care for you? I loathe you! Even the old men, who come to me with their silver and gold, with lecherous lips and limbs marred by disease, are not as loathsome as you. They are at least human. . . !"

She stamped angrily out of the room.

'At least human!' reverberated in my ear, as the other phrase which I always tried not to repeat, even mentally. Not human! Not human! I was set apart from all other men. I was alone. Everybody would sooner or later point at me: Stranger! Outcast! Alien!'

I dressed myself and went to consult the most famous physician of Jerusalem, an old rascal, addicted to strange drugs and stranger vices. I explained my case to him. He laughed. "You are the first patient who complains that he is too young. I need prescribe no medicine. Time will remedy matters."

"I am not jesting. I bring gold, but also a—dagger."

He bade me strip. His lecherous eyes devoured my naked body. He felt every muscle, tested every nerve with the strange instruments known to the priests of Isis, analyzed my saliva, measured the pressure of my blood. He consulted his books and pondered over old diagrams.

"You tell me that you are sixty. I tell you that you are thirty. You may bring any witnesses you please. You may swear a solemn oath by your mother. I shall never be convinced that you are more than thirty. You may even slay me, Captain, but that will not alter my conviction."

"Doctor, can I have children?"

He summoned a slave girl. Hovering near, he waited upon us

like the obliging maid in a house of pleasure. Then, assuming once more the cold severity of the physician, he brought strange vessels from his laboratory, and made curious tests.

After pondering over his retorts, he turned to me: "No, you will have no progeny, Captain. Fate which has given you much has denied you this."

'However long your life may be, Cartaphilus,' I thought bitterly, 'you must walk without kin,—alone!'

VII

I AM ACCUSED OF DEALING WITH THE DEVIL— I LIQUIDATE MY ESTATE—I LAUGH—FAULTY ARITHMETIC—I SEEK—WHAT?

ENVY disguised itself as hostility. My friends insinuated, laughed, mocked. An old woman, whom I had befriended for a long while, refused to accept the silver coin that I was in the habit of offering her.

"Have you become so rich, good woman?"

She shook her head.

"Do you need more, perhaps?"

"I need God's alms, not the Devil's."

"What do you mean?"

She glared at me, and ran off.

The gay women who used to accost me, shrank away at my approach. No doubt Aurelia had spoiled my reputation in the demi-monde of Jerusalem.

I visited another physician for some trifling disorder. He hardly listened to me. "All diseases are curable, provided the patient lives long enough to overcome the initial cause of the complaint. You, Captain, can overcome all diseases."

I was on the point of drawing my sword, but stopped, reflecting that the murder of the physician would require a longer explanation than I could afford to offer. I laughed. "Here is a gold coin, leech. You are a philosopher."

The beard I raised only emphasized my youthful appearance. I shaved it off.

I lived alone. My only servants were two country boors, morose and taciturn. I realized that before long popular envy against me would burst out, like a volcano. What would happen to me, whether I could really be killed or hurt, I did not know. But I was certain that it would be unpleasant. I liquidated my estates, a matter which I already found very difficult to accomplish, resigned my position in the Roman army, and left the city on horseback.

The sea was like a vast liquid jewel. I walked up and down the deck of the boat, thinking of Lydia. For a long time now she had disappeared from my memory, and I felt a pang of conscience for this neglect. I laughed. My very name predisposes me to laughter. Isaac is Hebrew for laughter. Nevertheless, my laughter startled me. I understood, as if by some revelation, that laughter was to be my weapon from now on—to laugh and forget, much and quickly.

The boat was crowded with people of many nationalities. Suddenly a tall, thin man exclaimed in a Latin tinged with the accent of some Oriental tongue, "He is the Messiah! He is the Christ!" He stopped, looked upward, and made a gesture with his right hand, first horizontally, then vertically. His enormous Adam's apple moved up and down as if the shock of his voice continued to stimulate its activity.

"He died upon the Cross; three days later He was resurrected, and rose to Heaven."

Some nodded, and made the same curious gesture with their hands. Others smiled.

"All who believe in Him shall live forever, for His death was an atonement for our sins."

"Did you know Jesus?" I asked.

"How could I know Him since He was crucified thirty-nine years ago? I am only thirty-two."

"Thirty-nine? That must be an error. It's only thirty-four."

He shook his head. "Thirty-nine."

Jesus was becoming a legend.

"Tell me—have you heard of a man by the name of Cartaphilus, known among the Jews as Isaac Laquedem?"

"Cartaphilus, the cursed one!" he exclaimed. "He must tarry on earth until the Master returns!"

"And where is this Cartaphilus—the cursed one?"

"Who knows? He must be roaming about, like a starved beast, seeking the Master."

'Like a starved beast seeking. . . . ' It was true. When I left Jerusalem, I thought I was merely fleeing for safety. But I realized now, because of the remark of this tall man, with an extraordinary Adam's apple, that there was a deeper meaning in my pilgrimage. Seeking—but what and whom?

I began to walk once more up and down the deck. I thought of John—gentle and handsome youth, as I knew him—and of our great friendship. I thought of Mary—of her magnificent body, of our passionate embraces. It was so long ago! They had become characters, more or less fabulous, in a greater fable. The hundreds of people I had known, and the many women I had possessed—all were shadows now that had merely crossed my path. These two alone were real.

VIII

I ARRIVE IN ROME—I TEMPT THE GODS AND—SNEEZE— I TRANSLATE NERO'S POEMS—MY FIRST AMOUR WITH AN EMPRESS—I AM EMBARRASSED— "HOW STRONG YOU ARE CARTAPHILUS"

I ARRIVED in Rome just as the sun was setting. Its immense reflection in the Tiber resembled a great conflagration.

I was walking slowly along the shore, analyzing a half dozen emotions that besieged me, when I heard a piercing cry. "Help! Help! Help!"

The mock fire upon the river rose into tongues of flame as a boy beat the water desperately. Several people rushed to the spot. A woman pulled one, then another, by the toga. "Save him! Save him! My son! Save him!"

"I cannot swim."

"The Tiber is too rough. It will swallow us both."

"Save him! My son! Help! Help!"

'You are eternal, are you not?' a voice distant, extraneous, as of another person, rang in my ears. 'Prove it now!'

'I cannot swim,' I answered.

'That's just the reason. . . . Tempt fate!'

I made a motion as if to disengage myself from an invisible hand. 'Prove that your life is inviolate!'

I meant to continue my walk. What strange power then, hurled me suddenly, dressed as I was, and against my will, into the river? By what stranger instinct did I find myself swimming, when I had never swum before?

I caught the boy, just as he was sinking, and held him in one arm; with the other I beat the water. The Tiber pulled at my body like a great iron weight. I beat it, as one beats a living enemy—a wild beast.

A fisherman's boat arrived. I felt a power pull me upward. The great iron weight became light. I heard a shout—and then,—a long silence.

I opened my eyes. My lids were a little heavy. I tried to keep them from pasting together again. A man was bending over me. I sneezed in his face. He remained grave and unperturbed. Wiping his face, he said: "Only a cold. A few days of rest, and this drug both for him and the boy."

I noticed then that he was talking to a man and a woman, standing in back of him. In the opposite corner, a child coughed. I realized that I was in the home of the boy I had saved from drowning. If immune from death, I was nevertheless susceptible to colds.

For weeks I was the guest of Lavinius, an enormously wealthy patrician. He introduced me to the Imperator. I translated Nero's poems into Hebrew and Chaldean and gained his favor by flattery. I was prejudiced against the Imperator because his face was red and covered with pimples, but I was fascinated by the Empress Poppaea. Was it her finely etched nose, was it her lips, indented at each corner, making two exquisite dimples, was it her voluptuous posture revealing the dazzling fragment of a breast that made me whisper 'Mary'? And Sporus, the Emperor's minion, how his large blue eyes gazed directly into the distance. 'John!' Was it an illusion? Was it my loneliness that invested with similitude unrelated things?

It was bruited in Rome that Poppaea was a Jewess. I do not know. Judaism was the one topic that we avoided when we exchanged confidences. Nevertheless it is possible that the consciousness of our racial consanguinity established a secret tie between myself and the Empress.

Nero, after one of his vulgar banquets reeking with drink and retching with food, disappeared in the vomitorium to relieve angry nature with the aid of a peacock feather. He did not return. The guests departed. I found myself alone with the Imperatrix. She was reclining on the sofa as was her wont, and Sporus sat at her feet. The boy, concerned about the health of his imperial Master, to whom he was deeply devoted, kissed her hand, bowed to me, and walked out.

The Empress made a sign to two slaves who were standing at the door with arms crossed, a mode learned in Egypt. Making deep obeisance the two eunuchs closed the door behind them.

Poppaea's eyes smiled. Her lips curled like the hungry petals of a carnivorous flower. The message of her blood to mine made her silence eloquent. My blood rushed to my head.

Did she mean to accept me as her lover? Should I, Cartaphilus, the shoemaker's son, venture to touch the Empress of the world?

Apparently Poppaea, imperial even in her love-making, preferred to make the advances. She caressed my cheek and pressed her finger-tips against my eyelids.

The tumult in our blood leaped over the abyss that separated the cobbler's son and the Empress. Poppaea drew me gently upon the couch. She caressed my body.

What cruel divinity interfered? Was it too great a privilege to touch the Mistress of Rome? What secret sense of inferiority stopped the onrush of the blood? Perhaps the very aggressiveness of her passion paralyzed mine. . .

In a sheet of flame, yet incapable of quenching the fire, I beat my fists against the couch. My limbs trembled as if a sudden spell had been cast upon them. Impotent to break the ensorcelment, I cursed in Hebrew and in Latin. I raged against myself, but my wrath was of no avail. Flushed and ashamed, I whispered, "Poppaea, Poppaea, I do not understand."

She made no answer. Her eyes glistened. Her teeth clenched. The futility of my gestures became tiresome and, no doubt, ridiculous, for suddenly she burst into laughter.

Her laughter unleashed wild beasts in my bosom.

White with anger, no longer master of myself, I struck her brutally across her imperial mouth. I grasped her arms roughly, leaving upon them, like wounds, the imprint of my hand. My passion, expending itself in fury, I shouted obscene insults. Poppaea's bosom shook, but no longer with laughter.

"Strike me, Cartaphilus, strike hard!"

She groaned, her eyes closed, her mouth opened.

A drop of blood, falling upon my hand like a red petal, brought me to my senses.

"Forgive me, Poppaea."

The features of the Imperatrix relaxed. She opened her eyes. "Cartaphilus, I love you." Her voice was unexpectedly strident.

"Hurt me, crush me," she gasped.

I rushed out of the palace. The night was cool, the stars hung in thick clusters like grapes. To my left I could hear the Tiber beat softly against the shores like a dog lapping.

The tempest aroused by the Empress raged in my brain for hours after I had reached my home.

My slave, a young girl from Damascus, brought in my night-robes.

"Wine!" I commanded. When she brought the wine, I ordered

her to remain. She trembled. She had never seen me in such a mood.

"Don't be afraid. Come, drink with me!" I poured a cup for her. "You will share my couch, tonight. Are you glad?"

"Whatever pleases my master, pleases me."

It was already morning, when the slave, exhausted, placed her head upon my chest.

"How strong you are, Cartaphilus!"

'If Poppaea could only hear you,' I thought.

"When you rise, my child, you are a free woman."

"I don't want to be a free woman. I want to be your slave."

She fell asleep. Her regular breathing lulled me to sleep as well. The sun was high overhead when we rose.

IX

SPORUS MISUNDERSTANDS—NERO FIDDLES—I BLAME
THE NAZARENES

The Imperator was draping the folds of his robe when I entered.
He received me cordially. "Look, Cartaphilus, is this perfect?"

"It is the fold of the statue of a god carved by a master."

The guests were coming, generally by twos or threes. Nero continued to fix the folds, now and then raising his eyes to notice
the effect it produced on the visitors, who seemed entranced.

His arm tired, he seated himself.

We spoke of various matters. The conversation drifted finally to
architecture which interested him greatly.

"Alas," the Emperor remarked moodily, "the Romans prefer to
keep their old wooden shanties instead of building magnificent structures of stone and marble. Rome . . . Rome . . . the city of
lumber! I love stone, Cartaphilus. Eternity lingers in stone. If I
had it my way, I would burn Rome and rebuild it . . . make it a
thing of perfect beauty."

He drank deeply out of his cup as if to drown his regret, and
smacked his heavy lips.

Sporus walked out, slim, graceful, cat-like. He was not drunk,
but the intoxication of the Imperator had communicated itself to
him. His eyes were like torches. At the door, he motioned to three
soldiers to follow him. The Imperator did not notice his departure.
Poppaea feigned sleepiness to disguise her boredom. The guests were
becoming noisy. Their conversation rose and fell like the din of giant
insects. Some couples upon the floor interlaced in amorous postures.
A few sang. I was weary, and should have gladly taken leave, but
the Emperor continued to speak of architecture, of beauty, and
of beastly landlords, interested solely in their investments.

"What is this—the dawn?" one of the guests asked. A few laughed.
"Dawn! Dawn!"

"But it is very light," another one suggested.

"The wine of Nero has the power of changing night into day," someone remarked.

I looked at the open door. "Your Majesty," I said calmly, "fate has granted your wish. Rome is burning!"

Nero glared at me. I pointed to the columns of smoke embracing the city like serpents. Flames were rising from the seven hills.

"I am lost, Cartaphilus!"

"Fire! Fire!" several guests shouted, rushing out. Poppaea opened her eyes. Nero ran out. I followed him, slowly, unperturbed. I knew that whatever happened to the others, I was immune. For the first time since Jesus had hurled his imprecation against me, I felt that my predicament was not without its benefits. I could be dignified in a crisis that frightened an Emperor.

Poppaea touched my arm. "You are not afraid, Cartaphilus?" she whispered.

"No."

"Nero is afraid."

"Are you?"

"I love fire. Like passion it devours."

The wind, which had set in toward the evening, fanned the fire. The tongues of flame united into gigantic scarlet masses. People rushed to and fro, shouting and wailing.

Nero turned to me. "Is it right for an Emperor to run, Cartaphilus?"

"He can conquer himself even if he cannot conquer the elements," I answered.

With trembling hands Nero fixed the folds of his garment—and, mastering his impulse to flee, ordered one of the slaves to bring him his harp.

"Is not fire beautiful?" he exclaimed, but his voice quivered. "Shall we not celebrate in its honor?"

His teeth chattered.

'How,' I thought, 'could man survive amid the hostile forces of nature without a touch of madness or delusion of grandeur?'

Sporus reappeared, pale, disheveled, his hand bandaged.

"Recite the burning of Troy, Sporus, while I play."

People running in terror, stopped a moment to listen to the music.

"The monster!" a woman shouted, "He plays the harp! He is roasting our children alive while he plays!"

I do not know whether Nero heard the remarks.

"Cartaphilus, I am immortal now. The world shall remember me by this gesture."

'True,' I thought to myself, 'the human mind remembers the picturesque, not the essential.'

Hungry for admiration, the Imperator turned to Sporus. He noticed for the first time the boy's hand.

"Sporus, look at me!" he ordered. The boy obeyed.

"You?"

"You said you wished to consign Rome to the flames— —"

Nero boxed his ears.

Poppaea whispered, "Sporus."

For the first time the boy seemed to her more than merely the Emperor's plaything.

Nero, now very serious, listened to the distant grumble from the populace.

"This may mean revolution, Cartaphilus," he whispered.

An idea struck me. "No, Your Majesty, not if you take my advice."

"Speak!"

"We should not be overheard, Your Majesty."

We walked aside.

"Your Majesty, when dealing with angry crowds all logic is futile— —"

"Yes, Cartaphilus."

"Also their attention should be distracted, should it not?"

"Yes."

"The Nazarenes— —"

"I have heard of them."

"Have secret meetings, Your Majesty."

"That is against the law!"

"To them Rome is secondary to the world, and the Emperor inferior to their God. They deny the Emperor's divinity. Men who deny the divinity of the Emperor are capable of any iniquity. . . . "

Nero looked at me long.

"The Nazarenes have set fire to Rome!"

"Yes, Your Majesty."

"Their leaders shall be thrown to the lions! Cartaphilus, you are my friend. I shall make you the Governor of a province."

"What province is comparable to the friendship of Nero?"

X

THE GREAT GOD ENNUI—THE WIND'S WILL

NERO would never forgive me: I had seen him weak. Poppaea could never forget that I had sought no repetition of our ferocious amour. If Nero discovered the singularity of my fate I would not fare well. He would put me to the test. Perhaps it would amuse him to see me swing from a rope for years, without dying; or be flogged for months, and still breathe; or be cut to bits, retaining consciousness. Nero was subtle and insatiable in his curiosity! Or perhaps, angry that I could outlive and outlove him, it would enter his diabolical mind to mutilate me to deprive me of pleasure. I could not face eternity as a eunuch . . .

The seven hills began to stifle me. I decided to disappear.

I stood at the crossroads and asked: 'Whither?' I turned to the east; I turned to the west; to the north, to the south. Whither? Every path was open to me, but I was like a man whose feet are nailed to the ground. At each extremity I saw an enormous figure, squatting, his face between his palms,—Ennui, ubiquitous and everlasting.

It is not enough to live. One must find a purpose, a reason for existence.

What did I desire? What purpose could I make my own? How should I conquer the terrible god who squatted, his face between his hands, at the end of each road?

"Whither?"

A man passed by on a brown donkey. I asked him where the road to my right led to. "All roads lead to Rome," he smiled and passed on. Was his remark a warning, or an oracle? What did it mean? Should I return to the Eternal City?

What god was entrusted with my well-being? Reason, not faith, was my guidance. That was the cause of my quarrel with Jesus and his disciples. I would not—perhaps could not—believe. I must investigate, weigh, reject . . . waiting for time and space to expose, hidden like some black pearl, Falsehood, the Kernel of Truth.

Even the miracle of my own existence did not make me believe in the supernatural. Somewhere there was a mystery; but I refused to worship it. I refused to call it God, or the Son of God, merely because it baffled my reason.

Waving my fist in the air, I exclaimed: "Jesus, did you imagine you could frighten me into belief? Did you imagine you could persuade me by some trick of hypnotism, by the subtle power of certain words? My defiance shall outlive your curse! I am he who does not believe! I am he who accepts no truth as final!"

The sky was very red. Two clouds above me seemed to shape themselves into a fiery cross. Did my words provoke such anger in heaven? I racked my memory to discover how the sky had looked previous to my harangue. I could not tell. I could only doubt and speculate. Doubt—always doubt—yes, that would be the symbol of my life: doubt never assuming the hue of certainty, certainty always dissolving into doubt!

But whither?

I raised a bit of dust, and threw it into the air. The wind blew it to the east. "It is the hand of God!" I exclaimed.

I laughed.

XI

I ENTER DELHI ON AN ELEPHANT—A FAITHFUL SERVANT—THE LEVITATION—MY FRIEND THE FAKIR—I BECOME A MAGICIAN

I ENTERED Delhi, riding on an elephant. The driver walked ahead of the animal, shouting. "Make way for my master! Make way for my master!" The elephant flapped his great ears and raised his trunk toward me. I fed him on small hazel nuts. He was as gentle and playful as a young dog. I had bought him some months previous from a blind merchant, and I became very fond of him. I hired the driver the same day, upon the recommendation of a shopkeeper. The man was worthy of the beast. He was as kind and as sportive, and, with the exception of a few phrases, as taciturn. I was frequently tempted to feed him on hazel nuts.

At the crossroads, a crowd of people encircled a very dark-skinned man, with a long white beard, who waved a black cloth and uttered incomprehensible sounds mingled with prayers from the Upanishads. At his feet, a shrub was rising. He sprinkled water upon it, while continuing his incantation and the waving of the cloth. The trunk spread into branches upon which blossomed large leaves. When the tree reached his knees, the man stopped, breathed deeply several times, and mopped his face.

"Make way for my master!"

"Wait! Wait! Don't disperse the people. I want to see more of this."

The driver helped me jump off the elephant, which turned around and struck my arm gently with his trunk. I filled it with the nuts. "Take him to the empty space yonder, and wait until I come. But be careful," I whispered into his ear. "My valuables are in that sack."

Animal and man skipped off. I watched them for a few moments, delighted, and mingled with the crowd. The fakir drove several swords into the ground, and asked a boy to stretch out upon the hilts. He covered the body with a black cloth, and motioned to the

68

people to make room. For several minutes, he uttered queer sounds, discoursed on life and death, prayed, all the time waving his arms to east, west, north and south.

The body began to rise slowly, constantly, until it overtopped us all. It remained in the air a few moments, then descended, as leisurely as it had risen. The man removed the cloth, rubbed the boy's forehead and nostrils, made strange gestures over him. The boy opened his eyes, looked about bewildered, and jumped off the swords. The spectators laughed. The fakir bowed profoundly and passed around a wooden bowl. The people dispersed.

"I amuse them; I make them laugh, and they do not give me enough to eat."

"Is it possible?"

"See for yourself."

He showed me the bowl which was almost empty.

"I know a place, my friend, where you would be considered a god, if you performed miracles of this sort."

"Where is it? I am not as old as I seem and can travel for days without tiring."

"Crucifixion, however, is apt to precede apotheosis."

He looked at me and smiled. "The penalty is disproportionate to the honor, I fear, sir."

"You are wise."

He was about to go. "Wait. Since you do not wish to become a god . . . do you wish at least, to make money?"

He bowed very profoundly. "At your service."

"I come from very far off countries. I am a man of leisure, have nothing to do. If you should care to teach me some of your tricks— —"

"Not tricks, sir, I beg you . . . art."

"Art . . . it would be a most entertaining way of spending my time and a means of amusement for my friends."

"It is not easy to teach, sir."

"Does it not depend upon the reward you obtain?"

"My master is wise."

"My servant and my elephant await me yonder. Come along."

We reached the spot, but I saw neither elephant nor servant. "Strange. I ordered my man to wait for me here but— —"

We walked up and down. We looked into the distance.

After an exhaustive search, I came to the conclusion that my very gentle elephant and my gentler servant had disappeared.

"There are many such rascals around here," the old man suggested.

"You can't imagine how faithful he seemed."

"He only awaited his opportunity. If you wish it, I can direct you to the authorities, who will search for the rascal."

"Are they very severe with thieves?"

"No . . . they merely cut off their hands."

"I prefer not to find him."

He looked at me for a long while. "You are not a Hindu, and probably not a Buddhist. How can you be so humane?"

"Other religions and philosophies also teach charity." He shook his head.

I had told my servant that all my valuables were in the sack. As a matter of fact, however, I had nothing there, save some clothing and a few trifles. I wished to direct his attention from where I really kept my valuables, for I never stretched to its limits the elastic faculty of man's honesty.

For several months the old fakir and I retired to a solitary villa, where he taught me many remarkable tricks. In a long life, such as mine, it was well to know things that dazzle the onlookers. I rewarded him handsomely.

"It's strange," he said, "you pay to learn what I should gladly forget."

"That is often the case, my friend."

"Will you allow me to praise you, sir? You have a marvelous faculty for the art. You should continue with it."

"Are there better teachers than yourself?"

"Not better, but more accomplished."

He mentioned several Hindu names. Then scratching his head, "But I'm thinking of another man . . . the greatest of them all . . . a Greek . . . but he is not a fakir like me. He is a saint. His great wisdom and the purity of his life, enabled him to perform miracles—not trifles, such as these. His name is Apollonius the Tyanean."

XII

APOLLONIUS OF TYANA RAISES THE DEAD—DAMIS THE FAVORITE DISCIPLE

APOLLONIUS was not in. The door to his house being open, I entered nevertheless. A very simple home, a few pieces of furniture, Greek statuary, Hindu vases, and large piles of manuscripts. I seated myself on the floor, my legs under me, and waited. 'You have always time to wait, Cartaphilus. You need never be in haste.'

It was early afternoon, and the sun basked upon the threshold— a luminous, tamed serpent. I closed my eyes. Peace caressed me like a kind, smooth hand, and I was on the point of falling asleep when two young men broke the reflection of the sun, and entered the room.

I rose and bowed.

"I have come to see the Master. Having found the door open, I took the liberty of entering. Have I transgressed the laws of courtesy?"

"Our master's door is never closed, and he who seeks truth is welcome always," answered one of the young men, motioning to me to sit down.

We were silent for a while.

"Damis, you were recounting the conversation between our Master and the prisoners."

"Oh, yes. He touched the arm of the thief, saying: 'While we live, my friend, we are all prisoners, for the soul is bound to the body and suffers much.'

" 'Ah,' remarked the thief, 'but we are not all cast into jail. Some of us live in palaces.'

" 'He who builds a house,' replied our master, 'builds one more prison for himself. Cities are only common prisons and the earth is bound to the ocean as by a chain.'

" 'Ah, but life even in prison is very sweet,' replied the murderer, who is. to be quartered tomorrow.

" 'True freedom,' replied our master, 'consists in loving neither

71

life nor death overmuch.' The prisoner wept, paying no attention to his words."

"The people marvel at the miracles of the master but they cannot grasp his thoughts."

"The people clamor for miracles, not for truth."

"A philosophy degenerates in proportion to the number of those who embrace it."

"Still— —"

"I know, my friend. You would like to go among all the nations of the earth and preach the Master's gospel."

"I feel in me a great passion . . . a need to wander, Damis."

They remained silent. I watched Damis. He was fair, and his traits were delicate. If his nose had not been perfectly Hellenic, his resemblance to John would have been startling.

The sun receded until only one thin strip still remained on the threshold. In a few moments, it also slipped silently off.

Apollonius entered. He was tall and thin. His full snow-white beard, hung leisurely upon his chest. His eyes were large and black. He wore a white silk robe and a silver belt of exquisite design. Upon his left wrist he had a wide bracelet studded with a large emerald. He bowed and bade me welcome.

"Master! Master!" some voices shouted at the door.

Apollonius turned, unperturbed. "What is it, my friends?"

"Master!" An elderly woman in mourning, knelt before him. A young man remained standing on the threshold, his head bent.

"Master! Do a miracle!"

"There are no miracles, woman."

"Master! Bring my daughter back to life. Only a little while ago she was talking to us, laughing, jesting, when suddenly she placed her hand upon her heart . . . and fell. We threw water upon her, called the physician, prayed to the gods! . . . She is dead, master! She is dead!"

"Is she not happier now?"

"No, master. She was to be married in a week. There is the young groom."

"Master, give life again to my bride, I beg you! We loved each other as no one ever loved."

The master smiled. "Do you like to be awakened rudely from a profound sleep, young man?"

"Awaken her, awaken her, Master!"

The woman embraced his legs. The young man knelt at the door, weeping.

"Give me back my daughter, Master!" she sobbed.

Apollonius meditated, his eyes half-closed, his left hand protruding from his belt. "Where is your daughter, woman?" he asked at last.

"She is in the cart, outside, Master," the young man answered.

"Bring her in!"

The corpse was brought in.

Apollonius rubbed the girl's forehead gently and pressed her limp hands.

The girl's eyelids trembled; her chest heaved slightly.

"Master! Master!" the mother exclaimed.

Apollonius raised his forefinger, demanding silence. He continued rubbing the girl's forehead and hands, whispering, "Awake!"

The girl opened her eyes, and sighed deeply.

The people who had meanwhile gathered at the door, fell upon their faces.

The mother and the bridegroom knelt at the sides of the resurrected girl, mumbling words of endearment. Apollonius stretched out his right hand. His voice, as he spoke, was like the cool waters of a brook, tumbling softly over stones whose edges have been smoothed and rounded.

"Death and Life," he remarked, addressing his pupils, "are two facets of the same jewel—sleeping—waking. What reason is there, then, to seek either Death or Life? . . . Seek rather freedom from both!"

The girl sobbed. Her mother and her lover helped her rise. She hid her face in her hands.

The people dispersed. No one remained, save a dog, who wagged his tail lustily for a few moments, and ran away.

Apollonius was walking silently, his hands clasped behind him. Damis walked on his right. The master looked at me.

"Master," I said, "how can such a miracle be accomplished? How can you resurrect the dead?"

"To recall a person from death into life is no more miraculous than to arouse him from sleep. Dying and living are equally mysterious and equally simple," Apollonius replied.

"But you are thwarting Nature, master. All living things must die."

"Are you sure?" Apollonius responded, looking strangely at me. His eyes, like the eyes of Jesus, seemed to penetrate the core of my being. He added, "Life and death depend upon a slight readjustment-balance. The skillful merchant may lift or lower either side, by adding or subtracting a tiny weight."

Apollonius had replied to my unspoken question.

My mysterious fate presented itself to me in a different angle, much simpler, much less marvelous. It was almost commonplace. I felt for the time being, neither sad nor joyous. I was neither a man in plight nor a man specially favored. Life and death were too much akin.

Apollonius said, guessing my thought, "Life and death, my son, are one. They are different beats of the same rhythm."

We re-entered.

"Master," I asked, "can a man find his soul in the space of a single life?"

"It is not a question of finding, my friend, but of seeking."

"Why seek, then, that which cannot be found?"

"That which can be found . . . is it worth the seeking?"

XIII

DAMIS, APOLLONIUS AND JESUS—THE DOUBLE BLOSSOM
OF PASSION—"CARTAPHILUS DO YOU WANT
TO DIE?"—"SEEK—AND PERHAPS—
YOU SHALL FIND."

BEYOND my name, the Master asked me nothing. Our minds met
where the accidents of flesh were meaningless.

Damis was the favorite disciple. Apollonius considered him as
a son. But he was as dear to me as he was to the Master. Hand in
hand we walked for hours, discoursing on the remarks of Apollonius,
trying to grasp his subtleties. Frequently, I would call him "John."
He would smile.

"Why do you call me John, Cartaphilus?"

"I can think of no name half as beautiful for you as John." I
preferred not to tell him my story—for the time being, at least.
Damis had learnt from his master the art of discretion.

"Perhaps something of our ancient prejudices still linger in our
souls," Apollonius once said. "Perhaps we might be inconsiderate
enough to judge a man by his race or ancestry. It is better to know
nothing of him, except as he appears to us in manner and speech."

Apollonius was fond of the full moon. "The sun is too strong for
our eyes; the earth is beneath our feet, and we cannot see it; the
moon allows us to understand the meaning of the cosmic harmony.
She does not attempt to convince us of her glory by either scorching
or blinding us."

I looked at Apollonius. He squatted on his doorstep as radiant as
the moon and as unperturbed.

"Master, have you ever heard of Jesus?"

"Yes, in our youth—we were of exactly the same age—we were
both the disciples of the same master in Thibet."

"In Thibet?" I asked surprised.

"Yes."

This, then, accounted for the long absence of Jesus from Jerusalem. He never spoke about it even to his intimate friends. 'A

god,' I thought, 'must be mysterious.' Addressing Apollonius, I said,—"Master, do you know that Jesus has become a god?"

Apollonius smiled. "He was always ambitious. Has he many followers, Cartaphilus?"

"Yes, but they are, with few exceptions, recruited exclusively from the very poor. To follow him, a man must relinquish his wealth. A rich man, according to one of his parables, can no more enter his Heaven than a camel can pass through the eye of a needle."

"How characteristic!" Apollonius remarked with an amused smile. "Always a Jew! Only a Jew—albeit a philosopher or a god—would attach so much importance to wealth as to make its denial the basis of salvation."

The clarity of the idea startled me.

We continued watching the moon for a long time in silence.

"Master, I have been with you for an entire year. You have been as a deep and an inexhaustible fountain of delight to me. I would lower an empty bucket into it, and always it would return filled to the brim with wisdom that cooled and refreshed me."

"The water sought the throat as eagerly."

"Master, I have traveled in many lands and have seen many things. I have loved and lived much."

He nodded.

"I see before me a dreary desert of years, a desert without end. Can life offer me nothing except repetition?"

"Time, Cartaphilus, is elastic. It may be stretched or it may be shortened."

"Alas, Master, time must stand still for me—perhaps forever."

He looked at me.

"What is the difference between a man condemned to die on the morrow and ourselves, except that our sentence is indefinite?"

"No, no! I am not speaking in metaphors. I must actually tarry on earth for thousands of years, maybe until the end of time."

He was interested, but not startled.

"Is it not a strange thing, Master?"

"All things are strange, Cartaphilus. But tell me what powerful factor disarrayed so violently the processes of your being?"

Apollonius listened to my extraordinary recital. The moon thinned and became amorphous like the torn fragment of a cloud. The sun rose silently, as if on tiptoes, afraid perhaps of the Great Dark that had so recently devoured it. I spoke on, omitting nothing. A young water-carrier passed by, and offered us sweets and cool water.

"Master, am I not accursed?"

"Life is not an evil, Cartaphilus, nor is death. No one is really ever born, no one really dies. There is but one Life, and of that we all partake—to a lesser or greater degree."

"How had Jesus the power to inflict this upon me?"

"I have seen greater marvels, Cartaphilus. Jesus, too, has seen. The subtle powers that govern the life and death of the body may be arrested or paralyzed, by a shock. People die of fear or of joy. Is it inconceivable for the reverse process to occur? The shock that can end life, by acting upon the chemistry of our being, may intensify or prolong it. . . . "

"Will he ever appear again, Master? Must I tarry until he is reborn?"

"In infinity the same note is sounded again and again in the identical pitch. The same type recurs."

'Infinity!'

Apollonius looked at me critically.

"Tell me, Cartaphilus, would you really relinquish life if it were possible? Do you want to die? . . ."

"Is it possible?"

"Only if your passion for death is greater than your passion for life."

"I am no longer certain, Master."

"Then you must carry your fetters, Cartaphilus, or if you please, your garland. Make it a garland of roses," Apollonius continued. "Be not afraid of yourself, Cartaphilus. Be strong!"

"Can we be strong? Are we not tossed about by the whim of an irrational fate?"

"The will is both free and not free. If you fling a dead leaf into the air, it is carried hither and thither without volition. If you toss a bird upward, the wind may hamper its flight and dash its brains against a rock, but while life persists it will struggle: its will modifies the wind's will. The average man is a leaf tossed hither and thither. He who has lifted the veil from the face of life resembles the bird. He cannot dominate but, within limits, may direct his fate."

"Master," I said, " the bird has no conception of boredom; he rapturously sings the same note forever. He has no purpose beyond existence. But a man . . . must not a man's life have a purpose, Master, if he is to escape from the clutches of the great God Ennui?"

"Even so."

"What purpose can last centuries? Can knowledge, for instance, suffice?"

"Knowledge is repetitious. One lifetime suffices to recognize its sameness."

"Love, Master?"

"The difference between one love and another becomes finer and finer, until it disappears."

"Hate, Master?"

"Hate may be mightier than love, but hate dies out like a fire. Time is a great sea."

"What then . . . what then, Master?"

Apollonius meditated. "Have you not spoken of John and Mary, Cartaphilus?"

"Yes."

"You loved both."

"Both."

He leisurely turned his bracelet.

"It is doubtful whether you will ever find a purpose which will run parallel to Time's strange zigzag."

I sighed.

"And yet if a purpose should be robust enough and capable of a long endurance, would it not suffice?"

"It would, Master."

He combed his beard, twisting the end into a sharp point.

"In Damis you see something of John. Even in Poppaea you caught a glint of Mary. All types reintegrate. All return, with infinite variations.

"The ideal you seek is neither Mary nor John, but a synthesis of both, a double blossom of passion, combining male and female, without being a monster. . . . If you could find John and Mary in one, Cartaphilus, so that touching Mary, you might feel the thrill of John . . . and speaking to John, you might hear the voice of Mary . . . would it not rejoice you, Cartaphilus?"

"It would be the supreme felicity, a devastating joy—a divine surprise, an inconceivable rapture."

My head turned, my ears rang. I shivered. "Yes, Master. Yes. That is what I desire . . . that is what, in his heart, every man yearns for. Master, you are wise beyond wisdom."

Apollonius smiled.

"But Master, is it possible? Is it possible to find them both in one?"

"All things are possible, Cartaphilus. The World Spirit, in his ceaseless experiments, may evolve your dream. . . . Seek . . . and perhaps . . . you shall find."

"Did you not say, Master, 'that which may be found is it worth the seeking?' "

"There are many truths, Cartaphilus, and every truth carries within itself its own contradiction."

He rose and walked into the room.

Damis, seated in the semi-darkness behind us, had listened to my story without uttering a sound.

"Damis," I said, "you have heard my recital, but you have said nothing."

"Cartaphilus, why was John's love not great enough to embrace both Jesus and you?"

"The Jewish God is a jealous God," I replied. "Jesus inherited the jealous strain from his Father. . . . He enjoined children to forsake their fathers, and lovers their sweethearts, before accepting them as his followers. He recognized no human tie. 'Woman, what have I to do with thee?' was his reply to his own mother when she upbraided him for his selfishness."

"Our Master makes no conditions. He demands nothing. I love both him and you."

Tenderly I took his hand in mine. Then, weary beyond endurance, I placed my head upon his chest. "Damis, let me sleep."

"Sleep, Cartaphilus."

When I awoke, Apollonius was standing over us, pale, his head bent upon his chest. In his right hand, he held a tall staff, the large branch of a cherry-tree, planed and surmounted by a gold knob, the shape of several snakes huddled together.

"My children, the time has come when I must depart."

"Master!" we both exclaimed.

"The day has come. I must go."

"Whither?" Damis asked.

"Wherever the spirit leads my feet."

"Master, must you conceal the path even from those that love you?"

"If a man cannot conceal his life, should he not at least conceal his death?"

"Master, speak not of death!"

"Life is a symbol. Death is a symbol."

Damis threw himself into his arms. "Master!"

I kissed his hands.

"Apollonius, although we are of the same age, I think of you as my father . . . a father whom I love. I understand better than Damis what you mean. You must go. Damis, make not our Master's departure difficult."

"Shall we meet again, Master?" Damis asked.

"The moon begins as a crescent and grows until it becomes a perfect disk. The clouds tear it, then, and smother it, until it vanishes. But the moon is born again . . . and grows again . . . eternally. Is it the same moon always—or is it a new one?"

When we looked up, the white head of Apollonius was disappearing in the distance.

XIV

DAMIS FALLS ASLEEP—ETERNAL COMRADES—THE MARRIAGE OF THE BLOOD—"YOUR BLOOD IS POISON!"

Toward morning, Damis fell asleep in my arms. He clutched at me, muttering: "Don't go! Don't go!" I do not know whether his invocation was addressed to Apollonius or to me. He woke up with a jerk, and looked about, bewildered. "The Master is gone, Cartaphilus," he said hopelessly.

"Your loneliness is not comparable to mine, Damis."

He caressed me shyly, pressing his lips against my cheek delicately like a younger brother.

"Do not carry the past like a chain about your neck, Damis."

"You speak like the Master."

"His voice would have been gentler," I said, "and his words more beautiful."

"Your voice, too, is gentle, and your words are beautiful, Cartaphilus."

"Damis, if I could share with you the strange vitality that defies the years! What marvelous vistas would unfold themselves if we wandered, eternal comrades, arm in arm through the centuries!"

"Even if it were possible, Cartaphilus, would it be desirable? Who knows what changes time may work in us? Who knows if our friendship so dear to us now, would not become a chain about our necks?"

He remained silent for a while, then continued: "Besides, unlike you, I could not endure the loss of those I cherish. My heart would be bruised. I would pray for death . . . and death would not come."

"One learns to forget and to laugh, Damis," and I laughed almost unwillingly.

Silence descended upon us with brooding wings.

After a while, Damis asked: "Will you ever desert me, Cartaphilus?"

"How shall a man be certain of the future, my friend? Are we the masters of our fate? But if my heart desired ever to fly away from you, would I consider it a joy to make you my traveling companion on my pathway to infinity?"

Damis placed his head upon my shoulder. Again silence nestled about us. "Cartaphilus, is it really possible for you to transfer to another something of the mysterious gift that sets you aside from all human beings?"

"I do not know, Damis. If it were, would you wish to face eternity with me?"

"The thought frightens me, Cartaphilus, but it also lures me. The gift of eternal life may be a blessing to you and to me a curse, and yet who can refuse a drink from the cup of the gods? But am I strong enough to bear the deep darkness and the fierce light of the path where the immortals wander?"

I caressed his head, soft and tawny like John's. "It is difficult to be strong. The heart, like the athlete's muscle, does not harden except by blows." He smiled at me through the tears that rolled down his cheek.

"Come with me, Damis. Let our destinies mingle and merge together!"

"So be it, Cartaphilus."

A small house on the outskirts of the town was the home of the most celebrated doctor in Delhi. The door was low, and we bent our heads in order to enter.

The doctor was a tiny old man, whose long white beard constituted almost half of him. The physician, satisfied that his services would be handsomely rewarded, begged us to sit down, treated us to sweets and water, and recounted his marvelous deeds. He had given life to the dead, limbs to the crippled, sight to the blind, virility to those shipwrecked on the tides of love.

"But, Doctor," I finally managed to interrupt him, "can you prolong human life? Can you stretch its span indefinitely. . . .?"

"I have cured people of mortal diseases. Thus their span of life— —"

"Can you make a man live for centuries . . . ?"

He looked at me quizzically. "The gentleman deigns to mock me."

"Is it not possible?"

"Everything is possible, sir. In medicine, however, one must deal with what is at least probable. Experience is the Father of Knowledge."

"Is the prolongation of life by divers magics and devices an unknown scientific phenomenon?"

"No, I have heard of a few extraordinary cases of longevity. I cannot see the benefit of such a state, since a man must re-don the garments of the flesh again and again until at last, by saintliness, he enters Nirvana."

'Does man pretend to scorn long life,' I thought, 'because the grapes are beyond his reach? Does he simply console himself? Or is there in the depths of our being, a will to die as well as a will to live? Does all life yearn for the perfect peace of the womb . . . ?'

"Doctor," I said smilingly, "I am much older than you."

He laughed, his beard dancing upon his chin.

"Older perhaps in wisdom, but not in years," he cackled drily. "Surely you exaggerate your age."

I remained silent, noting the strange instruments, many-shaped knives and multicolored phials that crowded the room. Pleased by my curiosity, the physician explained their manifold uses.

"Doctor," I said, "I did not exaggerate when I said that I am much older than you."

"It is possible to look younger than one's age," he answered, straightening up. "I look older than mine."

I shook my head. "I am probably twice your age. I have lived more than a century and still my vitality continues to burn with undiminished intensity."

He frowned, then smiled, his eyes almost closing. "I hope your years have brought you joy."

"Joy is the sister of pain," I remarked, careful not to arouse his jealousy. Man might be envious of anything that another possesses —even his cross!

"I am very lonesome, Doctor. My friends die, and I remain to mourn always."

He looked at me quizzically, still uncertain if I was telling the truth, or if I was jesting. Perhaps he doubted my sanity, although miracles were commonplaces in India.

"Lonesomeness, Doctor, is a canker that gnaws at the heart.'

He sighed sympathetically.

"Doctor, is there a means by which I could communicate my vitality to another?"

The Doctor pulled at his beard and coughed, at a loss for an answer.

"My companion, because of the friendship he bears me, is willing to brave fate with me, to walk with me to the end, if there is an end. . . ."

"Friendship is a priceless jewel," he remarked sententiously.

"If you can devise some way by which I can give half of my life to my friend I shall make you as rich as a Rajah," I continued quickly.

He waved his hands. "That is a mere incident. I serve Truth and Science first."

"Is there a way, Doctor?" I asked anxiously.

"I am not certain."

"Wisdom always wavers at first— —"

"Perhaps . . ." He spoke to himself. "Perhaps . . ."

"— —but triumphs in the end. Am I not right, Doctor?"

After a long silence, he said: "I must meditate for nine days; for nine days I must read the secret books of India and of Egypt; for nine days still, consult the stars, and go into a long trance. On the last day of the full moon, I shall know definitely if I can conscientiously take your case."

"Very well. Meanwhile, I know that books are expensive, and the stars will not allow themselves to be consulted, save by means of costly charts. Therefore, permit me, Doctor, to ease your task."

I filled his hand with silver.

He thanked me. "Buddha will be propitious."

The physician received us gleefully. "I have found it! I have found it!" He pulled at his long beard, until the pain made his eyes tear. I pressed the hand of Damis.

We seated ourselves. The physician told us, in minute details, about the labor and pains he had endured to learn the mystery I sought. He had fasted, thirsted, fallen into a long trance, and nearly became blind over charts and books.

"Your reward, Doctor, shall be proportionate."

He was indignant. "Is it for this I was working? Are not Science and Truth supreme? Are they not a reward in themselves?" He seemed so sincere in his expostulation that I almost believed him.

"Shall it be said, however, that Science and Truth remained unrewarded?" I asked.

"That is another matter, sir, and it depends upon you."

"Science and Truth shall have both honors and gold."

He bowed until the tip of his beard touched the ground. We were silent for a while. Then he began again. "Where is the spirit

of life housed? In the blood. Remove a few jars of the red elixir
from the body,—does not man die? Is it not because the blood is
hot that we are young; and when the blood freezes, like water in
winter, are we not old? And how do we live once more in our children, if not through the blood? The blood is the man. Blood is the
symbol and the truth of Life!"

I nodded.

"Therefore, if your blood fills this young man's veins,—he will
partake of your life."

"It seems logical," I said.

"It is the truth of all the Buddhas. It is a great discovery, and
the stars are propitious."

"When can this transfusion of my blood into my friend's veins
take place?"

"At once, if you will. I have prepared a couch in my other room.
You will both stretch out upon it. I shall open a vein in his arm, and
a vein in yours, and let the stream of your blood ·trickle into his
body."

I looked at him somewhat unconvinced.

"Have you ever performed such an operation before?"

"Several times, but for other reasons. The quantity of blood
tapped from your body need not be large. The intermingling of your
life and his will be sufficient. The marriage of the blood will be
consummated."

I kept silent.

"No other leech in all India would undertake this operation."

"Why not?"

"Because," he whispered mysteriously, "I found the method in
the Book of Forbidden Lore."

"Will you permit me to consult with my friend for a few
moments?"

"Certainly."

"Damis," I said, "I believe his idea is the true one, for I, too,
have long ago come to a similar conclusion. My blood must mingle
with yours, that you may partake of my life."

"Yes, Cartaphilus."

"Damis, are you still willing to risk—immortality? The marriage
of our spirits, alas, may be shorter-lived than the marriage of our
blood. . . ."

"Cartaphilus, Apollonius was as a father to me; you are my
brother. I cannot face the future alone. I need you as the vine needs

the oak. Let me lean against you forever!" His pale features were flushed, his eyes were restless like torches reflected in water that is stirred. "Unless," he added suddenly, "you think I will be a burden— —"

"Your delicate weight shall be as natural to me and as pleasurable as upon my shoulders is the weight of my head."

I turned to the leech.

"We are ready."

He asked us to strip, and offered us a potion. "This will deaden the pain, although I expect it to be very slight."

We stretched out upon the couch. He looked at us, took our pulse, examined our eyes, tested each limb. Over Damis he stopped much longer, troubled by the boy's epicene beauty. His aged hands trembled. 'His senses are not dead,' I thought. "My friend is very handsome," I whispered. He looked at me guiltily. "Yes, very handsome."

Damis was asleep. The potion and the loss of blood had weakened him. I was quite conscious, and felt no pain, save a tiny itching sensation. The little doctor had bandaged our arms to stop the flow of the blood. Seeing that I watched him, he made many curious motions and mumbled extravagant sounds. I smiled. I had lived long enough to know that every trade had its tricks.

"Is my friend still asleep, Doctor?" I asked.

"I shall wake him now."

He touched him gently over the face. Damis did not stir. He shook him, at first lightly, then a little more energetically. Damis remained stock-still. He rubbed his temples, tickled the soles of his feet, pricked him with a needle. All in vain.

"What is wrong, Doctor?" I asked, jumping up. He did not answer, but pressed his ear against the heart, and applied a small metal object to the nostrils. He glared at me.

"What is the trouble?" I shouted. "Quick, tell me!"

"You have killed him. Your blood is poison," he hissed.

"I killed him! You scoundrel, it was your potion— —"

"My potion?"

"Yes, your potion."

"The drug was harmless, mainly water."

I hurled him against the wall, where he crouched, groaning and grumbling, "Your blood is poison! Your blood is poison!"

I bent over Damis. His features were pinched and his limbs had already the rigidity of a corpse. "Damis, Damis," I wept. "Damis, do you not hear me? Cartaphilus calls you, Damis,—my friend!"

The physician did not dare to move from the spot. I rushed at him again. "Fool!" I shouted. "You consulted the stars, and went into trances . . . and now, look! See what you have done! You have killed him! You have killed my friend!"

"How should I know that your blood is poison? The stars did not mention that, nor the voice in the trance."

"My blood is poison?"

"Look at him, look at your minion! He is turning black!"

It was true. I covered my face with my hands. 'Your blood is poison!' The sentence maddened me. It seemed like the echo of another sentence years ago that had rung in my ears, with the violence of a storm.

"Help me carry him out."

We placed the corpse upon a pile of wood, sprinkled it with perfumes and aromatics. The red fangs of the fire devoured the body of him to whom the gift of life was the gift of death.

I turned to go. The physician held my arm. "Go away!" I shouted. "Clumsy fool!"

"Am I to get no reward for my labors?"

I glared at him. He followed me. "Master, Master! Are you breaking your promise?"

"What promise?"

"My fee!"

"Impudent wretch!" I walked on. He followed me, mumbling, "Was it my fault that your blood——?"

Before he could finish the sentence, I struck him on the mouth. He fell. "You have killed me!" he shouted. I threw a purse at him. He rose, seized it, and ran off with the agility of a young animal.

XV

GOD OR DEMON—I AM STILL A MAN—THE RAJAH'S SISTER ASI-MA—NUPTIALS AT SEA

I DID not leave my room for a long while. I do not know what perturbed me more: the loss of Damis, or the knowledge that my blood was accurst. Was I fated to slay those I loved? Was my love a serpent, whose fangs are fatal? Must I wander henceforth uncompanioned and loveless? I walked up and down my room, talking to myself in all the languages I knew.

It struck me that I did not even possess a language quite my own. "Who am I, what am I?" I shouted, and the walls answered, "Stranger! Wanderer!" I envied the pariah who dared to call himself by his true name, who could mention the place and date of his birth, without fear or confusion.

"A human being," I expostulated, "has significance alone in time and space. He can be neither a star, whirling in infinity, nor a feather blown about by whimsical winds." I thought of Jesus, and a great hatred overcame me. "Who was he to impose upon me a life suitable for a god or a demon, but not for a man? By what right, natural or supernatural, did he wish this doom upon me? We shall be enemies," I shouted, "eternal enemies!"

My nature had become very elastic, however, and I could pass rapidly from despair to a rational understanding. 'After all,' I thought, 'had you been like other men, Cartaphilus, you would have turned to dust long ago, after dragging your body through wearisome years of decrepitude and pain. What have you lost that you cannot replace? Love? Is not one love the antidote of another? And if your blood be poison, if you are brother to the rattlesnake, Cartaphilus, what of that? The serpent is not venomous to its mate. Find the mate to whom your blood is a balm.

'What have you known of love? What have you known of life? Ten times the span of man's life are not sufficient to slake your thirst for knowledge. Time is your ally. He will bring back all your loves, even Damis, even Mary and John. Time holds for you under the cloak of the years, unimaginable delights. Apollonius the Tyanean, has said that a great, a supreme love waits for you in some far away corner of the corridor of infinity,—a love which will be both Mary and John. You shall yet find it, Cartaphilus.

'You can laugh at the sands as they run through the hour glass. You need not hurry. You can walk through life with slow, deliberate steps,—an aristocrat in the midst of slaves!'

Nothing consoled me save thought. This sharp blade that hurt most men, was like a cool, smooth hand caressing me. In Reality, I found the Great Fiction which other people endeavor to snatch from Illusion.

'Cartaphilus,' I said to myself, 'if your life is suitable only for a god or a demon—be a god or a demon!'

I soon discovered that I was still human. Drouth was parching India. In vain the priests sacrificed victims to the implacable gods. Moved to pity, I tried my arts as a rainmaker. It was one of the lesser tricks which I had learned in the house of Apollonius. I do not know whether natural causes or my incantations produced the rain, but I was regarded by the natives as their saviour. This made my position unpleasantly conspicuous and aroused the jealousy of the Rajah.

"Miraculous coincidences," he remarked, to me, as he bade me farewell, "sometimes save the faces of prophets and of kings."

"Not only their faces," I replied, "but also their necks."

He smiled.

Two black eyes peered at us from behind the curtain of a window. Was it one of the Rajah's wives? The Rajah's enormous belly shook with suppressed excitement.

Touching the rug before the throne three times with my head, I departed.

My elephant had carried me several miles beyond Delhi when suddenly I heard someone shouting. A man ran towards me waving his hands. His body heaved grotesquely and he wiped the foam from the corners of his mouth with the back of his hand.

"My mistress, Princess Asi-ma, is more beautiful than the full moon in whose reflection the leaves of the great palm trees carve their gorgeous patterns."

"I doubt it not."

"Her love for my new master whose word brought rain to the city is deeper than the seas."

"Your new master accepts both you and the Princess."

We were silent for a while.

"If Buddha is propitious, and we can escape the Rajah's men, my mistress shall be my master's wife."

"Your master's joy is great."

"If not, we shall all three be crushed by the elephant's paws, for the Rajah wished to marry my mistress, himself."

"Is it permissible for a brother to marry his sister?"

"The Rajah's sword is very sharp, Master."

I knew now what face had peered at me from behind the curtain.

Asi-ma approached us, and knelt before me. I raised her, and looked at her. "You are indeed more beautiful than the full moon." She lowered her lids. Her skin was much lighter than that of the pure Hindu type. Her hair, however, was as black and lustrous. Her breasts were full-blown, as well as her hips, although she could hardly have been more than about fifteen or sixteen years old. She turned to her slave. "Ra-man, have you delivered my message to our master?"

"I have."

"Come," I said. "We have no time to linger, Asi-ma, adorable child."

The two of us mounted one elephant while Ra-man mounted another, and we galloped away.

When we reached the harbor, we descended from our animals. Ra-man ran ahead of us. We followed slowly in the same direction, my arm tightly wound about Asi-ma's waist. The time we had ridden together, her head upon my chest, sufficed to endear her to me. Ra-man waved to us. We approached. A small sailboat was anchored at some distance, but a rowboat scratched its nose gently against the shore. We entered into it. The slave rowed vigorously so that in a few moments we reached the boat. Ra-man jumped into it, lifted Asi-ma, and assisted me. I helped him raise the rowboat, and in another moment we were sailing.

"Look! Look!" exclaimed Asi-ma. "They just missed us." She laughed like a little child. On the shore, a number of armed men upon elephants looked in our direction, and either waved their hands or shook their fists, I could not tell.

"Make me your wife, Cartaphilus."

"You are my wife."

"Make me, now . . . now. . . ." She drew my head to her lips and kissed me. "Now . . . Cartaphilus."

I pointed to Ra-man.

"He is not a man. It does not matter if he sees."

"Asi-ma, you are a great joy to me."

"Undress me, Cartaphilus."

I was a little clumsy, and at one or two points, perplexed. She laughed, and clapped her hands, but would not help me. She stood at last in the full reflection of the moon, more dazzling than that cold divinity.

"Asi-ma, beloved!"

I spread a lion's skin on the deck, and laid her down gently upon it. For a long while I caressed her. Her body was as smooth as the surface of a still lake. Her breasts were tinged with thin blue veins, which appeared and vanished under her skin. She drew me to her. I relaxed my grip.

The reflection of the moon danced upon us with her soft, silver feet, then lay quietly over us like a head that sleeps.

Ra-man, his arms crossed, looked silent and thoughtful as a sphinx.

"Cartaphilus, you were my husband before."

I did not answer.

"Don't you remember, beloved . . . long, long ago? And you will be again . . . and again . . . until we are one in Nirvana."

"Yes, Asi-ma."

I tried in vain to find any resemblance between her and Lydia, or any of my mistresses. Only the perfume of her hair reminded me of someone whose face I could not recollect.

XVI

I BUY A VILLA—I WATCH THE STARS—"TIME IS A CAT, CARTAPHILUS"—ASI-MA WEEPS

AFTER a few days of sailing, we landed in a small town situated upon a hill that had the shape of a sharp cone. I bought a villa with a large orchard, and built a high, stone wall around it. I was weary of the world and longed for seclusion.

"Asi-ma, my wife, here let us spend the rest of our days in love-making, and peace."

"I am the slave of Cartaphilus."

'The rest of your days, Cartaphilus?' I thought. 'Who knows how many more there will be?'

"I have brought a little gift to my husband." She clapped her hands. "Ra-man, where is the casket?"

Ra-man placed before me a gold casket, an exquisite piece of workmanship. "Open it, Cartaphilus." I opened it. It was filled almost to the brim with jewels—the crown jewels of the Rajah.

"Asi-ma, I will not accept your gift. I have enough wealth."

She did not answer, but played with the jewels, raising them in half-fistfuls and letting them drop back in tiny cascades. "Cartaphilus does not love his wife."

"How can she say that?"

"He scorns her gift, for which she nearly lost her life."

"She herself was a gift beyond compare."

"Is not what she possesses part of herself? Why should he scorn any particle of her?"

I remembered what Apollonius had said in reference to Jesus. Was I still so much a Jew that property mattered to such a degree? Did not my refusal to accept the jewels indicate what importance I really attached to their value? Had her gift been a flower, say, or a trinket, should I have refused?

"My dear, I accept your gift."

"Ra-man, Ra-man! Cartaphilus accepts my gift."

I was happy. With the exception of Hindu philosophers, who initiated me into many of the greater mysteries of the East, and one or two shipowners, with whom I invested some capital, my house was closed to the outer world.

I studied the pathways of the stars. I watched the growth of my trees and flowers. One hundred and twenty different species of birds sang for me; deer gamboled at my approach; an elephant extended his great trunk to be filled with nuts,—and at my feet, like a magnificent lioness, purring delicious nonsense mingled with profound wisdom, stretched out lazily my beloved, my wife.

Asi-ma was standing before the tall, Corinthian silver mirror which I had recently imported for her.

"Cartaphilus, look!" she cried.

"What is it?"

"Cartaphilus, does the mirror lie?"

"Not if it tells you how beautiful you are."

"The mirror tells me something else; alas its voice is more honest but less honeyed than yours."

"Then we shall break the mirror, my love. It is blind, and its tongue is poisoned with falsehood."

"Look, Cartaphilus! See how Time has scratched the edges of my eyes; and also the edges of my lips; and here . . . look . . . look at this long scratch upon my throat! Time is a cat, Cartaphilus."

Her eyes were studded with two, hard tears, which must have smarted her, for she tightened her lids.

"How shall a cat scratch a little kitten? Besides, I know a positive cure for this."

"What, Cartaphilus?"

"My kisses have the power of erasing all such scratches."

"Kiss me!"

I kissed her eyes and her lips. "Now look in the mirror, Asi-ma!"

She looked for a while, then covered her face with her hands. "Time is mightier than your kisses."

I took her on my lap and tried to console her. I called her a dozen pet names, I jested, I was serious, I promised her endless affection, I assured her that she was capable of perennial beauty. She wept quietly, uninterruptedly.

"What a child you are, Asi-ma! What does it matter if you have a few scratches? Besides I see none."

"Must I wait until you notice them, Cartaphilus?"

"What do you mean?"

She did not answer. I did not press her. I feared her decision. I knew that although she had been a slave to my desires, she was capable of obstinate resolution. As long as she had not yet pronounced the words, however, I still hoped it was possible to comfort her. I thought of a new transfusion of blood, but "your blood is poison" struck against my ears like the blow of a fist.

"Besides, my dear, am I not getting older, also? Does not Time scratch my face as well?" I asked.

"No, Cartaphilus. You never grow older. You are a god; you brought rain to the city."

"That . . . that . . . was merely a coincidence."

She shook her head. "You have been since the beginning of things, and will continue forever, Cartaphilus."

"You exaggerate my age a little, beloved."

"No."

We remained silent for a long time. I knew that she was planning what to do, and how to break the news to me.

"There is a full moon tonight, Cartaphilus."

"Yes, my love."

"That is a good omen."

"Yes."

"Tonight you shall make me your wife again under the moon, like the first time, beloved, and . . . and at dawn . . . I shall go away."

"Go away?"

"I shall go back among the people that become old like myself. I shall marry, and have a child whom I shall name after you, Cartaphilus."

"Asi-ma, your words are like so many daggers that stab my heart."

She ruffled my hair playfully. "Those were the words you always spoke when we parted."

"What do you mean, dear?"

"At every incarnation, after I had been your wife, when Time scratched my face, and I told you I was leaving, you always used the same words."

"Asi-ma, that is only a dream."

"You said even that."

"Asi-ma, it is you who are a goddess."

"No, not yet. At some future incarnation, you shall make me a goddess, Cartaphilus, and I shall remain with you always. But the day has not come yet."

"Asi-ma, my dear, my perfect wife . . . since it is the will of Buddha that we separate, it is not you, but I, who must go."

She thought for a while. "Yes, that is true. I had forgotten. It is always you who must go. You must wander about until we meet again."

"Where and when shall I meet you again?"

"Who knows? It may be ten thousand miles from here. It may be ten thousand years. . ."

I opened the gate. Asi-ma accompanied me to the roadway. She threw herself into my arms.

"Farewell, Cartaphilus!"

"Farewell, my Much Beloved!"

"You must go on, Cartaphilus."

Where had we met before? Had I lived other lives before I was Cartaphilus? Was the vista behind me as unending as the road before me?

Shuddering, I drew my cloak about me.

XVII

CAR-TA-PHAL, PRINCE OF INDIA—MARCUS AURELIUS— FAUSTINA TOYS—JESUS IN THE PANTHEON—THE FEMALE WORSHIPER

ONCE more I stood at the crossroads on the outskirts of Rome. I remembered the remark of the man made to me long ago: "All roads lead to Rome." The man had turned to dust by this time; Nero, Poppaea, Sporus, Nero's Golden House,—all dust. But all roads still led to Rome, and I, Cartaphilus, was still living, still young! I felt exalted.

The sun was setting very slowly, and like long streams of pollen dropping silently from some crushed, gigantic flower, its rays gilded the world. The day's heat, dispersing in the cool breezes, scattered a perfume of grass and flowers and vine leaves.

This time it pleased me to enter the Eternal City neither as a Roman citizen nor as a Jew. I was Car-ta-phal, a Hindu Prince. In a splendid chariot and dressed in the Hindu fashion, with a belt and a turban glittering with jewels, I dashed into Rome. The sparks danced about the hoofs of my horses like small stars, and the populace, blasé and sophisticated, gaped in awe and admiration. Their Emperor was a philosopher affecting the black garb, but their instinct was for magnificence and display.

I succeeded in gaining the ear of the Emperor Marcus Aurelius by presenting him with rare manuscripts from the East. He invited me to hear him read one of his essays on virtue.

The reading room of the imperial Palace was poorly lit. Marcus Aurelius could not endure any glaring light. The large statues about the walls mingled their shadows, making curious and grotesque patterns. The guests were reclining on the couches, or standing in small groups, talking. I walked from one statue to another, approaching or standing at distance, feigning admiration. As a matter of fact, they were chiefly imitations from the Greek, and too bulky.

"Rome," sighed an elderly artist, Apollodorus the sculptor, "is no longer the Rome of our fathers. The Christians are destroying our love of beauty. Even," he whispered cautiously, "the Imperator's philosophy has been influenced by them."

"To what do you attribute this hatred for art?"

"They are really Hebrews whose god hates images."

"Are the Hebrews a source of danger?"

"The Hebrews," he laughed, "are no longer a nation."

"Is that possible?"

"Ah, don't you know? Their capital was burnt to the ground, and they were dispersed. It was about time."

"Jerusalem has been razed to the ground?"

"Yes, some years ago."

"And their temple—I heard the Hebrews had a marvelous temple— —"

"We are building a temple to Jove on its site. If I were not so old, I would be sent to administer the work."

I turned my face away. My eyes had filled with tears. Jerusalem . . . the Temple . . . burnt . . . and my people dispersed. All, all of us, wanderers like Cartaphilus!

The Emperor entered, his arm about the waist of the Empress. Everything was average about him. He was neither tall nor short; neither stocky nor thin; neither homely nor handsome. Even his hair was a mixture of gray and black, and his eyes were an indefinite brown that easily changed to gray. The Empress, Faustina, on the contrary, had very pronounced features: a sharp nose, sharp chin and black eyes that seemed sharp as daggers. Her teeth, as she smiled, were white as a young animal's.

Marcus Aurelius seated himself on a throne at an angle of the room, and Faustina upon another one opposite him. Behind her cushioned chair stood a young slave with black curls and long slumberous lashes, waving a fan of white ostrich feathers. The Emperor did not like to be fanned, saying that a Stoic endured heat as well as cold, imperturbably. Apollodorus, who reclined on the couch next to me, whispered: "He catches cold too easily, that's the reason, and he sneezes like a thunderclap."

I made believe I did not hear him.

The Emperor began to read. His voice, too, had nothing distinctive, neither pleasing nor displeasing, running in a straight line somewhere between a bass and a tenor, except occasionally when it rose to a pitch and broke abruptly. Then he would clear his throat and begin again in a straight line.

"Everything which is in any way beautiful is beautiful in itself.

and terminates in itself, not having praise as part of itself. Neither worse than nor better is a thing made by being praised," continued the Emperor.

The Empress yawned. She motioned to the slave that fanned her to come to her right.

"Thou art a little soul, bearing about a corpse, as Epictetus used to say."

Faustina's right hand dropped leisurely over the chair and touched the boy.

The boy shivered.

"Does another do me wrong? Let him look to it. He has his own disposition, his own activity."

The slave continued to fan his mistress, obedient to his training.

"Thou canst pass thy life in an equable flow of happiness, if thou canst go by the right way, and think and act in the right way."

The Empress turned her head. This compelled the boy to move nearer.

The boy trembled.

The Empress smiled.

"Neither the labor which the hand does nor that of the foot is contrary to nature, so long as the foot does the foot's work and the hand the hand's."

The fan almost dropped from the boy's hand.

"Be thou erect, or be made erect."

The boy straightened up as if in obedience to the Imperial command. His face was flushed but he still maintained his courtierlike demeanor. However, as he moved, the fan for a moment touched the face of the Empress.

"Different things delight different people."

The Empress yawned. The boy bit his lips till they bled. The fan fluttered, tipped somewhat, and like a butterfly alighting on a rose, touched her breast lightly.

"Whatever one does or says, I must be good."

Faustina was not listening to Marcus Aurelius. Amused by the perturbance of her toy she again, almost negligently, brushed the lad with her fingertips.

"Men will do the same things, nevertheless, even though they should burst."

The boy's heart must have been near bursting. He almost swayed, but he did not dare to interrupt the fan's rhythmic motion.

Faustina continued to tantalize the lad.

"When thou wishest to delight thyself, think of the virtues of those who love with thee."

Suddenly the gleam in the eyes of Faustina went out like a lamp. Her hand dropped slowly.

The Emperor arose. The audience exclaimed, "Magnificent! Profound! Unequaled!"

Marcus Aurelius motioned to the Empress to lead the guests into the banquet hall.

Lazily the Empress draped her garments. The boy knelt at her feet. She ignored him. He crawled after her.

"Augusta! Faustina!"

The Empress looked straight ahead. The boy had ceased to exist.

Bewildered, the boy attempted to halt his mistress. She stepped upon his hand as if it were a thing of stone or an insect. The boy shivered from pain, but he crawled on, embracing her knee.

The boy's lips moved. "I love you, I adore you," he whispered.

The Empress motioned to a gigantic slave. Her face smiled but her lips said, "Flog him."

The boy disappeared between the great arms of the man.

At the banquet messengers from the north and east reached the Emperor telling of the reverse of the Romans and the struggle with the Barbarians.

Marcus Aurelius spoke of the superiority of virtue and intelligence over brute force.

"I long for peace, Car-ta-phal," he said to me. "Alas, the gods will it differently."

He lowered his head, and kept silent for a while. He liked to attitudinize. "Much worse than the Barbarians are our enemies at home."

"The Christians——"

"Particularly the Christians. I have burnt them and thrown them to the lions and hounded them as unclean beasts, but all my efforts have been in vain."

"Their religion, Your Majesty, glorifies martyrdom. If they are tortured to death, they are promised a whole eternity of pleasure in heaven. Who would not barter a few hours of agony for endless joy? The Christians, particularly, have the sense of the merchant. They were originally Hebrews."

"That is true. But how shall I exterminate them?"

"What is more damning than half-praise?"

"An excellent aphorism, Car-ta-phal, but I fail to discover its application."

He had already adapted several things I had said, and I knew that sooner or later my remark would appear in his Meditations.

"Recognize Jesus as a minor divinity . . . some half-forgotten Hindu god."

"Perhaps," the Imperator remarked, "he is a minor god. The world's imagination is stale. People rarely invent new gods."

"Your Majesty, why not admit Jesus officially to the Pantheon? Make him one of the gods, and he will be no longer the one god. Both Christians and Romans will forget their political grievances, buy sacrifices, and by invoking one additional divinity, will triumph against the Barbarians."

"You are indeed my good counsellor, Car-ta-phal. I must propose your plan to the Senate."

The temple was crowded with soldiers and women. The priests were busy taking offerings and sacrifices to the gods. Mars, above all, was invoked. But Venus was not neglected. It was difficult to push through the crowd, but I was obstinate. I would not leave the temple until I had seen the statue of the new god.

"Car-ta-phal," some one called. I managed to turn my head, but could not swing my shoulders about.

"Apollodorus."

"You are seeking what I seek, Car-ta-phal."

We reached an angle which had the shape of a large alcove. "This must be it," I said. Apollodorus, a little near-sighted, asked, "Which one?"

"The cross, look!"

He approached and looked intently. "What a hideous thing! A god upon a cross! A god with a writhing face and holes in his hands and feet! Car-ta-phal, it is horrible!"

Apollodorus laughed. "And I feared that Christianity would supplant our gods and our temples! A religion with a god on a cross, bleeding from his hands and his feet!"

I joined Apollodorus in laughter.

A woman, dressed in black, her face partly veiled, approached the cross, and knelt before it for a long while, then rose and, kissing the feet and hands, left.

"Apollodorus, we may still be wrong. We have forgotten woman. She is the mother. She pities. . ."

XVIII

THE EMPEROR-EMPRESS—HELIOGABALUS DANCES— THE GIANT

MARCUS AURELIUS was dead. Heliogabalus, the crowned transvestite, cuddled himself daintily on the throne of the Cæsars.

The people vociferated at the top of their voices that they were robbed to support an army too weak to cope with a band of undisciplined and uncouth Barbarians, and a monarch—from the East —who danced and painted his lips. Foreigners preferred not to accept the honor of Roman citizenship, and many Romans pretended to have been born in the provinces, for the taxes imposed upon the citizens were much higher than those upon subjects.

The mother of the Imperator was too hysterical and his ministers were too frivolous to govern; while he himself had become engrossed in the friendship for his adopted cousin, a taciturn young athlete, Bassianus Alexianus. His grandmother, however, who still retained a modicum of serenity and common sense, insisted that something had to be done, or the nation would rise in rebellion.

"What?" Heliogabalus shouted, exasperated.

"Augustus, High Priest of the Eternal Sun, man appreciates an unexpected gift a great deal more than that which is due him."

The Emperor made no comment, but turned to me with the smile of a young coquette.

I remained silent.

He sighed, moved with profound pity for himself when I failed to respond. His effeminacy was too grotesque to intrigue me.

"Her Majesty's logic is convincing," I remarked, somewhat flatly.

"I hate logic." Heliogabalus placed his small, soft hand upon his cousin's shoulder.

"We are all children, Augustus," the old Empress continued, "and children must be placated with gifts."

"What shall I give them?"

"Your ancestors used to give them the circus, but they are bored with the games."

"What shall I give them?"

"Your ancestors waged wars and returned triumphant, followed by captive kings and princes and chariots overbrimming with precious jewels and gold."

The Emperor's face, delicate and small, flushed. His nostrils shivered and his lips, fleshy but well-chiseled, lengthened in disdain. "I hate war! It is the work of butchers and cutthroats." And addressing Bassianus, he continued: "Not that I dislike blood. The High Priest of the Sun knows the beauty of sacrifice. But it must be shed delicately, at leisure, amidst joy and merriment. Blood, like wine, should be drunk out of golden goblets. Am I not right, Bassianus?"

He rose coyly from his throne, arranged the folds of his robe, and reseated himself.

"Augustus," the old woman began once more, "since you will not give them wars,—give them baths."

"Baths?"

"It is a Roman fad. The physicians claim that bathing keeps people young. Everybody wishes to be young. Give them the baths. The water may quench the smouldering fire."

"The old woman is clever, Bassianus. Shall I give them the baths?"

Bassianus nodded.

"Let them have the baths."

"The gods are with the Imperator. The sun shines upon his High Priest!"

A holiday to last three days was proclaimed. Roman citizens were invited to take possession of their new baths, the magnificent gift of their incomparable Emperor. Day and night the stones were to be kept hot that the steam might rise, dense like smoke; and the pools were to be replenished with spring water that the bodies might be refreshed and rejuvenated. Wine, too, was to be distributed without measure, and enormous piles of wreaths were at the disposal of the merrymakers.

Rome had not been so joyous for a long time, and the Emperor, just turned eighteen, wished to partake of the gayety. He dressed himself in a flowing toga, embroidered with gold and studded with tiny jewels, which reached the ground in the manner of the robes worn by patrician women. Upon his head he placed a wreath of fresh roses. His fingers were covered with rings, and his arms were

wound with long bracelets, the shape of fantastic snakes and grotesque crocodiles.

"Any one recognizing me forfeits his life!" he exclaimed.

We nodded.

"I am Erotius, the son of a rich merchant."

"Erotius," we all repeated.

The moon, large and white, was encircled by an enormous aureole.
Its reflection silvered a large part of the pool and overbrimmed the
bank.

The people shouted, "No torches! No torches! It is light
enough." The torchbearers blew out their lights.

The Emperor threw off the linen blanket which dried his body
and warmed him, when he came out of the pool.

"I am the brother of the Sun. I am the sister of the Moon!" he
exclaimed.

The people laughed.

"Let there be music that I may dance!"

"Your Majesty," a Senator whispered in his ear, "I fear——"

"Tomorrow you die, wretch!"

At first a little unsteady on his feet from the strong wine he had
drunk, Heliogabalus managed to regain his equilibrium. People sang
and played on various instruments, producing a strange cacophony,
not entirely displeasing. The Emperor danced. He did not stir from
the spot in the reflection, turning only his torso, delicate as a girl's
and twisting his arms in the manner of the Orientals. The slow
sensuous movements became more and more rapid, more and more
irregular, until they seemed the mad paroxysm of uncontrollable
passion.

The Emperor danced on. The moon wound about him like a white
veil, torn in spots and blown by the wind. The people clapped their
hands and stamped their feet, shouting from time to time, "Magnificent! Fine! Fine!"

The music became more clamorous.

The Emperor breathed heavily through his open mouth. His
movements slackened, became disjointed. Exhausted, Heliogabalus
fell, suddenly, his head between his hands. The people laughed,
applauded, made obscene remarks, and dispersed. One man placed
a wreath upon the Imperator's head. "Terpsichore,—Queen of the
Dance!" he exclaimed.

Heliogabalus raised his head. A few steps away, he beheld a man
of gigantic stature staring at him. The Imperator frowned. The

man lifted his powerful arm slowly, and waved his immense fore-finger commandingly.

Heliogabalus rose, fascinated. The man continued to motion to him. The Emperor made a movement to withdraw, but something mightier than his will kept him nailed to the spot.

The two stared at each other; the giant's eyes small but very sharp, stabbing the large dreamy eyes of the boy. The latter lowered his lids. The silent battle lasted for some time.

What strange premonition troubled the Emperor? What stranger power overcame fear, anger, disdain? Heliogabalus, like a girl in a trance, like a bird spellbound by the glittering eyes of his ancestral foe, approached the giant, making slow, indeterminate steps.

"Come!" the giant whispered.

Heliogabalus wavered.

"Come!" he said, and placing his large hand upon the Emperor's shoulder, pulled him gently.

They walked toward a dark corner,—two shadows, one long and broad, the other short and rotund, preceding them.

An hour later a sharp shriek pierced the air, like the cry of a murdered bird.

Cruelly lacerated, crushed by gigantic hands, the body of Helio-gabalus, the Master-Mistress, the Emperor-Empress of Rome, brother to the Sun and sister to the Moon, was found in a pool made scarlet by his blood.

"I shall not die tomorrow!" breathed the Senator, leaning upon my arm.

XIX

I BECOME A GOD—PRAYERFUL BUTTOCKS—THE HOLY CAMEL—CAR-TA-PHA YAWNS

AGAIN I turned my steps to the East. After a long sojourn at Palmyra, it pleased my fancy to bury myself in the desert. I amused myself by teaching a parrot to pronounce my name, "Car-taph-al."

"Carr-tarr-pharr" the bird shrieked back.

Tempted to face fate alone, I dismissed my retinue.

Toward dusk, I was within sight of what seemed to be a village or the home of some tribe. My only companions were my camel and my parrot, which had become quite tame, and perching upon the animal's head, formed a bizarre and radiant crest. I waited until it was dark. Meanwhile, I drew upon the center of my turban the shape of the sun with a chemical an alchemist of Egypt had taught me to use and a large crescent moon upon the camel's forehead; while the beak of the parrot I dotted with many points to represent the stars.

A heavy smoke that smelt of tallow rose leisurely, punctured at times by sparks that were immediately stifled and devoured. Around the fire, in a wide circle, men and women were squatting, their heads bent. Their backs were black, and in many cases, scarred with wounds. At an angle, a white-haired man was beating ceaselessly a large kettle, with an iron stick, growling at intervals. The sound of his voice was like the mooing of a lonesome cow. My approach was unnoticed, for the steps of my camel were slow, and the ground was wet with recent mud. Suddenly my parrot called out: "Carr-tarr-pharr."

The natives jumped up: men with colossal mouths and jaws, and tiny eyes, and women with enormous breasts that fell below their big, circular bellies.

"Carr-tarr-pharr. . . . Carr-tarr-pharr. . . ."

They seemed paralyzed. The chemical I had applied to my turban and my companions, was shining like a white fire. A woman shrieked and groveled at the feet of my camel. The rest did likewise. Soon the entire tribe, swaying to and fro in rhythmic exaltation, prostrated themselves before me. For hours they continued the prayerful swaying of buttocks and bellies.

Weary at last of this adoration, I motioned my worshipers to rise. I spoke to them in a dozen languages. They did not understand. I clapped my hands. They groaned and beat their heads. I urged the camel to move. They held his legs.

"Divinity is a precarious occupation," I thought. "I may be forced to die astride my camel."

My hope lay in the fact that human backs could not endure forever the same posture; also that the enormous nostrils of these people would soon detect, as I did, that the lamb they were roasting, was beginning to burn. I was right. One woman, by long instinct, no doubt, forgot the divinity she was worshiping, and turned her head, her breast beating against her side. I caught her eye, and bade her rise. She growled something. The rest growled in return, and rose. I made a motion with my fingers to my mouth. They began to dance. The old man, who had beaten the kettle, looked at the sky, then at me, and bowed very deeply. I understood that he meant that I was Heaven-descended. I nodded. He no doubt thought of me in terms of both the camel and the parrot. I was one, and yet three. It was an amusing idea, which pleased me greatly.

"Carr-tarr-pharr. . . . Carr-tarr-pharr. . . ."

They imitated him: "Ca-ta-pha . . . Ca-ta-pha. . . ."

My parrot was making my name divine, and no doubt immortal, but by the time it was uttered by these enormous mouths, it was hardly recognizable.

The dance continued,—a wild lifting of legs, slapping of bellies, and waving of arms, accompanied by raucous sounds and the ceaseless beating of the iron kettle. Meanwhile, however, three of the women lifted the lamb from the fire and placed it upon the ground to cool.

I descended. The people saw nothing curious in this disentangle- ment of the three personalities, nor did they consider it extraordinary that Heaven should accept the piece of roast lamb which they offered. My fingers were burnt, but to show my friendliness, I did not relinquish the morsel. They ate not alone with their mouths, but with their entire faces, including the hair that nearly reached their eyebrows. I was too amused to feel nausea, but I could not help thinking that my camel was more genteel in her habits. The parrot called out my name from time to time, and always the rest answered him, like a distorted echo.

"What a High Priest you would have made in Jerusalem, my polly!"

Their gorging over, they began to dance again, with even greater gusto. They were not at all embarrassed that Heaven was watching them, squatting on the stump of a charred tree. Heaven was kindly, it was quite evident. He did not broil them, like mutton; he did not blind them with the white fire of his turban. Like the stars above, he smiled upon them.

I thought their dancing would be eternal. My head became heavy. I began to doubt my own consciousness. Perhaps, after all, I was the sun, and they colossal black stars dancing a mad dance in my honor. My eyes closed. I fell asleep. . . .

"Carr-tarr-pharr . . . Carr-tarr-pharr. . . ."

"Carr-tarr-pharr . . . Carr-tarr-pharr. . . ."

I woke up with a start. It was already morning. The parrot, perched upon the camel's head, was screeching my name and flapping his wings, while all about me, in a large circle, the natives kneeling, their faces to the ground, were echoing the bird.

Already somewhat accustomed to the idea of my apotheosis, I stretched and yawned.

XX

CA-TA-PHA UP AND CA-TA-PHA DOWN—I MAKE A SAINT —MAN OR MONKEY—KOTIKOKURA

WHEN I had learnt sufficiently of the language, I engaged in conversation with the white-haired man. "Who is your god?" I asked.
"Ca-ta-pha."
"But before he came among you, who was your god?"
"Ca-ta-pha."
"How do you explain that?"
"He was up, now he is down."
"Is he not still up? Look!"
He pointed to a tree. "The tree is up." Then to its shadow: "The tree is also down."
His subtlety pleased me. It reminded me of the priests in Jerusalem. "But during the day, the sun does not shine on his forehead. Is he a god during the day, as well as at night?"
"Always. When he is tired of shining up, he shines down; when he is tired of shining down, he shines up."
"Is the camel also a god, and the parrot?"
"You are the father, the camel is the mother, the parrot is the son."
"How can the camel have a parrot as a son?"
He shrugged his shoulders, and his large mouth opened as if to swallow an enormous piece of meat. "Ca-ta-pha is god."
I gave him a gold coin. He did not know its significance, but his joy in receiving it was immense. He bent to the earth, rose, danced about me like a top. He shouted: "God Ca-ta-pha has given me the sun."
I thought, "You are doing the Universal Dance of the Golden Calf, my poor gorilla!"
Ever after, he was considered as a saint by the rest, who trembled at his approach. He assumed the dignified air of a high priest.
I was the mighty god of war. Marching at the head of my people, I vanquished tribe after tribe. At the sight of me, our enemies either

ran madly away, leaving behind them booty and food, or falling
upon their faces, accepted my divinity, and relinquished their independence. My tribe became rich beyond its wildest dream. The
smoke, thick with the smell of animals roasting, mounted like an
endless offering to the Lord of Bounties, and the dances and orgies
never ceased.

I asked why it was that a woman was not presented me as wife.

"Ca-ta-pha is God. There is his wife."

They pointed to my camel, which, overfed, was munching like
a giant cow, a wisp of hay between her enormous wet lips. I accepted
their logic. A successful god must never contradict his worshipers.

I grew weary of hearing my name invoked several times a day
at the caprice of the parrot, and seeing the black bodies surround
me, faces in the mud, and posteriors raised upward like hillocks. I
realized why the gods prefer to live upon the tops of mountains,
or in the sky.

But a god must disappear, as he appeared, suddenly and unexpectedly. On the morning decided upon, I ordered my tribe to go
into the woods, and not to budge until the moon rose, when they
might return. They shivered and fell on their faces.

"Rise! Fear not. No harm shall befall you."

"Ca-ta-pha . . . Ca-ta-pha . . ." they groaned.

"Ca-ta-pha is mighty and just, is he not?"

"He is mighty and just."

"Are not you his chosen ones?"

"We are."

"Therefore, chosen people of Ca-ta-pha, fear not."

As they were about to turn away, one of them shouted: "Look!
Look! Ko-ti-ko-ku-ra! Ko-ti-ko-ku-ra!"

My parrot repeated "Korr-ti-korr-kurr-ra . . . Korr-ti-korr-
kurr-ra. . . ."

Was it a man, or a monkey? I could not tell. His face was much
lighter than that of the others, almost yellow; the features were
much finer; but his body was covered with a heavy black fur, and
his back was bent, as if he preferred to walk on all fours. Several
men dashed upon him, and by their looks, I understood that they
were on the point of tearing him to pieces.

His hazel brown eyes blazed defiance.

"Stop!" I shouted. "Do not touch him! Bring him here! Who is
he?"

"Ko-ti-ko-ku-ra . . . Ko-ti-ko-ku-ra. . . ."

"Who is Ko-ti-ko-ku-ra?"

Everyone answered at the same time, making a noise like a menagerie. I raised my arm. "Silence! Let him to whom I gave the sun speak!"

The white-haired fellow was too clamorous and excited. It was only after much difficulty that I finally grasped the trend of his chatter. Kotikokura meant something like "accursed." This interested me. He had laughed, it seems, at one of their elders, who had prophesied no less a fact than the arrival of Ca-ta-pha. I realized that the exact nature of his crime had been forgotten, but that he was, nevertheless, Kotikokura, the Accursed One who dared to laugh.

I looked at him again. His eyes danced to and fro, like two enormous fireflies.

"Let him remain with me! I shall devour him myself. Go to the woods at once, and do not return till you see the moon!"

'You are like Cartaphilus, Kotikokura,' I thought. 'We ought to be good company for each other.' I touched his face, and looked into his small phosphorescent eyes that moved incessantly.

"Do not fear, Kotikokura, I shall not harm you."

He grinned.

His teeth were very large and yellowish.

"Who are you?" I asked.

He grinned.

"Would you care to accompany Ca-ta-pha the god?"

He continued to grin, but he made no answer. Had he understood me? Could he speak? It did not matter. His muscles looked like iron, and I needed a servant. "Come along!" The camel galloped, but Kotikokura ran still faster, and the parrot screeched, as he flew over our heads: "Carr-tarr-pharr. . . ."

I awoke with a start. A snake had bitten me. I could see the tip of his tail disappear in the sand. My arm began to swell. Was I to die at last, and in the desert? Had Jesus forgotten to bind the snake? Was I, after all, vulnerable? Kotikokura grasped my arm, and began to suck it. His lips pulled at my skin like a leech. "You will die, my poor fellow. My blood is a worse poison than the venom of a snake."

My arm assumed its normal size, but Kotikokura did not die. Had one poison neutralized the other, or being an outcast, was the blood of this curious fellow, akin to mine? Would he, like me, continue to live indefinitely? I decided to keep him, and see what would happen.

Suddenly an idea struck me. Perhaps . . . perhaps the years had attenuated the power of the poison. Perhaps I had become like the others. I would put it to a test. I sprinkled some drops over the parrot's food. He swallowed a few of the seeds, and began to screech: "Carr-tarr. . . ." He stopped, rolled his eyes. and fell upon his back, as if struck by lightning.

I was still Cartaphilus.

Kotikokura plucked the bird, and devoured it, grinning. 'A beast,' I thought. A few moments later, he chose the largest plume and stuck it in his hair. 'But a man, nevertheless.'

XXI

KOTIKOKURA SHAVES—I MAKE HISTORY—THE CROSS
AND THE SWORD—THE CHRISTIAN EMPEROR—THE
CRESCENT MOON HANGS UPON THE BOSPHORUS

KOTIKOKURA understood me in whatever language I spoke. Was
he a linguist, or merely an animal, sensitive to the tone of my voice
and the change in my features? His answers were a grin, a growl,
some inarticulate sounds, or a movement of the shoulders and
head.

"Kotikokura, we are going into civilization. You must look
civilized." He grinned. "I shall teach you how to shave the few
threads of hair on your face, and the fur upon your arms and chest,
at least. Also, you must get accustomed to wear clothes, according
to the country you happen to be in. The meaning of civilization is
to look like the rest."

He still grinned. His eyes galloped from one corner to the other.
He was on the point of dropping upon his palms. "Be thou erect, or
be made erect!" So said an Emperor, Kotikokura,—an Emperor who
was also a philosopher, which is an extremely rare thing."

Kotikokura stiffened up, his head thrown back.

"Not quite so much, Kotikokura. Man should not be always looking at the stars. One's eyes should watch the solid earth. All good
things grow out of the earth, Kotikokura; the stars generate mad
dreams, harmful for those who harbor them."

A man was standing upon the steps leading to the Capitol.
About him was gathered a large multitude. Some shouted: "Maxen-
tius! Maxentius!" Others, in greater numbers, drowned their voices:
"Constantine! Constantine!"

"He alone will rule who believes in Jesus!" exclaimed the man,
making the sign of the cross. "The cross shall conquer!"

I saw many crossing themselves; others frowned; some grumbled,
but no one assaulted the speaker, no one even hissed him.

"Is Jesus the new god of war? Has Mars been replaced?" I asked.

"Jesus is the only god. The rest are idols."

Not even this answer disturbed the populace.

"Is not Jesus one of the gods of the Pantheon?"

"Jesus is god of the world, and he who believes in Jesus shall conquer the world."

I made a careful investigation of the military situation. Constantine was stronger and cleverer than Maxentius, it was universally recognized. The armies of both leaders were encamped within three or four miles of Rome, and it was but a matter of days now before they would strike the final blow. I decided to join Constantine.

"It is always advisable, Kotikokura, to side with the strong, for the gods favor them." He grinned and bowed. I had taught him by this time the necessary rules of etiquette. He learned very rapidly, and imitated perfectly.

"He who draws the sword shall perish by the sword," Jesus taught. Did not this also refer to nations and religions? If Constantine should win because he had drawn the sword in the name of Christianity, should not Christianity perish by the same gesture?

"Things are most illogical, Kotikokura, and yet, an intelligent man must act as if life were governed by reason."

I shaved Kotikokura's back, and blackened it. Upon it, with my chemical, I drew the sign of the cross, and underneath it, I wrote: *In hoc signo vinces!* "In this sign thou shalt conquer." I ordered him to dress again. "Kotikokura, I am making you immortal, perhaps." His back itched him, and he scratched himself. "No, you must not do that until I allow you." He bowed.

The hillock that faced Constantine's army was almost perpendicular, and terminated in a sharp point. The night was darker than usual. "Things favor us, Kotikokura. I depend upon your agility. Climb the hill, and stand with your back turned. Do not move until I call you. I shall remain at the base."

In a few moments, Kotikokura appeared upon the peak, or rather merely the cross and the words I had written. They dazzled and shivered against the sky like a new and splendid constellation. I was almost prompted myself to bend my knee in adoration and exclaim: "I believe!"

Suddenly Constantine's camp flamed with the lights of many torches. I knew that Kotikokura's back had accomplished its work. "Come down, Kotikokura!" Almost instantly, as if he had flown,

Kotikokura stood grinning before me. I ordered him to dress again, and follow me home.

Near the Capitol, many people were kneeling. I asked the reason for it.

"Have you not seen the great miracle?"

"What great miracle?"

"The sky shone with stars in the shape of the cross."

"Really?"

"I have never seen or heard of such a marvelous thing."

"I am a Roman. I believed in the gods of my forefathers, but this very hour I have become a Christian."

"The whole world shall become Christian now, for do not the same stars shine everywhere, and who, having seen what we have seen, will continue to doubt?"

I felt uneasy. Had my ruse defeated my very purpose? "We shall see, Kotikokura, if a religion that preaches love can long exist by the sword." Kotikokura grinned, and scratched himself violently. "You may scratch as much as you wish now. You have become history."

I bent over the balustrade of my balcony. To my right, the Bosphorus rose in jerky waves, tipped with foam, like some angry giant cat spitting; to my left an immense cross of gold glittered over the ancient Greek temple; while below me, massed on both sides of the street, the multitude awaited the Emperor's arrival at the New Rome, Constantinople. The silver trumpets and the cymbals could already be heard by the keener ears. People exclaimed: "They are coming!" in Greek, Latin, and several dialects.

Immediately behind the trumpeters, who served primarily to disperse the crowds, came with deliberate, proud steps the Christian High Priest, recently appointed by Constantine. He was dressed in a white silk robe with gold stripes; in his right hand he carried a large golden crucifix, studded with precious stones, the gift of the Emperor. He seemed to be of pure Roman blood, and looked more like a soldier than a martyr or a man versed in the mysteries of the spirit. On either side two boys were scattering incense, and behind him about forty or fifty priests, in white silk robes, but without the gold stripes, and carrying crosses, chanted an old Hebrew homily in Latin words.

Although doubtless many of the spectators were not Christians, everybody made the sign of the cross. Had not the Imperator proclaimed Christianity the State religion? Besides, there was a rumor that the priests employed spies, and that unbelievers were to expect punishments as severe as the Christians had received at their hands, when the Roman gods were in power.

Several officers of the Imperial Guard, erect and almost motionless on their horses, carried tall banners on which were painted the cross with the words: *In hoc signo vinces.*

"Kotikokura!" He appeared almost instantly. "Look! Do you remember?" His eyes darted to and fro. "The Cross . . . have you forgotten?" He did not understand. I burst out laughing. "Of course not. How could you remember? You never saw it! You flamed like a heaven, but you only saw the darkness in front of you." Kotikokura grinned.

The Emperor, reclining upon a couch, a diadem upon his head and a mass of jewels upon his hands and arms, was carried by four giants. *Vivat Imperator! Vivat!*

The great dark hand of night covered the Bosphorus and hid the cross upon the Greek temple. Over it hung, like a scimitar, the crescent moon, tipped with a star.

XXII

MY VINEYARD ON THE RHINE—ULRICA—ROME IS A
WITCH JEALOUS OF YOUTH—THE TREE MUST EN-
DURE FOREVER—KOTIKOKURA GRINS—LIFE IS CIR-
CULAR

THE Rhine barely stirred, and our boat glided upon it, lightly,
like a giant feather dropped by some mythological eagle. For a
long time, I continued to see the tall, wooden fence that surrounded
my vineyards. I remembered the dingy shop of my father and the
poverty I had endured in my childhood. My present wealth delighted
me, like the fragrant wines that my slaves squeezed out of the
grapes.

My childhood! Strange! It seemed as if it had just been; as if it
recently merely turned a corner. Had centuries really passed? Was
it only a dream? But if a dream . . . where were the people I had
once known . . . the kings, the emperors, the empresses, Lydia,
Asi-ma, Damis, Poppeae? What boors were stepping upon their dust?
Time was a motionless, frozen river, over which shadows flitted and
vanished, but I was as a tree congealed within it, and my shadow
carved upon its face a permanent pattern.

In a corner of the boat, Kotikokura curled up like a dog, his face
turned toward the sun. Was he, too, a congealed tree; or had he
become a branch, as it were, of me?

Ulrica sang. Her golden hair, coiled into two heavy braids, whose
tips rested on her lap, shone like the sun that was setting in back of
us. Whom did she resemble? Mary? Perhaps. But she was not as
voluptuous. Lydia? She was as sentimental and tender, but at unexpected moments, too haughty or too timid,—a little incomprehensible like the woods she came from.

"Ulrica, in Rome they would call you a Barbarian."

"Rome!" she sneered. "Rome is an old witch, jealous of youth."

"Have you not heard, dear, that Rome is eternal?"

"The city may be eternal, but the people are dying."

"What makes you think that the people are dying?"

"Rome sneers at virtue, Cartaphilus, and no longer believes in the gods."

"Rome believes in a new god, Ulrica."

"How can a god be new, Cartaphilus? Are not gods older than heaven and earth?"

"Are you sure, my dear, that the gods live?"

She looked at me, her blue eyes opened wide, as if scared.

"May they not all be just . . . stories? Tales to put to sleep little children?"

She burst out laughing. "Cartaphilus, you say such fantastic things. You know, at times, I think that you too are a god . . . maybe Fro . . . the god of love."

"You called me a god, Ulrica, many years ago . . . in a far-away country . . . do you remember?"

Ulrica kissed my hands. Is she Asi-ma, I wondered? "Do you remember?"

"I never traveled to a far-away country . . . and many years ago . . . I was not born then, Cartaphilus." She placed her head upon my knee.

"You were a princess then, Ulrica."

"And did you love me then, Cartaphilus?"

"I loved you then."

"Do you love me now?"

"I love you now."

Why did I seek always the past in the present? Was my life of centuries merely the endeavor to capture again and again my first experiences, my initial sensations?

The sun disappeared, drawing after it the last semicircle of its reflection that lingered on the edge of the horizon.

"Dear, when you were the princess of that far-away country, you became my wife on a boat like this."

She closed her eyes, and pressed tightly against me.

"Now that you are a princess of the woods, will you become my wife again . . . on a boat?"

"Cartaphilus, am I not your slave; did you not purchase me from a merchant? Am I supposed to have a will?"

"You are not my slave. I purchased you because you were beautiful, and because you whispered: 'I love you.' Do you remember?"

"Yes."

"Was it not true?"

"It was true."

"Are not two lovers as free as monarchs?"

"Cartaphilus . . . make me your wife . . . again."

It was true—Rome was dying. The Barbarians were becoming more and more daring. Some day, I was certain, they would attempt to capture the Eternal City. My vineyards lay between them and Rome. The boots of the conquerors spare nothing. A Roman, formerly the Governor of one of the provinces in Asia-Minor, more confident than I, in the prowess of his country's army, bought my property.

"Ulrica, I shall soon leave. Will you come with me?"

"Where?"

"Perhaps to Rome . . . perhaps to some farther country. I do not know."

She shook her head. "I belong in the woods."

"Think it over, my dear. We shall not leave for a few days."

"I will not go." She walked away.

Kotikokura approached me, out of breath, and pulled my arm.

"What is the trouble, Kotikokura? What has happened?"

He uttered some sounds which I could not understand, but I noticed that his hands were covered with blood. "What's happened? Quick, tell me!"

He pulled me. "Ulrica! Ulrica!"

Ulrica lay upon the ground, her head thrown back. A stream of blood was flowing out of her chest, passing over her arm and one of her braids, and making a large, red pool that separated into several branches. In her right hand she held a short sword.

"Ulrica! Ulrica!" I bent over her. She opened her eyes, already blurred. "Cartaphilus," she whispered, "when I was a princess, did I also kill myself?"

"I do not know, Ulrica. I went away."

"You always go away."

"I am he who wanders forever, Ulrica."

She was about to say something, when her mouth filled with blood. Kotikokura, bent almost to the ground, groaned.

"Come, Kotikokura. You must be a man. Men suffer less noisily." He stood up and stared at me. "Or perhaps, a man should not suffer at all, seeing that he deals with mere shadows that flit across a frozen river."

His jaw fell.

"Many birds shall perch upon the tree for a while . . . and fly away. The tree must endure forever."

The loss of Ulrica pained me more than I had expected. There was a freshness, a purity in her that resembled the perfume of the fields after a rainstorm. I felt that I had not breathed deeply enough, that I had walked by quickly and a little absent-mindedly . . . and suddenly found myself upon a long, dusty road.

Kotikokura was shaving his body. He had become very skillful, and no longer needed assistance.

"Kotikokura, how long must a man live to learn how to live fully, so that he may not know the meaning of regret?"

Kotikokura grinned. Was he the incarnation of some grotesque sphinx? Did he know the wisdom of the ages, and therefore would not speak?

"Do the gods live in eternity, Kotikokura, because they find mere time insufficient?"

He grinned on.

"Or, is eternity as futile as an hour?"

"Ow-w-w!" Kotikokura tried to shave while looking at me, and cut himself.

"Thought, Kotikokura, generally produces pain,—in one form or another."

He sucked the wound, and continued to shave, his eyes riveted on the razor.

He had acquired—or so it seemed to me—a much more human appearance. His yellow face, high cheek bones, small eyes, grinning mouth, reminded me of someone I had seen once.

"Who are you, really?"

"Kotikokura," he answered gravely.

"One is always someone else. What ancestral ghost, swaying in tree-tops, speaks through you? What thoughts can you call your own?"

"Kotikokura."

"From the beginning of things to the end of things . . . Kotiko-kura?"

"Kotikokura."

"Kotikokura, be unto me as the handful of dust I once threw into the air, which indicated the path I was to take."

Kotikokura rose and turned about me quickly, raising his knees almost as far as his chin. His gait became slower and slower, until he remained stock-still, his head stretched out. I understood what he meant. He was the dust. He was whirled in the wind for a while, then blown in the direction his head indicated.

"So be it, Kotikokura. The East! Life is circular, and our steps move always about its circumference."

XXIII

KOTIKOKURA SCRATCHES HIMSELF—A FUNERAL PROCESSION

To be a Roman was no longer an incomparable honor; no longer a magic word with which to conjure safety and protection. To be a member of any of the Barbarian tribes, however, was just as precarious. To be a Hebrew meant nothing. People had almost forgotten about Jerusalem or Judea. The cross might incur favor or animosity; the ancient gods likewise. The boundaries were no longer well defined; the roads no longer led to accustomed and secure spots.

"What shall we be, Kotikokura, as we travel through this cauldron of uncertainty?"

Kotikokura scratched himself. It was his manner of indicating doubt or unconcern.

"Kotikokura, we must change our identity as the chameleon changes the color of its skin . . . remaining, nevertheless, unchanged . . . Cartaphilus and Kotikokura, doubters and laughers."

He grinned.

"We must appear neither rich enough to excite envy, nor so poor that we become contemptible and pathetic."

He grinned.

"Let us not seem strong enough to provoke conflict, nor too weak to defend ourselves. Mediocrity, Kotikokura, is the salt of the earth. In mediocrity, all things flourish. Below ,it they wither; above it they are struck by lightning."

Kotikokura's eyes slacked their pace.

"If you are a giant, Kotikokura, you must not rise to your full stature in public, or else the others will become weary of craning their necks to see you, and sooner or later, they will chop your head off that they may equal you in size."

Nothing seemed as safe and agreeable as being a merchant of mediocre means, traveling to the nearest seaport with a small load of goods. A gentleman of leisure would have been suspected as a spy, and a poor pilgrim might have been forced into slavery. My caravan consisted of two large wagons, drawn by two teams of powerful oxen. I hired drivers, black-skinned men from one of the Roman colonies, who could not be suspected of taking an interest either in the military or political situation. Kotikokura and I rode on horseback. His dress was similar to mine, but of a cheaper material. It was advisable, always, to make him feel my superiority, for equality breeds contempt. He might think not of his advancement, but of my degradation. Did not Jesus, in spite of his democratic preaching, stand apart and remain unidentified with his followers? He had twelve disciples . . . but he was the master!

Melancholy pervaded all things: the sharp cries of migratory birds, the last feeble croaking of frogs, the large yellow vine-leaves dropping, dropping always, to be crushed by the hoofs of the animals and the heavy iron wheels of the wagons— —

"Kotikokura, we are a solitary funeral procession leading the dead year to its grave."

Kotikokura tried in vain to grin. He was sentimental.

My horse neighed. The oxen bellowed. Kotikokura sighed.

XXIV

THE WALLS OF CHINA—I DO A MIRACLE—A CHINESE
APOLLONIUS—FLOWER-OF-JOY

STANDING near the Wall, it was impossible to see the top. It seemed
to melt into the sky. We moved away.

"Kotikokura, man is tiny, but he builds high walls."

He grunted.

"Look at those pretty daisies and blades of grass, Kotikokura,
which grow out of the crevices of the stone. Trifles like these proclaim
Nature an artist, not merely a colossal ox pulling at the plow of
life."

Kotikokura measured the height of the wall with his eye, his
fingertips moving as if they desired to try their prowess.

"No, no, Kotikokura, not that way must we enter this most
ancient of countries. Besides, even if you should manage to crawl
over, how should I?"

He scratched himself.

"There is a gate a little farther on. Watchman's eyes are generally
weak, and they close at the glitter of gold."

The gate was narrow, and two yellow giants blocked its passage.
At the sight of us, they pointed their long spears. I dropped, as if
by error, a handful of gold coins. They looked, but never deigned
to stir. They grumbled something which I could not understand;
the tone of which, however, augured anything but hospitality. One
of them raised his spear into the air and almost touched me. Kotikokura rushed to his throat.

"Stop, Kotikokura!" I commanded. "This is not the way to
treat people we wish to visit. Besides, am I not God Ca-ta-pha?
Have you no confidence in my power?"

Kotikokura fell on his face. "Ca-ta-pha!"

This disconcerted the watchmen a little. Meanwhile, I looked into
the eyes of the one who seemed a trifle more pacific. I waved my
hands about his face, and pronounced the word "Sleep" in Chinese,
which I had learnt before my arrival "Sleep . . . sleep . . . sleep!"

The giant began to yawn. "Sleep . . . sleep." He stretched out upon the ground and began to snore. The other, frightened, dropped his spear and ran away, screaming.

"Come, Kotikokura, let us enter."

Kotikokura, dazzled by what I had accomplished, continued to bow and touch the ground. I did not discourage his adoration.

"Rise, Kotikokura, and follow me!" I ordered.

The Wall was several feet deep, and when we reached the other end, people were running toward us, weapons in their hands, and shouting.

"Lie down, Kotikokura, and do not budge. Fear nothing!" I covered him with a black cloth. I waved my arms, describing large semicircles, reciting the while most dramatically, stanzas from the Upanishads. Two small mirrors concealed in my palms, reflecting the sun, made strange patterns of light. The people, disconcerted, watched.

"Rise, Kotikokura!" I commanded. "Rise!" The body of Kotikokura ascended slowly, steadily. The people, their mouths agape, dropped their weapons. "Return, Kotikokura!" I ordered. The tips of my fingers united. The mirrors shed a milky way, through which Kotikokura descended slowly, almost elegantly. When he reached the ground, I uncovered him. He looked about, startled, and fell at my feet, calling: "Ca-ta-pha! Ca-ta-pha!" The others knelt also, and repeated "Ca-ta-pha! Ca-ta-pha!" Like the parrot, Kotikokura proclaimed my apotheosis.

"Go back!" I commanded, pointing with my forefinger. The crowd obeyed.

One elderly man, only, remained. He was dressed in a many-colored silk robe. He smiled and his eyes shone with intelligence. I bowed to him. He returned the greeting. I spoke to him in several of the European languages. He shook his head. I asked him if he knew Sanskrit. He was delighted. He had learnt the language in his youth, when he studied philosophy and the wisdom of Guatama the Buddha.

"My esteemed friend," he said, smiling, "the levitation was beautifully done. I have read about this strange phenomenon, but I have never had the pleasure of witnessing it."

"I am happy to meet so wise a man."

"Wisdom is a rare flower. It is sufficient for a man to just breathe a little of its exquisite perfume."

"I have read the words of Kong-Fu-tze, the greatest of philosophers. Anxious to meet the people whom he taught so wisely, I risked my life and the life of my faithful servant."

He smiled. "You have noticed, my learned Master, that the people are not apt scholars. I suspect that wisdom is rare among the people everywhere."

"You are right, excellent friend."

"There are, however, in each generation, and in every locality, a handful of men who love truth. . . . "

"I shall esteem it a favor beyond recompense, if I am allowed to speak with that handful of men who live in this city."

The Chinaman's lips curled into a smile. "Accept the hospitality of my humble roof."

I bowed, and thanked him profusely. "I am most anxious to be converted to the teaching of Kong-Fu-tze."

"Kong-Fu-tze desires no converts. It suffices to quaff his wisdom. . . . "

'Apollonius!' I thought suddenly, 'except for the slanting eyes. . . . The tall stature, the white beard, the slow intelligent gestures of the arms are unmistakable. . . .' I scrutinized him. He smiled politely.

"Forgive me," I said "your words recalled and recaptured the voice of a friend. . . . "

"Living or dead?"

"Alas! He died . . . if he died . . . at Ephesus, at the age of one hundred. I tried to discover in your face, the beloved features of my friend."

"Wherever one goes, one always discovers one's friends."

My host begged me to make myself comfortable in his library. We smoked.

I watched the smoke, my eyes half closed. The shadow it threw upon the opposite wall assumed the shape of a woman.

"Are the women of your country desirous to afford pleasure?"

"The wiser ones among them make a devout study of the ways of pleasure."

"I should like to meet such a student."

"You shall, Cartaphilus."

She pushed gently the door of my room and looked in. I pretended to be asleep. She entered, and on tiptoes, much lighter than a cat, approached me. With the corner of one eye I observed her,—a tiny creature with a face hardly larger than a doll's, illumined by two long eyes that seemed to be dreaming something weird, or merely reflecting the strange smile that appeared and vanished in rapid succession about her mouth.

I opened my eyes. She bowed. "Has Flower-of-Joy disturbed Cartaphilus, Master of Wisdom?"

"Flower-of-Joy has entered more gently than a ray of the sun, and disturbed Cartaphilus no more than the perfume that leaves the heart of a flower and mingles with the air he breathes."

"Cartaphilus is beautiful and wise and Flower-of-Joy fears she cannot delight him."

"Her very presence is a great delight to him."

"Flower-of-Joy is a little tired. May she lie down with Cartaphilus?"

"Flower-of-Joy will be as a dainty dream that visits him in his sleep."

She was a bit of chiseled ivory, animated by the seven devils that Jesus drove out of Magdalene.

Like a labyrinth made of deeply perfumed flowers, within which one wanders certain at every turn to discover an issue, but always finding that it is merely another bend, was the pleasure she afforded me.

Mung Ling greeted me, as always, most cordially. He apologized for having sent me an inexperienced girl.

"Inexperienced?"

He smiled, closing his eyes. "When I was a young man, Cartaphilus, and lived in the Capital, pursuing my studies, I discovered the meaning of unendurable pleasure indefinitely prolonged. . ."

I thought it was merely an old man's exaggeration of his youthful delights, but nevertheless decided to visit the Capital. 'Unendurable pleasure indefinitely prolonged!' His words stirred ancient echoes in my brain. My thoughts returned to Jerusalem. I heard Aurelia's soft voice insinuate the very phrase.

"Your fine phrase is worth a long trip, excellent Mung Ling," I remarked.

XXV

TAXES AND PLAGUES—STONY FINGERS—I GO—A PRISONER OF ATTILA—KOTIKOKURA PULLS HIS MUSTACHES

THE people were clamorous in their complaints against the tax-collectors. The harvests had been very poor, but neither the Governor nor his subordinates showed any clemency. Even the few fistfuls of rice and the small portions of dried, salted fish were dwindling from the hands of the coolies and the small merchants. Many refused to work. If it was one's fate to starve, why add to it the pain of labor?

Fishermen, with baitless lines, were sitting at the shore of the river, their thin legs up to the knees in water; the small merchants, their shops closed, reclining upon the threshold, gossiped with their neighbors across the narrow alleys; the coolies wandered about like lean dogs or cats, seeking among the refuse something to eat.

The Governor sought to subdue them by force. He imprisoned whole families; sold children into servitude; put men to torture. An obstinate silence supervened. People grinned or frowned, but said nothing. They understood one another perfectly. The newlyborn were carried hastily to the shore of the river and left to die and decompose in the sun. The stench was becoming unendurable. It was rumored, hardly above a whisper, but which chilled like the half-motionless shadow of a venomous snake, that some men and women had died of the plague.

"What should a man do, Mung Ling,—stay among the people or go away?"

"Kong-Fu-tze, the Incomparable, said that when law and order prevail in the Empire, the man of sincerity and love is in evidence. When it is without law and order, he withdraws."

> "While the storm is raging,
> The fragile, sensitive butterfly
> Hides deeply among the hospitable petals
> Of the lotus-flower,
> His tremulous wings pasted
> Tip to dazzling tip."

127

We were silent for some time. Kotikokura pulled my sleeve, and bade me listen.

Soldiers on horseback were galloping through the street, and men and women shouted after them. "Thieves!" "Thieves!" "Murderers!" "Wolves!"

Mung Ling nodded. "Sooner or later a river breaks its dikes."

"Will you accompany me, Mung Ling? Let us go to the Capital."

"How kind you are, Cartaphilus, and how can I have the heart to refuse your offer?"

"Will you come then?"

He shook his head. "I remember a poem of an ancient master. He was speaking of the uselessness of taking too much care of one's self." He stopped awhile, then recited:

> "The rose
> However nurtured
> Must wither
> Crushed
> Between the stony fingers
> Of the inevitable Autumn."

"I am too old, Cartaphilus, to care where I die."

"Apollonius," I whispered.

He smiled, ordered his servant to light his pipe, and addressed Sing Po, who was meditating, his head between his hands.

"May I disturb you, Sing Po, pride of all poets?"

"How can Mung Ling ever disturb me?"

"Do you remember the two verses you once wrote to Gen Hsin, who complained that one could no longer keep his soul intact . . . that the days of beauty had passed away?"

Sing Po wrinkled his forehead.

"Our friend is like a bird . . . sings, delights his hearers, and flies on . . . unaware of the joy he has afforded."

"Mung Ling knows how to praise better than all men, and his words are as delicious as wine."

"This is what Sing Po answered Gen Hsin, the skeptic:

> "On the crests of turbulent waves
> Petals of roses ride."

Outside the tumult increased. Kotikokura gripped my arm.

"Do not fear, Kotikokura, Ca-ta-pha shall protect you."

He grinned.

Mung Ling placed his hands upon my shoulders. "Farewell, Cartaphilus."

I looked at him astonished.

"It is time for us to separate, alas! You must go, dear friend."

"Always Cartaphilus must go, Mung Ling . . . always."

"Man is like the wind, Cartaphilus."

"Like the wind . . . it is true, Mung Ling." I remained silent for a few moments, pressing his hands. "But the wind, Mung Ling, at times blows through a garden and is impregnated with a rare perfume."

Mung Ling turned his face away.

"Can a man hide himself, Sing Po? Can a man hide himself?" I asked.

"That is exactly what Kong-Fu-tze asked, Cartaphilus. He, too, was a wanderer. . . ."

"What do we seek always, Mung Ling?"

"Ourselves. We cannot hide, and yet we cannot find ourselves, Cartaphilus."

I twirled the tips of my long mustaches. Kotikokura pulled at the few sparse threads that dotted his upper lip.

"It is not well to look too different from the others, particularly in times of revolution, Kotikokura."

We came upon smoking villages and weary women. The steeds of war were stamping through the land. Our guide, a servant of Mung Ling, deserted us to save his wife and his children.

He kissed my hands, and weeping, galloped back.

"Kotikokura, we are destined to remain alone, always."

Kotikokura pulling at his mustache had the appearance of a gigantic yellow tomcat.

"There is room for everything save for logic, Kotikokura. There has been much kindness and much cruelty upon the earth . . . but very little intelligence."

Kotikokura wrinkled his brow like a puzzled dog.

We found ourselves in the midst of a camp of soldiers. We were immediately surrounded, and ordered to dismount. Our hands were tied behind our backs by heavy ropes. Kotikokura's legs were restless. He bent, ready to run away.

"Do not budge! Ca-ta-pha is with you!"

We were ordered to wait. Two soldiers stood guard. The others went away, to report to their superior. Kotikokura grumbled. "Silence!" I commanded. I wished to know in what camp I found myself, who was the leader, and whom they were fighting. With this information, I could easily extricate myself.

I smiled to one of the soldiers. "It is strange that you treat as enemy the friend of your master."

"What! Are you the friend of King Attila?"

"Of course, valiant soldier."

"Are you not the Emperor's spy?"

I laughed. "Would a spy ride as leisurely into the enemy's camp as I did? Would a spy travel unarmed?"

The soldiers seemed uncertain, but more kindly disposed. One of them said: "But if you are the Emperor's spy, you will learn the meaning of torture." The other grinned.

XXVI

I SMOKE A PIPE WITH ATTILA—TWO MEN WITHOUT
A COUNTRY

ATTILA was sitting at a long table, making drawings upon white silk. He placed his chin upon the hilt of his sword, and looked at me. His mustaches, uniting with his beard, hung heavy and low on either side of his face, and his long teeth shone like the ivory tusks of an elephant in the sun. I was determined to employ hypnotism, if necessary, to safeguard myself, but it amused me to try my skill without relying upon occult psychic forces.

"What is your name?"

"Cartaphilus, Your Majesty."

"Where do you come from?"

"I come from many lands."

"On the other side of the Wall?"

"Countries in which the people do not even dream of the existence of the Wall, Your Majesty."

He sighed, and raised his head.

"What sort of countries are they, Cartaphilus?"

"They are countries with noble and heroic histories . . . but on the verge of ruin."

"Why?"

"Corruption, vice and a false religion called Christianity."

Attila rose, and walked up and down the room. He was tall and rather heavy. The skin of his face was a few shades lighter than that of his soldiers and his cheek-bones were somewhat less protruding.

"Sit down, Cartaphilus." He offered me a gigantic pipe.

We smoked in silence for some time.

"You come from many lands, Cartaphilus; which one is yours?"

"I have none, Your Majesty. My country was destroyed and my people dispersed."

He looked at me not unkindly.

"I, too, have no country, Cartaphilus. I am not absolutely certain

131

who my people are. Perhaps I am a descendant of the kings of your people. . ."

"Then, Sire, my people are indeed fortunate."

"Cartaphilus, he who does not possess a country must make one for himself— —"

"Or else," I interjected, "wander . . . always a stranger in every land."

Attila pulled at his beards.

"Conquer Rome, Sire! Destroy her false, pale-faced god. The Mistress of the World is too old, and Christianity too young to withstand a determined blow."

The King drew circles upon the silk in front of him. "China is at my feet. I could proclaim myself Emperor . . . but I hate walls!"

"For a great general, it must be exasperating to find a nation too easily conquered!"

"Cartaphilus, you fathom my feelings. . . . I love valor and glory and hard combat." He stamped his sword.

"The Romans still love glory, and Christianity is ambitious."

"These people send messengers at my approach and beg me to be their ruler. I cannot fight open doors. . . . "

"The doors of the Romans are still locked. Your sword shall rattle against them like a thunderclap."

At dawn, I was ordered to appear again before the King.

"Cartaphilus, Heaven has sent me a sign . . . this golden chain shall bind at my feet . . . the world beyond the Wall."

I bowed reverently.

"Stay with me, Cartaphilus. Teach me the roads. Draw the maps for me. Attila is not the leader of wild hordes, but the ruler of a disciplined army."

'Jesus of Nazareth,' I thought, 'You have vanquished Julian the Apostate. Attila shall conquer you!'

For three days three Ambassadors of the Emperor begged in vain to be admitted to the presence of Attila. The King had not yet finished his plans: my map was not yet completed.

"Is it not sufficient that I do not order their heads chopped off? Let them wait! Attila is busy."

Finally, at my intervention, he consented to see them and concluded a truce with the Son of Heaven.

The Ambassadors were on the point of leaving when I begged them to remain a while longer.

"Attila, magnanimous monarch, may I speak?"

"Speak!"

"Attila must march forward from conquest to conquest. This is the meaning of his life, is it not?"

He nodded.

"Cartaphilus, lacking the passion and might that are in the blood of the great King, must wander from knowledge to knowledge. . . . He too may not remain still."

Attila nodded.

"If Cartaphilus has helped to save the Celestial Empire, may he travel unmolested from province to province?"

One of the mandarins extended his arm, the rim of the sleeve touching his large ring, whose soft glittering harmonized with the sheen of the silk. "Cartaphilus shall be our honored guest."

"May he enter the Capital?"

"The gates will swing wide open."

"In the company of the Ambassadors of the Perfect Emperor?"

"Carried upon the shoulders of His Majesty's slaves."

Attila's voice was as gentle as a woman's. "Cartaphilus, you must go, even as I must go, that is true. In you, my unrest has a brother. Three days, however, you must spend with me. Three days we shall spend in revelry. Then I shall go forth to conquer the world."

The Mandarin bowed very deeply before me, his hand heavy with jewels, upon his chest.

I smiled.

"In the capital, Cartaphilus, my excellent friend, you are my guest. Meanwhile, we can travel at leisure. I have already sent several messengers at top speed to inform the Emperor of the good news. I have asked him to make Cartaphilus a Mandarin of the First Order."

He presented me with a transparent red ruby, as large as a sparrow's egg.

"The honor is too great."

"It is not a question of honor, excellent friend, but of comfort . . . and elegance."

XXVII

UNENDURABLE PLEASURE INDEFINITELY PROLONGED —THE LORD PROCURER TO THE SON OF HEAVEN— FLOWER-OF-THE-EVENING—THE PALACE OF PLEASURE AND PAIN—I SEEK PERFECTION—SA-LO-ME

"Unendurable pleasure indefinitely prolonged?" To Fo smiled. His eyes closed, until only two thin horizontal lines shone between his lashes. "Cartaphilus is young."

"To Fo is also young."

He shook his head.

Our cups, lighter than lotus-leaves, were filled once more with tcha, whose perfume delighted our nostrils while its color soothed our eyes.

"Cartaphilus, I know who will best afford you what you desire."

"To Fo is a peerless host."

"The Mistress of the Palace of Pleasure and the Palace of Pain is my friend. She is beautiful and very clever. Since the age of ten she has been a profound student of the mystery of the senses. Because of her great talents, I advised His Majesty to appoint her the teacher of the Large Harem and also of the Small Harem, which must not be mentioned in public, under the penalty of death, and which is guarded by two regiments of giant eunuchs. I am the Lord Procurer of the Son of Heaven. . . . "

I bowed profoundly. He clapped his hands. A slave fell on his face. "Go tell Flower-of-the-Evening that your master will visit her shortly."

Flower-of-the-Evening raised her head, then bent over me, her small round breasts perfumed with the essence of two hundred flowers.

"Has Flower-of-the-Evening pleased Cartaphilus?"

I bowed assent.

"My pupils, gratified, plucked for you the fruit from the tree of pleasure that is within easy reach. . . . In the subtler arts, where the line between pleasure and torture is finer than the wing of a butterfly, Flower-of-the-Evening trusted only herself. . . ."

Flower-of-the-Evening unlocked for me the secret gardens of delight. . . . Her hands, tiny as the petals of a delicate, yellow rose, caressed me.

"Has Cartaphilus known pleasure more delectable than my caress?"

"He has not," I lied.

"We have exhausted the two hundred and sixty ways of love, Cartaphilus. I have revealed to you the thirteen ways that are known only to the Emperor . . . but I have not yet revealed the ultimate secret.

"Cartaphilus, Flower of the Evening knows seven more ways of pleasure, ways that are unknown even to the Emperor himself—the secret of unendurable pleasure indefinitely prolonged." She stopped to see the effect of her words upon me. "I have kept the secret as a nuptial gift for my lover."

Her hands continued to caress me.

"Cartaphilus, no mere man could dwell unscathed in the Palace of Pain and the Palace of Pleasure uninterruptedly for seven months as you have done. A giant would have perished on the wheels of its pleasure; its pain, no less exquisite, would turn a demigod into a wraith of himself. Whence do you draw your strength? Who are you?"

"I am . . . Cartaphilus."

"No . . . you are more than Cartaphilus . . . you are . . . a god . . . or a demon."

I laughed.

"Cartaphilus, do you not desire to discover the seven ultimate ways of pleasure, the final essence of the perfume of joy? Flower of the Evening shall teach you the secret ways of love . . . but Cartaphilus must initiate Flower of the Evening into his secret."

"What secret?"

"How to remain young always, and always strong, and always beautiful."

"How should he know all that?"

"He knows! He knows!"

I remembered how I answered the hetaera of Jerusalem, and how she fled out of the room, insulting and cursing me. The intervening centuries had taught me better. I was determined to learn the secret of unendurable pleasure indefinitely prolonged.

"I know, it is true, and I shall teach you how to remain always young, always strong, always beautiful."

She clapped her hands, and pressed herself upon me.

"Flower of the Evening will startle her master with unimaginable delight."

We remained silent for a while.

"What is the drug, Cartaphilus?"

"Not a drug. Drugs are but man's invention. A god needs no drugs."

She listened, her mouth open.

I whispered mysteriously. "Every seven years Cartaphilus shall visit Flower-of-the-Evening at the first hour of dawn. Every seven years Cartaphilus shall renew with his caress the beauty and strength and youth of Flower-of-the-Evening."

For seven days Flower-of-the-Evening taught me the seven ultimate ways of love and the meaning of unendurable pleasure indefinitely prolonged. Each day wrenched a sharper pain into a more exquisite joy. . . .

To Fo congratulated me. "Flower-of-the-Evening is generally inclined to be cynical about men, but she speaks of you with unequivocal satisfaction."

"Flower-of-the-Evening is the most perfect blossom of feminine loveliness. . . . "

To Fo dipped his fingers in perfume, and twisted his mustache.

We smoked our pipes and drank the delicate tcha.

"Are there no other ways, of delighting the senses, admirable To Fo?"

To Fo laughed. "Cartaphilus is insatiable."

"But do you not suspect some inconceivable pleasure beyond the delectable thirteen. . . . ?"

"Impossible. They exhaust every possible source of pleasure."

I smiled. Flower-of-the-Evening then had not lied to me. I was the only man to whom she had revealed the ultimate thrill of passion, the final essence of joy.

To Fo read a few poems. I watched him, my eyes half closed. His beard was becoming quite gray; his hand, as he held the manuscript, seemed a trifle emaciated and the knuckles too large.

"To Fo, your youth is dead."

I praised his work, and we spoke leisurely about life and glory and happiness.

"Are you happy, Cartaphilus?"

"I am not, To Fo."

"Perhaps it is my fault. Is there anything I have omitted? Am I a careless host?"

"You are the most perfect of hosts. My unhappiness lies within, not without. I still seek. . . . "

"What are you seeking?"

"Something beyond pleasure and beyond pain. The technique of love, however perfect, still leaves unslaked the hunger of the soul. . . . "

"What is the soul, Cartaphilus?"

"I do not know; I only know its hunger. . . . "

To Fo shook his head.

"Perhaps you are seeking something for which the world has not yet discovered a name. . . . "

"In my youth, To Fo, I had an incomparable love."

"In youth, love is always incomparable."

"If we drink the cup to the dregs, then we may be satisfied . . . but if the cup is snatched from our lips, our thirst is never afterward quenched."

To Fo pulled gently the sleeves of his gorgeous robe, until they covered his hands up to his long, hooked nails, like the curved beaks of birds of prey. Was he conscious of his large knuckles?

"What joy does Cartaphilus seek that Flower-of-the-Evening and her garden cannot afford?"

"I seek unimaginable perfection. . . ."

To Fo, playing with his beard, remained silent for a long while. Did he understand?

"In my youth, Cartaphilus, I heard of a woman, a goddess, who was perfection . . . the embodiment of all men's dreams. . . ."

"Yes?" I said anxiously.

"She was as old as the Black Mountain, and as young as the first ray of dawn. Witch or goddess, she passed from country to country. He or she who had the incomparable fortune of meeting her knew the meaning of heaven. But all this is merely legend, Cartaphilus. . . ."

"What was her name?"

"She had many names, as she wandered through the ages. Many have called her Lilith and Ashtoreth, but the name she loved best was: Sa-lo-me."

"Sa-lo-me!"

"Have you also heard the voice of Sa-lo-me from afar, Cartaphilus?"

"Perhaps."

"Like a will-o'-the-wisp she flits, in fevered nights through the dreams of youth."

Salome? Could it be she indeed . . . Salome . . . she who scorned me? Salome . . . Nemesis . . . the passionate and cruel . . . the exquisite, the magnificent Daughter of Night! She who beheaded those whom she loved and tortured with her disdain those who loved her? If she lived, who but I was her destined lover? Whom should she love, if not Cartaphilus!

The cup fell out of my hand, and broke.

To Fo smiled. "Her very name makes our hands tremble, Cartaphilus." After a while he resumed: "The cup always slips . . . and it always breaks."

"Kotikokura, we have been long enough in Cathay. Our friends are aging rapidly; Flower-of-the-Evening has noticed a gray hair in her head; the people have forgotten Attila and the events that invested me with a red ruby and the rank of a Mandarin of the First Order. A guest should leave before the host begins to yawn."

Kotikokura scratched his head, pulled at his mustache, and grumbled something.

"I understand, Kotikokura, you have made friends here, and feel comfortable. Comfort, however, is our greatest enemy, Kotikokura. When the goose is most comfortable in her warm grease, the time for her slaughter is near. Besides, my friend, Salome is probably in the West. You do not know Salome? She is the . . . Daughter of Night! She is cruel and beautiful, and disdainful! Like the Queen bee, she destroys those whom she loves!"

Kotikokura grinned.

"She is Lilith, perhaps—mother of demons, or Ashtoreth, goddess of love! We must seek her, Kotikokura."

Kotikokura placed his hands into his wide sleeves, and bowed.

To Fo accompanied us for several miles. The sun was about to set. He gave me a letter sealed with the Grand Seal of the Dragon from the Son of Heaven, exhorting his fellow sovereigns, as well as his subjects, to respect my wishes.

"Cartaphilus, best of friends, now and then when you will see the sun disappear, drink a cup of wine to To Fo."

XXVIII

IN QUEST OF THE PRINCESS—MOON, TORTOISE, OR WITCH?

My eyes sought the faces of all the women I met. Is this Salome? Or this one? Kotikokura imitated me. He squinted his eyes and sighed.

"Are you, too, seeking Salome, Kotikokura?"

He looked at me, his upper lip studded with his sparse hair, trembling.

"Are we running after our own shadows, Kotikokura? Are we in search of that which never was, and never can be?"

Kotikokura did not hear. An enormous fly persisted in tormenting the tip of his nose.

"If Apollonius were but here, he would console and instruct us. Perhaps his ashes are mixing even now with the dust of the road!"

We stopped at every village, and every town. The Emperor's letter brought to my feet mayors, governors and generals. Of all I asked: "Have you seen Salome?" Not knowing whom I meant, and guilty perhaps of some secret misdeeds, they would stammer: "No, no, my Lord, we have not heard of Salome." But when I explained who Salome was, their lips would stretch slowly into a long smile. "Perhaps our poets or our philosophers can inform our Lord. We are so ignorant."

Some of the poets had heard vaguely of a beautiful woman, wandering about the great Celestial Empire, who once in a century upon a certain day, and a certain hour shared the couch of the Son of Heaven. The philosophers, however, smiled at their simplicity. Salome, they claimed, was another name for the moon, revealing the fullness of her beauty to the Emperor, once a month in his garden.

The philologists ridiculed the philosophers, considering their explanation as childish as that of the poets. Salome, they argued, was a tortoise. The tortoise lived for hundreds of years, and moved about so slowly that it needed a century to return to the spot whence it started. Among the ancients, they said, the sight of a tortoise was considered a happy omen. Salome was merely a corruption of an obsolete word for tortoise. The two words were derived from the same root in one of the two hundred forgotten dialects of the Celestial Realm.

We reached the town which had seen our arrival years previously. Nothing seemed to have changed; the same small wooden houses, the same narrow alleys, darkened by wet clothing and fishermen's nets, which hung on poles nailed to opposite roofs; swarms of naked children and shopkeepers smoking on the thresholds. An unpleasant stench rose now as then.

I approached a group of men. They bowed to the ground.

"Where is Mung Ling, the great philosopher?"

One of them answered: "Mung Ling is at the Lake, excellent Lord, but he is not a great philosopher. He is a poor, and not over-intelligent fisherman." The others smiled.

"Is he the son of the philosopher?"

"His father has been dead for many years, great Lord," an old man added. "It may be that he was a philosopher. There are so many things to remember, and the memory of man is like a sieve. . . ."

"Is Sing Po, the poet, alive?"

They shook their heads.

"Have you heard of Li Tung, the sculptor?"

"No, my Lord."

"Kotikokura, things are stronger than men. Men pass; things remain. Often, however, man believes he is stationary, while things disappear about him. Even thus the swift-footed river wonders why the shores fly past it forever."

The gates of Cathay opened and closed behind us, the watchmen hiding their faces in the dust.

"Kotikokura, it is no longer necessary to hide our lips with hair. We must not belong too conspicuously to any country."

XXIX

ISPAHAN PLAYS CHESS—THE PRINCESS SALOME HAS NO
LORD—SALOME CLAPS HER HAND—ORGY—THE
ULTIMATE PORTAL—KOTIKOKURA'S ADVENTURE—
THE GOD LI-BI-DO

A CROWD gathered about the two players, who, sitting on small
carpets, their legs underneath them, were twisting their long beards,
meditating. Some of the spectators whispered to one another, pointing with their fingers to a board. Chess had recently been invented
by one of the prisoners of the Shah, and Ispahan, the capital, had
forgotten about her story-tellers and jugglers and mummers in her
enthusiasm for the new game. The narrow roads were blocked by
players and watchers, and mule and elephant drivers complained in
vain to the city authorities for relief. The authorities promised to
attend to the matter but, being themselves enamored of the game,
were too sympathetic with the violators of the traffic, to interfere
with their pleasure.

"Make way! Make way!" a dark-skinned driver shouted. No one
paid heed to him. A few grumbled, "Take another road."

"Make way for my mistress!" the man insisted.

I looked up. Upon a tall elephant, royally caparisoned, reclined
a woman. Her eyes were half-closed, as if in meditation or in voluptuous revery. Her forehead was encircled by a gold band studded
with jewels, and her cheeks were partially hidden by heavy tresses
of red hair. I could not tell her age. I remembered To Fo's remark:
'As old as the Black Mountain and as young as the first ray of dawn.'

"Make way!"

"Take another road, fool!" several exclaimed.

I approached the driver and placed a coin into his half-closed
palm. "Who is your mistress?"

"Princess Salome."

"Make way!"

I slipped another coin into his hand. "Where does she live?"

"Yonder. This side of the palm trees."

"Make way!"

I dropped a third coin. "Who is her lord?"

"Princess Salome has no lord."

"Checkmate!" one of the players called out. The crowd dispersed, and Princess Salome, still dreaming or thinking, rode slowly past me, rocking lightly on her giant animal.

Kotikokura beat a monotonous tune upon a kettle, like the white-haired man of his native tribe.

"You, too, Kotikokura? You, too, yearn for your youth? Must man revert forever to his pristine lusts? Is there nothing in life, except the ghost of the past?"

Kotikokura continued to beat upon the kettle.

"Stop! We have no time to lose. Go, hire the finest animal. This very evening we shall be the guests of Princess Salome!"

The eunuch, watching the gate, was a colossal mass of flesh, motionless as a stone. His semicircular sword glittered like an evil eye. I placed a purse into his hand. "Tell your mistress, Princess Salome, that His Highness Prince Cartaphilus begs for the favor of an audience with her." He took the money, but did not budge. I tried to put him to sleep, but his small black eyes opened and closed, unperturbed. I dipped my fingers into the chemical which accompanied me on all my journeys. My hands dazzled like stars, but he was unmoved.

"Inform your mistress that Prince Cartaphilus is at her gate," I repeated angrily.

He did not stir.

"You evidently do not know who Prince Cartaphilus is. Here—" I waved before his eyes the letter with the seal of the Imperial Dragon. He looked at the curious characters on the parchment, which of course he could not decipher.

I whispered, "A message from the Shah." He dropped upon his hands, like a lifeless thing. "Rise," I commanded, "and announce my arrival!"

The palace was surrounded by a garden, in the center of which a tall fountain rose and fell silently, like a stream of light. A flock of peacocks first screeched at our approach, then spread slowly like magnificent fans their luxurious tails. Several small monkeys climbed rapidly the giant palm trees, and crouching upon the tips of the branches, glared at Kotikokura, whose uncovered teeth shone like whetted knives.

Salome was reclining upon a low sofa, covered with a silk canopy, embroidered with one enormous eagle, whose wings of red gold seemed to flap in the glitter. I kissed her hand. She bade me sit opposite her.

"I am Cartaphilus, gracious Princess."

"Do not speak in Hebrew, I pray you, Cartaphilus. I hate words that gurgle in the throat. Speak in Greek. Greek undulates like a river, which is stirred by the breezes."

She understood Hebrew,—that was what I wished to know, to ascertain if she was indeed Salome.

"It is natural to dislike the language of the vanquished, Princess, and Greek is certainly more beautiful."

She patted gently the spotted back of a leopard cub asleep at her side. We were silent. Was she really the Princess who once upon a time praised the subtle and impersonal love of flowers, but accepted the personal embrace of a swarthy Nubian? Was she the reincarnation of the most delightful and most detestable Princess, or a composite of the women I had known? She partook of each; but was different nevertheless. Was she Salome, Princess of Judea, or the Perfect Woman? Was she all things, being still herself?

She guessed my thoughts. "The body is a house wherein dwells a multitude of beings," she remarked.

I did not know how to begin the conversation, and Salome refused to help me.

"I have traversed the land of Cathay to meet the incomparable Princess."

She nodded.

"Have you also visited that marvelous land, whose walls encircle so much wisdom and beauty?"

"It may be. I have traveled much."

"The poets of the Celestial Empire sing of Princess Salome rapturously. She is the magnificent goddess, appearing every hundred years in incomparable glory."

Salome smiled. "Poets."

"Poets, Princess, see beyond the walls that encircle others— —"

"They deal in symbols."

"Are not all things symbols?"

We remained silent again for some time. The cub opened its eyes, yawned, and licked the hand of his mistress.

"What does the Shah desire?"

"The Shah?"

"Yes. Did you not show my slave a letter from the Shah?"

I smiled. "It was the only way I could gain admittance."

She looked at me angrily.

"I beg your forgiveness, Madam, but is not any strategem lawful, in love and war?"

"So the proverb goes, but I dislike proverbs. It is a facile manner of thinking."

"Quite true, Princess. The letter, however, is from a monarch greater than the Shah,—it is a missive from the Son of Heaven. Do you care to read it?"

She shook her head slowly, and patted the young 'leopard. I wondered whether she refused to see it because she did not know Chinese.

"The Chinese language," she said, answering my thought, "is not as difficult as people believe. With a little imagination, and the ability to draw, one can master it within five or ten years."

"Princess Salome must be well versed in it, then, I am certain."

She did not answer. I was making no impression. My words seemed unconvincing and futile.

'It is she, Cartaphilus!' I thought, 'and once again, she treats you as a Princess treats a commoner.' My hand itched, as it had itched centuries before, to penetrate the armor of her insolence if not with my love, at least with my sword.

The cub opened wide his mouth. Salome placed the tips of her fingers between his jaws.

"Even the wild beasts adore your beauty."

She lifted slightly her left brow, as Poppaea had been in the habit of doing, when disdainful.

"In my travels, O Princess, I have mastered the secret laws of love."

She smiled.

"I have been as a bee that gathers the perfume from a thousand flowers that its honey may taste the sweeter."

She clapped her hands. A young slave appeared. She whispered something into his ear.

"Does Cartaphilus enjoy music and dancing?"

"Of course, Princess." I was piqued at the idea of being interrupted.

What I had taken for marble walls, dissolved and vanished, and the room in which we were became as large as a street. The ceiling was studded with enormous diamonds, which shed a light, soothing and cool like the sun at dawn, when the lower part of its circumference still touches the thin blue line of the mountains.

In the farther corner of the room, several girls were playing Oriental melodies, which were the passionate pulsation of a lover's blood. Suddenly, strident and insistent, the music changed into a raging sea beating against metal shores.

Naked giants, red-bearded and black, dashed into the room. Their dance mimicked love's final siege. Was it an amorous embrace? Was it wrestling? Their limbs united, separated and clenched again, until one half lay panting, outstretched under the colossal weight of their conquerors.

The Princess watched the play of their enormous sinews with half-closed eyes.

The bearded giants were followed by clean-shaven men,—black, white and yellow, dancing native dances to which they added movements reminding me of the convulsive spasms with which the body responded to the caresses devised by Flower-of-the-Evening.

These were followed by youths with fleshy hips, whose hair fell over their shoulders in long silken ringlets. Their dancing was almost motionless, like half-congealed waters or wary snakes that creep among the grasses more silently than summer breezes.

The Princess threw a bracelet to one of the dancers. He walked over to her with tiny, mincing steps, balancing his hips like a young Hindu girl, who carries upon her head a crystal vase filled with perfume. Salome caressed him, and bade him sit at her feet. His head against her knee, he remained motionless in an attitude of adoration.

The music played softly a Lesbian air, stirring epicene dreams and shadowy atavistic desires. Girls entered, some tall, slim, with wiry muscles; others, with full-blossomed breasts, wearing like a badge of love, the triangle of Astarte. They formed a semicircle, in the center of which a tall woman, her body half hidden by many veils of various hues, began to dance, first slowly like the young men; but gradually quickening her movements until she seemed like a wind of many colors, turning in a mad spiral.

Salome bade her approach, placed around her neck a gold chain, and embraced her.

The girls sang to the accompaniment of a harp. Slaves shook perfumes out of ivory bowls the shape of roses.

Salome waved her hand. It was as if some divinity had commanded a storm. The bearded men fell upon the women with groans of anguish and delight like wild beasts mating. The women, like maenads, encircled the youths and embraced each other. Bearded giants, full-breasted women, girls indistinguishable from boys, boys hardly distinguishable from maids, curious figures in the chasm between the sexes, all danced to a music that was like a madman's joy. It was a feast of Priapus, an orgy of sex in which sex overflowed its limits and blood mingled with kisses. It was a battle of lust punctured by the crash of cymbals and the swish of lashes.

The music died slowly; the dancers, exhausted, dropped to the floor in heaps of two, three or four; the lights dimmed until one could distinguish merely motion, like some ocean tossed by winds blowing in many directions. . . .

Salome clapped her hands. The walls moved back into their original position. The lights shone once more. The storm abated. One heard nothing save the loud yawning of the cub.

Salome brushed aside one of her braids, and looked at me, smiling. I understood what she meant.

"You wish to convey to me by this exhibition that you too have explored the ways and the byways of pleasure," I said.

"I too," she said, "have discovered unendurable pleasure indefinitely prolonged. I have traversed the two hundred and sixty ways of love, the thirteen secret ways that are known only to the Emperor, and the seven ways that are not known even to the Emperor himself. I seek something beyond the ultimate portal of pleasure. . ."

"Is this orgasmic medley your definition of love, Princess?" I queried.

"Love, Cartaphilus, what is love?"

The silk curtain stirred a little, and the long, hairy arm of Kotikokura moved slowly in, followed by his head.

"Who is that?" Salome asked.

"My slave, Your Highness. His fidelity is so great that he fears to leave me alone."

Kotikokura withdrew.

"Is he a man . . . or a beast?" She sat up, wrinkled her brow a little, as Damis used to do, when very much interested. "Who is he, Cartaphilus?"

"A denizen of the forest, Princess. I found him in Africa."

"In Africa?"

"A curious country . . . peopled with extraordinary beings."

"What is his name?"

"Kotikokura."

"Kotikokura. . . ." The name seemed to float like music from her throat.

"It means 'The Accursed One.' "

"The Accursed?"

"He dared to laugh at the gods. . . ."

She looked at me, fathoming my thoughts.

"It is not difficult to become a god, Cartaphilus. . . ."

Again her eyes traveled to the curtain where the eyes of Kotikokura gleamed.

"Cartaphilus, will you sell me your slave?"

"He is not really my slave. He is my friend, who has saved my life on several occasions."

"Your life, Cartaphilus?" There was a touch of irony in her intonation.

"Not my life, then, my skin. . . ."

She remained silent for a while. "I will give you in exchange three of my slaves, a maid, a boy and if you wish, my favorite hermaphrodite . . ."

"I cannot barter my friend for your slaves."

"Take six of them . . . twelve, Cartaphilus. They are marvelous people, past masters and past mistresses in the art of pleasure . . . and pain."

I made no answer.

"Well?"

"Kotikokura!" I called.

He appeared immediately. I made a sign. He returned with a casket of jade, and walked out again. Salome watched him with a curious fascination.

"Princess, deign to accept this." I opened the casket, which was filled with exquisite trinkets of jade and ivory. I recounted their history and their symbolism. I spoke of the great artists who had imprinted them with their dreams. Salome, paying no attention to my explanation, toyed with the tiny figure of Li-Bi-Do, an obscene god, long forgotten, even in the Celestial Realm, and carelessly tossed the others aside.

"Kotikokura has an extraordinary head . . . and what arms!"

'Did she need a headless lover to excite her emotions?'

"A strange head," she mused.

Was it her intention to decapitate Kotikokura?

'Should I offer his head for her love?'

"Let me have Kotikokura, Cartaphilus."

I remained pensive.

"Does Cartaphilus believe that Salome desires to repeat the same sensation forever?" she remarked, again reading my thoughts.

"Kotikokura shall remain with Princess Salome, if she commands, for one night," I said angrily.

"What will you take in exchange?"

"Cartaphilus does not bargain."

XXX

SALOME WRITES A LETTER—MAGIC RUINS—THE TOKEN—I LAUGH

At dawn Kotikokura appeared, bringing me a letter. It was in Hebrew, on thin parchment:

"What Cartaphilus seeks Salome must also seek. In strange things and strange places she seeks her soul. Farewell!"

I looked intently at Kotikokura. He lowered his eyes, and bent nearly in two. I raised my fist to strike him. 'Cartaphilus, are you jealous . . . jealous of an ape?' I laughed, opened my fist and caressed his head. "It is well, my friend. Salome preferred Kotikokura, as she once preferred . . . but no matter. . . ."

I asked him many things. He merely grinned or grumbled. Nevertheless, my desire to possess Salome did not abate. She must pay for her pleasure! I was a Jew, and required payment. My generosity had been merely a gesture.

"Salome shall be mine! We go there again this evening, Kotikokura. Am I not God Ca-ta-pha?"

Kotikokura knelt. "Ca-ta-pha! Ca-ta-pha!"

The gate stood wide opened and unwatched. No sword, no eunuch. Two owls, perching upon it, hooted at our approach, and rocked it by merely flapping their wings. What the previous night had been a gorgeous garden was now a wilderness of giant weeds, which scratched our hands and faces, as we tried to make a pathway to the house. I looked in vain for the peacocks, and Kotikokura watched the palm trees, whose withered leaves were covered with a heavy white dust, to discover the monkeys. Only large bats brushed threateningly against our faces.

The steps leading to the palace, shook under our feet, and the door, hanging from one hinge, swung against us like a broken branch. We lit a torch. Rats, enormous worms and lizards, scurried into the large holes of floors and walls, or remained in the corners in menacing attitudes. Our faces became entangled in the cobwebs,

149

which hung from the ceilings where diamonds had been glittering like lamps.

The couch Salome had sat upon crumbled at my touch; the canopy was devoured by sharp-fanged moths and other insects; the skeleton of a small animal, yellow and frail, like the tendrils of a large, fantastic leaf, cracked under Kotikokura's step.

"Kotikokura, are we dreaming?"

He scratched his head vigorously.

"Were we not here last night? Was not this a palace, luxurious, gay?"

His eyes galloped from corner to corner.

The rest of the furniture was an indescribable hill of débris, except one huge bed which seemed intact. We approached it. Pathetically, like a living thing, in a vast cemetery, shone upon it Li-Bi-Do the exquisite tiny god of jade I had given Salome.

"It was not a dream, Kotikokura!"

He bent his head.

I struck the bed a heavy blow. It crumbled into a shapeless mass. The foul air stifled me. My throat tightened. "Let us go out."

As we reached the spot where the fountain had been, I noticed a large stone basin, made white by the moon.

"Was this basin here when we entered this evening, Kotikokura? Did you see it?"

He scratched his head.

"Are things changing under our very eyes, Kotikokura? Are we enchanted?"

The basin was deep. I looked into it. A large tortoise, whose back glittered like a great yellow and black jewel, lay within it motionless save for a tiny, sharp head which moved rapidly like the tongue of a bell.

"A tortoise, Kotikokura! Is this Salome? Was the Chinese philologist right? Was it this animal with whom you spent the night?"

Kotikokura grinned.

"We shall take it with us. Its name shall be Salome, in honor of the magnificent Princess."

I inquired about Salome of many people. No one had ever heard of her. The castle had been in ruins for generations. It was a place haunted by evil spirits and queer beasts, but as I insisted that I had seen and spoken to a beautiful Princess there, whose retinue was enormous and magnificent, that peacocks spread their gorgeous fans at our approach, and monkeys hung on the branches of palm trees, the people smiled or laughed, and as I turned my face, pointed to their foreheads significantly.

One old woman, thin as a skeleton, with eyes as dazzling as the beads of a stuffed animal, hissed: "Salome? A witch, who died three hundred years ago."

I would have considered the whole matter a dream, a nightmare, had I not found the little obscene divinity upon the bed. "And the letter!" I exclaimed suddenly. "You brought me a letter from her, did you not, Kotikokura?"

He nodded.

As I reached for the missive, a thin stream of ashes fell to the ground, and I remained empty-handed.

For a very long time, I could think of nothing save Salome. I was quite certain that I had actually met her and that, much better versed in magic than I, she had been able to transform ruins and death into life and magnificence for a night. But why had she treated me so disdainfully, preferring an ape's caresses to mine? Was I he whom she must shun?

Perhaps—and this pleased me and comforted me more than any other idea—she feared that if she yielded herself to me, her personality, weaker than mine, would be submerged and conquered.

Perhaps possession would slay desire.

No! Seeking was better than finding. . .

I laughed aloud. Kotikokura, frightened, crouched behind me.

XXXI

THE ELOQUENT HAMMER—KOTIKOKURA DISCOVERS
TEARS—MOHAMMED OR JESUS?—I REACH THE OUT-
SKIRTS OF MECCA

"He is the Prophet!" shouted the horseshoer, dropping the animal's leg, which he held in his lap.

"He is not the Prophet!" shouted back the owner of the horse, placing his foot into the stirrup.

"He is the Prophet!"

"He is not!"

A crowd gathered. The two men shouted back and forth their absolute convictions, adding insults, dealing with their physical appearance, their professions, their morals, their intelligence, and the probity of their ancestors.

Infuriated, the horseshoer struck his opponent a powerful blow. The man fell, his face covered with blood. The horseshoer raised his hammer over the victim's head. "Do you believe he is the Prophet?"

The man grumbled, "I believe."

Turning to the rest, his hammer still in the air: "Is there any man here who does not believe that he is the Prophet?"

No one answered.

"Is he the Prophet?" he asked Kotikokura, who was grinning. Kotikokura nodded. He glared at me. "Is he the Prophet?" "Certainly he is. How could it be otherwise, when I see so much zeal! Is not zeal the sign of truth? Could a lie inspire such passion?"

The horseshoer replaced the hammer upon the anvil.

"Stranger," the blacksmith said, "you deserve a place with the true believers in Paradise, where soft couches, delicious fruit, and beautiful virgins await us. So says the Prophet."

"Whatever the Prophet says is truth."

"The unbelievers refuse such delights, but we shall find ways to persuade them. Where kind words fail the hammer shall speak."

"The eloquence of the hammer is indisputable."

Kotikokura walked behind me, his body bent, his arms dangling. Since the affair with Salome, I had neglected him, and he was unhappy.

"Forgive me, Kotikokura," I said.

He kissed my hands. His eyes filled with tears,—for the first time it seemed to me.

"If Mohammed is truly the Prophet, Kotikokura,—who knows . . . perhaps . . . we shall be parted forever."

"Ca-ta-pha! Ca-ta-pha!"

I took his arm. "Kotikokura, you have been a great consolation to me."

Kotikokura threw his head backward and walked upon his heels, his face radiant.

Rumors of the new Prophet had reached me from many quarters. These rumors strangely disturbed me. Could it be Jesus returned to earth? Was it the second coming of the Messiah which John and Mary ceaselessly prophesied?

"Tarry until I come" he had said. If the second part of his command should prove as true as the first my pilgrimage was at an end. I was not prepared for such an issue. Every year had added new zest to my life. I did not want to relinquish it now. Nevertheless, some force beyond my own volition drew me inexorably to Mecca.

Soft couches, delicious fruits and beautiful virgins?

It could hardly be that the Paradise of Jesus was so earthly. It was possible, even probable, that the horseshoer had misinterpreted his words. Even Paul and Peter and his immediate disciples had misunderstood him; why not this simple fellow, whose arguments were the fist and the hammer?

I tried to visualize Jesus, to hear his voice. I could recall nothing save his luminous eyes, which I preferred not to remember.

We reached the outskirts of Mecca and it began to rain,—a heavy perpendicular rain. We struck up our tents.

Kotikokura was snoring. The tortoise stretched out its thin head at intervals and munched the large leaf of cabbage in front of it. The rain beat upon the canvas.

Should I turn back? Could I avoid my destiny? Was I master of myself? Why should I fear? Was it not ridiculous to think that Jesus had returned? And yet . . . was it more impossible than the miracle of my own existence?

I remembered suddenly Nero. I could see him arrange the folds of his toga. He was dust. I remembered John and Magdalen, Lydia, Damis, Asi-ma, Ulrica, Flower-of-the-Evening. All were dust. Should I become dust as well? I shuddered. No! I must live on! I had permitted life to pass me by as a dream. From now on I would grasp at realities! I would begin to live!

The night was interminable. I yearned to pray. Who was my God? I could not choose from the long array that passed before me—old gods, new gods, even myself riding upon the camel, on whose head, like a crest, the parrot perched, screeching: "Carr-tarr-pharr . . . Carr-tarr-pharr . . . !"

Toward morning the rain stopped. The sun shone like the eye of some mischievous young divinity. Kotikokura continued to sleep. I descended, patted the animals, and offered them food. Kotikokura woke up with a start, and jumped off the cart.

"Come, my friend, we must face our destiny, whatever it may be. Life . . . death . . . who knows the difference?"

Kotikokura yawned, stretched, breathed deeply.

"Being accustomed to the earth, Kotikokura, one hates to leave it. There is something delicious in merely existing."

Kotikokura rubbed the long noses of the bullocks.

"The earth is beautiful. The earth is like the lap of one's mother. Who can leave her, Kotikokura, without weeping?"

Kotikokura knelt and took my hands. "Ca-ta-pha, Ca-ta-pha! Live . . . always."

"But after all, should we disdain death, Kotikokura? May she not be as beautiful as life? May not her kiss be as delicate as the kiss of a virgin?"

"Live always ، . . Ca-ta-pha. Live always."

"Better than either death or life is the calm acceptance of fate."

"Live always, Ca-ta-pha."

XXXII

I FACE MY DESTINY—MY FRIEND ABU-BEKR—THE ANGEL GABRIEL DICTATES A BOOK—MOHAMMED STROKES HIS BEARD—"DARUL HARB"

MECCA was a cauldron of argumentation and mysterious stabbings. The camps had not yet been clearly formed, and it was dangerous to say "I believe" or "I doubt." Believers and doubters alike had their faces set, and their hands upon the handles of the semicircular knives which protruded out of their wide belts.

"Neither nod nor shake your head, Kotikokura. We are strangers from far-off countries passing through Arabia. We have not heard of Mohammed, the new Prophet, but are certain that truth will conquer."

Kotikokura grinned.

"Truth always conquers, Kotikokura, for that which conquers is truth."

But if my lips were tightly sealed, my ears were opened wide and attuned to the whisperings, as well as to the tumult of the storm.

'Was Jesus, Mohammed? Was Mohammed, Jesus?' I must face my destiny. The uncertainty was intolerable. But where was Mohammed? Neither the believers nor his enemies could tell with precision. The former promised that he would soon appear, a dazzling prince at the head of a great army, leading them to victory; the latter laughed ironically, and called him a coward, hiding behind the skirts of his women, afraid to face them.

Meanwhile, the name of Abu-Bekr crawled into the argumentations, subtly, quietly, with something of an ominous significance. No one knew how powerful or how weak Mohammed's father-in-law might be: no one could tell when or how he had acquired his wealth, nor what had prompted him years ago to give his daughter into marriage to a mere stripling, almost destitute. And now that his daughter was dead, and Mohammed remarried for the third time, —what were the relations between the two? They could neither praise nor condemn Abu-Bekr. He eluded them like water that one tries in vain to keep in one's fist.

I sought out Abu-Bekr. I won his confidence by quoting ancient prophecies announcing the coming of the Messiah. I offered him my wealth for his camels. The old man was moved. We became blood brothers. Abu-Bekr consented to lead me to the hiding-place of Mohammed.

"Follow me, Cartaphilus."

Abu-Bekr led the way through a subterranean passage which meandered in various directions. At every turn, a watchman demanded the password. Abu-Bekr answered each one differently, and each one replied: "Allah is God, and Mohammed is His Prophet."

We climbed several steps and found ourselves in a large room, which led into other rooms by openings on the right and left. Afterwards, I discovered that the roof of the house was completely covered by a vine, which hid its existence, and that there was no other entrance save the circuitous catacomb.

"Allah is God and Mohammed is His Prophet," Abu Bekr called out. A slave appeared and bowed three times. "Tell the Prophet I must speak to him." A few minutes later, the slave reappeared. "The Prophet—may his name prosper forever—has converse with the Archangel Gabriel."

He bent three times to the floor, and we did likewise.

"The Prophet will see you as soon as the Archangel returns to the Throne of God."

We entered the room to our right. A middle-aged man was reclining on a couch. A pretty girl, one of his wives or concubines, was anointing his head and washing his beard with perfume.

"Mohammed, my son, and Prophet of Allah, I have brought a stranger with me,—Cartaphilus, a great merchant of India." I used the Latin form of my name by preference.

Mohammed motioned to the girl, who walked out immediately. I felt a curious dizziness. Was it merely my own excitement, or the presence of him whose return would mean my destruction, as long ago it had meant my life?

Mohammed raised his eyes. They were very black and dazzling. But they were not the eyes of the Nazarene!

"Welcome, Cartaphilus."

His voice was deep and vibrant. But it was not the voice of

Jesus! My faintness disappeared. He bade us sit down, and ordered sweets for us.

"Has the Angel of Allah visited you today, my son?"

"He has."

"Is it permissible for our ears, Prophet of Allah, to hear the angelic message?"

Mohammed looked at me critically.

"Our sacred books," I said, "foretell the advent of the true Prophet . . . who was born in the desert . . . they were dictated by God himself."

"I know. So were the words that Moses carved on the tablets of stone. Jesus, too, heard God."

"Moses," I remarked, "was a great lawgiver. Jesus was a young prophet who had heard merely the beginning of the prophecy and mistook its purpose."

Mohammed caressed his beard. His hand was large and fleshy. It was not the hand of Jesus.

Abu-Bekr smiled, closing his eyes slowly. "How should it be otherwise, my son, if a man dies so young? Do not all our books speak of the wisdom of old age, and the errors of youth?"

"Every great event is foreshadowed by a lesser one. Jesus is the moon, Mohammed the sun," I added.

'If he is Jesus,' I thought, 'it matters not if I belittle him. If he is not Jesus . . . he shall be the sword with which I destroy the Nazarene! Attila was merely a warrior. The sword rusts in its scabbard or breaks with usage. Mohammed is a man of words . . . words dictated by an angel, directly descended from Heaven! Words rust not.'

"Jesus spoke beautifully," Mohammed remarked.

"Beautifully? Who heard him, Prophet of Allah?" I asked. "His disciples were long dead before the words were put upon parchment."

"Besides," interrupted Abu-Bekr, "what does it mean? The poets speak beautifully. Are they, for that reason, the true prophets of Allah? Shall a man speak beautifully, or truly?"

"Truth shuns beauty, knowing that she ensnares like a woman," Mohammed replied.

Would Jesus have spoken thus? Mohammed spoke as a man of worldly experience, and with something of the bitterness which is the heritage of all who have known the joy and the profound disillusion of sex. No. These were not the words of Jesus!

"Woman is the mother and mistress of man. She must be faithful and obedient to him," Mohammed added.

"How true, Prophet of Allah! But what has Jesus said of woman? Did he not accept a gift of the courtesan and forgive the woman taken in adultery?"

Mohammed clenched his fist. "Against those of·your women who commit adultery, call four witnesses among yourselves, and if these bear witness, then keep the woman in the house till death release her, so God has ordered."

"The words of the Prophet are full of wisdom."

"And God has also commanded this to the wives of the Prophet: O wives of the Prophet, whosoever of you shall commit a manifest wickedness, the punishment thereof shall be double!"

"Jesus forgave Mary instead of punishing her. Was he a true prophet?" I asked.

His eyes blazed, his heavy lips pouted.

No, he was not Jesus, or if Jesus, so changed that he remembered neither himself nor me.

"Prophet of Allah," I said, "is it true that Europe is nearly all Christian?"

"It is, Cartaphilus."

"The boundaries between Europe and Asia are no longer very formidable. I have heard that even the great wall that encircles the Celestial Empire yields to the hoofs of horses and camels."

"They who wait to be attacked are already half conquered," added Abu-Bekr.

"If Christianity has conquered Europe and converted the descendants of Attila— —"

"May his name be cursed!" exclaimed Abu-Bekr.

"Then," I continued, "is Arabia safe?"

Mohammed listened intently, smoothening his black beard. His large chest rose and sank quickly.

"Christianity is the religion of woman, Prophet of Allah . . . woman glorified and forgiven."

"Woman is the servant of man!" Mohammed exclaimed.

"Christianity belittles man. It condemns the sword. It sanctifies the eunuch!"

"What!" Mohammed stood up. Only then did I realize how tall and masculine he was, as compared to the Nazarene. He waved his clenched fist. "Christianity shall never pollute the East!"

"The East, then, shall continue to feel the joy of the senses. The

East shall continue to sing of the lips and breasts of women; of the prowess of men in battle. The East shall exclaim forever 'Allah is the only God and Mohammed is His Prophet!' "

Abu-Bekr raised my hands to his lips. "Stranger, your words are sweeter than honey, and your thought deeper than the ocean. You have opened the door wide, and let the light of truth fall at the feet of the Prophet—who was born in the desert and whose advent the ancient and sacred books of your great country announce."

"Prophet of Allah, what is the symbol of Christianity . . . a cross . . . a man wriggling upon a tree, helpless and ridiculed! And to what purpose this suffering? Is it that a man may receive forever in Paradise an incomparable reward? Shall his joy make up for his agony?" I laughed. "The Paradise of the Christians knows neither man nor woman, but vague sexless wraiths, wandering aimlessly and disconsolately about, remembering how much more agreeable was the earth, even when enduring pain."

"Who can accept such a religion?" asked Abu-Bekr.

"It is the creed of eunuchs and of women!"

Mohammed, his eyes burning with a curious mixture of passion and dream, stood gazing into the distance. Was he wrestling with himself to overcome the final doubt? Did he see beyond the walls of the room, his followers, lovers of the sword and lovers of woman, in endless phalanxes, march against the West, conquering the Nazarene,—the soft preacher of mercy and self-denial?

Closing his eyes, he spoke: "The sincere servants of God shall have a certain provision in Paradise . . . they shall be honored; they shall be placed in gardens of pleasure, leaning on couches opposite one another; a cup shall be carried around unto them filled from a limpid fountain, for the delight of those who drink. Near them shall lie the virgins of Paradise, refraining their looks from beholding any besides their spouses, having large black eyes, and resembling the eggs of an ostrich covered with feathers."

He breathed rapidly, and tottered. We grasped him in our arms, and stretched him gently upon the couch. Two spots of foam dotted the corners of his mouth, and whitened his beard.

His breathing became gradually regular again. He opened his eyes. "Thus speaks Allah,—may his name be praised through Mohammed, his Prophet."

"Allah is the only God and Mohammed is His Prophet," we answered.

Mohammed stood up again and exclaimed: "Every spot of the

earth that believes not in Allah and Mohammed shall from now on be *darul harb,*—a place of endless conflict!"

Mohammed turned toward the East and knelt. We did likewise.

"Thy will be done, Allah, God of the world."

"Allah is the only God and Mohammed is His Prophet."

XXXIII

KOTIKOKURA LOSES A FRIEND—MECCA GLOWS LIKE A RUBY—THE PROPHET CONQUERS—"I MUST GO, CARTAPHILUS"

KOTIKOKURA came running toward me. "Ca-ta-pha! Ca-ta-pha! The tortoise . . . the tortoise!"

"What about the tortoise, my friend?"

"Gone . . . gone! Ca-ta-pha!"

"Did you not watch your sweetheart, Kotikokura?"

He nodded violently as if to frantically deny my aspersion.

"Then how could the tortoise be gone?"

"Gone, Ca-ta-pha! Gone!"

Kotikokura seemed so disturbed that I promised I would help him search for it. We looked through the streets, in deserted gardens, in abandoned houses. Kotikokura called out from time to time: "Salome! Salome!" I asked many people if they had seen a tortoise. Most of them had never heard of such an animal, and my description only made them smile. "Can such an animal live?" they asked. One old woman hissed through her toothless mouth, "Tortoise? I saw one when I was a child. A tortoise lives forever . . . and always changes masters."

"Were you ever in Persia?" I asked.

She walked away, grumbling.

Kotikokura's eyes filled with tears.

"Salome deserts even her favorites, it seems, Kotikokura."

"Salome," he muttered.

I could not tell whether he meant the woman or the tortoise.

"Salome does not matter just now, Kotikokura. We are called by more important affairs. Christianity must be destroyed!"

Kotikokura grumbled, "Salome."

"Mohammed, the true Prophet of Allah, shall vanquish the Man on the Cross."

"Salome."

"And we shall live, Kotikokura! We need no longer tremble before the name of Jesus! We shall live!"

"Salome."

"Comfort yourself. We shall meet her again, Kotikokura. We have passed the bend of the road. Once more the path before us is endless. . . ."

"Oh, that I had a daughter who might find favor in your eyes, Cartaphilus!" exclaimed Abu-Bekr, as I crossed the threshold. "Alas! My two remaining daughters are aged, and already married."

"Cartaphilus considers you as a father, nevertheless, Abu-Bekr."

He embraced me.

"Abu-Bekr," I said, "does not blood always speak?"

"More powerful is blood than swords and spears."

"And more enduring than rock, Abu-Bekr."

He nodded.

"I am a Hindu, Abu-Bekr . . . but my ancestors came from a far-off country."

"Arabia?" he asked, anxiously.

"From Arabia, also, but more recently from Palestine. My ancestors were Jews, Semites as your people, speaking a language akin to yours and worshiping the same God."

Abu-Bekr raised his arms: "May Allah be praised, and His Prophet live forever!"

"I was drawn to your country, as the water of the rain is drawn by the thirsty earth. The country of my fathers has been destroyed, Abu-Bekr. What part of the world is left me, save Arabia?"

"Arabia is your country, Cartaphilus."

"Arabia is my country, and Abu-Bekr my father."

"As true as Allah is the only God, and Mohammed is His Prophet."

I stood up. "My country has been razed to the ground, and my people dispersed by those who profess the weak and effeminate religion of the Nazarene. Abu-Bekr and the Prophet shall avenge us!"

He stood up in his turn. "They shall avenge you, Cartaphilus, I swear it by Allah, and the beard of the Prophet!"

We reseated ourselves.

"Mohammed is wiser than all men, and nearer to Allah,—but for that reason, a little visionary."

"Very true. Had it not been for me, he would have gone into the desert to speak with the angels, while our enemies slaughtered his followers."

"It is for us, then, to attend to all practical affairs."

"Yes, Cartaphilus."

"It is not meet for me, a stranger, however, to be too much in evidence."

"That is true."

"Let it be known, then, that the Hindu merchant has bought all your camels and your wheat, and that he has gone home. Let the people see the animals laden, driven through the streets by many slaves. But the faithful slaves at night shall drive them back. Our enemies will think us weakened, and will attack us. Then shall Prophet of Allah triumph, and conquer the world!"

Abu-Bekr was silent.

"I understand, Abu-Bekr. You need the gold. That is why you wished to sell the animals. Well, you shall have both gold and animals."

He raised my hands to his lips. "Allah has sent His angel Gabriel to His Prophet, that he may tell him the truth, and his other angel Cartaphilus, that the truth may be heard by all men."

Mohammed's camp seemed deserted. Many of the believers were sent about the town, instructed to look dejected and humble. Our enemies jeered at them, shouting: "Where is your Prophet, fool? Has he spoken to the angel again? What did the angel say to him?" Frequently, they slapped their faces or spat upon them. The believers, more Christian than the followers of the Nazarene, bent their backs and grumbled, "Mercy, masters."

Meanwhile, Abu-Bekr, and ten chiefs, planned the attack. I moved into a secluded house on the outskirts of the city, where I received daily reports. From time to time, Abu-Bekr came to consult me. I suggested some of the methods used by the Romans, and illustrated them by means of chess.

Abu-Bekr presented me with two virgins, that time might not weigh too heavily upon me.

"Woman is after all the best toy that Allah has invented, provided she is obedient and faithful," he said.

Abu-Bekr decided to attack the enemy at night, as I had advised. Thanks to my gold, his men were well equipped and the granaries filled to the brim.

The people, considering themselves quite secure henceforth, slept peacefully. A few watchmen wandered about the city, calling out from time to time: "I see you! I see you!" Novices only trembled, but the more experienced thieves laughed in their beards, knowing that human eyes could not pierce the heavy black curtain which Night, their friend and benefactor, had lowered over the earth. Nor were they afraid of the dogs that barked disconsolately, answering one another, like endless echoes. They could easily be bribed by a piece of meat, dipped in poison, or be silenced by a firm grip about the throat.

We stood upon the top of one of the hills. A crescent moon, sharp and dazzling as a scimitar, and a star like a diamond upon the hilt, hung above us.

"Day shall break much sooner than usual, Cartaphilus. Allah will shorten this night for the sake of His Prophet, Mohammed."

Masses of flames began to appear at many angles of the city. The black window of Night cracked, as if large rocks had been hurled against it.

"Allah be praised, and His Prophet live forever!" Abu-Bekr exclaimed, and looking at the moon, began to intone an ancient Arabic war-song:

> "We are the children of Allah,
> When our spears grow rusty,
> We make them bright
> With the blood of our enemies."

'Is he Nero?' I thought. 'Am I witnessing once again the burning of Rome?'

The officers sang the last words of each verse. I hummed.

Mecca glowed like an enormous ruby in a dark hall. The singing mingled with the wails and lamentations of men and women, and the weird and desperate howls of animals.

"Allah is the only God, and Mohammed is His Prophet!"

"Assassins!"

"Scoundrels!"

"Incendiaries!"

"Allah is the only God, and Mohammed is His Prophet!"

> "We are the children of Allah,
> When our spears grow rusty,
> We make them bright
> With the blood of our enemies."

The flames paled in the morning lights, while the smoke became darker and heavier.

For two days, messengers dropped at our feet, and when their voices became articulate, exclaimed: "Allah be praised! Our enemies wallow in their blood like slaughtered oxen! Allah is the only God and Mohammed is His Prophet!"

Upon a tall, white steed Mohammed, dressed in a cloak of white silk and a turban shining with jewels, rode slowly through the city. In front of him, a hundred priests chanted, and exclaimed from time to time: "Allah is the only God, and Mohammed is His Prophet." Behind him, Abu-Bekr, the staff of officers and I, rode on small black horses, and for a few miles in our rear, men, women and children walked or rode, singing martial airs and screaming from time to time, at the top of their voices: "Allah is the only God, and Mohammed is His Prophet."

"This was the ambition of Jesus,—to ride triumphantly amid believers, proclaiming him the King of the Jews. But instead, he dragged his cross, hooted and mocked by the populace,—for it was ordered by Allah that only his true Prophet should be victorious."

"Allah is just and His mercy is eternal," answered Mohammed.

"The Prophet of Allah is not only the King of his people, but the King of the world."

"Kings become old and die."

"Their kingdoms remain."

He turned and looked at me, his eyes dazzling like ebony ablaze. "I must go, Cartaphilus, but thou wilt tarry. . ."

I was startled. Was my destiny reiterated and reinforced? Was this the echo of the anathema, softened into a blessing?

As a hurricane that uproots mighty oaks, crumbles houses, and whirls in the air huge animals like withered leaves or feathers dropped from sparrows' backs, were the fury and the might of the Prophet's army.

The Word always succeeded the Sword, and the conquered were either persuaded of the truth, or considered it more prudent and more profitable to pretend belief. Thus all Arabia shouted: "Allah is the only God and Mohammed is His Prophet." The desert and the mountains trembled with the echo.

XXXIV

CATASTROPHE—I WORK A MIRACLE—I RAISE A COFFIN —ABU-BEKR PAYS HIS DEBT

KOTIKOKURA turned his face to the East, and bowing several times, grumbled: "Allah . . . Mohammed."

"Kotikokura, what is the meaning of this? Have you forgotten that Ca-ta-pha is the only God?"

"Ca-ta-pha is God. Allah is God. Mohammed is God."

"Heathen! Barbarian! Are you not ashamed to have more than one God?"

He looked at me, startled.

"Perhaps you are right, Kotikokura. If there is one God, why not many?"

He grinned.

Abu-Bekr entered, breathless, his beard disheveled, and his hands trembling. "Cartaphilus, the Prophet is dead!"

"The Prophet cannot die, Abu-Bekr."

"Alas," he whispered into my ear, "he was poisoned."

"Has the news spread among the believers?"

"Not yet. At this very moment, millions are praying to the Prophet . . . but the Prophet is no more!"

Abu-Bekr seated himself upon the floor, his head between his hands. "The Prophet is no more! The Prophet is no more," he groaned.

I seated myself next to him. "The Prophet cannot die."

"What shall we do, Cartaphilus?" He pulled at his beard nervously, and knit his brows until his forehead seemed divided into two.

"A Prophet must die that he may live forever. He who lives too long dies in truth."

"Cartaphilus, you have brought truth to the Prophet; bring truth to his followers."

"Has the culprit been discovered?"

"Who knows? Should not the culprit be among the fifty who have perished in the river at dawn?"

"It is always wiser to include many, that the one may not be missed."

He continued to groan, "The Prophet is no more! The Prophet is no more!"

"Abu-Bekr, return and announce to all that the Prophet has died."

Abu-Bekr looked at me, dismayed. "Shall we survive when he is no longer?"

I continued, without answering his remark: "————but that to-night, he shall be resurrected, and the Archangel Gabriel shall carry him to Paradise in his arms."

Abu-Bekr remained silent.

"It shall take place, do not fear."

"Have you the power to resurrect the dead? Are you a messenger from Heaven?"

"I am . . . Cartaphilus."

He looked at me, his left eye half-closed. "My plan was different, Cartaphilus."

"What was your plan?"

"To bury the Prophet secretly and permit one of the priests to assume his guise."

"What man can be entrusted with so much power and so great a secret, Abu-Bekr? Should the faithful believe, are not the eyes of our enemies sharper than theirs?"

"It is true, Cartaphilus. Their eyes are sharper, and their ears wide open."

"The Prophet shall rise to Heaven, Abu-Bekr, do not fear . . . and you shall be his Voice on Earth."

"But can it really be done?"

"Abu-Bekr, the bee travels over a hundred fields, but returns at last to the hive. The bird flies over seas and mountains, but in the spring finds his old nest again. The ant builds palaces under the ground, and the mole considers the sun superfluous. Angels, invisible, visit the Earth and the souls of holy men rise to Heaven. Who shall fathom Life's mysterious forces, Abu-Bekr? Who shall understand Allah's will?"

Abu-Bekr nodded thoughtfully.

"The Hindus are an ancient race, and their priests are learned beyond all others."

"Have you ever made a man rise, Cartaphilus?"

I related my entrance into China. He remained silent for a long while, his hands upon his knees.

He rose. "Allah himself inspires you."

"Go then, Abu-Bekr,—announce the death and the resurrection of the true Prophet, and order all believers to come at sunset to the Mountain of the Light."

"It shall be done as you say."

"Then—return to me, unseen by the rest."

"I shall return . . . unseen."

The sky was heavy with clouds, and a storm seemed imminent. No more propitious moment could have been desired. The people, awed by the weather, attributed their emotion entirely to the great event which was about to take place. The old men remembered that on the day of the Prophet's birth, the heavens were just as black, and a terrible storm followed,—but only the wicked were hurt, and their houses demolished. The good remained unscathed.

"Let the unbelievers purify their hearts now, and repent!" exclaimed, at intervals, the priests. "God shall have mercy only upon those who believe. So says the Prophet."

Thousands sang, wept, or called to Allah to witness the anguish of their souls. Abu-Bekr, Kotikokura and I were hidden by a rock which had the shape of a great bowl, halfway overtipped. The body of Mohammed, dressed in a white silk robe, his face dazzling, lay outstretched in the open coffin at our feet.

Suddenly the clouds were rent as if by a long white whip. "Now, Abu-Bekr!" I whispered.

"The Prophet lives forever!" he exclaimed.

The priests burst into a wild chant. The people shouted: "The Prophet lives forever!"

The coffin began to rise out of the enclosure, overtopped the rock and remained in mid-air. A gasp, as if a colossal smothered abyss suddenly flooded with air,—and then a shout that stifled the thunderclap.

"The Prophet ascends to Allah!"

"The angels are lifting him up!"

"Look! Look!"

"Allah is the only God and Mohammed is His Prophet!"

"He is rising! He is rising!"

"He lives forever!"

The lightning flashed in quick succession. The thunderclaps beat against the mountain like Herculean hammers.

The people fell upon their faces, weeping, groaning, singing.

"Allah is the only God and Mohammed is His Prophet!"

Still hidden by the rock, Abu-Bekr called out: "Hearken all!"

"He speaks! He speaks!"

"The Prophet speaks!"

"Hearken all!"

"The Prophet lives!"

"The Prophet speaks!"

"Hearken! Hearken!"

Out of a cloud of smoke rose the voice.

"Go forth among the rest of men and proclaim the Word of the Prophet!"

"We shall go forth, Prophet of Allah!"

"We shall go forth!"

"Accept all those who believe as brothers, and slay the infidels everywhere. So commands Allah!"

"Allah is the only God and Mohammed is His Prophet!" Abu-Bekr chanted.

"We obey the Prophet."

"You have seen the Prophet rise."

"We have seen him rise."

"The angels are lifting him to Heaven, where all those who believe in him shall follow him."

"We believe! We believe!"

Again, but more distant, the spectral voice proceeded out of the clouds.

"That you may never forget, I bequeath unto you the Kaaba upon which I have placed the crescent moon, taken from Heaven for a night. It is my gift to the faithful ones, that they may never forget."

"We shall never forget!"

"Allah is the only God and Mohammed is His Prophet." From the peak of the hills, the voice continued: "Return now, children of Allah. Let not your eyes gaze again upon the Mountain of Light, until the morning, lest you be stricken blind."

"We return, Prophet of Allah."

"Return!"

The priests sang:

> "We are the children of Allah
> When our spears grow rusty
> We make them bright
> With the blood of our enemies."

The people repeated the refrain. Their voices mingled with the thunderclaps.

The coffin with the body of the Prophet descended slowly as if held by a rope. We carried it to a ditch which we had dug previously, and buried it, covering the grave with a rock. Suddenly, the clouds began to disperse, as if some over-industrious divinity had swept them into a corner. We mounted our horses.

"Behold I too can work miracles, Jesus of Nazareth!" I exclaimed. "Your name and your followers shall be as dust underneath the hoofs of Mohammed's horses."

"Allah is the only God and Mohammed is His Prophet!" Abu-Bekr shouted.

The resurrection of Mohammed gave his religion a new spiritual significance and united the followers as if a gigantic hand, stretching from the Red Sea to the outer rim of the desert, closed into a firm fist. There was no doubt that Mohammedanism—as the new sect was beginning to be called—would prosper luxuriantly as a young and powerful tree.

My work was accomplished. The Crescent would overtop the Cross, I was certain of it. Meanwhile, I could abide patiently my time, catching once more the thread of my soul, entangled among the recent events.

I decided to leave. Abu-Bekr did not persuade me to remain. He had begun to think of me in terms of the superhuman, and accepted my word as irrevocable. Perhaps, too, he feared me. Could I not, if I wished, claim to be Mohammed returned to life, or his appointed successor?

True to the word of the Prophet, however, he paid his debts with a large interest, and we took farewell of each other, promising to meet in Paradise, and sit on opposite couches, rejoicing in the bounties of Allah and His Prophet, Mohammed.

XXXV

I SEEK MY SOUL—BAGDAD CHATTERS—I HIRE FIVE
HUNDRED CRAFTSMEN—ALI HASAN AND MAMDUH
BARAZI—THE MULTIPLICATION TABLE OF LOVE

"Kotikokura, I must find my soul. Cartaphilus cannot live without a soul, or with a soul, entangled among trifles, like the roots of a
tree. Cartaphilus must hold his soul in the palm of his hand, like
a perfect crystal. He must watch the shadows of his existence dance
upon it, and guess what strange things are the realities casting
them."

Kotikokura grinned.

"But my soul, Kotikokura, will not stay motionless upon my
palm. It is quicksilver, not crystal. It slides off, breaking into many
pieces. I must gather them together, and it is not easy."

"Ca-ta-pha will find."

"Where? Once—long ago—you whirled about me, Kotikokura
and your head pointed the way; but it is not wise to address Fate
twice in the same fashion. She remembers, and being a woman of
caprices, may purposely misguide us. This time, my friend, we
must reason our path . . . and what is more fallacious than reason?
Here, however, we cannot remain. Come! Let us wander aimlessly,
and perhaps our feet, wiser than our heads, shall tell us whither to
go and where to stop."

In front of us four slaves urged the oxen that pulled the two carts
filled with our belongings,—mainly books, curious bits of art and
part of my gold and precious stones hidden in statuary and vases.

Kotikokura rode at my side. From time to time, I would tell him
something. His answers were invariably a grin or a half-articulate
growl. Nevertheless, I felt that somehow he understood me, perhaps
better than any human being I had known through the centuries.

What united him to me? Was it merely because he had been my
companion for so long, or because he had rebelled, as I had, against
some irrational divinity? Was the Hindu doctor right, perhaps,

that the blood contained the soul and the life of man, and Kotikokura having partaken of my blood had become, in some mysterious
way—myself—an inarticulate elemental self,—a self long buried
within me, which I no longer knew or recognized?

Had I always been a rebel, from the very beginning of life? How
many gods had I mocked or destroyed? Was Jesus but the mightiest
of them all? Was he the only god—who could not be mocked with
impunity?

"What god did you laugh at, long ago, in Africa, because of
which you have become—Kotikokura?"

"Ca-ta-pha."

"What! You laughed at Ca-ta-pha?"

He nodded.

"You believe in God Ca-ta-pha, and you laughed at him?"

He grinned.

"Do you still laugh at him?"

He nodded.

Did he understand me? Was he merely jesting? Could one mock
and believe at the same time . . . perhaps love and hate also? Was
it possible that I, too, believed in, and disbelieved, hated—and
loved, Jesus?

Bagdad was in a chattering and disputatious mood. Abu-Bekr had
just died, and his successor had not yet been named. But since
the Prophet was no longer doubted, nor his ascension to Heaven,
nor his Word, which had been copied by a thousand scribes, and
memorized by all the priests and saintly men, I had neither anything
to fear, nor anything to suggest. Whoever might be the man of
destiny, the destiny of the new religion was to conquer the East—
to crush the religion of the Nazarene.

"Kotikokura, upon that hill yonder, hidden by palm trees like
a canopy, through the long thin rents of which one sees the Tigris
flow quietly toward the Red Sea, there is a castle with an enormous
orchard and a magnificent garden. We shall retire to it, Kotikokura, and forget for a long while the futile clamor of things."

Kotikokura grinned, delighted.

The castle belonged to a Prince who had squandered his patrimony
in gambling and orgies and needed ready cash to pay his debts.

I hired five hundred craftsmen and gardeners, whose labor turned
the palace into a dazzling jewel, and the garden into another Eden.
I wandered about the great halls and the magnificent flower-beds,

vastly bored. Kotikokura followed me, generally silent and as disconsolate. He reflected my emotions like a sensitized shadow.

"Kotikokura, my friend, life has no meaning in itself, and the days are like great iron balls chained about our necks, if we cannot discover an all-absorbing passion; if we cannot immerse ourselves in some labor or pleasure.

"When I feared that my life had reached its terminus I vowed I would not let time fly past me again.

"I would capture each hour, like a beautiful, rare bird and pluck from it whatever mystery, or good, or evil it offered. Nevertheless, my friend, here we are, both of us supremely bored in the most beautiful castle of Bagdad, and the most gorgeous garden in Araby."

Kotikokura sighed.

"I begin to understand and forgive the gods the torture they inflict upon us, seeing how much more bored they must be than we."

"Ca-ta-pha—God."

"Ca-ta-pha has but one believer, hardly enough to establish a new religion."

Kotikokura remained pensive. I plucked a rose, and gave it to him. He placed it between his teeth.

We seated ourselves upon a bench made of ivory. Its legs had the shape of many snakes intertwined.

"Two weapons only, two dazzling swords, can dispel the shadow, black and heavy, as a thing of iron, that God Ennui, squatting at all four corners of the earth, casts upon the world,—sex and knowledge. I am fortunate, Kotikokura, for what country offers more delectable women, and more profound mathematicians? With women and mathematics let us multiply pleasure."

Kotikokura grinned, and removing the rose from his lips, placed it over his ear.

I invited Ali Hasan, famous mathematician, and Mamduh Barazi, formerly Lord Procurer to the Vizier, to pay me a visit. They appeared at the same time, bowing many times before me, wishing me endless life and prosperity beyond the dream of man. They were about the same age, and dressed in the manner of princes, wide belts, studded with jewels, and turbans, in which dazzled the crescent moon. I could not decide who was the Procurer and who the Mathematician. I smiled.

"Can you judge a man's profession by his appearance?" one of them asked, guessing my thought.

"Marcus Aurelius, an ancient Emperor and philosopher of Rome, thought he could read a face like a manuscript. At the very moment when his lips formed this assertion, however, the Empress toyed amorously with a lusty young slave."

"Some faces, my Lord, are limpid like crystals; others, however, are like mother-of-pearl, changing colors at every angle."

The word 'angle' suggested the mathematician. I looked at the man who spoke. "I have the honor of addressing Ali Hasan."

He shook his head. "My Lord is mistaken."

We laughed. I invited them to spend a few weeks with me.

We were reclining on the wide benches that faced the lake, upon which twelve white and twelve black swans sailed motionless and silent, like dreams. A slave filled our cups with wine. Both Ali Hasan and Mamduh Barazi had joined the new religion of the Prophet Mohammed, but neither believed that water was to be henceforth the sole drink of man.

"The Prophet speaks of a limpid drink," said Ali. "Is not wine limpid?"

"The Prophet said that the understanding should not be beclouded. Is not wine like some cool, fresh wind, that chases the clouds from the face of thought, which shines henceforth like a sun?" added Mamduh.

"Abdul Ben Haru, my teacher and the greatest of mathematicians, drank deeply indeed, saying that only thus could he be in perfect harmony with the Earth, which he called the futile dolorous turning of a thing nearly circular."

"And what is more important and more beautiful than harmony?"

"My excellent guests, you have uttered the word that I have been seeking for a long time: harmony. But is it not more difficult to be in harmony with one's self than with the Universe?"

"The final proof of any problem, Cartaphilus, splendid host, is the balance of its equations," said Ali.

"The perfect satisfaction of the senses uniting with the perfect satisfaction of the mind, is the most perfect equation," added Mamduh.

"I have been more fortunate than the rest of mankind in having discovered Ali Hasan and Mamduh Barazi."

They rose, and bowed touching the ground with their foreheads.

"While Ali Hasan shall explain to me the mystery of numbers, Mamduh Barazi shall solve for me the mystery of the senses."

Our cups were filled again and again. Kotikokura made a wreath of wine-leaves, and placed it upon his head.

"Bacchus!" I called to him. He grinned.

My guests and I discussed the science of numbers in love and in mathematics. Our words came more and more lazily out of our mouths, and one by one, we fell asleep.

XXXVI

THE ORCHESTRATION OF DELIGHT—KOTIKOKURA'S HAREM—THE KING OF LOVE—THE BATH OF BEAUTY—UNSOLVED PROBLEMS

MAMDUH had both taste and understanding. The Vizier whom he had previously served was not merely a sensualist, but an æsthete and a poet. Mamduh appreciated my caprices. Every new denizen of my harem was to remind me, however obscurely, of some love that had delighted me in the past; at the same time, she must harmonize with her sisters. They must be notes in a large orchestral composition, conceived solely for my amusement. Thus I hoped to resurrect the past, and create a new present, achieving perfect unity out of diversity.

The result, always strange, was sometimes ludicrous or pathetic. I saw Lydia's eyes look out of Poppaea's face, Ulrica's hair blazed upon the head of Pilate's wife, Flower-of-the-Evening's tiny hand fluttered, accompanied by the voice of Mary. . .

Once I thought that I had discovered John and Mary in one envelope of feminine flesh. My heart leaped within me like some startled animal. I touched her. She laughed raucously. Her laughter sounded like Nero's. Her gums covered a large part of the teeth. Nevertheless, I made her my favorite, on condition that she never open her mouth in my presence. She was excessively ticklish, however, and could restrain neither her laughter nor her prattle.

Meanwhile, Mamduh, traveled from city to city in search of new beauty. My harem became famous throughout Arabia.

I built an enormous wall around my estate, and within it my mistresses wandered, displaying their charms, and chattering endlessly. Sixty giant eunuchs, with drawn swords, walked among them, settling disputes, punishing or admonishing like judges, and calling out at my approach: "Our master! Kneel! Kneel! Our master!"

Kotikokura became my chief steward, and relegated to himself a small number of women, black and yellow-skinned. He seemed to

176

relish mistresses in whom the attributes of femininity were enormously emphasized.

"What lost love do you seek among them, Kotikokura?"

He grinned.

"Even in our first amours, Kotikokura, we seek something that came before them perhaps in some dimly remembered dream, or in some dimly remembered life. . . ."

He scratched his nose, and rearranged his turban.

I distributed my harem, like a strange and complicated chess. Sooner or later, I hoped, by divers moves, to capture the King of Love—Perfection. I tried the ways of Flower-of-the-Evening, but before long her devices began to pall. They left the board in disarray, without checkmating the King. I invented new and fantastic moves by applying the law of permutation, which I had just learned from my wise teacher.

I achieved an infinity of variations.

I built many pavilions, the pavilion of color, the pavilion of perfume, the pavilion of touch, the pavilion of size. Pleasure was a thousand-stringed harp. Each note, each shade, melted almost imperceptibly into the next. Eyes, tiny and brilliant as beads, softened until I met the tender glance of the wounded gazelle. Blackest skin turned to brown, brown to yellow, yellow to white. There were breasts like hillocks rising upward; breasts like enormous grapes hanging from a vine; breasts like fists of rock; breasts like hazelnuts whose sharp points were dotted scarlet.

Love assumed numberless hues and numberless shapes. Hair short and stiff like quills, melting into masses of gold, flowing about the ankles; hips round and wide as hoops, dwindling until they became straight vertical lines; perfumes pungent as the taste of green apples upon the edges of teeth, luxuriant as of roses full-blown, delicate as the air at dawn; lips thin as a line drawn with the point of an artist's brush, thickening, broadening, until they filled the mouth like ripe fire-colored pomegranates, whose honey overruns.

I was the master harpist, playing string after string. The sound was often pleasurable, but the tune lacked perfection. I combined pavilion with pavilion; mingled incongruities, uniting the grotesque and the abnormal, the monstrous and the normal.

Always the King of Love eluded me, playing hide-and-seek, mocking, laughing. . . .

I consulted with Mamduh. His advice was intelligent and the result of much experience, but always in the end futile.

"I shall devise a tune that will bring all strings into play at once. . . . Do you think I can thus ensnare Pleasure?"

Mamduh combed his beard leisurely with his fingers. Evading somewhat my question, he answered: "Who shall play the tune more perfectly than Cartaphilus?"

Petals of flowers covered the garden with a heavy carpet. The resources of the entire harem were enlisted for the Bath of Beauty.

I was a rock in the midst of a vast sea of flesh, perfumed with a thousand scents, moving and undulating above and below me. . . . Billows rising and falling, accompanied by stifled murmurs and groans—waves caressing and laving, like soft tongues, or beating against me like open palms—my body ablaze in an ocean of concupiscence, delighted and tortured . . . an amorous delirium—a nightmare and a gorgeous dream—an orgy of lust. . . . Jets of love, quivering and hot, splashing back into the flames—billows rising and beating the rock—obstinate, determined. . . . Breasts and buttocks and mouths and hands and bellies—a fury of passion, laughing, weeping, groaning. . . .

A muscular rock, still inexorable, still unyielding—a thousand tongues of flame surrounding it, seeking to melt it—beating against it like hammers, scorching, tearing, lapping. . . .

A sea stiffened by the furious caress of the tempest. Then a sea without motion. The rock crumbled into the billows. Hot ashes smothered the flames, but left still unextinguished, the volcano beneath.

Where was the King of Love? My hand sought, but captured only shadows. . . . My eyes glared, but discovered nothing. . . . My ears heard, in the distance . . . laughter . . . like the laughter of Salome. . . .

"Do you believe that a thousand women equal one Salome, Kotikokura?"

He walked off, suddenly remembering something which needed his immediate attention.

"My excellent friends," I said to Ali and Mamduh, "is it possible to achieve unity through diversity?"

Ali shrugged his shoulders and replied with a long string of incomprehensible equations.

Mamduh, more practical, however, replied. "There is always some virgin, harboring some unsuspected delight."

"No, no, Mamduh, my harem is already more numerous than King Solomon's, who also sought—and in vain—the one perfect queen. The multiplication table cannot help me solve the problem of love. No, Mamduh, seek no more. Your exquisite taste has already accomplished miracles. But, alas, however many zeroes we add to a number, infinity remains distant and unapproachable. . . .

"Beauty, my friends, is a magnificent vase, broken into a thousand parts. However expert we may be at piecing them together again, some chip is missing, or is wrongly united, and if, by some supreme good fortune, we restore the vessel to its original form, we cannot hide from the touch, the cicatrice, the scar where we have joined them together."

My friends tried to console me.

"Perhaps man should not seek to remember, but rather to forget . . ." I suggested.

I ordered festivities, such as Nero and Heliogabalus had never dreamt of. I invited the Rajahs and the Princes of many cities. The most famous cooks of Arabia prepared dishes of so many varieties that names could no longer be invented for them. Wines of fifty nations flowed incessantly into golden goblets. My harem danced before us to the music of all races, and at night procured us tortures that delighted, and pleasures that agonized.

Some guests, unable to endure the torments of delight, left. Many, persisting, succumbed. Among these were my two dear masters, Ali and Mamduh. At last, only Kotikokura and myself remained,—perennial survivors of the cataclysm of joy.

"Are we owls, Kotikokura, perching forever upon ruins?"

He grinned.

My women, woefully decimated, wandered in the garden, like strange peacocks, endeavoring to entice me. I saw merely the ugly feet. I heard only disagreeable voices.

"What shall I do with these creatures, Kotikokura? I can neither take them with me, should I desire to continue my wanderings, nor can I leave them here, to starve. After all, there was something of beauty in them, something that reminded me of the unforgettable past. Should Ca-ta-pha imitate other gods, who send floods and earthquakes when they can no longer endure the sight of their creatures?"

He shook his head.

"Should not Ca-ta-pha be more reasonable and more kindly?"
He nodded.

"Very well, then, Kotikokura, since we have so much time at our disposal, we shall be merciful and just. We shall wait patiently until these creatures die, one by one, and when the last is gone, we can continue our journey. . . . Meanwhile, there are many problems that my late master, Ali—may he be happy in Paradise—has left unfinished; problems that merit solution."

XXXVII

THE MASTER OF THE HAREM—TIME DISAPPEARS—
I DISCOVER RELATIVITY — FUNERALS — KOTIKO-
KURA ACCELERATES FATE—THE MOSQUE OF A
THOUSAND GRAVES

ALI had found in me an apt pupil. My theories made the heart of
the mathematician leap. I unfolded to him the knowledge I had
gathered in the monasteries of Thibet. I recounted bold astronomical
formulæ which I had worked out, assisted by the secret lore of the
Hindus, while Asi-ma, the Rajah's sister, purred at my feet like a
magnificent lioness.

"Heaven descended into the eyes of my beloved, Ali, and it was
both easy and delectable to learn the secrets of the stars."

He sighed.

"Where is Heaven, in truth, Ali?"

"It all depends."

"Upon what?"

"Upon where a man happens to be."

Our discussion, purely sentimental, suggested an idea which I
could not formulate clearly at the moment it took place, but which
now, since the death of Ali and my futile orgies, had taken complete
possession of me. If heaven depended upon one's position, did not
the earth depend upon one's position also? Did everything depend
upon one's position? What, then, was Truth? An entity—eternal and
unchangeable—or a variable thing, fluctuating with one's position?
And Time—was that not purely an illusion, non-existent, perhaps?
Had not some years appeared to me shorter than hours, and could I
not remember some hours longer than years?

"Kotikokura, henceforth you are the lord of the harem, and
master supreme of my earthly goods. Ca-ta-pha retires to his tower,
to meditate upon time and space and the final meaning of truth."

Kotikokura took my hands in his, and looked into my eyes, his
own filled with tears.

"No, no, my friend, do not mistake my intention. Kotikokura will not disturb me. He may visit me whenever he pleases."

His face beamed. His eyes dashed so rapidly from one corner to the other that I could not look at them.

"Kotikokura, be a kindly master. Remember that justice is mainly pity. You are dealing with creatures whose years at best are few. Should they not endeavor to derive as much pleasure as possible from a world which is generous only in pain and in disillusion? Their life will be an attempt to avoid suffering. That indeed is the meaning of happiness. They will commit theft, adultery, and murder occasionally. They will tell lies, use flattery, and gossip. They will wallow in dirt like hogs, and pretend death, like foxes. And always will they be vain and obstinate.

"But all this is in the very nature of things, and should rather amuse than irritate. Be just. Justice, Kotikokura, is three-quarters convenience and one-quarter pity. All other definitions are the rhetoric of politicians and prophets and the vain words of poets. You and I are the masters of time. We can afford to pardon and to laugh. And when absolutely necessary, we may be cruel—or what may seem to be cruel—and laugh, nevertheless. Do not attempt to reform mankind or womankind. It is vainer than sweeping the refuse from one corner of the room to the other, and only raises dust and stench, which irritate the nose and throat. However, don't hesitate to grant favors, deserved or undeserved."

Kotikokura murmured, "Ca-ta-pha."

"Ca-ta-pha, meanwhile, must find out—how things should be judged, Kotikokura. No archangel whispers into his ear. He has no Father in Heaven, no Holy Spirit alighting upon his palm, in the shape of a dove. He must rely upon reason and logic—both precious jewels, hidden within a mountain of stone. Ca-ta-pha must become a hewer and breaker of rock. Hard labor harmonizes with the law of his being. He is not a fragile receptacle, but a huge hammer, hammering God."

The conclusions I reached astounded me. Infinity, eternity, dwindled into mere circles. Time disappeared. Space changed shape and size like clouds blown about by the wind. The earth lost its solidity, and spun under my feet like a toy. The stars were underneath and above me. Everything whirled about everything else, and nothing seemed constant, save a fantastic and passionate dance. Could this be the ultimate meaning of Life and of the Universe? I rebelled against it. I yearned for something less amorphous, more tangible, more comforting. I worked over my charts and my problems again and again. Always the result was the same. The equations, like an apothecary's scale, balanced perfectly.

I looked out of the window. A moon as clear and as dazzling as the one I had watched with Apollonius long ago from the threshold of his home, adorned as a perfect jewel, heaven's forehead. Some clouds crept over it for a while, and vanished.

Kotikokura entered, informing me that one of my concubines had died during the day and would, according to Mohammedan law, be buried that evening.

"I shall come to the funeral, Kotikokura."

Kotikokura looked at me, startled. It was the first time, since my seclusion, that I had spoken of my return.

"Are you glad, Kotikokura, that I shall be once again with you?"

His eyes filled with tears.

"You must not be too sentimental, my friend."

He kissed my hand.

"Or, perhaps, it is just as well. Sentiment is a more pleasant companion than reason."

A large part of the orchard had been cleared and turned into a cemetery. Already ninety stone slabs glared in the wide reflection of the moon, throwing their own shadows, like wraiths of the dead. Upon each tomb was engraved the name of some dead concubine, and a prayer to Allah.

I read aloud each name, trying to evoke the faces of my dead mistresses. Their names were empty sounds, like strokes of a stick upon a tin pan. I could not remember whether they had afforded me pleasure, or had merely skimmed the surface of my senses.

Kotikokura walked behind me, grumbling something from time to time.

"Kotikokura, the man who possesses but one woman may, after all, possess more than he who possesses a thousand. His memory does not waver, as the light of a torch in the wind."

We walked in silence for some time.

Two slaves were running, a wooden coffin upon their shoulders. The surviving women followed them, more leisurely, wailing and beating their breasts, and invoking Allah and the Prophet. Some chanted, repeating at intervals the name of the deceased. The coffin was lowered into the grave, a slave refilled it, and leveled the ground, beating it with a spade. The cortège, chatting and calling to one another, returned. The eunuchs walking among them admonished them to be less noisy.

The youngest of the women had already acquired the rotundity of maturity, while all about me I saw faces seared by wrinkles. I walked among my concubines, caressing them, or complimenting them, and telling them amusing stories. They laughed, and touching me furtively, whispered promises, lascivious or sentimental. They all remembered the Bath of Beauty.

"Were you very lonesome without me?" I asked.

They sighed. "Very lonesome. Fatima and Chadija wept and wept, until they died. The rest of us gradually became accustomed, knowing that the will of Allah is supreme."

"Who were Fatima and Chadija?"

"Fatima had brown hair, tied in a knot, and eyes out of which all the sadness of the world seemed to peer. She was your favorite for an entire night. . . ."

"Lydia," I muttered. "And Chadija?"

"Chadija's hair was like the new flax, and she rolled it into braids that reached to her knees. Our lord praised her beauty and called her by a heathen name."

"What name?"

They remained silent.

"Does no one remember?"

"It sounded like Rica . . . or Urica," one answered, her tongue slipping over her toothless gums. "She stabbed herself, master," she whispered.

"And where is she who was so ticklish that I could not touch her, without making her laugh uproariously?"

"It is I, master. Don't you recognize me?" She began to laugh, but stopped suddenly, and conscious of her bare gums, covered her mouth with her hands. "I am no longer ticklish, master," she whispered significantly.

I looked at her, and wondered how every trace of John and Mary had vanished so utterly from her face. Would they, whom I loved so much, have looked like her, had they lived long enough? Did they look like her when they died. . . ?

"Was Kotikokura a lenient master?"

They nodded. One looked around and whispered. "He was too indulgent, my lord. He allowed the eunuchs to fondle us."

Kotikokura had evidently obeyed my instructions.

"Are you satisfied with your table?" I asked, realizing that as youth disappears, culinary raptures take the place of amatory delights.

"Our master has always been very generous," one of them remarked. "But the new cook," she whispered, "does not stew lamb with fresh almonds. His almonds are hard. . . ."

"Our women are aging, Kotikokura. It is a pity."

He nodded.

"But what is even more pathetic is that they still desire: their passions still smoulder. Alas, there is no harmony in the world! Passions are awakened long before we may express them, and continue long after we can. But why speak of harmony in a whirlwind?"

Kotikokura scratched his face.

The cemetery, having become too crowded, I ordered the remainder of the orchard to be cleared. Only four of the eunuchs were still alive, stout and hairless individuals, grumbling and scolding incessantly. At my approach, they still ordered the women to kneel. "Our Master! Our Master!" Most of them would no longer obey, finding it too difficut a matter to bend or rise. They preferred to lie outstretched upon the couches or carpets, and relate to one another their ailments, begging me to give them ointments and drugs to relieve their pain. Several had become deaf, three blind, some had succumbed to a second childhood. They sang ceaselessly or wept bitterly.

Kotikokura sighed.

"By the way, we too, my friend, must at least appear affected by the passing of time, or else, who knows what the jealousy of man is capable of? We must paint our faces yellow, walk with difficulty upon our canes, and make wry faces."

Kotikokura dropped his jaw. His face seemed a thousand wrinkles. Senility crept into his joints.

I applauded.

Every few days another woman died,—peacefully, save for a slight cramp. Kotikokura smiled secretively. His visits to the laboratory where I had stored my favorite poisons were mysterious and frequent. The eunuchs, too, passed away, and were buried during the night near the rest, as if they were still to guard their honor and virtue.

The swans, like boats with broken masts, continued to sail on their sides, their long stiff necks half drowned in the water. The dogs, each in a tiny coffin, were buried in one grave, and Kotikokura ordered a tombstone, upon which the names were inscribed, and their souls entrusted to Allah and His Prophet Mohammed.

I freed and rewarded my slaves according to their ability and my caprice.

"Kotikokura, once more we are ready to go. The banquet is over, life has turned to death, and noise to silence. Such is the fate of things and of men."

Kotikokura nodded, fixing his turban.

I paid a visit to the Vizier. I told him that I felt death approaching, and that I preferred to breathe my last in Mecca, where the soil, trodden by the feet of the Prophet, was holy.

I signed a document, bequeathing all my possessions to the city of Bagdad, for the purpose of building a great mosque to the glory of Allah and His Prophet. Since the thousand faithful ones were buried there, I suggested that the place be known as The Mosque of the Thousand Graves.

The Vizier considered it a most appropriate and propitious name. He embraced me, and wished me a fine couch near the Prophet.

XXXVIII

I MEET A JEW—EVIL OMENS—THE DISAPPEARANCE OF ABRAHAM—SHIPWRECKED

THE Caliph's armies captured Alexandria and the northern part of Africa, as far as the Atlantic Ocean. Europe's feet began to scorch under the conflagration. Before long, the flames would rise and consume the entire body. Why was I so delighted? Was Mohammedanism more desirable than Christianity? Was it less an amalgamation of superstitions? Neither Christ nor Mohammed tolerated reason, and I would be an outcast whether the golden cross or the silver crescent glittered. And yet I exulted in the idea that the Nazarene must succumb to Mohammed.

I decided to investigate the progress of Christianity. Once more I was a wanderer. Once more the sea carried me away in her arms to a new destiny. The waves beat against the sides of our boat drearily, as a dog asleep wards off with his tired paw a pestiferous fly.

In an angle of the boat, some one played a Hebrew melody upon a reed. In my childhood, I had heard it played in just that manner by an old shepherd, owner of a dozen sheep, whose ribs nearly pierced through the skin. I used to follow him to the top of a hill, where the animals could graze unmolested. Unlike most Jews, he was not disputatious, and utterly unconcerned about the perennial quarrels of the clergy and the prophets.

"Who knows who is in the right, my child? Maybe they are all in the right, or all in the wrong. And what difference does it make, anyhow? If a man lived a thousand years,—then he would have time to find out the truth,—but since he doesn't live much longer than his sheep, it is better to keep quiet or play a tune upon a reed."

He was wrong. A thousand years sufficed no more to discover the truth than sixty. At sixty or at a thousand the best thing was to play a tune on a reed!

I approached the player. I was struck by his resemblance to the shepherd I had known in my childhood. Or, did I perhaps imagine a resemblance? Would my memory really have retained the image so clearly?

I praised his music. He thanked me. I asked him where he came from, and his destination. He smiled sadly. "You may never have heard of my country, sir, and as for my destination,—who knows? Wherever the boat stops, I must land, must I not?"

I understood perfectly what he meant, and something gripped my heart like a fist. After seven centuries, was I still a Jew?

"I have traveled through many lands, my friend. It is very likely that I have been in yours."

He laughed. His voice sounded like several dice shaken together. "My country? I have none. Hundreds of years ago, my ancestors were driven out of it. My country? Any place where I can earn my bread; where I am not beaten and spat upon too often; where I can pray to God in peace."

"Your demands are certainly modest, and I am sure you can find welcome in any country."

He stared at me. "You say you have traveled in many countries, and you do not know that it is often better to be a leper or a dog than a Jew!"

"A Jew," I muttered.

"Ah, you see! A Jew! It sounds terrible to your ears, doesn't it? I suppose that like the rest of the travelers here, you will shun me from now on. You will laugh at me as I pass by. You will call me ugly names. I suppose I ought to consider myself lucky if I am not thrown overboard."

"Oh no, my friend. Is not a Jew a human being?"

"Thank you, sir, thank you," he answered, half in irony, and half in humility.

'The eternal Jew,' I thought. 'Proud and vain,—and ingratiating. And how much like myself'! I liked him and hated him for it.

"But it doesn't matter, sir. Our enemies fare no better than we. They hate and slaughter one another, and the day will come, when they will atone for the cruelty to us. Meanwhile, I have my reed, my sack of goods,—and my God."

I remained silent. He mistook it for anger. He laughed a little. "I am sure you do not take my words seriously, sir. I am but a fool, and my tongue utters silly things. Our enemies are powerful and eternal. I beg your pardon." He bowed, and was about to go away.

"Stay a while longer. I am not at all angry at your words."

We were silent for a while. The edge of the horizon was a scarlet flame.

"It will be windy," he said.

I nodded. I looked at the large sack next to him. He caught my glance.

"Perhaps the gentleman would like to buy a scarf for his wife, or a turban for himself?"

Without waiting for my answer, he opened the bundle and showed me one thing after another, talking ceaselessly, and swearing by his children and his own life, that never were such goods sold at such a price,—that indeed such goods had never been made before.

I chose a few things, and paid him the price he asked. He was a little taken aback, and as he remade his bundle, he muttered in Hebrew: "What fools these Gentiles are!"

The moon hid her ghastly face behind a fan of clouds.

The azure waters of the Mediterranean changed to a dark ominous blue which at times appeared jet black. The waves which had ruffled gracefully like silk became gigantic hills dashing angrily against our boat.

Food became scarce.

Several members of the crew died from some mysterious malady.

To the east of us the clouds gathered like a gigantic black fist. The sailors, grumbling and taciturn, rushed up and down the deck.

Suddenly it occurred to me that I had not seen Abraham an entire day. We looked for him at his accustomed places. I asked one sailor after another "Where is Abraham?"

They glared at me.

I asked the captain. He shrugged his shoulders and made the sign of the cross. I was about to return to my cabin when I heard a piercing cry, followed immediately by the splash of a heavy body in the water.

"Adonai! Elohim! Ado——"

The voice died in a gurgle.

Three more sailors died and were thrown into the ocean. The crew made the sign of the cross whenever they passed me or Kotikokura.

"We must act quickly, Kotikokura. It is not pleasant to have a knife thrust through your body."

Kotikokura did not answer but his fist opened and shut spasmodically.

Next morning the deck was strewn with the corpses of the crew and of the captain. We threw them one by one into the ocean.

Kotikokura had a few cuts on his arm which a sailor not entirely asleep from my potion had managed to inflict. He licked his wounds like an animal. I was struck by the enormous size of his tongue.

At times we drifted. At other times I steered the vessel. Kotikokura scrubbed the deck, his immense muscles pressing against the hairy skin.

Kotikokura was shouting and dancing about me. His eyes, much keener than mine, had espied land. He had become very restless recently, and complained steadily against his work. He considered it a positive pain, and longed for the solid earth where he never overstrained his muscles. It was one thing to please a Princess, and another to keep a boat in good condition.

"We are reaching land, and you are overjoyed, Kotikokura. You shall be free."

Kotikokura danced more wildly.

"Yes, my friend, but if you are free of the boat, you will be a slave to the earth. You will have to act in accordance with the foolish customs and notions of whatever country we may happen to live in. Who knows which is a worse slavery? Perhaps it were best to continue forever on the water, where we do not have to pretend any religion, or nationality. For such people as we— —"

Kotikokura shouted: "No! No! No!"

"You do not believe that— —"

"No! No! No!"

"All right. It shall be as you say. But where shall we land? And what shall we be? It is never sufficient to be a man, Kotikokura. It is not even essential. It is absolutely necessary, however, that we praise the right Prophet and shout 'Long Live!' to the right Emperor."

Kotikokura was not in the mood for listening to me.

"Land! Land!" he exclaimed, pointing to the west. By this time, I had begun to see the gray peaks of a long stretch of rocks or mountains.

'Where shall we land, and under what pretenses?' I asked myself, again and again. But finally I burst out into laughter, which startled Kotikokura.

"Why should we trouble our minds about our welfare, my friend? The gods who are anxious to keep us alive as symbols of perversity, will see to it that all things are adjusted in our favor. Are we not their perennial prisoners; and their eyes,—are they not a million times sharper than ours?"

Kotikokura grinned.

"God's will be done!"

My words astounded me. I realized how close blasphemy was to prayer.

The sky darkened with heavy clouds, and the wind beat against our masts like iron whips.

"Kotikokura, have we blasphemed the gods, or overestimated our importance?"

He looked worried. I patted his head.

"Come, be cheerful, Kotikokura. The storm will pass."

"Ca-ta-pha! Ca-ta-pha!" His eyes filled with tears.

"We have no time for sentiment, my friend. We must be alert."

He did what I ordered him to do, but he continued to be very sad. Was he afraid? Did he, as on previous occasions, feel a premonition of evil?"

The storm became more and more violent. The waves dashed against our boats, as if intent upon crushing it. We were approaching rocks. If the storm did not abate, or the wind change direction, the boat would be dashed to bits.

"Kotikokura, we must be ready for anything. Tie about you this belt, within which are hidden many precious stones. I shall do likewise with this belt. If we are shipwrecked, and survive, our jewels will buy us a cheerful welcome."

The storm continued its mad career. All my efforts to save the boat were fruitless.

"In a few moments, Kotikokura, we shall have to battle against the waves. If this is to be the end, let it be."

Kotikokura wept. "Ca-ta-pha! Ca-ta-pha!"

I embraced him. Then we leaped into the angry sea to escape the wreckage of our ship. We struggled with the ocean, bruising alike our dignity and our skin.

"Don't give up, Kotikokura!" I shouted from time to time.

"Ca-ta-pha!" he replied.

"Keep your head up, Kotikokura."

"Ca-ta-pha."

At times, very near each other, at times barely within hearing distance, we battled against the waves that showed no mercy.

"Kotikokura," I whispered. "Kotikokura."

Was it merely my own imagination, or did I hear him answer:
"Ca-ta-pha. Ca-ta-pha."
"Ko-ti-ko— —"

The waters were quiet and still like a bed of feathers.
"Kot— —"

XXXIX

SOFT HANDS—"WHERE IS KOTIKOKURA?"—ULRICA
ONCE MORE—A HUSBAND WADES TO SHORE—
"FAREWELL"

A SOFT hand caressed my forehead.

I looked up. I saw a young woman, with long braids the color of
flax, and light blue eyes.

"Ulrica!" I whispered.

"I am Ulrica. How did you know my name?"

"Ulrica!" I whispered again, and closed my eyes. I tried to understand where I was, and how I happened to have gotten there. Slowly,
painfully, I reconstructed my boat, the storm, the shipwreck. And
who was this woman? Ulrica? Who was Ulrica? Oh, yes . . . my
beloved . . . long, long ago . . . on the Rhine . . . my vineyards.
. . . But what was she doing here? Where was I? Was it really
Ulrica? And Kotikokura . . . where was he? What had happened
to him? I opened my eyes. The young woman was sitting near
my bed, holding a cup out of which rose a thin vapor, delicately
scented.

"Drink."

I drank, breathed deeply, and stood up.

"Are you really Ulrica?"

"I am."

"Where is Kotikokura?"

"Who is Kotikokura?"

"My friend . . . my brother."

She patted my hand, and said very softly: "Everything will be
all right, you will see. Don't exert yourself too much."

"Don't be afraid, Ulrica. I am already well. Kotikokura is not a
creature of my imagination. He is a real person. I understand everything now. I was shipwrecked, was I not?"

"Yes."

"Well, Kotikokura was with me. We swam for a long while, and
suddenly as I was about to lose consciousness, I felt someone or

393

something lift me out of the water. I was saved! But life will be worth very little if my dear friend was drowned."

"Perhaps he was saved also. When you get well enough to walk about, we shall look for him."

I kissed her hand. "Why are you so good to me, Ulrica?"

"Should we not be good to those who suffer? Our Lord Jesus Christ commands us to love our neighbors."

I was in a Christian home, and in a Christian country.

"Blessed be His name," I piously added.

"I am so happy that you are a Christian, and not a Mohammedan," Ulrica exclaimed.

Her language was a mixture of the Barbarian language of the first Ulrica and Latin.

"And what is your name?" she asked.

"Cartaphilus."

I inquired everywhere for Kotikokura. No one seemed to have seen another sailor who was saved on the day of the great storm. If I remained alive, could he drown? Were we not of the same blood? Was not my fate his? Was he perhaps at the bottom of the ocean, in constant agony, yet unable to die? Was he a prisoner of the monsters of the sea? If Kotikokura was not drowned, he was somewhere among men, and I was happy to think that I had given him enough precious stones to make him wealthy for centuries.

Ulrica and I were sitting on the verandah looking at the sea.

"Ulrica, who are you indeed?"

She looked at me, astonished.

"I am Ulrica."

"Of course. But who is Ulrica?"

She looked at me again.

"No, no,—don't be worried. I am very well. I must have given you much trouble."

"No, Cartaphilus."

"You are kinder to me than a mother."

"Is not woman always the mother?"

"I have traveled all over the world, Ulrica, and have read the books of many nations, while you have been here your entire life watching the sea and helping people in distress. And yet, we have reached the same conclusion. Is it not strange?"

"Why should it be strange, Cartaphilus? What can one see in

other lands . . . but the earth, the water, the sky . . . and men and women?"

"How true."

"And is not God everywhere . . . and do not all people worship Jesus?"

"All people, Ulrica?"

"All except the Moors. But our King will convert them or kill them."

"Who is our king, Ulrica?"

"Charles —the great Charles."

"How do you know these things?"

"My husband, who was a sailor like yourself and had traveled everywhere, told me how Charles, after conquering all of Europe, was conquered himself by Jesus."

"Your husband is dead, Ulrica?"

She nodded.

We remained silent for a while. The sea splashed the rock lazily, as if playing with it.

"The sea hides a man for years sometimes, and suddenly washes him back to his home. Your husband may return."

She shook her head.

'Just like the other—Ulrica,' I thought. 'Is this her reincarnation? Is she Asi-ma and Lydia too?'

"Did you love your husband much, Ulrica?"

She sighed, and claiming that she had to take care of the cooking, begged me to excuse her.

Did she love me?

"Ulrica, I shall tell you a story."

"You tell such wonderful stories, Cartaphilus. They do not seem to be stories at all . . . but truth."

I related my love for Asi-ma, and then for the other Ulrica. She wept. I caressed her hands.

"Ulrica died because of love. . ."

She nodded. "Always."

Ulrica's love and tenderness consoled me a little for the loss of Kotikokura. Meanwhile, I gathered information about the political and religious conditions of the country, and planned my new attack. I broached the matter of travel to Ulrica, but like the other Ulrica, she obstinately refused to leave her place of birth. I was becoming restless. 'What does it matter, Cartaphilus?' I asked myself again and again, 'if you spend a quarter of a century in this spot, with Ulrica? Be compassionate, have mercy, be a man, not a god!'

The desire to leave beat against my brain as an impatient stallion paws the ground. Vaguely the thought of abandoning Ulrica shaped itself in my brain. One evening, as I was telling Ulrica a story, playing with her hair which she had unfolded upon my knees—someone knocked at the door. Ulrica asked who it was.

"Open, Ulrica,—it is I, your husband!"

She staggered to the door, like a person who has received a heavy blow on the head.

A man, tall, gaunt and unshaven, appeared on the threshold.

"Ulrica!" he exclaimed, but stopped short on seeing me.

"Who is that man?" he shouted.

Ulrica did not answer. She groped her way to the wall, and hid her face against it.

"So that's it! Your husband fights the king's wars while you are another man's bedfellow."

"She thought you were dead, sir."

"What of that? A whore's a whore—"

"You misjudge, sir. She is faithful—"

"Faithful?" He laughed, and turned Ulrica about, pulling her by the hair.

"Can you swear by Holy Writ that you are faithful to me?"

She remained silent, her head bent upon her chest.

He raised his fist. "Shameless bitch!" he shouted. "I'll kill you!"

"Don't touch her!" I remarked quietly.

"What? You! You! How dare you step between husband and wife? Yes . . . that is true . . . first I must kill you! Then I shall square my account with her."

It was a novel situation. Should Cartaphilus, lord of a thousand women, suffer injury for the sake of one?

"Calm yourself, sir. I can explain my presence—"

"Cur!" he shouted, and drawing a knife from his belt, raised it, ready to strike me. Ulrica screamed, and trying to divert the blow, received it full in the chest. Without uttering one sound, she fell in a heap.

He bent over her, caressed her face a little, closed her eyes, arranged her hair. He motioned to me to help him. He held her head, and I her feet. His back turned toward me, he led the way to the rocks. We climbed the highest of them. We swung the body and threw it as far out as we could into the sea. A small jet of water splashed our feet.

I planted myself firmly on the rock, expecting a furious combat. Instead, however, he turned about quickly, descended the rock, and walked off. It was too dark to see the direction he took.

"Ulrica!" I called. "Ulrica!"

No answer! Only the echo of my voice striking the rock and mingling with the waves.

I seated myself on the rock, and meditated on my life. What was it, save a panorama of dreams and of graves? What could it ever be but more dreams and more graves?

It became chilly. I shivered, and rose with a start. I walked toward the house where Ulrica had nursed me to life, that she might forfeit her own. I looked in. It was empty and quiet, as if nothing had happened.

"Nothing matters, Cartaphilus," someone seemed to whisper in my ear. "Everything flows."

"Ulrica," I muttered, "farewell."

XL

CHARLEMAGNE HAS A PAIN IN HIS LEG—INCESTUOUS LOVE—I PREPARE TROUBLE

AACHEN fluttered with pride. Charlemagne had recently returned, crowned Emperor of the West by the grace of God, and possessor of the key to the grave of St. Peter. To show his gratitude to the Pope, he issued an order to behead all subjects who refused to accept baptism. He founded several schools of theology and paid large salaries to teachers of Greek, Latin and Hebrew.

Charles had chosen Aachen because of its warm springs. In spite of his Herculean figure, he suffered from rheumatism. But the springs did not prove as miraculous as he had expected, and a new physician, I knew, would be welcome. Dressed as a monk, but wearing around my neck a large cross studded with precious stones to indicate opulence, I begged admission to the Great Monarch, claiming to be a doctor of medicine as well as a master of theology, conversant with all languages. The messenger, an officer of the Guard, whose large hand I filled with gold, bade me wait at the gate. A little later he reappeared.

"His Majesty will receive you at once."

I was ushered into a large hall, in the center of which at a long table, Charlemagne and a dozen men, officers and bishops, had evidently just finished eating, and were munching nuts now, and drinking wine.

I knelt. The Emperor bade me rise. His voice was sharp and thin, curiously out of harmony with his enormous body and his short, heavy neck.

"Who are you?"

"My name is Isacus, Your Majesty. I was born in Rome, a descendent of the early martyrs who were burnt and tortured for their love of Jesus. Several of my ancestors are buried in the catacombs. Early—in childhood, almost—I heard the Lord command me to travel to all parts of the world, and preach His Holy Word. I have been in every country of Europe, Asia and Africa. I studied the mysteries of drugs in India, and of the stars in Arabia, and everywhere I preached the truth of the Lord Jesus Christ."

"In Arabia, Isacus, I have a great friend, Haroun-el-Raschid, Caliph of Bagdad. Although an infidel, he is a man of courage and heart. Have you met him?"

"He sends greetings to the Great Emperor of the West, and this large ruby, whose scarlet symbolizes brotherly love."

The Emperor showed the jewel to his guests, while eulogizing the Caliph.

"Tell me, Isacus, is it true that you speak all languages?

"It is, sire."

"My friends who are masters of various languages, will speak to you, and see if it is really possible for one man to possess as much knowledge as you claim."

The Emperor's companions addressed me in several languages. I answered each in the tongue he selected. The sounds we uttered made the Emperor laugh uproariously.

Suddenly the Emperor's face twitched. His enormous hand gripped his leg. The rest stopped midway in their laughter and drinking, and looked at one another, distressed.

"You are a doctor, Isacus?"

"Yes, sire."

"Can you relieve my atrocious pain?"

"Your Majesty, I have brought with me strange and secret drugs from Samarkand, the country of marvels. With the help of our Lord Jesus I shall relieve your pain."

"Try your drugs, Isacus."

I massaged the Emperor's leg, whispering passages from the Vedas and invoking Jesus and Mary.

Gradually, Charlemagne's face relaxed, and he breathed freely.

I was offered a cup of wine, and we drank the Emperor's health.

"Will the cure be permanent, Isacus?"

"I dare not hope it, sire."

"How long must the treatment continue?"

"It is not possible to say, Your Majesty, but at least a year or two."

"You shall remain with us, Isacus."

His Majesty's rheumatism necessitated frequent massages. He showered me with gifts and praises, and had I been ambitious, he would have included high honors.

"You are a fool, Isacus, not to desire a bishop's mitre."

"I aspire to no higher honors than to serve my sovereign."

"You have served me well. My leg is much better. Though the pain has not disappeared entirely, I have not had any violent attack since good fortune sent you to the gate of my palace."

"Lord Jesus be praised!"

The Emperor struck me lightly on the back, and bade me accompany him into the garden.

"What is your opinion, Isacus,—should the Emperor be the head of the Church or should he relegate his spiritual authority to the Pope?"

"It is very difficult to rule a great empire, Your Majesty."

"It is."

"Should the Emperor be concerned as well with the souls of men?"

"Perhaps not. But who should be supreme,—the Pope or the Emperor?"

"Is it not self-evident, great King? The sword is mightier than the cassock."

"You are the only man of the Church who holds this opinion."

"I am not ambitious, Your Majesty."

A young woman whose hair glittered in the sun like gold that's poured from one vessel into another, was walking slowly, bending now and then over a flower.

The Emperor whispered: "Is it a sin to love one's own sister, Isacus?"

"It is not a sin, but a duty, sire."

"I mean—as a man loves a woman."

"In Egypt it was considered sacrilege for a royal brother not to marry his sister. Thus the dynasty was kept undefiled."

"Very interesting," the Emperor remarked, his eyes following hungrily the slim figure, whose blue silk gown fluttered a little in the breeze, like an enormous leaf.

"The daughters of Adam and Eve, our first parents, were the wives of Cain and Abel, their brothers," I added.

"You are learned indeed, Isacus. I had never thought of this before. I always wondered how they had populated the world. But," he added after a while, "would the Pope approve of this—now?"

"The Pope? The Emperor can make and unmake popes. Laws, Your Majesty, are for the people, dispensations for Kings. If the Pope does not admit this, he must learn the lesson. . . ."

"I shall teach him his place!" Charlemagne shouted, his voice breaking like a thin needle.

This was what I sought—to instil in Charlemagne a desire to dominate the Church, without being part of it. Thus sooner or later the two powers would clash and destroy each other. The proverb about a house divided against itself still held true.

My position at the Court was all the more important and influential because of its indeterminate character. I was merely a monk, officially,—but in reality, I was His Majesty's physician and chief adviser in scholastic and political matters: also frequently in religious controversies. It became very soon apparent that I was impervious to bribes of all kinds. My enemies sent maidens, delicate and voluptuous, to gain my confidence. When the feminine messengers failed, the subtle priests entrusted their mission to ingratiating and complaisant young men. When those seductions proved equally ineffective it was whispered about that I was a eunuch.

My experiments with a balloon inflated by gas proved my undoing. It gave the church a pretext to accuse me of witchcraft, and to rob me of my wealth.

Even the Emperor resented the invention which, crossing the borders with impunity, reduced the might of princes to nothing.

Once more I fled.

XLI

WHITHER?—THE NEW JEW—THE LAND WHERE MEN WEAR SKIRTS—A CLUE

For a long while I lived among prostitutes and beggars. I experienced stark poverty, even hunger. It was a new, and therefore not unwelcome sensation. I regained wealth, however, by being a saint and dwelling in a tower curing the lame and the blind in the name of the Cross.

Two generations passed. Once more I was a rich man. Fortune, like an obedient bitch, comes to him who waits.

Weary of incense and sanctity, I sailed upon the Mediterranean! Oh beautiful sea, eternal and unchanging, and unperturbed! Cartaphilus may also be eternal, but he must change always, and always in his heart must be a storm and a great wind, and now and then, a shipwreck.

Whither? To what part was the boat sailing? What did it matter? All things were relative,—time, space, and Cartaphilus. Cartaphilus more than all else. Just now, he was a Greek of Constantinople, a merchant of moderate means and moderate tastes.

Several merchants, tried to interest me in their business, promising me great fortunes. One in particular was persistent. He was a very handsome Arab, who had read much and travelled extensively. What he desired to do, if only he could obtain sufficient funds and a partner as clever and as presentable as I, was to open an establishment—very exclusive and elegant, of course—where men and women could find delectation.

"Nothing is as profitable in this world, sir, as sex and religion. A young man like you," he added, "must be very careful how he invests his money."

I smiled. "I am older than you think."

He scrutinized me. "Not one day older than thirty."

"True. But is not thirty a sufficient age for understanding?"

He laughed. "I am thirty-five. You would be astounded how much I had to learn—and lose—from thirty to thirty-five."

"What then would you call the age of reason?"

"Thirty-five."

The Arab alternated his remarks about business with pungent aphorisms about life and women.

"The Koran is right. Woman must always be man's slave. He must crack the whip, else— —" he laughed. "They say that in Africa there is a nation where men wear skirts. Imagine that! A nation ruled by woman, where men are women's slaves, where female chieftains have harems of males!"

"What is the religion of this country?" I asked.

"They worship a parrot."

'A parrot,' I mused. 'Women having harems of men.' How much was truth, how much invention?

"In Africa, you said?"

"Just beyond the desert."

'Just beyond the desert—a woman ruler and a parrot god.' Something within me cried out: 'Salome—Kotikokura.'

The Arab pulled me aside and showed me a ring with a small opal. "Anyone who wears this is bound to be lucky, for it was worn by the Prophet's nephew—may he be blessed forever! I shall present it to you for a trifling sum."

He mentioned a price about ten times greater than its actual value. I had learned enough from him to pay for my lesson.

"It fits your finger as if it had been made expressly for you. You are the Man of Destiny."

"What destiny?" I asked.

He smiled. "Who knows?" Walking off, he muttered in Hebrew: "What fools these Gentiles are!"

I was startled. This Arab was a Jew—the new Jew, the Jew that had drifted from Palestine—but nevertheless, a Jew!

Meanwhile, something much more important occupied my mind. Was it possible to find both Kotikokura and Salome again?

Who but Salome would think of establishing a matriarchy, with a harem of men? Where would Kotikokura go, if not to his native land? Curiosity, vanity, natural instinct, would prompt him to revisit Africa. Also, perhaps, the feeling that I would seek him where I had originally found him.

Was it possible that so much joy awaited me? I turned the ring about my finger. Would it really bring me good luck? Life was illogical. If two bits of wood nailed in opposite directions could work miracles, why not this ring?

XLII

THE SACRED PARROT—MASCULINE REVOLT—SALOME'S SACRILEGE—THE HIGH PRIEST OF CA-TA-PHA— THE SEX OF GOD

I BOUGHT camels and hired four experienced drivers who had crossed the desert several times. I asked them whether they had heard about the country where men were the slaves of women and a queen ruled. They answered that beyond the desert everything was possible.

I bought a young parrot, whom I taught to say.—"Carr-tarr-pharr . . ." and perch upon my camel's head. The drivers were much amused at my whim, and made many puns on the word.

With the exception of a mild sandstorm, the passage was uneventful and suited my mood exceedingly. One morning, the drivers pointed ahead of us. "Look, Prince! Smoke! We have reached the end of our journey."

I paid them what we had agreed upon, to which I added valuable gifts. I kept only my camel and the parrot and one day's food and water. The other animals and the rest of the provisions I allowed the men to take back with them.

I waited until sunset, and having painted the sun upon my turban, the moon upon the camel's forehead and dotted the parrot's beak as of yore, I began my ride in the direction of the smoke.

As I approached, I heard the violent beating of an iron kettle and I saw many men run from various directions. I thought it advisable to hide within hearing distance. A large tree served my purpose admirably. The parrot was asleep, and the camel, weary from the travel, did not stir.

A man waved his arms violently, and shouted at the top of his voice. The rest formed a circle about him.

"How long will you endure the tryanny of this terrible queen and of her women?"

The language was that of my tribe, with the exception of a few words, which seemed a corruption of some European tongue.

"Are you such cowards indeed? Are you not men?"

"Yes, yes!" growled the others.

"Has not God Ca-ta-pha made man in His image?"

"Yes, yes!"

"Woman is an unclean animal!"

"True! True!"

"Have we not found comradeship more pleasant than the love of our women?"

"More! More!"

"Shall we obey the order to become the fathers of their children?"

"No! No! By the Sacred Parrot, a thousand times, no!"

"Should we not rather die?"

"Yes, yes!"

"Can you forget the great history of our country, as our old men tell it to us, from generation to generation? Can you forget that Ca-ta-pha, Supreme God of Heaven, came Himself among us?"

"We shall never forget!"

"Has He not commanded man to rule woman?"

"He has!"

"Was He a man or a woman?"

"A man!"

"Shall you violate his commandment?"

"Never! Never!"

Meanwhile, more men came, some of them carrying long spears, others hatchets. In the reflection of the fire, which was burning a little away from them, they appeared like animated black shadows of invisible people.

"Have they not tortured us enough? Have they not tickled hundreds to death? Have they not given us refuse to feed upon?"

"True! True!"

"Her knives!"

"Her spears, chief!"

"Her sorceries!"

"What of it? If we are defeated, we can at least refuse to be fathers!"

"Right! Right!"

"How can we refuse to beget their children?"

"Her virgins inflame our passion . . ."

"The Queen's wines and spices set our blood on fire . . ."

"The Queen's instruments of pleasure incite the flesh in spite of itself . . ."

"We formed a Sacred Band to resist her enchantments. Emasculate yourselves to assert your manhood! Better castrates than slaves!"

"Better castrates than slaves!"

Knives flashed.

One man laughed hysterically.

"Who laughs?"

No one answered.

From the distance several men shouted, "Chief! Chief!"

The Chief shouted back, "Hurry, brothers, hurry!"

The men approached.

"The Queen . . . has driven . . . the High Priest out of the Temple."

"What!"

"Is it true?"

"She has broken the altar!"

"She has outraged the Keeper of the Holy Camel."

"Hear, men!"

"She has opened the cage of the Sacred Bird."

"She shall not live!"

"She cannot live!"

"Heaven will strike her blind!"

"She proclaims herself God!"

"Sacrilege!"

"Ca-ta-pha will destroy us all!"

"Death to the Sorceress."

"The High Priest is coming with the sacred image of Ca-ta-pha!"

"Here he is! Here he is!" some shouted.

Kotikokura, dressed as a Bishop, carrying in his hand an immense golden image of a rider upon a camel, upon whose head perched an open-mouthed parrot, approached pompously, preceded and followed by several priests. All men dropped on their faces, calling out: "Ca-ta-pha!"

I did not know whether to shout for joy or to laugh uproariously. My parrot, awakened by the noise and hearing my name pronounced, screeched: "Carr-tarr-pharr! . . . Carr-tarr-pharr! . . ."

There was a deadly silence.

I struck the camel's back with my open palm and the animal, half asleep, trudged slowly toward the people, who at my approach, began to roar and howl and shout. They beat their faces with their fists, rolled upon the ground, kissed the camel's hoofs.

"Carr-tarr-pharr! Carr-tarr-pharr! . . ."

The frightened parrot screeched, flying from the camel's forehead to a bush and back again.

"Ca-ta-pha! Ca-ta-pha!" the people repeated ceaselessly.

Kotikokura saw me.

"Ca-ta-pha! Ca-ta-pha! My Master!"

He gave the image to one of the priests, helped me descend from the animal, and embraced me, weeping on my chest. I called him endearing names. He turned to the men, who, seeing how I treated their High Priest, remained stock-still, their mouths and eyes wide open, their bodies bent.

"Look! Ca-ta-pha! God has come . . . Ca-ta-pha . . . God!" Kotikokura exclaimed.

The men howled: "Ca-ta-pha! Ca-ta-pha! God!"

They rolled upon the ground, struck one another's back; several turned somersaults.

Weary of their infernal vociferation, I ordered them to stand aside, silent, while I discussed with their spiritual ruler, what means to take against the terrible Queen who violated the customs of the tribe by her refusal to sleep for eight days with the corpse of her chief male concubine, and who desecrated my holy house.

"Kotikokura, how did you disappear? Where have you been, Kotikokura, my friend,—my brother?"

Kotikokura growled and chattered inarticulate sounds. He danced about me, embraced me, kissed my hands, kissed the camel's nose. His tiara, tilted now to one side, now to the other. A hundred years of civilization had fallen off him like a scab, and he resembled, for the moment, his aboriginal self.

The others, unable to restrain themselves, and besides, seeing Kotikokura's jubilation, began to dance. They made a large circle about me, and jumped, their legs reaching their chins. Two of them beat the iron kettle and sang hymns to my glory. The parrot screeched from time to time my name, to which they never failed to answer. Exhausted, finally, they dropped upon their hands, growling quietly.

"Who is this Queen, Kotikokura?" I asked, my voice trembling a little.

"Salome."

I had expected to hear the word, and yet, it almost gave me the vertigo. I grasped Kotikokura's arm to steady myself.

"Salome wants to be God in place of Ca-ta-pha. She must die."

"Do you forget, Kotikokura, that she cannot die?"

He scratched his nose violently.

"She is one of us, Kotikokura, whatever she may do."

He shook his head.

"Yes, yes, Kotikokura. Besides, is not Ca-ta-pha here? Shall not he bring justice? Is he not God?"

"Ca-ta-pha—God always."

I realized that if I did not act quickly, my enraged people would attack Salome. They must not mar her incomparable perfection!

"Hearken, my people!"

All knelt.

"By the sacred Parrot, let no one touch the Queen! Ca-ta-pha your God, will destroy her himself."

"Carr-tarr-pharr . . ." the parrot screeched.

"Ca-ta-pha," the people echoed.

"Rise and follow me!"

I mounted the camel. Kotikokura preceded me, the rest followed. The women who watched the gate of the city, tall creatures, hipless and breastless, seeing us, threw their spears to the ground, and ran, shrieking: "Ca-ta-pha! Ca-ta-pha! Ca-ta-pha!"

As we proceeded, men and women prostrated themselves before us, shouting my name.

When enough had gathered together, I stopped.

"Hearken, ye women! Ca-ta-pha has come to chastise you."

"We deserve it! We deserve it!"

"You have been unkind and unjust to your men."

"We have been unkind and unjust."

"I could no longer endure your ways, and I have come to punish you."

"Ca-ta-pha will punish us!"

I remained silent for a while. The women sobbed: "Woe is us! Woe is us!"

"But Ca-ta-pha is a kind God."

"Ca-ta-pha is a kind God."

"I shall have mercy on you."

"Ca-ta-pha shall have mercy on us. May his name be praised forever!"

" I shall neither broil you on spits, nor chop your heads off with a hatchet, nor shall I inflict upon you the tortures which you have inflicted upon your men."

"Ca-ta-pha will not kill us! He will not torture us!"

"Hearken and obey!"

"We hearken and obey."

"I have created man in my image, and I created woman to be his servant. Have not your High Priests and your elders told you this?"

"Yes! Yes!"

"Therefore man cracks the whip and woman obeys."

"Man cracks the whip and woman obeys."

"Deliver unto your men all weapons and kneel before them."

"We shall deliver unto our men all weapons and kneel before them."

"The chief of the men shall be the chief of the tribe."

"He shall be the chief of the tribe."

"So long as you obey man, and worship me, you shall not perish, neither shall you suffer."

"Ca-ta-pha is a merciful god."

"As for your Queen, touch not one hair of her head, but leave her to the wrath and vengeance of Ca-ta-pha and the Holy Camel."

"We shall leave her to the wrath and vengeance of Ca-ta-pha and the Holy Camel."

Turning to the men, I said: "Hearken, all ye men! Your High Priest I shall take with me to Heaven."

"Happy High Priest!"

"Choose the next one in rank among your priests, to be my vicar on earth."

"We obey, Ca-ta-pha."

"Take possession of your rights then, O men! Accept your masters, O women! Thus you shall be strong and mighty always, and you shall multiply as the sands of the sea, and conquer all nations. Ca-ta-pha shall watch over you forever."

The women, taller and stronger than the men, but awed by my words, knelt, and the new masters placed their feet upon their necks, pronouncing pompously: "Slaves!" A man, with large hips, small beardless face, and much bejeweled, waved a fist at his late mistress, who towered over him. "Obey! Or you shall feel my lash!"

She bowed her head submissively.

Another, more arrogant still, pulled his woman's hair, commanding: "Slaughter a lamb for me, and broil it!"

"Master," she answered, "how is it done?"

"How is it done? Learn! You have lazied long enough."

"Yes, master."

"And mind you, if you do not prepare it to suit my teeth, prepare your hide to suit my whip."

"Yes, master."

Delighted, the men laughed and danced. Children were pushed disdainfully toward the women. "Take care of your brats!"

The latter, weeping, hid their faces in their mothers' unlovely laps.

"Stop weeping there!"

"Sh-h!" the women repeated, "Your fathers do not like noise." Their voices were deep and heavy, and ill-suited for tender consolation.

Kotikokura and I rode to the residence of the Queen.

The palace was unguarded. I asked Kotikokura to remain outside, and await my orders.

Salome was sitting upon her throne, in the fantastic garments of savage royalty. She was alone. She had not changed since our meeting in Persia. I bowed and remained silent.

"Ca-ta-pha, you have won!"

"I come to save you from serious discomfiture."

"I know. I am grateful to you."

"Your people are enraged at you. You must not remain here another moment."

"I know. I expected you."

"You expected me?"

"Yes."

"You anticipated my thoughts in Persia, but how could you prognosticate my arrival?"

"It is easy to read a man's thoughts, and to guess his moods."

"Easy?"

"Of course. And don't forget that a woman, too, may learn something in India. . . ."

"I do not forget that Salome is incomparable."

She smiled. "Cartaphilus, too, is incomparable."

I kissed her hands. "Shall we go?" I asked.

"Yes."

"Kotikokura will come with us."

"Of course," she said, a little annoyed.

"Has he been a source of displeasure to you?"

"He was too faithful to you!"

"He is as a brother to me."

"No brother is half so faithful."

"Kotikokura," I called.

He came in.

"Kneel before Salome, she is your mistress while she remains with us."

He knelt. Salome bade him rise, and gave him her hand to kiss.

"We shall leave by my secret exit, Cartaphilus, which leads to a road unknown even to Kotikokura. Three camels are waiting for us behind a cluster of trees."

"And my parrot, who has been screeching 'Carr-tarr-pharr' . . . ever since I entered the palace?"

"The Sacred Parrot can remain here, to remind the people of Catapha." She laughed a little sarcastically.

"Is Ca-ta-pha inferior to other gods?" I asked.

"Few in the profession are his superiors," she answered.

"Then why did you wish to depose him?"

"I am weary of men-gods."

"Is not God always . . . man?"

"The womb of woman gives birth to man!"

"Perhaps God is both man and woman in one. . ." I suggested.

"Cartaphilus, at least, is a master of gallantry."

She touched my hand gently. I was too delighted to discuss gods or creeds.

XLIII

THREE IMMORTALS RIDE THROUGH THE DESERT— SLAVES OF THE MOON—CONFESSIONS—KOTIKO- KURA PLAYS ON A REED

Our camels rocked like tall weird boats, shaken by a sea slightly ruffled. Salome rode at my left, and Kotikokura behind us. The sky seemed like a luminous desert covered with stars instead of sand.

Salome chuckled a little.

"The Queen is amused?" I asked.

"Somewhat."

"By what?"

"By Ca-ta-pha, Kotikokura, and Salome,—the three immortals, riding together into the desert."

We rode in silence for some time.

"Did you think that a nation ruled by women could maintain itself permanently?" I asked.

"Why not?"

"Man's rule is based on the laws of nature. . ."

"Cartaphilus," she exclaimed, "you are incorrigible! Woman was the first ruler. Her rule was before man's, whatever legends man may devise to soothe his vanity."

"I am humble, Salome."

She laughed. "Cartaphilus humble!" Her teeth glittered, her curls struck lightly her checks. Sparks seemed to dance from the fire within her eyes.

"Cartaphilus is vain only because Salome rides at his side."

"I do not deny that you are gallant, Cartaphilus, and however childish flattery may be, I cannot but be pleased by it. Alas, I am a woman."

"Alas?"

"Yes, for you are right, after all. Woman must remain man's inferior while she is enslaved by her body."

"Oh!"

"She is the mother, the bearer of progeny. Even when her organism is not engaged in the function of reproducing the race, she is weakened by the rhythm of her purification. As the moon waxes and wanes, nature draws the blood from her brain into the organs of procreation. Every month she gives birth to a bud destined in most cases never to blossom. Every month her body goes through the agony of childbirth without child. Man is free to go his way. She is the slave of the moon! . . ."

"Many of your women, Salome, seemed more robust and more capable than the men."

"Those women, alas, are neither women nor men, they are a disinherited sex. Even they are pleased to be slaves once more. Had I remained among them for many generations—I could have established a new type perhaps—but I was bored. Like Cartaphilus, I feel the irresistible urge of wandering. If I had really desired to remain Queen of the Land of the Sacred Parrot, I would not have been overthrown."

"Even your women were enraged because you violated their most holy traditions."

Salome laughed.

"You are referring to my refusal to sleep for a week with the corpse of one of my husbands. . . ?"

"Yes."

"That would have been a little uncomfortable, of course, but it would have been easy to make the situation tolerable by the use of a little magic. . . Cartaphilus ought to know. . . He is a god."

I laughed in my turn.

"What a curious notion this, to sleep with a dead man, and gather the worms of the corpse!"

"Not so curious, Cartaphilus. A little disgusting, no doubt, but quite rational. Is not the soul supposed to lodge within the body?"

"Such seems to be the essence of most creeds."

"Man attempts to preserve the soul. . ."

"Undoubtedly—he even preserves the ashes of the dead."

"There is more life in the worms than in the ashes that he guards with such care. Their writhing persuades the savage mind that the soul is a living reality. It continues to live in the worm! Man, Cartaphilus, is always logical. Whatever he does, proceeds from reason. The customs of your people, while nasty, are logical." She laughed ironically.

"And life," I replied, "continues to remain beyond logic and reason,—a whimsical thing, wriggling its thumb upon its nose and laughing uproariously."

"How very true, Cartaphilus."

Kotikokura laughed, slapping his thighs.

"Why do you laugh, Kotikokura?" I asked, turning around.

He shrugged his shoulders.

"What makes you so merry, my friend?"

He continued to shrug his shoulders.

Salome smiled, her eyes half closed. Was she thinking of the time when she had rejected me for Kotikokura?

Salome laughed a little.

"Cartaphilus still is angry at me a little."

"How shall he hide his emotions before Salome? It may be true, he may be a little angry, or a little sorry . . . but he is happy that Salome rides at his side."

The stars were dimming like old eyes covered with thin cataracts. Salome yawned and laughed. "Salome must yawn now and then, Cartaphilus. Sleep is another form of slavery."

"Kotikokura," I called, "the Queen is weary. Raise the tent, that she may sleep quietly within it, and not be disturbed by the Sun, when that great Slaughterer of Dreams stamps his golden feet upon the sand."

Salome stretched out her arms. I helped her descend from the camel. Her hands were small and white, as a child's almost. I kissed and caressed them.

"The desert makes us sentimental. The realization of our cosmic insignificance stirs pity in us, and creates new measures of values, purely human. We become important to one another, when we no longer matter to the universe."

"Yes, Cartaphilus. Besides, are we not both children of that strange race, most bitter and ironic, and yet how sentimental?"

We watched Kotikokura arrange the tent.

"And who is Kotikokura?" I whispered. "Is he perhaps also one of us,—a scion of the Lost Tribe?"

"He is the link that unites man to animal, Cartaphilus. He is yourself, perhaps, as you were a thousand generations ago. . ."

"I love him, Salome."

"I have vainly sought a woman companion like him! I tried to discover one whose blood could mingle with mine. . . ."

"Is your blood, too, poison to others?"

She nodded.

"Some day," she added, "I may find a vessel strong enough to bear life of my life."

"A blossom of your own body?"

She shook her head.

Kotikokura grinned and clapped his hands. The tent was ready. I wished Salome happy dreams, and withdrew.

Kotikokura stretched out beside me.

"Are you sorry that you are no longer the High Priest of Ca-ta-pha?"

"Kotikokura always High Priest of Ca-ta-pha."

"Tell me, are you not curious to know where Ca-ta-pha has been these many years, and what he did?"

"Ca-ta-pha was in Heaven."

"In Heaven?"

He nodded.

"Don't you remember the time we were both shipwrecked?"

He nodded.

"And you believe that Ca-ta-pha went to Heaven?"

He nodded vigorously.

"Who carried him to Heaven?"

"Ca-ta-pha is God."

"And how did you get back to Africa?"

"Ca-ta-pha carried me."

I meditated on the curious mechanism of the human mind.

"Oh, by the way, Kotikokura, what became of the belt I gave you? There were enough precious stones within it to purchase a caliphate."

Kotikokura laughed a little, like a small dog barking, and pointed to his waist.

"You still have it?"

He explained how he showed the belt to his tribesmen as a proof that Ca-ta-pha had sent him to be his High Priest. The belt remained on the altar. Anyone but himself touching it, died. But since Ca-ta-pha had come in person, it was no longer necessary to leave it there. Besides, the sacred parrot would remind the worshipers of their God.

"Kotikokura, you are too subtle for an honest man!" I exclaimed.

He laughed.

"Tell me, did anyone ever touch the belt and die?"

He nodded.

"How did he die?"

He made a motion which indicated that he had strangled him.

"Did anyone see you do it?"

He shook his head.

"Kotikokura, you are almost clever enough to be a god yourself.'

He shook his head. "Ca-ta-pha God."

XLIV

LOVE MAGIC—PARALLEL LINES—SMOKE—SALOME SMILES

THE moon was surrounded by an immense aureole, whose reflection flooded the desert like a white sea. Salome her eyes half-closed, looked at me and smiled.

"Cartaphilus, will you forgive me for my little jest in Persia?"

I remained silent.

"Are you really still angry at me? Do not two hundred years suffice to cool a man's ruffled vanity?"

"This time the incomparable Salome has not guessed my thoughts."

She smiled.

"I was merely shaping in my mind a reply which would prove most convincingly that the pleasure of being with Salome atones for the ancient pain."

"Was it really pain . . . ?"

I nodded.

"Are you less sensitive now, Cartaphilus?"

"Perhaps. I have lived. . . ."

We both laughed.

"Of course, you were so young in passion! How many centuries, Cartaphilus?"

"And you?"

Kotikokura laughed.

I turned around. He was too far in back of us to hear our conversation.

"Did he always laugh so much, Cartaphilus?"

"He hardly ever laughed. It is something he has learned recently."

"He, too, is growing up."

The white sea of sand continued to flow in utter silence in front of us.

"Salome, were you really in Persia,—or was it illusion?"

She laughed. "Of course I was."

"Were you in a magnificent palace, mistress of a thousand slaves, guarded by eunuchs?"

"Do you not know the power of mirrors and shadows dancing upon them? Are you not an adept in magic?"

I looked, incredulous. She patted my hands. "Cartaphilus will be a child . . . forever."

"The happiest child in the world, if Princess Salome remains at his side."

She shook her head. "No, no! That must not be."

"Why not, Salome?"

"Cartaphilus desires most to be alone, and unhampered until he finds himself. Delve into your soul, and see if I am not right."

I remained silent for a long while.

"Well, Cartaphilus," she said quietly, a little sadly, "am I not right?"

"Perhaps. And yet . . . are we not logical companions, predestined mates, bound by one race and one fate . . . forever?"

"We are two parallel lines drawn very close to each other . . . so close indeed that no third line, however thin, could be drawn between them."

"Will the two parallel lines ever meet?"

"Yes. In infinity."

"Ali Hasan!" I exclaimed, "had you ever dreamed that there was so much poetry and pathos and sorrow in mathematics?"

"Who is Ali Hasan?"

"My master of mathematics, an Arab of incomparable wisdom. He died of sheer pleasure."

"Of sheer pleasure?"

"In Damascus, that I might forget Salome, I bought a harem of a thousand women. Now and then I invited my friends. Many could not endure the delights, and died. Ali Hasan—may he sit at the right side of Mohammed—was among them."

"And did the thousand women make you forget Salome?"

"They only intensified my yearning for her."

She closed her eyes.

"While all the time Salome never even thought of Cartaphilus. . ." I said, a little bitterly.

She did not answer for some time. "We may force ourselves to forget what we dare not remember. Forgetfulness may indicate deeper depths of emotion than recollection."

"Have you, too, reached the conclusion that there are no fixed

stars in the firmament of emotion . . . all things are relative . . .
everything flows . . . ?"

"Cartaphilus!" she exclaimed "Will you never overcome your
masculine conceit? Will you never understand that woman's brain
may work as subtly . . . or more subtly than man's?"

"It is difficult, Salome, to overcome an idea held by hundreds of
generations preceding us, and transmitted to us with the milk of
our mothers."

"Well, that shall be the mission of Salome—to overcome this
idea! To combat man and his arrogance! To give woman, the great
mother, justice!"

"Cartaphilus will not combat Salome!"

"Yes, always . . . whether he wills it or not. Man and woman
are the eternal antagonists. And for this reason, too, it is best for
Salome to forget Cartaphilus. It is better for the two parallel lines
not to meet . . . save in eternity, where all things are one."

"Kotikokura, is not Salome God, like Ca-ta-pha?"

He screwed up his nose. "Salome . . . female."

"But she is wiser than Ca-ta-pha. She has discovered the great
law of life, which Ali Hasan and Ca-ta-pha found after much labor,
—that all things are relative, that nothing is permanent."

Kotikokura puckered his lips, contemptuously. "Salome . . .
woman."

"Is not woman man's equal?"

He shook his head.

"Is not God, perhaps, both man and woman . . . ?"

"Ca-ta-pha is God."

"Is not Ca-ta-pha, perhaps, both man and woman . . . ?"

He shook his head violently.

"Kotikokura, you are the eternal ancestor in me,—aboriginal,
masculine! You speak for me. Because of you, Ca-ta-pha cannot
accept Salome as an equal, or woman as a god."

He grinned.

Salome and I were sitting, our legs underneath us, upon a leopard's
skin. At a distance, Kotikokura made drawings in the sand,—heads
that resembled his own, and curious libidinous symbols.

Salome filled two small ivory pipes, and offered me one. We
watched in silence the smoke raise thin hands, trying to capture
the moon.

"Kotikokura has developed artistic tendencies. Is it a sign of advancement, or of degeneration?"

Salome smiled. "He is passing through the various stages of human existence. Some day, he will become like Cartaphilus."

"Salome is always slightly ironic when she speaks of Cartaphilus."

"Irony is a shield."

"Is Salome afraid of her own emotions? Does Cartaphilus touch her heart at all?"

"Could it be otherwise? Who, save Cartaphilus, can understand Salome?"

"Then why does she refuse to remain with him always?"

She drew vaguely at her pipe. "Are you not afraid of 'always,' Cartaphilus? Do you not tremble at the very thought of it?"

"Always would be as a day with you."

I took her hands in mine, and caressed them gently.

"You are as romantic as you were in the days of Pilate, Cartaphilus . . . you remember, when you were my royal guard."

"And you . . . are as cruel as you were then."

"I was not cruel, Cartaphilus. I resented your air of invincible masculinity, which made you strut about like a young turkey. You were handsome and clever. But what right had you to assume that Princess Salome would accept your caresses?" . . .

"One evening, you smiled, and spoke of the love of bees and of flowers . . . of a conquest, subtle and strong. . . Was it so wrong to hope?"

"Had you only hoped, perhaps. . ."

"And in Persia?"

She laughed. "That was merely a little lesson in magic."

She stretched out her arms underneath her head. I took the pipe out of her mouth, filled it again and replaced it between her lips.

"Is it right to always torture me . . . always, Salome?" I asked. My words seemed to rise on the edge of the smoke, high, high.

"Am . . . I . . . torturing you . . . you?" Her words came down from where mine had stopped, and entered the bowl of my pipe

"Yes. . . ."

She chuckled.

"I love you, Salome."

"I know. . . ."

"Do you . . . love me?"

"Perhaps."

"Say yes, Salome . . . for once!"

"For once, yes . . . yes."

"Salome, my well-beloved!" I exclaimed, and lifting her head a little, kissed her mouth.

"Salome . . . your lips are more delicious than crushed honey, daintier than the perfume of violets. Salome, my love. . ."

Her robes disappeared suddenly, and I could not tell which gleamed the more,—the moon or her body. I embraced her rapturously, murmuring: "Salome . . . my love . . . my love . . . Salome."

Our bodies mingled, merged, interpenetrated, until we were like one great marble column, inextricable.

"Do you love me, Salome?"

"Yes, Cartaphilus, I love you."

"But you are not Salome."

"Who am I?"

"You are . . . Mary Magdalene!"

She laughed a little.

"I have found you at last, Mary! And your eyes are not yours."

"Whose are they?"

"They are John's . . . the friend of my youth! You are Mary and John. Cartaphilus has found at last love's perfection!"

"But you are not Cartaphilus!"

"Who am I?"

She whispered: "You are he. . . ."

"Who?"

"He who returns from the uttermost rim of time, who was one with me before the soul split asunder into male and female—my lover before Adam and Eve were shaped by the Potter."

Her voice died in the distance, and the smoke wreathed itself like a serpent around her naked limbs.

Salome greeted me. "You have slept profoundly, Cartaphilus."

"And you?"

"I could not sleep. I watched the moon all night, meditating on the meaning of time and space."

I stared at her.

She smiled. "Cartaphilus is still a little asleep."

"Perhaps. How shall one distinguish between sleep and waking?"

"It is very difficult, for frequently they merge into one another."

What had happened? Had I only dreamed? Had I really possessed

Salome? Was it merely the effect of my poppied pipe? Was that exquisite pleasure a woman . . . a demon . . . or a cloud of smoke? I scrutinized Salome's face. Did she really resemble Mary and John? Did I remember them sufficiently to be certain?

"Yes, Cartaphilus, all things are relative . . . dream and waking . . . memory and forgetfulness . . . and even our stay in the desert. We must go on. Kotikokura, is everything ready?"

Kotikokura nodded and grinned.

"Kotikokura, have I dreamt or was it reality? Did I at last find my perfect love? Was Salome mine for a night?"

He grinned.

I shook him. "You must tell me."

"I don't know."

"You were there."

"I slept."

"You lie, Kotikokura."

He shook his head.

"Cartaphilus must know!"

He grinned.

I raised my fist. "Tell me!"

"I slept."

I dug into my brain, picked each infinitesimal detail, constructed pattern after pattern. Could this be a dream? Could that? Was this reality? Or this? Had I mistaken the reflection of the moon for the glamour of her body? Was it merely the smoke, assuming the shape of Mary Magdalene. . . . Was it the stars I saw or the eyes of John . . . ?

I passed from doubt to certainty, from certainty to doubt, from elation to profound depression,—and always at the end, I rejected everything, as if I had been pouring sand from one hand to the other, spilling a little each time until nothing remained.

"Woman, even Salome, always prefers mystery to truth and simplicity."

"And man—even Cartaphilus—always makes the mistake of dividing the human race into distinct elements, calling certain characteristics masculine, and others feminine. Yet, he has lived long enough to know that there is no clear division between the sexes. A woman may have everything save the loins of man and may still be a woman. A female's hysterical scream may issue piercingly from

a masculine throat. Every creature possesses the stigmata of both
sexes. . . . Every man is a fraction of a woman. Every woman is
a fraction of a man. Each retains some aspect—some reminiscence,
mental or anatomical—of a time when both sexes were one. . . .
Is not the son of Hermes and Aphrodite a god?"

"All this is true, Salome. Nevertheless— —"

"It is Kotikokura who speaks in you, Cartaphilus!"

"Alas! I can blame no one for your perversity!"

"I am surprised," she laughed, "that you have not invoked Lilith,
the demon woman who was before Eve!"

"Lilith! Lilith!"

She continued to laugh.

"You are as wise and as cruel and as beautiful as Lilith! You
are Lilith!"

"And you . . . Lucifer, perchance."

"And Kotikokura . . . Adam, the seed."

"We have reconstructed the cosmos, have we not, Cartaphilus?"

"We have forgotten Jehovah."

"True . . . Jehovah and Eve."

"Eve,—is she not merely the earth?"

"And Jehovah the clouds?"

"How easy it is to build a universe, Salome! How difficult to
know whether one has kissed the lips of Salome or the libidinous
lips of a Succubus who steals the strength of men's loins in their
sleep . . . ?"

We were in sight of civilization again. I took Salome's hands in
mine. I looked at her long. "You are beautiful beyond compare,
Salome. Your mouth inflames more than the kiss of a thousand
lips . . . but it is no doubt best for Cartaphilus not to taste it,
except in dreams. . ."

"You say this, Cartaphilus, because you no longer desire me."

"It may be I no longer desire you," I said, irritated. "It may
also be that we have analyzed ourselves too minutely, to accept
love as reality. . . . We have crushed a star into fragments, and
the winds have blown the flames and the ashes across the
cosmos."

"Cartaphilus and Salome are the two sides of a coin . . . forever
together, yet never facing each other," Salome replied.

"Neither," I conceded, "is complete without the other."

"Quite so, Cartaphilus."

"We shall soon part."

"Yes."

"It is best so."

"It is."

"This time, however, let there be no pranks when we meet again . . . no magic."

"Perhaps, a little before infinity, the two parallel lines will meet. . ."

At the gate of the city, we embraced. Her lips tasted like Mary's lips, and as I looked up into her eyes, they were John's.

"It was not a dream," I whispered.

She smiled.

XLV

COUNT DE CARTAPHILE AND BARON DE KOTIKOKURA, KNIGHTS—THE ARMY OF JESUS—ETERNAL SCAPEGOAT

WE rode slowly on our small Arab horses. Our armors creaked and moaned gently, while our long swords swung against our sides, like pendulums of clocks that have not been wound and are about to stop. We raised our helmets, looked at each other, and burst into laughter.

"Kotikokura, we have lived long enough to become Christian Knights, fighting for the deliverance of the Holy Sepulchre. Who knows what other curious and ridiculous things we shall fight for in years to come?"

Kotikokura slapped his thighs in merriment.

"Remember, my friend, that I am Count de Cartaphile, and you Baron de Kotikokura, of Provence. Remember, Kotikokura, that we are infinitely more precious than all the princes and the knights of the world and all armies put together. They are mere shadows, moving grotesquely about for a while, and vanishing into the abyss of nothingness. We shall use our swords only in self-defense and remain at a respectable distance always, when a fray is on, for a wound may plague us forever. . . ."

Kotikokura grinned, and clanked his sword.

"Do not forget the magic powder concealed in your belt, in case we are disarmed and in danger. Hurl it against the face of the enemy. He will totter for a few moments. Then gently, silently, he will cross the fine line that separates being from not-being. . ."

In front of us, the Crusaders, the clamorous army of Jesus,—pedestrians, riders on horseback, on asses, on oxen; wagons and carts, loaded with people and food,—and crosses, crosses, always crosses, rising above the heads of animals and people, stiff like masts of boats, undulating with the rhythm of the carriers, leaning to one side or another.

The army of Jesus! What a strange and uncouth army! Murderers escaping the noose; thieves; bankrupts; unfrocked priests; monks whom even the Church, best of mothers, would no longer shield from the wrath of secular penalty; gamblers; squires whose lands had been confiscated; the younger sons of noblemen, titleless and empty-pursed; and now and then, a poet, a mystic, a mountebank, a jester too caustic for a prince's court. . .

Apart from these, as if fearing to be smothered by the stench and the dust and the noise, small companies of knights, luxuriously caparisoned, riding to conquest and fame, or death.

Attila redivivus! The Scourge of God! More terrible the footsteps of these than the horses' hoofs of their predecessors! Nevermore shall the grass grow again upon these lands! Ah, Jesus, was it this you meant by 'love ye one another?' Was this your conquest; were these the followers you dreamed of; was it for this you allowed yourself to be nailed to the Cross?

Are delicate John and beautiful Mary sitting at your feet, Jesus, and approving of this? Do they exclaim triumphantly to the stars that dance about you forever: 'Master, you have conquered the Earth.'

"Kotikokura, I cannot rejoice in the defeat of my enemy. It is too terrible, too inhuman . . . and my heart is still the heart of man! This was a city, Kotikokura, a Christian city. Look at it now, my friend! Look at the ruins, the corpses, the awful devastation wrought in his name! Our horses are splashing through blood, as if a scarlet rainstorm had flooded the place! I cannot laugh or jubilate, Kotikokura. . . I am not a god!"

"Ca-ta-pha god."

Slowly the army moved, swaying clumsily like a wounded rhinoceros.

"The army of Christ, Kotikokura,—decimated, but trailing after it still death and torture and disease! The army of Christ! What irony, Kotikokura! How he abhorred soldiers and princes and governors and high priests!"

"High Priests!" Kotikokura exclaimed angrily.

"Don't be offended, my friend. He never realized that there could be a high priest like Kotikokura."

Kotikokura smiled, delighted.

A number of women and children were running in our direction, screaming. They were followed by three men on horseback from whose raised swords blood dripped.

We interceded to save them from the wrath of knights who accused them of sniping. The women blessed us in the name of the Saviour.

We had ridden a few minutes, when once again we heard shrieking and shouting. The women we had just saved from the sword were running after an old man, white bearded and almost naked.

"There he is! There he is! The Jew! The cursed Jew! Kill him! Kill him! He brought the wrath of the Lord on us. Kill him!"

I thought it would be too hazardous to try to save the Jew, and I was too weary and too disgusted to help humanity in distress.

"Kotikokura, by saving the life of a human being, we merely endanger the life of another. It is futile to be kind and generous. 'Homo homini lupus.' Wolves all,—devouring one another,—and always the Jew the final scapegoat. So be it! We cannot help it. We must laugh or go mad."

Kotikokura laughed heartily. I joined him.

"Kotikokura, I am weary of splashing through blood and tumbling over ruins. Besides, it is becoming increasingly more dangerous. We can go to Jerusalem by far safer and pleasanter means. The Mediterranean still runs on as calmly as ever."

Kotikokura grinned, delighted.

"Let us cast off this armor, and become merely prosperous citizens, unconcerned with the Holy Sepulchre, with doing chivalrous deeds, with witnessing this horror, in the name of Jesus. One glance suffices. We need not witness the entire performance."

XLVI

I REVISIT JERUSALEM—THE PLACE OF SKULLS—IS TIME
AN ILLUSION?—THE TEMPEST—THE RED KNIGHT
—"DON'T YOU KNOW ME, CARTAPHILUS?"—TREAS-
URE TROVE

"Kotikokura, I do not understand it at all. How did this army,
ragged, famished, undisciplined and almost weaponless, defeat the
splendid troops of the Mohammedans? What magic did it use? What
strange power? Is it true indeed that Jesus wished to free his
Sepulchre from the hands of the infidels? Did he strike fear into
the hearts of his enemies, or . . . ? But why rack our brains, my
friend, to understand a game which seems to have no permanent
rules, and whose players—the gods—have no sense of honor?"

Kotikokura grinned.

Jerusalem! Was this Jerusalem indeed? The hills and the sky
were unchanged,—but where were the houses, the streets, the cemeteries? I wandered about as in a dream, trying to find something
that I recognized, that could serve as a guide. As in a dream, everything dissolved, shrank, united grotesquely together. I drew a map.
Like a lost dog, I followed each line carefully, my eyes riveted to
the soil.

Where my father's shop used to be, there was a marsh now.
Large frogs croaked, and a million insects buzzed ominously. Where
the temple was, moss-covered rocks piled together. The palace of
Pilate,—a highway upon which a driver urged a donkey whose ribs
were piercing his sides like sharp elbows.

Kotikokura accompanied me silently, like a dog, faithful but
puzzled.

I assiduously avoided one spot. Something told me that it had
not changed, had remained perfectly intact, expecting my arrival
—and perhaps another one's. And yet, like some magnet that draws
metal toward it, draws it and will not relinquish,—so the spot drew
me, drew me.

"I must go, Kotikokura. I must go."

He looked at me, not understanding.

"I must go alone . . . without you, alone!"

He looked startled. His arms fell and he bent almost in two.

"No, do not fear, Kotikokura. Ca-ta-pha must go only for a day or less . . . must see something . . . alone. He will return."

I walked as a somnambulist walks, choosing neither one road nor another, allowing my legs to find their way. They would lead me to the place, I was certain.

The sun had climbed half way the hill to my right. The moon, like a bit of gray gauze, already torn to shreds, was vanishing quickly; two or three stars winked a few more times in great effort. Now and then my steps echoed noisily, as if to announce my arrival.

Had I whirled about myself many times? Did the earth under my feet rock as a boat? What whirlwind was blowing against my ears? I seated myself upon a rock, my head tightened between my hands. I dared not stir.

Why had I come alone? Why had I not fled away? The hurricane howled on. The earth rocked. If I only dared to raise my head to see where I was . . . if I only— — What was there to fear? If death, let it be death!

I stood up. What was this? Had I gone insane? Had all these centuries been merely a dream? Was I a captain in the Roman army? Was I no longer Cartaphilus, the wanderer?

"Thou must tarry until I return! Thou must tarry until I return! Thou must tarry until I return!"

"Stop!" I shouted.

The Cross shook. Was it the wind? Was it the earth? His eyes like two long swords pierced my head. I screamed. It was the same agony I had once experienced. A thousand years had not obliterated its memory.

"Tarry until I return!"

"Stop!"

I tightened my head with my hands, and began to run desperately. I fell.

"Tarry— —"

I staggered to my feet again. I looked at my hands. They were covered with blood. I wiped them in the dust.

"Tarry until— —"

I dared not look back.

"Tarry— —"

It was like a far-away echo. I began to run again and did not stop until I reached the city. I seated myself on a curbstone. For a long time, I panted, my mouth open. I rose and walked homeward. My legs were weak and unsteady, like a man's who had just recovered from a severe illness.

A knight in armor galloped by. Two monks, hiding their hands in their sleeves like Chinamen, were grumbling against the rations of food they were receiving; several crusaders, ragged and thin, were sitting propped against the fence; in the distance, the tinkling of a leper's bells. . .

"What a storm we had," I said to a sentinel on his way to the barracks.

"Storm? When?"

"Just now . . . a little while ago . . . I thought the whole city would be shattered to pieces."

He glared at me. "My good man, you had better go home and lie down. You must be drunk or ill."

"Was there no storm?"

"Of course not. It is as fine a spring day as you have ever witnessed. Hunger must have driven you out of your mind. The good Lord Jesus doesn't seem to be particularly overjoyed with the fact that we have recovered His Sepulchre. He lets us starve. Well, He knows best."

How silly of me to have asked about a storm! I should have known that it was my own excitement, my own over-sensitiveness,—the storm in my breast. . . . And yet, who knows? It seemed so real! Those eyes! The voice! Why had I not taken Kotikokura with me? He would have comforted me. He could tell me if what I saw was a phantasm or the truth. No, perhaps it was better this way! Some things must be suffered alone! Jesus suffered his Cross alone! Every man. . . .

A soldier interrupted my thoughts.

"Sir, my master entreats you to follow me."

I accompanied him a few steps. He helped his master, a knight in full armor, from the horse, and left us alone.

Was I in the presence of a great monarch? The armor made of red gold, was encrusted with precious jewels. The helmet was surmounted by a large rare plume, the tips of which were studded with pearls. The buckle on the scabbard of his sword was a tortoise of lapis-lazuli.

I bowed deeply.

The knight raised the helmet. I looked bewildered.

"Don't you know me, Cartaphilus?"

"Salome!"

"You have just come from there . . . Cartaphilus?"

"Yes."

"I was there yesterday. . . ."

"Was there . . . a storm?"

She nodded.

"Jerusalem is not for us, Cartaphilus. We are stirred by too many memories."

"Is it only that?"

"Who knows?"

"Did you see . . . him?"

"Yes."

"Did he speak?"

"Yes."

"Was it magic, Salome?"

"If magic . . . it was stronger and stranger than ours."

We were silent for a while.

"Were you with the Crusaders, Salome?"

"I am the Red Knight, famous for many exploits," she smiled.

"You should not have run any risks."

"I have not run any. Can we afford to be hurt? I have heard of the chivalrous deeds of Count de Cartaphile of Provence, planting the Cross over the Crescent. . ."

"What a sorry victory for Jesus, Salome!"

"All victory is sorry. . ."

"Save only— —" I looked steadily into her eyes—"the conquest of Salome."

She shook her head and tapped me on my shoulder.

"I must go, Cartaphilus."

"May I go with you?"

"No. The time is not yet ripe. We must still seek . . . and must seek alone."

"What?"

"I do not know. Perhaps that which when found is not worth the seeking."

We remained silent.

"Salome, what shall it profit a man to be a thousand years old, if he cannot understand more than at thirty?"

"What are a thousand years, Cartaphilus? Only to those who live one generation or two, a thousand years seems a.very long stretch of time. To us, ten thousand years are no longer than ten thousand days."

"Ten thousand days are long without you. . . ."

"Farewell, Cartaphilus!" She barely touched my cheek with her lips.

"Since you command it,—farewell, Salome, Queen of Women!"

She kissed my other cheek. "Even in hell, Cartaphilus would be gallant."

"And Salome a Queen, even in hell."

We set out the next morning by the road I had taken at my first departure from Jerusalem. The second evening, as we reached the foot of a rocky hill, we saw two men fighting desperately, their faces covered with blood, their clothing torn to shreds. At our approach, they stopped, caught their breaths for a while, and were about to begin once more.

They were two brothers fighting over a piece of silver.

I asked them for information as to the roads, and rewarded them each with a purse.

When they were out of sight, I laughed heartily. Kotikokura looked at me, puzzled.

"Kotikokura, my friend, this is the most delicious bit of irony I have witnessed for some time,—not the desire of the two brothers to kill each other. That is as old as Cain and Abel. . . ."

I examined the ground.

He looked at me puzzled.

"Wait . . . first let me ascertain if I am right."

I scrutinized the stars, studied a map, made some calculations on a piece of parchment.

"Yes, this is it."

Kotikokura tied our horses to trees.

"Help me roll away this small rock. And now, Kotikokura, you will see why I told you to bring a spade. Clear off this mud and dust. We can work with perfect freedom here. Nobody, save two silly brothers trying to murder each other for a silver coin, would think of passing this way."

The mud and dust was so deep that for awhile I thought I had

made an error in my calculations. At last, however, the spade struck
something metallic. I was elated.

"Kotikokura, what if rocks become as overgrown with mud and
debris, during the course of years as people with superstitions and
prejudices? The stars are at their ancient posts, and mathematics
is eternal. We shall be guided by both. We cannot but find what you
will see presently."

I inserted a key into the iron trapdoor, which opened readily in
spite of its rust.

"Follow me, Kotikokura."

We descended a few steps.

"Pull this cord. The door will shut over us. We must not take
any useless risk."

We descended a few more steps, and turned to the right. Guided
by the light of my lamp, we finally reached an alcove. I turned a
knob, and a small door opened. I pushed my hand within it, and
brought out three iron boxes, which I unlocked. Kotikokura's mouth
opened wide, as if his lower jaw had suddenly dropped away from
the rest of his face.

"Look, Kotikokura!" I raised and dropped fistfuls of jewels.
"Diamonds and sapphires, and pearls and rubies that blind your
eye and burn your hand! Play with them awhile, Kotikokura. It is
a delicious sensation. What skin of woman rejoices as much as this?"

He touched the stones lightly as if afraid of being burned indeed.

"In this third box, I have gold coins. They are of far less value
than the jewels just now, but when they become ancient enough, they
may surpass them. He who lives long enough can never be poor,
Kotikokura."

Kotikokura's eyes continued to be riveted upon the jewels.

"Those two brothers nearly killed each other for one silver coin,
while underneath their feet, there was the wealth of a dozen kings!"

I took only one of the coffers.

"We shall leave the others here. We may need them some day. I
shall teach you how to find this spot and others, Kotikokura. You
may have to ransom me some day, or save a precious part of your
own precious skin."

He grinned.

We returned, Kotikokura covered the trapdoor with the debris,
and stamped upon it. He smoothed the place with a spade. Everything was peaceful. Only our horses were impatient. We mounted
them and galloped away.

XLVII

THE ISLE OF BLISS—I MEET AN ARMENIAN BISHOP—
KOTIKOKURA GROWLS—MY HEART IS IN MY
MOUTH—THE ILL-TEMPERED SON OF AN IRASCIBLE
FATHER

"What trees! What flowers! What a sky! The moon must be three times the size of all other moons I have ever seen,—and the people, Kotikokura, how generous, how kind, how honest! They never asked us who we are, where we come from, why we stop here. They offered us this little house and a bower of a thousand flowers. They have given us food and these garlands and leaves, which they call cloves. Tomorrow, we shall be given each a beautiful virgin as a wife."

Kotikokura danced, his head upon his chest like a goat.

"You have known the joy of woman, Kotikokura, but you have never known the comfort of a wife. A good wife is the very bread of life. A bad wife . . . nothing is quite comparable to her. But can you imagine a shrew among these charming people?"

He shook his head.

"Alas, whether a woman be good or bad, she must inevitably become old. The lips that were red and full as cherries become pale and thin like parchment; the teeth that dazzled like small pearls in the sun turn yellow and drop out; the breasts that just filled the cupped hand, hang heavy and loose or become shrivelled and wrinkled. Alas, Kotikokura, that is the fate of a wife."

Kotikokura's eyes glistened, one tear in each.

"It is very fortunate, however, my friend, that women resemble one another very much, and one may supplant the other."

Kotikokura grinned.

"Have you noticed, my friend, that these people have no religion, no churches, no bishops, or high priests? They greet the rising and the setting sun—symbols of Life and Death—a most beautiful and rational habit. Hail Life! Farewell Life!"

Kotikokura continued his goat-like dance. I took his hand, and we danced together. Many natives gathered about us, clapped their

234

hands, kept time with their feet, and soon formed a large circle about us, imitating us.

How long did we live upon this island? Was it centuries or merely years? I could not tell. Our days passed on as smoothly, as noise-lessly, as the river that faced our home. I had forgotten everything, —even Salome, even Jesus. It was like an exquisite dream that barely touches our sleep, but which makes us sleep longer and more pro-foundly.

One day, however, as I was sitting on my threshold, I was awakened with a start, as if someone had struck my head a violent blow. On the side of one of the hills, I saw the shadows of three men and three large crucifixes.

"Kotikokura, we are not destined, it seems, to live here peacefully forever, like those great trees which no one, for the last twenty generations, has ever remembered as young saplings bent by winds. Look!"

Kotikokura rose, his head forward. I pulled him down.

"The Christian Church not content with the misery and ignorance and cruelty it has brought upon the people of Europe, must spread cruelty and misery everywhere—even upon this beautiful little is-land, uncharted on any map."

Kotikokura placed his head between his palms, and his elbows on his knees.

"But we shall not let them spoil these people, Kotikokura. We shall tell our friends to beware of them, to shun them like leprosy."

Kotikokura opened and closed his fists.

"I fear, however, that our struggle will be futile, for after the visit of the monks, the Pope always sends armies. If the people are not persuaded by sermons, they must accept the eloquence of the sword!"

I warned the gentle natives not to listen to the words of the mis-sionaries,—a bishop from Armenia accompanied by two monks. I told them that they were more ferocious than tigers, and sooner or later, they would destroy their homes and kill them. The people hid themselves in their houses or in bushes, and ran away at the sight of the Christians. I watched intently the movements of the Bishop. He was a man of about fifty or sixty, dressed in a white silk robe, in the manner of the Orientals, and wore a headgear that was nearly a turban. He reminded me of Mung-Ling and Apollonius, except that his eyes were clouded and sad, and his mouth too thin. Because of this resemblance, I suspected a good deal of kindness and intelligence in the man.

I sat on the threshold of my house one evening. The Bishop, unaccompanied by the monks, approached me. He greeted me very cordially, and began to speak to me with his hands, uttering at the same time sounds that he had learned from the people. He believed he was addressing me in an intelligible language, but the words he uttered were devoid of all meaning. His efforts to make himself explicit seemed so ludicrous that I could not help laughing.

He was not irritated, but on the contrary, laughed with me. I liked him. He seemed so different from the dignitaries of the Church I had known. He seated himself next to me and pointed to the moon, which was unusually beautiful. He made gestures to indicate how happy that made him. I remembered how Apollonius had loved the moon.

He placed his hand upon my shoulder and pointed to the cross which hung about his neck. I shook my head. He did not insist. We remained silent for a long while. He was not impatient.

Suddenly, I said in purest Greek: "Why do you come to torment these people?"

He looked at me as a man awakened suddenly from a profound sleep looks at some strange creature sitting at his bedside.

"Who . . . who speaks in you? Is it Satan or is it an angel?"

"I have seen neither heaven nor hell. . ."

"By what miracle have you acquired your impeccable Greek? Has the gift of tongues suddenly descended upon you?"

I laughed. "If I told you that God or Satan speaks through me, you would believe me."

"Before God, all things are possible, my son," he said quietly. His voice was a melodious echo of Apollonius. 'The spirit of the Tyanean must be lodging in this man,' I thought, 'but distorted by theology and the dark superstitions which now prevail in the world.'

"Though all things are possible, Father, it is always best not to stretch forth our hands for the most far-fetched explanations."

"Yes, you are right, my son. One should seek the simplest explanations, and the most natural. You are a Greek who, weary of civilization, its iniquities, its futile glamor, has settled here. Now you fear that your peace may be interrupted again."

I nodded.

"In a sense, I am here for the same purpose,—to forget the indignities heaped upon our Lord Jesus by false teachers, and the selfishness of man. Perhaps here, these simple, kind people will accept the Word of Jesus as it comes undefiled from His lips."

"They are perfectly happy now. Why disturb them?"

"Life on earth lasts only a day, but in Heaven . . . or in Hell, it is eternal. Those who do not believe in our Lord cannot dwell in His Heaven."

"Are there not many mansions in my Father's House. . . .?"

"True, but the door is barred to all heathens except by the long road of purgatory. Even saintly Plato, and Apollonius the Tyanean, must travel the road of darkness."

"Apollonius?"

"Yes,—for whatever the ignorant rabble may say, he was a saint. Alas, he was not baptized!"

"Where is he now, Father?"

"In the outer rim of Purgatory, where he knows neither pleasure nor pain. But the Lord will soon shine upon him as a sun, and he will know indescribable joy."

"I am glad to hear you speak in this manner of Apollonius, my great Master."

"My Master too."

I looked at him.

"His mind was too mighty for his heart. It is the heart, not the mind, that saves us."

"Do you believe that God's mercy extends to all men?"

"Eventually . . . certainly. His mercy is limitless."

"Will it embrace Judas?"

"Even Judas."

"Even Ahasuerus?"

"Even Ahasuerus—if he accepts the Cross he refused to bear."

Unconvinced by his arguments, I was nevertheless touched by the generosity of his spirit.

One of the monks approached. In the chiaroscuro of the moon's reflection, I thought I saw Damis. My heart beat against my chest like a hammer.

"I shall soon be with you, Francis," the Bishop called out.

The monk bowed, crossed himself, and walked away.

"A charming fellow—perhaps a trifle too pious and too serious. He even scolds me upon occasions, you understand—not openly, but with a countenance so hurt that I cannot but accept the rebuke."

"Man needs a thousand years to mellow him."

"Why live so long, my son? Can one really learn much more in a thousand years than in seventy? Life merely repeats itself."

"Are seventy years sufficient to understand even one's self?"

"Neither seventy years nor seventy times seventy, my son,—not until we meet our Lord face to face. Then, in the fraction of a second, we understand all."

Kotikokura, dressed in his gaudiest attire, filled our glasses with solemnity and pomp, while his wife, on tiptoes, her head bent, brought in the food,—a young lamb, slaughtered in the morning, prepared with a dozen vegetables and fruits whose perfume delighted the nostrils of the Bishop.

"My son, I have often noticed that a sensitive palate does not exclude a sensitive soul," the Bishop remarked, as he helped himself to another plate.

"Apollonius, too, rejoiced in delicate viands."

"Our Lord Jesus was seen frequently at the table with His disciples," he added.

I could have related some gossip about Jesus that was current in Jerusalem, but I preferred to discuss my own fate with him—the first man in centuries who was the intellectual equal of Apollonius. I was determined to tell him my story. However, I waited for the most opportune moment.

Kotikokura glared at his wife who, either forgetting, or her toes aching, walked on her soles, making a noise like the slapping of a large tongue against the palate. She did not see him. He uttered a low growl. Frightened, she rushed out of the room, and returned immediately on her tiptoes.

"Your valet is an extraordinary person," the Bishop whispered.

Kotikokura stood motionless at a distance, approaching the table only from time to time, to refill our glasses.

"Father, are you in a mood to hear a strange story?"

"I am delighted to listen to you, my son."

We rose. He took my arm, and walked leisurely.

The river flowed on silently as the hours in sleep, and upon it, the moon trembled vaguely, like the wing of a giant butterfly perched upon a flower.

"Father," I said, "is Jesus God?"

"Of course, my son."

"Was he not a man when he was crucified?"

"He was both man and God."

"It is difficult to conceive of such a union."

"Not at all. I find it very easy."

"Strange. Some people are born with a predisposition to believe; others are born to doubt."

"There is much joy in Heaven when those who doubt see the light."

I smiled ironically.

"You, too, will accept Jesus," the Bishop gently added, "Jesus is inescapable."

"No!" I exclaimed. "He is not inescapable,—and I will not accept him!"

The Bishop smiled kindly, drawing his robe tightly about his legs. "Perhaps you have already accepted Him, but are unaware of it . . . and something inexplicable in you restrains you from confessing it. Our minds are prouder than our hearts,—and less wise. . . ."

"Father, what will always prevent me from accepting Jesus is not inexplicable, but perfectly rational."

"What is it, my son?"

"I knew Jesus and spoke to him, as I speak to you. He was not a god."

"Many of us have spoken to Him, and many have found that He is God."

"I am not speaking in metaphors, Father . . . I knew Jesus, knew him physically. I broke bread with him. I walked with him, I talked to him even as I talk to you. . . ."

The Bishop rubbed his chin and eyes vigorously. He smiled. "My son, you are pleased to jest."

"I do not jest, Father."

"Jesus died twelve hundred years ago. Then you must be more than twelve centuries old. . ."

"I am. . . ."

"Who— —?"

"I am . . . Ahasuerus. . ."

The Bishop withdrew a little. He made the sign of the cross. Then, placing his hand upon my shoulder, he said: "Whoever you are, I bless you!"

"You say this, Father, because you still do not believe me."

"You expect me to believe the miracle of your longevity—but you reject the miracle of Christ's divinity, which millions have found so simple, so natural of acceptance."

"Truth should be demonstrable."

The Bishop smiled. "You of all men should accept His divinity. He made His power manifest in you. . ."

"I refuse to be bludgeoned into belief by a miracle that defies my reason. . . ."

I looked at him intently. He resembled Apollonius more than ever.

"Father, do you not remember,—long, long ago,—I spoke to you of this? Do you remember?"

The Bishop squinted his eyes and rubbed his forehead several times. "I think . . . I remember. . . It seemed, indeed for a moment . . . that I had really met you before. . . . Memory alas, is a sieve. . . ."

We remained silent for a long time.

"But I beg you, tell me your marvelous experience under the seal of the confessional. Your words shall remain a secret for all time."

He made the sign of the Cross.

"There are some things I should like the world to know, Father."

"I shall divulge to the world any message with which you may charge me."

I pressed his hand. "So be it! Look at me well, Father. What is my nationality or my race?"

The Bishop scrutinized me carefully. "You may be of any race or nationality. And you may be of any age . . . thirty, perhaps, or sixty. There is something unreal about you . . . or maybe it is only the reflection of the moon."

He shivered a little, and recoiled slightly.

Then, collecting himself, he said: "Tell me your story. My lips will be sealed after you unlock your breast—even" he whispered, "if you are Anti-Christ."

The sun had already risen, but I continued to relate my adventures. The Bishop, spellbound, listened motionless, fearing perhaps that it was all a dream, that he might suddenly awaken, and the story remain untold.

At last my tale was finished. The Bishop, his head bowed, meditated.

"Father, do you believe my story?"

He nodded.

"Is it not too extravagant to be true?"

"Before God all things are possible, my son."

"Except my conversion to Jesus."

He looked at me sadly. "You will never know the meaning of happiness if you are not willing to accept Jesus. You have sought happiness for twelve hundred years; your eyes have beheld marvelous things—yet, what have you gained except disillusion?"

"Disillusion and a sense of humor."

"Deep in your heart, you are still seeking happiness. Disillusion and humor merely protect you from pain."

"I can conceive of no happiness based on the denial of reason."

"Reason is only an ornament; it is not life itself. The futility of your struggle against Jesus proves that the universe moves by something greater than reason."

"Is it greater . . . or is it smaller? Divine Unreason, perhaps!"

The Bishop smiled. "Forgive me if I say that your obstinacy proves you are still a Jew."

"A characteristic I share with the founder of your religion, Father. Life requires obstinacy. Man accomplished his growth from savagery by his unconquerable tenacity. Nature is a mountain of iron and rock. Man is a hammer!"

"Ah . . . if Jesus could persuade you through me! What glory and power you would bring His Kingdom!"

"Who knows, Father? Perhaps he lives only because I am his enemy. . ."

"He lives because He is."

"And I. . . ?"

"Because He wills it."

"He also willed that I suffer always, that I consider life an endless torment. . . and yet. . ."

"How do you know what He really willed? The love of Jesus is infinite. . ."

"His love was not infinite, Father."

"His hand heals, even when it seems to smite."

"It is not true, Father. Jesus hated. Jesus was irascible. . ."

"What do you say, my son?"

"The Council of Nicaea rejected several authentic narratives of the gospel. . . ."

"Those that were of divine origin rose from the altar, as if possessing wings. The others dropped to the earth," the Bishop interjected.

I smiled. "I was present. What you say never occurred. The fathers wrangled and fought. I never saw a more obstinate and self-willed gathering. A militant minority, backed by Emperor Constantine, imposed its will upon the Council. Finally, they compromised upon the Bible, as the Christian world knows it, but the books of Thomas and the gospel of the Infancy of Jesus were rejected, for they related things unpalatable to your theology. . ."

"What things, my son?"

"The cruelty of Jesus. . ."

"Impossible!" the Bishop exclaimed.

"You forget," I remarked, "that I knew Jesus as a boy. I knew his tantrums as a child. I knew him when he was an apprentice in his father's shop. I remember how, on one occasion, my father commissioned him to do a job for him. The work was not satisfactory. When my father pointed out certain flaws to him, young Jesus flew into a rage and smashed his own handiwork. If a god adopts a trade he should master it more completely."

"My son," the Bishop remarked, shaking his locks, "your hatred envenoms your tongue. You draw upon memories embittered by your own bias."

"If you will not accept my testimony, I can cite the evidence of your own sacred books. I shall draw upon sources regarded as sacred by the Fathers of the Church.

"His cruelty even as a boy became so frequent and so intolerable, according to the testimony of Saint Thomas and other witnesses, that Joseph, his father, said in despair to Saint Mary: 'Thenceforth we will not allow him out of the house; for everyone who displeases him is killed.' "

"That was a metaphor, my son," the Bishop smiled.

"No, Father! It was literal. Listen to a few incidents."

"Go on, my son."

"The son of Hanani, disturbing the waters of a fish pool, Jesus commanded the water to vanish, saying:— 'In like manner as this water has vanished, so shall thy life vanish.' And presently the boy died.

"Another time when the Lord Jesus was coming home in the evening with Joseph, He met a boy, who ran so hard against Him, that he threw Him down; to whom the Lord Jesus said, 'As thou hast thrown me down, so shalt thou fall, nor ever rise.' At that moment the boy died.

"Another time Jesus went forth into the street, and a boy running, rushed by His shoulder; at which Jesus being angry, said to him, 'Thou shalt go no farther.' And he instantly fell over dead. The parents of the dead boy, going to Joseph, complained, saying, 'You are not fit to live with us, in our city, having such a boy as that.

Either teach him that he bless and not curse, or else depart thou hence with him, for he kills our children.'

"Then Joseph, calling the boy Jesus by himself, instructed him, saying, 'Why dost thou such things to injure the people so, that they hate and persecute us?'

"But Jesus replied, 'They who have said these things to thee shall suffer everlasting punishment.' And immediately they who had accused him became blind."

I remained silent. The Bishop knit his brows, and meditated.

"It is merely a legend, the invention of some poet who liked cruel things. Your testimony is spurious. Jesus was as gentle as a lamb. Even as a child He was obedient and wise. . . ."

"That is also mere poetry, Father," I smiled a little cynically, piqued at the fact that he did not believe me. "Jesus snubbed his brothers. He neglected his family. He denied all family ties. He asked those who followed him to leave their fathers and mothers, their kith and their kin. I do not blame him for upbraiding his Father in Heaven on the cross. Yet why should he be surprised if his Father in Heaven forsook him, since he himself forsook his father and mother on earth? Only an unnatural son would deny his own mother with the cold insolence of Jesus. 'Woman, what have I to do with thee?' is not a quotation from the Apocrypha. It is part of the gospel, the gospel which, you claim, rose miraculously from the altar. He withered the lives of little children with the same petulance with which he blasted the innocent fig tree."

"My son, if what you relate were really true, would it not prove that He was omnipotent from His Mother's womb?" the Bishop exclaimed triumphantly. "He had a God's work to do even in His infancy."

"Then he who kills is God," I remarked.

"The Lord giveth, the Lord taketh away. His ways are inscrutable. If Jesus commanded the children to wither, it was part of His divine plan, I assure you."

I laughed. "He was cruel, and he was cruel to me. His eyes blazed with anger when he hurled his anathema against me, without attempting to understand my motives. If he had read my heart he would not have cursed me. He acted rashly, and he acted in anger. Perhaps he inherited his unreasonable irascibility from his putative Father in Heaven. . . ."

"He gave you the opportunity to find your soul . . . " the Bishop said gently.

"No!" I exclaimed. "He meant evil, but I have conquered him! By my will and by my intelligence, I have transformed his curse into a blessing."

"God's ways are incomprehensible to man," the Bishop repeated suavely.

"Let man be incomprehensible to God, then!" I exclaimed.

"Only man's vanity is incomprehensible to God, my son."

"Man's vanity, then, shall conquer God!"

"So Lucifer believed, and he was hurled to destruction!"

"Lucifer lives on, Father. He is not destroyed."

We remained silent. The Bishop placed his hands upon my shoulders, and looked at me, his eyes covered with a film.

"My son, believe me, if you understood Jesus you would accept Him."

"I understand . . . therefore, I cannot accept!"

"You have denied Him too long. He loves you. He waits for you. He will return whenever your heart calls Him. . . . You can end your long pilgrimage whenever you wish. You need not tarry until the end of time. . . Give up your age-long battle against His love and His Holy Word."

"How can I, a poor mortal, harm his Holy Word, if he indeed is God? You exaggerate my power, Bishop. In the great sea of humanity, is a man more than a wave?"

"One unruly wave may capsize a boat."

"If Christianity is the work of God, who is strong enough to destroy it?"

"No one!" he exclaimed. "And yet," he continued sadly, "people may so distort and misinterpret it, that it were almost better destroyed. . . ."

"Father, from the clash of mountains, there arises a conflagration; out of the struggle between Jesus and myself . . . who knows, something more beautiful than either Christianity or pure reason may be born."

"Christ is perfection."

His words startled me. It seemed as though I suddenly saw something—a Light—a Vision. I tried to grasp it, but it vanished immediately.

I smiled. "Father, that which we seek and find,—is it worth the finding?"

"Only one thing is worth the finding,—Jesus."

The two friars, the Bishop's companions, were approaching, and

at a distance, propped against a tree, Kotikokura was patting a large
cat and squinting his eyes in my direction.

"We are both very tired, my son. Let us rest a little. This evening
we shall speak again."

He arose, pressed my hands, and walked towards his friends. The
Bishop's face, as it broke the reflection of the sun, appeared strangely
different from that of Apollonius. Had I been laboring under an illusion? Had I made a grave error in recounting my story? My head
ached. My heart felt heavy.

"Kotikokura, we must leave this beautiful and happy place. We
must leave our two good wives."

Kotikokura shrugged his shoulders.

"I know you have long ago wearied of yours, and perhaps I have
a little of mine. However great a discomfort may be, there is always
a grain of pleasure in it. Thus, our leaving here will not make it
necessary for you to carry out your intention."

Kotikokura looked at me quizzically.

"Kotikokura, I know you too well. You cannot hide your thoughts
from me. You meant to strangle your wife . . . and perhaps mine
. . . and throw them into the river."

Kotikokura grinned.

"Nevertheless, I doubt whether we sha" ever discover another
place as lovely as this."

He shook his head sadly.

Kotikokura's cat crawled between his legs, purring. He raised her
and fondled her.

"You regret leaving your cat more than your wife—do you not
my friend?"

Kotikokura nodded.

XLVIII

THE EMPIRE OF PRESTER JOHN—"IF I WILL THAT HE TARRY TILL I COME WHAT IS THAT TO THEE?"— KOTIKOKURA DANCES—CAN MAN INVENT A LIE?

"Presbyter Johannes, by the power and virtue of God and of the Lord Jesus Christ, Lord of Lords," the friar exclaimed, "will deliver us from the infidels and the heathens. His power is limitless and his lands are the richest in the world. Even the pebbles of the shores of his rivers are pure diamonds and the mountains are replete with gold. In the center of the empire, the Fountain of Youth falls softly into a thousand cups, and he who drinks of it shall never die. Presbyter Johannes shall come to deliver us. He shall come with his hundred thousand knights and three hundred thousand footmen; with the princes and kings of the seventy-two states that pay him tribute; with his chariots and elephants and strange creatures that devour ten men at one meal."

His listeners laugh..., some pointed to their foreheads, one or two asked him a few questions. The friar expostulated against the Moors and the Saracens who had defeated the Crusaders, were knocking at the gates of Vienna, and threatened to destroy Europe and Christianity.

The people dispersed one by one. Only Kotikokura and I remained. Prester John—Presbyter Johannes—for some obscure reason, troubled my mind, like a word that one tries to restore in time and space but cannot.

"Brother," I said to the friar, "where is his empire and who is Presbyter Johannes?"

He looked at me startled. "Who is Presbyter Johannes?"

I nodded.

"He is . . . the Lord of Lords."

"I understand that . . . and yet— —"

He approached my ear and whispered mysteriously, "He is John, the Apostle."

"But John the Apostle is dead."

"How can he be dead, having drunk of the Fountain of Youth?"

"Of course," I said vaguely.

"The Lord Jesus has kept His beloved disciple alive and has made him great and powerful that he may save the cross from destruction."

'John,' I mused. Could it really be he? Speaking of John, Jesus said to Peter: "If I will that he tarry till I come, what is that to thee. . . ?" There was a rumor among the Christians based on these words that John could not die. But Jesus merely said: "*If* I will." Had he willed it? Had his love wrought for John what his hate had wrought for me. . . ?

"Whence, brother friar, will Prester John start?" I asked.

"From the center of his empire, which is the center of the earth— a far-off land, thousands of miles beyond Jerusalem, which, however, he will deliver first. . ."

"In the heart of Asia, then?"

He nodded.

I gave him a coin.

He bowed very low, making the sign of the cross over Kotikokura and me.

"Kotikokura, man is incapable of inventing a pure lie or discovering a pure truth. What this friar said today must have a grain of reality. . ."

Kotikokura grinned.

"And if John lives . . . alas, you do not remember John . . . that is true. It was a few centuries before I discovered you. You are a mere stripling, Kotikokura. . ."

Kotikokura laughed, and danced about me.

"Let us go in search of this fabulous land, Kotikokura, and see what scrap of reality suffices to create a legend. . ."

The reputation of Presbyter Johannes or Prester John was much more widespread than I suspected. Some laughed at the notion, some disputed; others proved his existence or non-existence by the Scriptures. But everywhere his name was mentioned and discussed.

We wandered about, taking now one road, now another, according to the vague and contradictory directions we received, stopping only to recuperate and replenish our supplies. The farther Europe disappeared behind us, the less resplendent became the empire of Prester John.

"We are on the right path, Kotikokura, for falsehood shines like a sun, but truth is a modest jewel."

"Where is the empire of Prester John?" I asked a very stout Buddhist monk.

He smiled leisurely. "The empire?"

"Yes."

"You are speaking metaphorically, sir, are you not?"

"Metaphorically?"

"A man's soul may be a vast empire."

"Is it in that sense only that Prester John has an empire?"

"Not quite in that sense, nor quite in the other."

'How strangely his empire shrinks!' I mused.

"Don't let me discourage you from visiting the empire of Prester John," the Buddhist remarked, as if reading my thoughts. "It is about two hundred miles in this direction———" He pointed toward the East.

I thanked the Friar very cordially, and gave him the expected alms.

"Kotikokura, truth is not even a modest jewel. Truth is a moss-covered stone pushed aside by angry travelers."

XLIX

THE CITY OF GOD—I RECOGNIZE PRESTER JOHN— PRESTER JOHN DISCUSSES THE BEAST—TIME HAS A HEAVY FIST

THE people were assembling in the public square, mostly fishermen and small merchants, dressed in the manner of the Hebrews of the time of Jesus. Their faces, too, their angular gestures, and their incessant disputations wrenched time back a thousand years.

Kotikokura whose foot was caught in the meshes of a fisherman's net pulled vigorously to regain his freedom.

"Who allows you to interfere with an honest man's means of livelihood?" the man shouted in Hebrew, discovering that several of the meshes had been torn.

Kotikokura was about to jump at his throat. I grasped him by the arm.

"I regret infinitely, sir," I addressed the fisherman. "We are strangers and know neither the name of the country we are in nor its customs. I am inclined to believe, however, that all such mishaps may be adjusted peacefully here as elsewhere."

I gave him a few pieces of silver. He looked at me critically. "This hardly pays for my loss."

I knew that he lied atrociously, but in order to avoid any further dispute, I doubled my gift.

"What is the name of this country, my friend?" I asked him.

"Ours is the Realm of God, and yonder comes our Patriarch, Prester John—may his name be blessed!"

A man, apparently seventy or seventy-five, approached gravely, followed by several priests, if judged by their garb, but rabbis by their long beards and curls. John carried in his arm the Torah, while from his neck hung a large crucifix.

The people bowed and crossed themselves, and made room for the procession which stopped where four fishermen deposited upon a stone platform a large arm-chair, in the shape of two lions from whose foreheads rose grotesque horns,—stars surmounted by crosses.

Presbyter Johannes seated himself. The people knelt. I did likewise. Kotikokura, dazed a little by the proceedings, remained standing. One of the priests glared in our direction.

"Kotikokura," I whispered, "kneel or we are lost."

He knelt.

Two priests sprinkled holy water and scattered incense, which was welcome to the nostrils, for the fishermen smelt rankly of their profession.

Johannes rose. I watched him intently. Was it really John? His eyes, perhaps,—but where was their brightness? His nose more likely,—but was it not rather a racial than a personal characteristic? John's face had been almost feminine in delicacy, and the down upon it was soft and silky. This man's beard was a mixture of gray and white, and his skin, whatever was visible of it, was yellow and thin like parchment.

He raised his hand, blessed the people in Hebrew, then made the sign of the cross over them. He reseated himself.

Could that be his voice,—a hard staccato thing that sounded like iron struck against stone?

The priests covered their heads with tallithim, and bowing and beating their breasts incessantly, chanted an old Hebrew prayer, mixed with barbaric Latin. The people, still kneeling, repeated at intervals a phrase or a word.

Johannes meanwhile, his head between his palms, meditated or prayed.

The ceremony over, the Patriarch rose. His right arm raised, he exclaimed: "Do not forget our mission, brethren! We are the chosen of the Lord to conquer the heathens and the unbelievers. We are the children of Jesus and of Moses. We are the Fountain of Youth. They who drink of our words shall inherit the earth and heaven forever."

"Amen," the people answered.

"We shall go forth embattled,—mighty knights who will deliver Jerusalem and the world. We shall bring perfection unto man. He shall be happy and rich beyond his present dreams. The mountains shall open at his command, and lo, he shall find them filled with gold! The sands on the river banks shall turn to precious jewels; the fish shall be odorous like flowers. Yea, we shall bring Eden once more unto the earth. In the name of Jesus, our Lord and David, His Father, and Moses whose Word is the Word of God, now and forever, Amen!"

"Amen," the people repeated.

Johannes made the sign of the cross over them. The people dispersed. The priests helped their Patriarch descend and followed him in silence.

I seated myself at the edge of the shore and meditated. Kotikokura, bored, threw pebbles into the water.

"Have you ever seen, my friend, greater poverty than here? Even in China,—you remember—during the Revolution, the people seemed more prosperous."

Kotikokura continued to throw pebbles into the water.

"Perhaps you are right, Kotikokura. It is just as rational to throw pebbles into a river as to endeavor to discover logic in the universe. I think I shall join you."

He laughed uproariously. We threw pebbles, vying with each other as to the distance and the height of the waves we could raise.

Suddenly, I felt someone grasp my shoulder. I turned around.

"Who are you?" the man asked stentoriously.

"We are strangers from far-off lands."

"Why are you disturbing the waters?"

"Forgive a little innocent pleasure, sir."

"There is no innocent pleasure. Every mundane pleasure is tainted with sin."

"Will you not forgive two strangers their great ignorance?"

"It is not for me to forgive, but for our Lord. Come along!"

Kotikokura's nostrils shivered, his fists opened and shut spasmodically. I looked at him, shaking lightly my head.

The man we followed was dressed as a priest, but about his waist dangled a long sword.

"Will you enlighten me, sir," I asked. "I am not quite certain, as yet, in what country we landed and who the king may be."

He did not answer. I repeated my question.

"He who does not recognize Virtue when he sees it, and does not distinguish God's own country from man's deserves no answer."

"How shall a man distinguish God's own country from man's?"

He turned around and glared at me. "How dare you blaspheme against Yahweh and Jesus! Is it not self-evident that our country is the most beautiful, the most blessed of all? Have you not heard the words to our Master this morning? Do you doubt— —?"

He placed his hand upon the hilt of his sword.

I remembered the horseshoer and the fate of the man who dared to question the divinity of Mohammed.

"How can I doubt when I see so much zeal? Is not zeal the sign of truth? Can a lie inspire such passion?"

He dropped his hand and ordered us to follow.

The Court of Justice was a long room dimly lit. At one angle, a large arm-chair, the exact counterpart of the one I had seen in the square—or was it perhaps the same one—upon two wooden lions with grotesque horns. Opposite an enormous cross with an agonizing Christ and the stone tablets of Moses.

"The Lord deliver us from justice, Kotikokura," I whispered, "particularly in this land of God. It will be a miracle if we escape unscathed. Be ready."

He nodded.

Presbyter Johannes entered, followed by four priests. He seated himself. The priests remained standing, two on either side.

My captor crossed himself, and made a long complaint against Kotikokura and myself. We were disturbing the peace of the river; we were blasphemous and cynical; we were frivolous, and preferred sin and pleasure to virtue and righteousness. He asked that justice be unadulterated with pity.

Presbyter Johannes stared at me, his brows knit. Did he recognize me? Was I merely a culprit?

He ordered everybody except myself and Kotikokura to leave the courtroom and continued to stare at me for a long while, saying nothing.

"Once more you have blasphemed against our Lord!" he thundered.

"John . . ." I asked mildly.

"Yes, I am John . . . and you are Isaac . . . Isaac Laquedem!"

"John," I whispered, almost pathetically.

"You rejected the words of the Lamb and you still wander like a hunted beast." His lips twisted into a malevolent snarl.

"John."

"I warned you, but you shrugged your shoulders. Do you believe in Jesus now?"

I shook my head.

"Cursed and damned forever!"

"John," I whispered, and my eyes filled with tears.

"Weep, for you have reason to weep if your heart is stone and your brain a forest of thistles that will not permit truth to pass through except bleeding and mutilated."

Kotikokura, not understanding the drift of our conversation, looked distressed and his eyes also filled with tears.

"Cursed wanderer and companion of men-beasts!"

"John.'

He looked up, crossing himself. "I thank Thee, O Lord, for having kept me alive long enough to meet Your enemy face to face again. I thank Thee, O Lord, for having permitted me to reach an age when my shameful sentiments toward Your enemy can no longer distort my reason. Amen."

"John."

His forefinger pointed at me, his words sharp and biting as a whip that is cracked, he continued: "And now you have come into God's realm, and once more you have mocked Him! Once more you have rejected Him. You are neither man nor beast, neither Jew nor Christian, but a monster possessed by the Evil One."

"John."

"I could release you from your bondage; I could give you peace at last,—but I will not until you accept our Master and kneel before His Cross."

I shook my head.

"No punishment that I can conceive can add to your curse. Go . . . wander again! Tarry, until the Lord Himself shall visit the earth again. And woe unto you, Isaac, when that day come to pass!"

I did not budge.

"Anti-Christ! Beast!" he shouted. Closing his eyes and raising his right hand, he continued: "I see the Beast rise out of the sea, having seven heads and ten horns, and upon his horns are crosses and upon his foreheads the names of his blasphemy."

He remained silent.

"I see the Lord coming to slaughter the Beast. I see seven golden candlesticks. And in the midst of the seven candlesticks, I see the Son of Man: His head and His hair are white like wool, as white as snow, and His eyes are as a flame of fire. He has in His right hand seven stars, and out of His mouth goes a sharp two-edged sword, and His countenance is as the sun, shining in its strength. . . ."

His teeth clenched, his legs stiffened. Two bits of foam dotted the corners of his mouth. I remembered that in his youth he had suffered from epileptic seizures. I was on the point of raising him in my arms as I did, so long ago, and speaking to him tenderly.

I yearned to whisper to him: "John, how have you forgotten your friend? I am Isaac,—he who loved you and whom you loved. Do you not remember the hours we spent together? Do you not remember that in each other's company we discovered Woman? Oh, the starry nights when we walked together along the shore of the Jordan and upon the hills that surround Jerusalem! Oh, the golden words we uttered! John . . . has your heart turned to stone?"

The foam trickled over his beard. He had the appearance of some unclean animal. Could not Jesus relieve him of his affliction? He gave life without improving upon it. I had improved mine, but in spite of him. . . .

John opened his bloodshot eyes.

"Go! Continue your devil's work that your soul may become blacker and blacker. Fight the Lord, neglect virtue and sanctity that your punishment may be the greater. I shall remain in this place. When the Lord returns, He shall find one spot where His gospel is inviolate, one disciple more faithful than Peter. . . ."

'Still jealous of Peter,' I thought. 'My search for John is ended. That which may be found, is it worth the seeking? If time has such evil power, may I never behold the face of Mary again.'

"Go!"

"Come, Kotikokura," I whispered.

I took Kotikokura's arm and walked out slowly.

L

"KOTIKOKURA, WHAT ARE WE?"—DO THE STARS HAVE A PURPOSE?—GROWTH

THE Mediterranean had never been so beautiful nor I so sad.

"You cannot imagine, Kotikokura, what I have lost. You saw John . . . if it was really John and not merely the wraith of an evil dream— —"

Kotikokura made a grimace.

"But had you seen him in his youth— —"

He shrugged his shoulders and twisted his mouth. Kotikokura was jealous. Whenever I mentioned John's youth and beauty, he became irritable or made gestures of depreciation.

John! John! Was it possible? Could a man change so, or was it merely a normal development? Was the youthful rebel destined to become the middle-aged hard and relentless zealot? Must the beautiful courtesan change into a hag, loveless and unforgiving? Had I escaped the inevitable only because I remained young? Were the mind and soul conditioned upon the functions of the body, upon a mere nerve, a slow or fast pulsing heart, a well-developed or atrophied muscle?

"Kotikokura, what are we? What are we?"

Kotikokura grinned.

"What shall I seek now, Kotikokura? Have I not already found what I sought?"

Kotikokura continued to grin. He was not at all displeased by my disillusionment.

"And yet,—I cannot live without a purpose. It is foolish. Do the stars have a purpose? Does the Mediterranean have a purpose? Why should I? . . . And yet. . ."

"Whither shall we go, Kotikokura? Are we indeed wanderers, aimless and hopeless? Is it not for us scorners and unbelievers to crush under foot gods and circumstances? Are we not the flame that rises above the ashes?"

Kotikokura knit his forehead and pouted his lips.

"Let us never acknowledge defeat! Crusades, Jerusalems, Armenian Bishops, Johns,—what are they to us? We shall survive them all, destroying their illusions and superstitions."

Kotikokura stamped his foot.

"Disillusioned? Why not? Disillusion is a sharp sword that cuts the chain about our necks. Pain? Sorrow? No matter! Does the mountain complain against the cloud that darkens it or the rain that beats against it or the snow that freezes its peaks? The mountain lives on. Living, after all, is what matters. If we live long enough, we shall conquer everything. We shall pluck and eat of every fruit on the Tree of Knowledge."

Kotikokura struck his leg with his closed fist.

"God defeats man merely because He outlives him. Give man sufficient time and what god shall survive? Or if a god should survive, what a magnificent god he would be!"

"Ca-ta-pha-god."

"Perhaps . . . but for that reason, Ca-ta-pha must be strong; must overcome himself, must step upon his heart as he steps upon withered leaves which trees shed in autumn; must grow—must become. . . ."

Kotikokura's eyes dashed to and fro.

"Kotikokura too must become— —"

He looked at me inquiringly.

"I do not know what, Kotikokura. That is unimportant. The seed which is sown does not dream of the possibilities that are within it. It must grow . . . it must break through the earth . . . it must rise high . . . high. That is sufficient."

Kotikokura stretched his arms upward, raising his heels.

"We shall never clutch the stars, Kotikokura. The higher we grow, the farther away the stars shall fly like birds teasing the rod of the fowler."

LI

THE GUADALQUIVIR CHURNS LIKE BUTTER—DOÑA
CRISTINA'S POLITE INVITATION—A TEMPLE OF
LOVE—UNPLUCKED ROOTS—I MEET DON JUAN—
DON FERNANDO—THE FURY OF DON JUAN—KOTI-
KOKURA BLUSHES

THE rain splashed into the Guadalquivir, churning it like butter.
Kotikokura and I, hooded, so that barely our noses were visible,
walked along the shore, making deep imprints into the mud which
quickly filled with water.

To the right, the Mezquita, now surmounted by an immense cross,
glittered through the long perpendicular trelises of the rain, like a
loving face playing hide and seek. Farther on upon the hill, the
Alcazar, its contours spoiled by recent repairs, looked disconsolate,
like a man who has outlived his glory.

The rain stopped suddenly. The sun broke through the clouds
which hung ragged-edged about his neck, like the hoop a bareback
rider has ripped. The Guadalquivir, no longer tormented, flowed
silently on, a little out of breath because of the new burden. The
puddles our footsteps made glistened like mother-of-pearl.

The eye ached from the glare of the whitewashed walls of the
houses, but rejoiced at long intervals at the remains of an ancient
building still untouched by the vulgar brush of the conquerors.

"Kotikokura, this is Córdoba, the pride of the Moors, when we
were on the road to Jerusalem to deliver the Holy Sepulchre. Whatever is beautiful and lovely was done before the Christians captured
the city. The hand of the conqueror has weighed heavily upon it.
Where are the palaces that once flourished upon the banks of this
lovely river,—the Palace of Contentment, the Palace of Flowers, the
Palace of Lovers? Nothing save arches and walls, like skeletons of
dead men. But even the arches are more beautiful than the new
palaces of the conquerors."

Keepers of wine-shops wiped their tables and chairs, wet from the
rain. Beggars, men and women, extended their hands, mumbling

prayers and benedictions, and if their requests remained ungranted, curses. Friars and nuns and priests passed in long procession, until the black of their garbs gave the impression of Night disintegrated, cutting fantastic figures upon the white canvas of day.

Three youths, their red capes thrown over their shoulders, were laughing uproariously, holding their stomachs. I turned to see what amused them so hugely. Two thin horses were pulling wearily a rickety hearse. The coachman, an old Jew whose face was entirely covered by an uncombed beard and curls, tried vainly to crack his whip, a small knotted cord, which seemed as voiceless as the corpse.

The cortège, a few men with red or black beards and women whose heads were covered with black shawls, beat their breasts from time to time and sobbed bitterly.

The youths continued to laugh. One of them shouted, "How many more of you are there, cursed Jews? When will the rest of you croak?"

Another pulled at his beardless chin, imitating a goat.

The third one, not to be behind in his display of wit, rolled a fistful of mud into a ball and threw it at the hearse. The mud stuck against the carriage in the shape of a large dahlia.

"We ought to burn them all!" the thrower of mud exclaimed.

"Except the young Jewesses. They are pretty lively in bed."

"Yes, they say that even Don Juan is in love with one."

"She will be the thousand and third queen of his heart."

"Do you think you will sleep with as many wenches, Miguel?"

"It is a trifle too many. Besides, I should not care to betray my friend's wives and sisters with the light-heartedness of Don Juan."

"Particularly not when the brother is my best friend," another remarked. "Fernando cannot get over it."

"Twins have a strange bond between them. Even physically, they say the sufferings of the one affect the other."

"And Fernando and his sister look so much alike you could hardly tell them apart—except in bed."

"What has become of her?"

"She has entered a convent."

"Don Juan will get into trouble some day—mark my words."

"He is the best swordsman in Spain."

"His back, however, is not immune from a good knife thrust."

I watched the hearse until it was out of sight, and the last member of the cortège disappeared.

"Kotikokura, my heart is heavy. There are roots within me which have not been plucked out. These poor people whose sorrow is ridiculed and mocked are my people."

Kotikokura looked at me surprised.

"Ca-ta-pha had a low beginning, Kotikokura. You cannot tell the shape of the roots by the perfume of the flower."

"Ca-ta-pha—god," he said emphatically.

I laughed. "You are not prejudiced against the Jew, are you? Why do all the races of the world hate him? What curse is there upon him? Wherever he goes, he brings wealth and culture and art, and receives in return an irreconcilable hatred."

Kotikokura looked perplexed.

"These people talk about a man who has possessed over a thousand women, Kotikokura. I am almost envious. It is too much for a mortal. . ."

"Ca-ta-pha . . . women. . ." He made a gesture to indicate that my harem was far more numerous.

"But Ca-ta-pha is god, and this fellow—what is his name—Don Juan—is only a man."

The youths fixed their capes, struck their heels together and left.

"What strange dissatisfaction must lurk in the heart of a man who possesses a thousand women in so short a career! Ca-ta-pha experiments. He has time. But Don Juan— —"

A woman approached us. She was dressed in mourning, but her face showed no indication of sorrow.

"The gentlemen are strangers, are they not?"

"Yes," I answered.

"Strangers are lonesome. . ."

"Generally."

"What is more consoling to lonesome gentlemen than . . . a woman,—young, beautiful . . . and loving?"

I looked at her.

"No, no, señor, I am not speaking of myself. I am Doña Cristina del Torno y Rodriguez, a poor widow," she sighed. "I have no claim either to beauty or youth, but— —" She approached my ear, rising a little on her toes. "I know where you can find both beauty and youth."

Kotikokura grinned.

"Not overexpensive either, señor, and not too far from here. Come, rejoice your body and soul, señores! You will not regret it. My Palace of Love is the finest in the city. Even Don Juan honors me with his visits."

"Don Juan?" I asked. "In spite of his thousand sweethearts. . .?"

"He is insatiable, señor. He is the handsomest caballero in the world, and so generous."

"Do you expect him in the near future?"

She knit her brows. "Why, yes . . . I expect him this very evening. I have— —" She placed a forefinger to her lips, "a virgin for him from the country—a real virgin. What does the excellent señor prefer . . . ?"

"Very well, take us over."

Taking our arms, she walked between us, proudly, chattering the virtues of her girls and the glory of Don Juan who once, while her husband was still alive, had honored her with his affection.

"Was he unusual as a lover?" I asked.

"He was cold and cruel, and that pleases me. I like men to dominate me, even as the lion tamer masters his beasts."

She looked at Kotikokura and squeezed his arm. He grinned.

The red shutters of the windows were slightly ajar, and two women's faces pressed against them. When they saw us approach, they bent their heads out and waved to us with their fans.

The door was opened for us by an old man who bowed innumerable times.

"My father, gentlemen."

I knew she lied.

"He was formerly a professor of mathematics at the university. He has become stone deaf, and besides suffers terribly from forgetfulness." She sighed. *"La vida es sueño."*

The walls of the waiting room into which we were ushered were painted with imitations of the Pompeian Catacombs. The furniture was of a neo-Moorish type,—heavy, bulky things, over-carved, overornamented. A servant helped us with our capes and hats; another brought us wine. Doña Cristina disappeared for a few minutes and returned dressed in a kimono of red silk, embroidered with large yellow flowers. Around her neck, she wore a rosary of immense beads.

She balanced her hips coquettishly, looking intently at Kotikokura whose eyes darted from one corner to the other, like young stallions.

She took our arms and led us into the salon. A stifling but not unpleasant smell of perfumes mingled with human flesh pervaded the place. The women greeted us with giggling and words of double meaning.

"Silence, geese! Do you not see that these are foreign noblemen?"

The women remained quiet. They reclined on couches and on the floor, their skirts raised to their knees and further, and their bodices half open, as if they had been suddenly disturbed in the process of dressing.

"Wine!" one called out.

"Sweets!" another one.

"Wine, sweets, wine, sweets!" they all shouted in unison.

"Silence! Their lordships have not yet deigned to indicate their choice. . ."

"Look, look,—your lordships!"

Doña Cristina pressed lightly Kotikokura's arm and sighed.

"Let there be wine and sweets!" I ordered.

The women clapped their hands, and shouted: "Long live los señores!"

One, blue-eyed and raven-haired, threw her arms about my neck. "My love, my Don Juan."

Doña Cristina pinched Kotikokura's leg. His face was flushed. His hands trembled a little. I whispered into her ear. "My friend is inexperienced. He is younger than he looks."

She raised her arms. "Santa Maria! Santa Maria! Jesus!" She pressed him to her voluminous chest. "My love, my bear, my lion!"

The girls laughed and applauded. They drank to our health and our strength, and munched noisily the sweets and the nuts.

The former professor of mathematics looked in. His head, bald to the neck, glistened like yellow ivory.

"Doña Cristina! Doña Cristina!"

"What do you want?" she asked irritably.

"Don Juan! Don Juan!" he stammered.

Doña Cristina shouted to the rest, "Don Juan, Don Juan!"

They echoed: "Don Juan! Don Juan!"

She dashed out and re-entered, preceded by a man still young, but already scarred by two parallel wrinkles on either cheek, and as he raised his hat upon which waved a large, white plume, his forehead and temples showed signs of baldness. He placed his left hand, covered with rings, upon his hip and looked about haughtily. Upon his chest glittered a small cross studded with precious stones, and the tips of his pointed, gilded shoes reflected the last rays of the sun.

"Foreign noblemen," Doña Cristina whispered into his ear, trembling a little.

Don Juan bowed. I returned the salutation.

"Don Juan," Doña Cristina said in a low tone of voice, "I have the virgin. She is as pretty as a flower . . . plump, red-cheeked, corresponding exactly to your specifications."

"Are you sure she is——?"

"I swear by the Holy Virgin Herself."

Don Juan turned to me. "It is an appalling state of affairs, señor. Girls of thirteen and fourteen are no longer virgins. I often think they are not even born untouched."

"Is virginity so important?"

"You are foreigners, gentlemen, and you are not aware, perhaps, of the terrible ravishes of the New Disease."

"What disease?"

"A kind of leprosy. The last Crusaders brought it with them from the Holy City. There is no safety except in virginity and in the *cordon de sureté*—the girdle of chastity. Romance has become more dangerous than warfare. You cannot be certain of any woman. Who knows how many of Doña Cristina's girls are capable of inflicting wounds more dreadful than those of the javelin . . . ?"

Doña Cristina threw up her arms in horror.

"Oh!" the girls shouted.

"Don Juan, my girls are all as pure as virgins. The gentlemen that visit them are the finest in Spain and— —" pointing to us, "in the world."

"Come, come, my little one, do not get exasperated."

He placed his hand upon her shoulder. "I only mentioned that by way of example." And addressing me, "It is true, indeed, señor,—this is the only safe Temple of Love in Córdoba."

Doña Cristina kissed his bejeweled hand. The girls laughed and drank another cup to Don Juan, the incomparable lover.

The former professor of mathematics stuck his head in once more. One ray of the sun pierced its center like a long golden horn. "Doña Cristina, Doña Cristina. . ."

"Well?"

"Don Fernando is at the gate."

Doña Cristina was flustered. "Santa Maria! Jesú!"

"Who is it, did you say?" asked Don Juan.

Doña Cristina was reluctant to answer.

"Who?" he demanded.

"Don Fernando, señor."

"Ah, that is a stroke of good fortune. We have not met for a long while."

"But . . . Don Juan . . . I thought— —"

"Perish your thoughts! Let him come in!"

"Let him come in!" Doña Cristina shouted in the professor's ear.

Don Fernando entered. He was a lad of about twenty, graceful and lithe; his aquiline nose and dark skin betokened an admixture of Moorish blood. Upon seeing Don Juan, the young man shook his fist in Doña Cristina's face.

"Fool! Why did you not tell me— —?"

Doña Cristina whimpered.

Don Juan smiled. "Is señor so angry at me that he would not even see me?"

Don Fernando glared at him without answering.

"We have no quarrel, I am certain. It is all gossip."

"No! It is not gossip—and we have a quarrel!"

Don Juan looked at him, his eyes partially closed and his lips stretched into a faint smile.

"I have always considered Don Fernando my friend."

"You have done wrongly, señor. Don Fernando is your enemy."

"It is ridiculous to break friendship because—of a woman."

"The woman is my sister."

Don Juan looked at the young man and breathed deeply. "I regret— —"

"What?" the young man asked.

"That she is your sister."

"And not your cowardly deed?"

"Señor, master your tongue!"

A white patch shone on Don Juan's forehead. His nostrils shivered. But his eyes, which I expected to glitter like knives, preserved a curious tenderness.

"Master my tongue? It is fortunate for you that I master my arm."

"What!" Don Juan exclaimed. "You dare— —"

"I dare! I am undaunted by Don Juan."

Don Juan opened and closed his fists. The patch upon his forehead shone like an ominous star.

Why was he so furious? And why did his eyes continue to be almost affectionate? A young man's taunt ordinarily, I felt, would have merely made Don Juan laugh uproariously. I remembered the conversation of the three youths.

Don Juan suddenly regained his composure. The patch upon his forehead disappeared.

"Fernando, for the sake of our former friendship, do not excite my anger. I am not able to control my sword, once it is out of its scabbard. You know that."

"Coward! You say that because you fear me in your heart."

"What! I fear you? Think of it, gentlemen! Think of it,—all of you! Don Juan fears this—child!"

Fernando raised his hand and slapped Don Juan's face. "I'll teach you to call me child!"

Don Juan straightened up, placed his hand upon the hilt of his sword, and exclaimed: "Impudent stripling, your own hand has sealed your death-warrant."

The young man placed his hand upon his sword, and drew it half way out of its scabbard.

The girls shrieked.

Doña Christina knelt between the two men. "Please, gentlemen, not in my house . . . please . . . you will ruin me!"

Don Juan pushed her away with his foot.

She clasped the legs of Don Fernando. "I beg you, gentlemen . . . not here!"

Don Juan laughed suddenly. "You are right—not here. He shall be dispatched elsewhere."

"At your service, wherever and whenever you wish," said the young man proudly.

"Gentlemen," Don Juan addressed us, "although I have never had the pleasure of your previous acquaintance, may I ask you to be my seconds?"

We nodded.

"For the friendship I once bore you, señor," he said to Fernando, "you shall die as a gentleman and not as a hog. I shall give you the opportunity to display your prowess."

"Within twenty-four hours, I shall send you my seconds," the lad answered proudly, and left.

"I am sorry for the boy," Don Juan remarked.

"Why not merely wound him to teach him a lesson, señor?"

"Hardly. Once in combat, my arm rules my sentiments."

He ordered drinks.

"The virgin . . ." Doña Cristina whispered into Don Juan's ear.

"This evening at ten," Don Juan replied, slightly bored.

Doña Cristina pressed Kotikokura's hand and whispered into his ear, "My bear . . . tonight, you are mine."

Kotikokura blushed.

LII

OUT OF THE WINDOW OF THE PAST—KOTIKOKURA,
THE LION—THE DISAPPOINTMENT OF DON JUAN—
I VISIT DON JUAN'S HOUSE—I DISCUSS LOVE WITH
DON JUAN—DON JUAN'S SECRET—I KILL DON JUAN

IT was nearly noon.

I opened the shutter, and looked out. At a distance, the Guadalquivir glistened like a long silver stripe on an officer's coat. Still
further, the hills rounded at the top as if a hand had smoothed
them. The whiteness of the houses no longer annoyed me. It served
as a fine background for the trees which cast long gray shadows,
trembling a little. The chimes of the Mezquita, whose belfry towered
about the city—rang slowly, lazily, inviting not so much to prayer
as to slumber.

A driver urged a team of oxen, swearing by all the saints that
if they would not hasten, he would deliver them into the hands of
the butchers.

Two nuns made tiny steps, counting the while their rosaries. An
officer on horseback rode proudly on, as if to an imaginary conquest.

I remembered myself dressed as a Roman captain. Lydia seemed
to pass underneath my window, her silken toga ruffled somewhat by
the wind.—Nero fiddled.—Poppaea smiled her lascivious, cruel smile.
—Charlemagne grasped his leg in sudden pain.—The Armenian
Bishop—Africa. The desert, the sand that rose like billows of the
sea.—Salome, the gorgeous, the incomparable Salome. Had I possessed her in truth? Was it a dream? Was not everything a dream?

The chimes continued to ring.

Who was I? Where was I? I rubbed my eyes vigorously, and
laughed. I was in the anteroom of Doña Cristina's Palace of Love,—
the purest in Córdoba which even Don Juan, the incomparable lover,
frequented. Don Juan—he was still with his virgin from the country
—and Kotikokura, the bear, the lion, had not yet unclasped the arms
of his love.

Poor Fernando—a fine face, almost feminine.—He would die

within twenty-four hours. It was a pity. But why not? A day, a year, a century—what matter?

And Don Juan—equally skillful as a duelist and as a lover. What did he seek? Was he a voluptuary or a philosopher? Did he find in women only a momentary spasmodic joy, or had he discovered some ultimate secret of sensual pleasure? Why the pride in the numbers? What secret motive animated his restlessness? What was the meaning of the affectionate look when he quarreled with the lad in the brothel? Why the regret? Why the inordinate fury?

He had mentioned the name of a Jewish girl—a rabbi's daughter —with his last cup. Ah, if he could possess her! But in the same breath, he cursed the whole race, would gladly have put them all to the sword.

He must not get her! Don Juan shall be frustrated by a Jewess! Something in me revolted at the idea that a woman of my race should be the toy of this man. Was my mother speaking through me? Was it something even more remote? Woman is a symbol, the foundation of her race. While she remains pure, the race continues. Why this partiality to the Jews? The fate of other races did not concern me. Was it because as long as the Jew lived, Jesus was still defeated? He might persuade the whole world, but not those who knew him. We were the thorn in his side. . .

Did I unwittingly love the rabbi's daughter whom I had not even met? A tenderness towards this unknown young person overwhelmed me. I had wandered long, I would return to my flock. It was always a woman who stretched her arms to welcome the prodigal. . .

Kotikokura entered quietly, and stood in back of me. I made believe I was not aware of his presence. He coughed a little and shuffled his feet. I turned. His head was bent, and he looked embarrassed.

"Well, my bear, my lion,—why the sheepish look?"

He pressed my hand to his lips.

"Has the lady bitten off—your nose, Kotikokura?"

He made a gesture of disgust. "Woman!"

I laughed.

He repeated, "Woman."

"Woman, Kotikokura, is an attitude. She is either the loveliest thing in the world—or the unloveliest. It all depends upon what you seek in her, and how much you are willing to forgive in advance."

He repeated, "Woman."

"How about Salome, Kotikokura?"

"Salome—woman!" he exclaimed.

"You are an old hag! I shall never cross your threshold again!" Don Juan shouted from the next room.

"But señor, is it my fault? How could I tell?" Doña Cristina whimpered.

"Why don't you instruct your women more adroitly?"

"She says she tried her very best, señor, but you were not in the mood to be pleased. . ."

The door opened brusquely. Don Juan came out. Doña Cristina, bent in two, her arms outstretched, followed him.

"Señor, señor!"

He threw her a purse. "Take it—and do not let me see your face again."

"What is money to me if——"

Don Juan placed his hand upon the hilt of his sword. "Go away —or I shall run you through like a sow."

She snatched the purse and rushed out. Around her neck I noticed two fingermarks, which I recognized as Kotikokura's.

"The stupid calf!" Don Juan exclaimed, walking up and down the room. His eyes were swollen a little from lack of sleep, and his face was drawn. He looked his age.

"Why do men rave about virgins, señor? They are awkward and clumsy and afford no satisfaction. Nobody wants wine which has been unfermented. Why do they insist upon virginity? The hen will cackle about it too. Don Juan was not in the mood! Is it for a man to be in the mood or for a woman to create it? Only boors are really hungry. A gentleman's appetite is stirred by an apéritif. Not in the mood! Had she had an ounce of brain or training, or lacking these, an instinctive flair——"

I remembered my experience with Poppaea. Had Don Juan failed to be—Don Juan?

"Perhaps, señor," I suggested, "you were distracted by something or other?"

"Perhaps. The fool Fernando came into my mind again and again. I do not wish to kill him. Why did he act like an idiot?"

"Is it really so important if he continues to live or not?"

He looked at me. "No! To the devil with him!" he shouted.

He walked up and down, his hands upon his back.

"And that Jewess has disturbed my thoughts. She is a virgin too—like all young Jewesses. But she cannot be so stupid! Besides, she is beautiful. How can such an abominable race produce such an exquisite creature, señor?"

"The roots of roses are set deeply in the mud."

"That is true, señor. She is a rose. Her roots are in the—Ghetto."

Kotikokura opened and shut his fists, grumbling: "Woman" from time to time.

"She is protected like a king's treasure. My very name is sufficient to alarm all Jews."

Don Juan resumed his walking. His shoes glittered like golden mirrors every time he broke the reflection of the sun, while his temples shone like thinly hidden ivory.

"Are the women of your country, señor, also mainly foxes and geese?"

"I have traveled in many lands, Don Juan, and have known women of all races and of all colors. Everywhere man complains against them. Woman has been compared to all creatures, wild or tamed, and still has not been explained."

He looked at me, placing his hand upon his hip and closing a little his eyes. "Señor, from the first glance, I recognized in you a kindred soul."

I bowed.

"You seek, evidently, as I do, the ultimate——"

"Unendurable pleasure indefinitely prolonged, Don Juan."

"Unendurable pleasure indefinitely prolonged," he repeated. "That is it! This is what I have been seeking. To know what one seeks is as difficult at times as to find it. Señor, you have the lasting gratitude of Don Juan. I swear it by the sword and the cross!" He touched both.

He muttered to himself, "Unendurable pleasure indefinitely prolonged! But señor, I forget the seconds of Don Fernando must be waiting for me at my home. May I ask you to be my guest?" Looking up at Kotikokura, "My guests, gentlemen, for the rest of your sojourn in Córdoba."

We bowed. I thanked him.

"The air here is stifling, putrid." He screwed up his nose. He reminded me at that moment of an oversensitive and fastidious young woman.

Don Juan's mansion was a neo-Moorish building, situated upon the bank of the Guadalquivir. A rectangular garden in which the flowers and trees were arranged with mathematical precision surrounded it on all sides, so that only the upper part of the house was visible when approached.

"I hate irregularity and disorder," he told me. "I prefer to dominate nature and arrange the colors and sizes of my flowers in a harmony which pleases my eye. But I suppose this is due to my masculine temperament. I am logical in all things."

This regularity, on the contrary, struck me as profoundly feminine. It seemed to me more like the fussiness of an old maid.

Two male servants helped us with our clothing. A third one prepared food.

"Even my servants are men. I cannot endure the whimsicality of women in my domestic environment."

The walls were covered with swords, weapons, heads of wild boars and other mementoes of Don Juan's masculine prowess. Two small parrots screeched "Bienvenido," ceaselessly. Several tiny birds in cages flapped their wings, warbling and whistling.

Don Juan invited me to sit at the table. Kotikokura, a large jug of wine between his knees, seated himself in front of the fireplace.

"A friend of mine," remarked Don Juan, "a young poet, has expressed my life in a poem. This poem shall be my epitaph.

> "At the flutter of my wings
> The breezes quivered,
> And a thousand flowers unclasped
> Their honeyed treasures.
> Alas! I died of sheer despair
> And lonesomeness
> In the golden chalice of a rose."

"And a thousand women were unable to dispel your gloom, Don Juan?"

"Only while their embraces lasted, and frequently not as long. A thousand women. . . What does it mean, señor? One obliterates the memory of the other, leaving us empty-handed. A man always says: 'This one is different. This one's lips will burn the flesh and touch the soul.'—But they hardly scorch the skin."

"Woman is an attitude," I replied, repeating my remark to Kotikokura. "It all depends upon what one seeks in her and how much one is willing to forgive in advance."

Don Juan drank another cup. His face flushed. "I do not know what I seek in her, my friend. Love is only a method to vanquish boredom. . ."

"Our lives are so short, Don Juan! Have we time to be bored?" Kotikokura grinned.

"The gods have mocked us with an unspeakable mockery, señor," Don Juan replied, "by making the temple of Eros an accessory of the cloaca. Only drink and the caress of a thousand women can make us forget the disgust and the indignity."

"Should not a great lover, Don Juan, overcome this fastidiousness—defeat the gods and their mockery, and discover beauty precisely where they had meant to create ugliness?"

He knit his brows and looked at me intently. "What man can do that?"

"I have done it, Don Juan."

He smiled a little bitterly, a little ironically. "Señor, if you have done that, then you are the Supreme Lover of all time—and not Don Juan!"

I smiled. 'How often we speak the truth unwittingly.' I thought. Was I more fortunate than Don Juan merely because I lived longer? Had Nature afforded me such an abundance of life, such torrents of vitality, that all the dikes of ugliness were swept away, and the fresh waters of beauty flooded my being?

"Perhaps," I said, "if our lives were stretched out for centuries, Don Juan, we might discover the secret of outwitting the irony of the gods."

"What an incalculable boredom would overwhelm us then, señor! We might have to possess a million women—and still remain unassuaged."

A servant whispered into Don Juan's ear that the seconds had arrived.

The seconds brought word that any attempt to effect a reconciliation would be futile. Fernando refused to apologize. After they were gone, Don Juan waved his fist. "The idiot! The idiot! He wants to die! He has seen me engaged in many duels. I never received a scar, señor,—never! He has never fought except in play. He was always so gentle and amenable—more delicate than his sister! What mania women have for confessing! Had she kept still about it, her brother would not be dead tomorrow! Ah, let us drink, señor. . . The world's a cackling hen."

We drank one another's health. With every additional cup, Don Juan became more melancholy. I had long ago observed that drink brings forth our true personality which, like a too passionate virgin, is locked within the castle of our beings. Drink is a daring Knight Errant who climbs the tall wall and descends a rope, carrying in his arms our secret.

Don Juan was a gentle lamb, bleating sadly—not a roaring lion of love.

Don Juan sighed. "I do not know why I tell you all this, señor," he said. "It is but the second day I have seen you. Never before have I spoken so freely——"

"I appreciate your confidence, señor."

The servant whispered something into Don Juan's ear.

"No, no—not today."

The servant seemed reluctant to go.

"Not today," Don Juan shouted. "To the devil with her!"

The servant left.

"The amiable Countess expects me."

He laughed suddenly. "I poisoned two dogs, bribed a half dozen servants, and nearly broke my neck climbing into her room. Besides her husband is a favorite of the King. I jeopardized my head to go with her through the absurd motions of conjugation. Why did I risk so much? Señor, she has a beauty spot on her left breast. . . A tiny spot the size of a pinhead. It is really a blemish, an imperfection of the skin,—yet it promised so much! . . . I assure you, señor, she was not one bit different from all the others. I should have known! . . . She was my nine hundred and ninety-seventh."

"Pardon me, Don Juan, but is it really possible to keep an exact record of every amour?"

He laughed. "I have an album, señor, in which I put the initials and the number of each woman with a few remarks, generally of a depreciating nature—too fat, too thin, too white, too dark, too insistent, too cold, bored me at the critical moment, reminded me of a parrot, a dog, a cat. Also the difficulties encountered—the duels fought, the husbands duped, etc., etc."

"A strange document which will be of value to posterity," I remarked.

Don Juan smiled, pleased.

"Many a poet will compose sonnets to the world's master lover. . ."

"But señor,—I have never loved."

"What!" I exclaimed.

"Love . . . love . . . what is love?"

"Not even the first woman who unlocked for you the sweet gateway of love . . . ?"

He shook his head. "Not even the first."

He seemed like a child with countless toys, enjoying none, stamping upon them, casting them aside, bored and irritated.

I too had experimented with many passions. I, too, had experienced the chill of a frozen kiss. But in spite of it, were there not Mary and Salome and Ulrica and Lydia and Damis and John? I had loved them! They had touched, in one way or another, my soul, leaving upon my memory the imprint of their exquisite loveliness. I had loved! I had not lived in vain! Why had Don Juan never loved?

Kotikokura, his eyes heavy, grinned constantly like a statue of mockery.

"Señor, my friend," Don Juan said suddenly, "you have mentioned unendurable pleasure indefinitely prolonged. The phrase sticks in my brain like an arrow."

"Yes," I said vaguely.

"What does it mean? Is it acquired by one of the drugs that the Crusaders have brought from the East, or the Moors from China? I have experimented with all. I have applied them externally; leeches have injected them into my blood; I emptied deep phials. The poppy whose sap I consumed never made me experience unendurable pleasure, or if it seemed unendurable, it was never indefinitely prolonged."

"It is not the poppy, not a drug, señor. Drugs, like apothecary's scales, weigh minutely their pleasures, demanding in return either an equal amount of pain or a diminution of capacity."

"Not a drug?"

He placed his elbows upon the table and looked at me closely. I remained silent.

"Señor, I swear by the cross that if it is a secret, I shall keep it until I am dust within the dust. Don Juan never breaks his promise —to a man."

"Don Juan, unendurable pleasure indefinitely prolonged is possible only for him who loves—woman."

He stared at me.

"It is neither a drug nor an incantation, but a long and profound study, a gradual training, until the senses perceive with the clarity

of an eye, a third eye, an eye that pierces like a sharp tool. It
transmutes the body into a conflagration. . . It turns the vulgar
metal to gold. . ."

Don Juan, his lips parted and brows knit, listened.

"Such knowledge, however, Don Juan, is only for the elect, for
those who truly love—woman."

"Señor," he said, slightly irritably, "this is the second time you
have mentioned the fact that one must love woman. I do not understand."

"Don Juan, is it the truth you seek or polite conversation?"

After a pause, he said a little hoarsely, "From you—the truth."

"The truth, Don Juan, as it appears to me. Naturally, I may be
wrong."

He nodded.

"Don Juan, you do not love woman."

"I have told you that myself."

"You said it without realizing the significance of your confession."

"What is the significance of my words?"

"You do not love woman, or else you would not pursue her
with such vehemence—and bravado. Each new conquest is proclaimed to the world. Don Juan has captured one more! Everybody
smiles, admires, and envies. If you loved woman, you would concentrate, would rejoice in the pleasure afforded by one, not in the
conquest of many. Your multiple amours are merely an attempt to
seek refuge from your own disgust. . ."

Don Juan breathed heavily and tightened his fist around the cup.

"Shall I continue?" I asked.

"Yes."

I realized that what I was about to say would strike him as a
dagger. Why did I not turn the conversation into another channel?
It was still possible. Why did I desire to hurt this man? Was it
simply to notice his reaction, to convince myself that my surmise
was correct,—or was it perhaps a secret resentment against the
enemy of my race . . . ?

"You do not love woman," I insisted, like a prophet of evil.
"Your amorous conquests rise from the endeavor to convince both
yourself and the world that you are capable of loving her, that there
is neither a spiritual nor physical deficiency in you. . ."

"Whom do I love, if not woman . . . ?" he asked, standing up
and glaring at me.

"You have asked me for the truth, señor," I said quietly.

"I beg your pardon." He reseated himself. "I do not know why I should be exasperated. You simply repeat what I told you myself, that I have not *loved* any woman."

I smiled. "Nothing exasperates us so much, señor, as the truth, particularly if we try to conceal it from ourselves. . ."

We remained silent for some time. Don Juan made small circles with his cup. The parrots screeched: "Bienvenido" from time to time drowning the exquisite music of the other birds.

"Señor, whom do I love, if not *woman?*" he asked.

"Perhaps no one now, but at one time—long ago—had you obeyed your nature, you would have preferred— —"

"What?"

"Narcissus-like, you were enamoured of yourself, or the image of yourself—in another man . . . !"

He burst into a hearty laugh but stopped short. "A man! Señor, what a jest! I am the most manly man of Spain, not an effeminate fop. Look at my arms! Touch the muscle! It is iron, señor!"

"Your eternal insistence upon your masculinity proves that you are not sure of yourself. . ."

"It is man's prerogative to be proud of his manhood. . ."

"When one is certain of it, it is unnecessary for him to emphasize its existence."

"Señor," he shouted, "you presume too much. . ."

"I merely obeyed your desire for my opinion. . ."

"That is right. Forgive me. I am an ungracious host."

I bowed.

"But what proof have you, señor, for your fantastic assertion?"

"Why are you so upset about Don Fernando, señor? Is he the first man you have killed in a duel . . . ?"

"He is so young. . ."

"Is he the youngest you have ever fought . . . ?"

"No."

"Well, then. . ."

"He was my friend. . ."

"And he resembles his sister as two drops of water resemble each other."

"How do you know, señor?"

"Everybody in Córdoba knows it."

"Supposing that were true,—what bearing has it upon your preposterous statement?"

"You would rather kill the sister than the boy . . . ?"

"Even if that were true, what then . . . ?"

"Don Juan, if you dared to look into your soul, you would see there . . . that you made love to the sister to escape from the brother. . . You love the man, not the woman."

"Señor!" he shouted, and struck the table a powerful blow.

Kotikokura awakened with a start. Don Juan was about to strike the table again when Kotikokura jumped forward and grasped his arm.

"How dare you!" Don Juan shouted. I made no sign. Kotikokura released his arm.

"Don Juan," I said, "if a guest's opinion so upsets his host, it is best for the guest to withdraw."

He became almost sentimental. "Forgive me, señor. Wine and the harrowing experiences of the day paralyze my understanding, and crush the instinctive hospitality of a Spanish gentleman. I beg you not to go." He stretched out his hand which I shook.

He clapped his hands. A servant entered.

"Jaime, go fetch Mahmud the Moor and his band. Tell him to bring a few dancers, men and women. Tonight we dine in the garden and make merry in honor of our guests."

The servant left.

Don Juan laughed, slapping his thighs. "Señor, you are magnificent! What you said was almost convincing. Your sense of humor is as keen as a blade. Your love of paradox is delightful. I am very fortunate to have met you." Turning to Kotikokura, "And you, señor—your fist is more powerful than steel. You nearly broke my arm. I congratulate you. One more cup, gentlemen, to our most catholic King and to—Woman!"

We drank. Don Juan recounted gallant anecdotes and amorous escapades. He laughed uproariously, but his eyes were melancholy and distracted.

The field of honor was a secluded spot on the outskirts of Córdoba. We drove in silence. Don Juan's face was drawn. The two long wrinkles on either cheek dug deep channels. The white spot upon his forehead appeared and disappeared at intervals. He kept his eyes closed. I knew that his fatigue was not due to the previous night's revelry—a very simple affair—but to my words which had been sharper and had struck deeper than the sword thrusts he was wont to administer to his adversaries.

I regretted having spoken. A mere mortal cannot endure the truth, uncoated with the sweets of illusion. It was too late to undo the harm. I had a premonition that Don Juan's last day had come.

Don Fernando and his seconds were waiting for us. The young man pretended a nonchalance out of harmony with the trembling of his body which he attributed to the morning chill. Don Juan scrutinized him, neither as an enemy nor as a friend, but as if endeavoring to discover whether what I had told him was true or false. He breathed deeply. Both the strange, affectionate attitude and the fury he had exhibited at their previous meeting, had disappeared. The lassitude of complete disillusionment possessed the great lover.

By the manner in which Don Juan handled his weapon, it was immediately evident that he was a master swordsman. Don Fernando was obviously a novice. Nervous, irritable, he exhibited the awkwardness characteristic of women in any purely masculine sport. Indeed, one might have taken him for a young girl in disguise, with his white skin, his delicate neck, whose Adam's apple was merely a dot that shivered nervously, his chest deeply indented in the center and bulging on either side, his arms rounded and hairless. . .

Upon three occasions in quick succession, Don Juan's sword touched his opponent's chest. Three times Fernando was at his mercy. One pressure, and the battle would have been ended. Don Fernando waved his sword wildly, striking always either the ground or the steel of his enemy.

Don Juan smiled faintly. He made small inconsequent movements, uncovering his chest. Was it a deliberate gesture, fatigue of life? Did he realize that he could no longer endure existence . . . ?

Fernando waved his weapon wildly, erratically. Suddenly, unexpectedly, it touched Don Juan. With the desperation of the tyro who sees himself vanquished, the boy forced it until half of it disappeared in the body of Don Juan. Then, surprised and awed by what had happened, he unclasped his hand from the hilt and stared, his mouth open.

Don Juan, closing his eyes in agony, tottered and fell. His mouth, flushed with blood, was contracted into a diabolic grin. His eyes rolled backward and glared at us with their whites, like newly polished porcelain.

The physician proclaimed him dead, killed in a lawful duel by Don Fernando in the presence of witnesses.

But I knew that I was his murderer.

LIII

I RETURN TO THE FOLD—AN ENCOUNTER IN THE GHETTO—THE RABBI'S DAUGHTER

THE gate that led Kotikokura and me to the Ghetto was of Moorish origin,—a fine piece of workmanship now almost in total ruins. From one pillar, the black mortar dripped slowly to the ground like blood from a fatal wound. The other shook under the weight of my hand. The top was garlanded by many birds' nests from which now and then a tiny inhabitant tried his unfledged wings.

On the side of the gate, which faced Córdoba proper, were carved and pointed threats against the Jews. On the opposite side in Hebrew letters, anathemas against the Christians, prayers, and prophecies of destruction.

Small ugly huts, surrounded by yards crowded with débris, goats, cows, and now and then a horse whose ribs pressed against his skin like the taut strings of a grotesque harp. Bearded men, their hands hidden within the sleeves of their long kaftans, their backs bent as if carrying an invisible load. Women with black shawls as if in perpetual mourning. Dilapidated shops upon the threshold of which the owners sat and gossiped with neighbors. Rickety carts dragged wearily through the mud by long-horned oxen or donkeys. Children —countless children—dirty, naked, noisy, ringlets over their cheeks or long braids upon their backs knotted with bits of string.

A thick stench—the stench of ancient and hopeless penury.

I stopped a young man and asked him to direct us to the home of Rabbi Sholom.

"I am going to the synagogue which is opposite our Rabbi's dwelling. If you will allow me, I shall show you the way."

I thanked him and bade him walk at my side.

The young man sighed from time to time. It sounded like the sighing of the Jews of Jerusalem, the sighing of hopelessness and futility.

'Will this always be the symbol of my race?' I thought.

277

"Is it true," the young man asked, "that Don Juan was killed in a duel?"

"Yes."

"Thank God."

"Why?"

"Rumor said that he planned to steal the daughter of our Rabbi, and kill everyone who defended her."

"Don't you exaggerate, señor?" I asked. "Are not your people somewhat too sensitive?"

"Sensitive?" He laughed ironically. "Is not a man whose skin has been flayed necessarily sensitive?"

He threw his head back. His face uncovered from the blond curls, disclosed a head emaciated and delicate.

I forgot that I was Cartaphilus, centuries old, walking in the ghetto of Córdoba. It seemed to me that I was Isaac, a youth of Jerusalem, walking with a companion of my age, talking about the Jews and their conquerors—the Romans.

Little merchants with baskets on their arms or upon their backs called out their wares from time to time. Here and there, groups of men discussed clamorously either their business or some difficult passage of the Talmud.

A woman, a pot in her hand, ran past us. Another woman stopped her.

"Where are you running, Sarah?"

"My clumsy husband has spilt some milk into the soup. I am going over to the Rabbi's to ask him if we may eat it, and if I can continue to use the pot for meat after this."

"Our men too," sighed the youth, "squabble and fight about trifles without consequence. My people have degenerated into ants seeking invisible crumbs while the feast is forgotten."

"But they are not allowed to go to the feast——"

"True, true," he sighed. "They are not allowed to go to the feast." Suddenly, however, he waved his thin, almost transparent hands. "Let them make a feast of their own! Let them show the merry-makers on the other side of the gate that they——" He stopped short. "It is ridiculous, señor, it cannot be done." He coughed, and sighed profoundly. "It cannot be done."

"Is it so difficult to get beyond the gate?"

He looked at me. "Difficult? It all depends. To some to deny their faith is very easy, to others death is preferable."

"Is denial of faith the only way?"

He nodded.

"A Jew remains a Jew, even if he accepts Christianity. Does the body," I asked, "change because the dress is different?"

He twisted one of his curls. "Who knows? Perhaps, after all, that stupid woman running with her pot to the Rabbi is right. Meticulous observance of trifles enables the race to persist."

We reached Rabbi Sholom's house. The woman with the pot of soup, now covered with a heavy coat of grease, emerged, her eyes dazzling with joy.

"What a man our Rabbi is! An angel, I tell you! What a man!"

The young man was about to bid me farewell.

"Your conversation has interested me a great deal, señor," I said to him. "It may be that I shall remain in the Ghetto. . ."

"Remain in the Ghetto?" he asked astonished.

I nodded. "I should like to have the pleasure of speaking to you again. May I know with whom I have the honor— —?"

He looked at me, unable to overcome his surprise and perhaps also, suspicion.

"My name, señor, is Joseph Ben Israel—a student."

"My name is—Isaac."

I extended my hand which he seemed reluctant to take for a moment. Then suddenly, he pressed it in his and rushed away.

Rabbi Sholom was sitting in a large armchair, underneath which the straw had gathered into a small heap. Two wooden benches on either side of him, and in a corner piled on a large table old books and manuscripts.

The Rabbi, a man of about fifty, dressed in white linen and felt shoes, rose and approached us.

"Welcome, señores."

"Rabbi, we are strangers—travelers. We arrived only a few days ago in Córdoba."

"Does Córdoba please you?"

"A beautiful city, indeed."

"I have not visited it for many years."

"Is that possible?"

"The younger generation dislikes our people. It is not prudent to irritate one's masters."

His voice betokened neither irony nor anger, merely resignation—resignation mingled with confidence. His eyes were deeply set and clear as a child's

"Is it not possible that the younger generation will realize that it is better to love than to hate their neighbors?"

Rabbi Sholom combed his beard with his fingers and shook his head. "This hatred is too young. It is still a little clumsy. It will increase and overthrow the last dikes. Only then may we hope for a reaction, for a better understanding."

Who was this man who could view unflinchingly misery and hatred? His features reminded me of no one, but his voice seemed familiar. Whose was it? I sought within my mind, as one seeks in a long dark attic, lighted only at intervals by the cracks in the walls.

A yellow curtain, faded and torn in a few places, was drawn aside slowly, and a young woman entered. Her hair, whose black glistened like a raven's wing, was woven into two long braids that hung down her back.

"I am busy now, my daughter," the Rabbi said in Hebrew. "I shall call you when I have finished."

She looked at me, blushed, and walked out. She was evidently the girl that had attracted the eye of Don Juan. It was for her he died,—for had it not been for his desire to possess her, I should not have spoken of the things that unnerved him. Don Juan died for a Jewess!

"Is it permissible, señor," the Rabbi asked, "to inquire from what country you come?"

"I come from many countries, including the Holy Land."

Rabbi Sholom opened wide his eyes. "The Holy Land?"

"Yes, Rabbi. Many times did I pass by the Temple—at least, the site of it."

He sighed. "The Temple."

"As an aged mother awaits patiently until the long hours of the night the arrival of a straying son, so the soil of Jerusalem awaits the return of Israel."

"You speak kindly of us and our misery, señor. We have so long been taught to fear the Gentile that— —" he smiled sadly.

"Rabbi," I said in Hebrew, "it is not a Gentile who is speaking to you—but a Jew."

He stood up, stared at me and breathed heavily.

"A Jew who has wandered into the enemy's camp, but who has never in his heart accepted the enemy's gods."

"Adonai be praised! But is it really true what you are saying, my son?"

I raised my arm. "I am Isaac Ben Jehuda who has wandered from land to land, without renouncing in his heart the faith of his fathers."

He approached and embraced me. "Sholom Alechim."

"Alechim Sholom," I answered.

"And your companion, Isaac?"

"He is neither a Jew nor a Christian, but an adherent of Ishmael."

"A cousin. . ."

"A cousin and a friend."

He extended his hand which Kotikokura raised to his lips.

"Rabbi," I said, "I am weary of travel. I am weary of being a stranger. I yearn to return to the fold. Will you accept me?"

"Israel is like an aged father waiting into the late hours of the night for the arrival of his wandering son," he said smiling.

"Rabbi, the wandering son has come with an impoverished heart, but not with an empty purse. May he be permitted to show his joy by helping his brothers crushed by the cruelty of the enemy?"

"Isaac, my son, had you returned as poor as a beggar, the joy of your brothers would not be less. But if you can help us in our misery, it is God Himself in His unbounded wisdom who chose the right hour." He clapped his hands. The sexton entered.

"Rejoice, Abraham, the lost sheep has returned to the fold! Make it known to all that Rabbi Sholom is as happy as when his daughter was born unto him! Let all men and women come to his synagogue where they shall receive wine and cake in honor of their brother! Blow the shofar in praise of the Lord."

Abraham ran out.

Rabbi Sholom drew aside the curtain and called out: "Esther, Esther, my daughter."

The girl came in, frightened a little.

"What is it, father?"

He kissed her forehead. "Do not fear, my dear. The Lord has led the steps of a lost son back to our house."

She looked at me, lowered her lids, and blushed.

LIV

THE BOOK OF ESTHER—THE VENGEANCE OF DON JUAN —KOTIKOKURA THE GOLEM—THE PLAGUE—THE SUICIDE OF JOSEPH—I ABJURE ISRAEL

THE feast lasted several days. I ordered unlimited food and drink and distributed gifts to all. Tables were spread in the yards and streets. Musicians with improvised instruments—pots, pans, iron and wooden sticks, flutes, one-string harps, made a ceaseless noise to which men and women, old and young, danced, their feet raised to their chins, or waved wildly in the air, clapping their hands the while. Only the morning and evening services interrupted the merry-making. The prayers were mumbled, the words half pronounced or omitted. Years of hunger and dreariness were smothered and stamped under foot.

"Rabbi Sholom," I said one evening, "you have received me as a son."

"You are my son."

"Are not the arms of woman as the ivy which winds itself about the trunk of the tree, keeping it rooted to the spot? Is not a single man like a bird always ready to fly away?"

"A single man is indeed as a bird."

"Rabbi, be my father indeed. Give me your daughter Esther as wife. Let me be rooted to my people for all time."

Rabbi Sholom smoothed his beard and meditated.

"Isaac, my daughter is more precious to me than the apple of my eye. I tremble before I open my mouth to say: 'Take her,' lest——"
He closed his eyes.

"Father, she shall be no less precious to me than to you."

Esther entered. Rabbi Sholom rose. "Approach, my daughter."
She obeyed.

"I love you more dearly than my life. You are my comfort and my joy. But the time has come when God commands you to be a mother in Israel. . ."

"Father," she said, pressing her head in his bosom.

I could not tell whether her voice denoted sorrow or joy.

"Our son Isaac—Isaac Laquedem—has asked for your hand in marriage. It is in my power to command you to take him. But he who uses his power against the will of his subordinate is a tyrant, not a father."

He patted her hand.

"Esther, do you desire to be the wife of Isaac?"

She nodded.

Rabbi Sholom embraced me. Greater than the delight of possessing a beautiful woman was the vanity of having vanquished Don Juan. Poor Don Juan!

Esther was as gentle and as faithful as Lydia, but found passion's rites, save those sanctioned by custom, abhorrent. The nuances of love, the subtle delicacies of the senses, she refused to learn. She clipped her beautiful hair much against my wishes, and covered her head with a black wig which seemed dusty always. Her meticulous insistence upon every trifle of the dogma palled upon me and her daily prayer that I raise a beard irritated me immensely.

Kotikokura who observed this, seemed to wait for a sign to dispose of her as he had disposed of some of my women in the Harem of a Thousand Graves.

Esther, with a woman's intuition scented his enmity. "Isaac, Kotikokura is not one of our people. Why should he remain with us?"

"He has saved my life on several occasions when the Gentiles discovered that I was a Jew."

"Pay him and let him go. Our people hate him. He has desecrated the synagogue by his bare head, and the Sabbath by riding on a donkey."

"He is not a Jew. It is lawful for him."

"Why should the daughter of Rabbi Sholom harbor one who is not a Jew, Isaac? It is for this reason, no doubt, that God refuses to give us children. We are tempting the Lord, Isaac! The women whisper that I am unfruitful. . . I shall soon be ashamed to face the world."

Every day and several times a day, she found occasion to speak against Kotikokura.

"Kotikokura, I have become a proverbial husband, disputing with his wife. Don Juan is avenged."

Kotikokura grinned, tightening his fists.

"No, no, my friend. It is not necessary—not yet."

My only friend was Joseph Ben Israel, the student I had met when I entered the Ghetto. We discussed for hours the bigotry of our people. He himself was not entirely free. Once I mentioned the beauty of images and the art of the Gentiles.

"You lived too long away from the truth," he exclaimed, "and you have become too tolerant of blasphemy."

I smiled sadly. "Joseph, it is too difficult for a man to cast off his environment. Having breathed the mouldy air of the Ghetto you cannot fully appreciate the deliciousness of fresh air. . ."

He stayed away for several days. One evening he returned. He pressed my hand to his lips. His face was drawn and white.

"Forgive me, Isaac. I have contradicted my wise brother. I am a fool and an ingrate."

I patted his hand. "Isaac bears no ill will."

"I have repented for it. For three days I fasted."

"That was quite unnecessary."

"It was, on the contrary, very necessary." He kissed my hand again.

"Joseph, have you no desire to go beyond the gate?"

"I desire to be with you always."

He covered his face and wept quietly. The shape of his head, his curls, reminded me of John, of Damis and of Walhallath, a boy whom I had known in Palmyra.

He looked up. "Isaac, you will leave, and I shall be forsaken. . . ."

"Why do you say I will leave?"

"I know it. You are cramped here as a man in a tomb."

"It does not matter. I shall remain. I shall try to break the walls of the tomb. Both my people and I shall breathe more freely. . ."

He sighed and shook his head. "Our people are obstinate, Isaac, and they mistrust you."

"Have I not given them money? Have I not helped the widows and the orphans?"

"They do not understand why you are good to them. They do not know how you obtained the money. Some consider you a spy and others regard you as a magician. Your companion they fear. They think he is a golem—a creature you have made out of yellow clay who obeys you like a machine and who is strong enough to destroy the town. . . One saw him uproot a tree, another raise a donkey with one hand, a third one, hurl a rock against the ground, and the rock disappeared."

I laughed.

"They even suspect me."

I consoled him. "Joseph, if ever I should go beyond the gate—will you come with me?"

He did not answer for a long while.

"Can one remain a Jew there?" he asked at last.

"One must at least pretend that one is not."

"Wherever you go, I go, Isaac."

Within two days, four men died of violent cramps. The Ghetto forgot its quarrels and its petty intrigues, and battered the doors of the Rabbi. "The plague! The plague! Pray to God to spare us! You are a holy man—pray!"

The synagogue was crowded to the brim. Rabbi Sholom, barefooted and covered in a shroud, called to God to spare his people. The shofar was blown seven times. The congregation beat their breasts. The women sobbed violently.

Two men fell dead on the threshold of the Holy House. The people scattered, shouting and waving their arms.

Rabbi Sholom asked a dozen men to confer with him. They shouted their opinions at the top of their voices. The fault lay in the sinfulness of the city and the lack of proper reverence for Yahweh. They suggested prayers, incantations, and sackcloth and ashes.

I entered the room. An ominous silence ensued. The men retreated and skulked. Rabbi Sholom, a little irritably asked, "What brings you here, my son?"

"Why do you ask me this, father? Is it not evident?"

"It is only for men who have spent their lives in the study of the Torah to discover why the Lord punishes us."

"You saw that even while you prayed, two men fell dead."

"Our sins are great!"

"The dirt and the squalor are greater."

"It is God's way of purifying our souls."

"God has given us water to purify our bodies."

"If our souls were pure, our bodies would need no purification."

"Very true," the Chasidim whispered to one another. "Very true. Our souls must be pure."

"Father, while you discuss the soul and its purification, our people die of the plague."

"It is God's will."

"Our obstinacy was our undoing, father. Even in the time of the Romans— —"

"May their memory perish!" Rabbi Sholom interrupted.

The others repeated: "May their memory perish!"

"Father, I am a Jew and have our people at heart."

There was grumbling among the Chasidim. I stared at them. They huddled together.

"Do you doubt, father, that I am a Jew?"

"How should I doubt it since I gave you my daughter in marriage?"

"Have I not proved my love for our people? Have I not given charity? Have I not— —?"

"It is not by charity that one shows love but by leading a godly life."

"Yes, yes," the others remarked.

"Have I not led a godly life, father?"

"Only the Lord can read our hearts. But there have been many complaints against you, my son."

"Complaints?"

"You are clean-shaven. Should not a Jew wear a beard? Should he rebuke God for causing hair to grow upon man's face? You have a Gentile friend."

"The golem! The golem!" some whispered.

"You object to your wife's wig. Should a virtuous woman look like a wanton? It pains me, Isaac, to tell you these things in public."

"Father, whatever the complaints against me may be, and however true, this is no time for words. Hearken to me! I have lived in many lands. I have seen many things, including plagues. Let me help my people. Let me save them from suffering and death."

"How are you capable of doing this, when our holy men know no remedy?"

"I shall pay large sums of money to physicians to come from the other side of the gate. I shall supply the funds necessary for purifying the sources of water and other necessities of life."

"But if our souls be impure, how can physicians purify us?"

"They know means by which the pestilence may be stopped. Later, we shall attend to our souls."

The Chasidim shook their heads.

"You begin at the end, Isaac."

"At least for the time being, the people should not gather in the synagogue. They infect one another."

"What?" the Chasidim shouted.

"Isaac!" the Rabbi admonished. "Not foregather in the synagogue? Not pray to the Lord in time of sorrow?"

"You are not a Jew!" one Chasid exclaimed, rising and pointing his forefinger at me. "You are not a Jew! Your words are the Devil's words and your advice is the advice of one who wishes to destroy our race!"

He stopped suddenly, pressing his hands upon his stomach, groaning with pain.

"He is the Devil!" some shouted.

"He has looked at him with his evil eye!"

"Look away, everyone!"

"He will kill us all!"

They turned their backs upon me and hid their faces. Rabbi Sholom covered his head with a tallith.

Late at night, Joseph entered my room on tiptoes.

"Isaac," he whispered, "Isaac—leave at once! They are planning to kill you and Kotikokura. They blame you for the plague. They claim that your evil eye killed a Chasid."

"I know, Joseph. I shall leave. Will you accompany me?"

He looked at me, his eyes filled with tears.

"Come with me, Joseph! The world is beautiful."

He looked at me reproachfully.

I placed my hands upon his shoulders. "Joseph, you are like the friends of my youth, long ago—longer than you imagine. It is for their sake I cherish you. Believe me, I am neither the Devil nor a magician. I do not mean to destroy your soul, but to show you the way to discover it."

He wept bitterly.

Kotikokura meanwhile was becoming impatient.

"Do not fear, Kotikokura, we have time enough to escape."

He looked at Joseph angrily.

"At most, he can be with us a few paltry years," I whispered.

Kotikokura grinned, pacified.

"Meet me at the gate, on the stroke of twelve!"

Joseph nodded and left.

As we reached the road that led to the gate, we saw dangling from a withered tree, like an immense and grotesque cat or monkey, the body of a man. We approached. The body remained perfectly still. Kotikokura, whose eyes glittered in the dark like a tiger's, recognized Joseph.

"Perhaps he is not dead yet. We may be able to save him."

Kotikokura began to climb up the tree.

I stopped him. "Don't! It is best not to disturb him. He can never overcome his environment; nor can he accept it again. Poor Joseph symbolizes his own existence—suspended between two worlds and belonging to neither!"

We walked along the shore of the Guadalquivir. The sun had not yet risen, but wide strips of red were already visible on the horizon. Here and there, upon the river, a fisherman's boat turned lightly about itself. From time to time, a dog barked and a cock crowed. Sea-gulls, fat and slick, uttered ominous screams.

"Kotikokura, you have seen my people and you have not found them to your taste."

He nodded.

"Poverty is like a horse's hoofs crushing delicate flowers. You must not judge my people too severely."

He nodded.

"Perhaps it was my fault, Kotikokura. I was indeed as a son returning to his parental roof. I was offered the toys and dishes I had enjoyed as a child,—but I am no longer a child."

He nodded.

"In the Christian world, I am not a Christian. Among the Mohammedans, I am a stranger. To the Jews, I seem a wicked magician, bringing about the plague. I do not belong anywhere, Kotikokura," I sighed.

Kotikokura sighed also.

"But that is the destiny of man. I am Man—and man is always a stranger among men. I am not the Wandering Jew, but the Wandering Man."

"Ca-ta-pha—god; Kotikokura—high priest."

"God or man,—I am. Life is. We are two parallel lines, running on always—perhaps. Life knows no favorites. Henceforth I shall know neither creed nor race. I am free, Kotikokura! Free!" I shouted.

Kotikokura echoed: "Free!"

"Kill the Jews! Burn the Ghetto! Drive the dogs into the sea!"

Córdoba had become a giant mouth, vituperating and threatening the Jews.

"Kotikokura, before long, there will be much slaughter here. We must seek fairer shores. Come!"

LV

THE QUEEN PAWNS HER JEWELS—I DO BUSINESS WITH ABRAHAM—I FINANCE COLUMBUS

THE snow fell leisurely, in tiny flakes like confetti. The sun shone, but a little dimly like an eye opening after sleep. The bells of all the churches rang. The people threw their hats into the air, shouting: "Long live the King!" A regiment of infantry preceded by officers on horseback passed by, laughing and calling their women. Children turned little wooden toys that made a deafening noise.

We entered a wine-shop crowded with people.

"What say you, Magister, to the notion that the earth is round and that we can reach the Indies by water?"

The Magister, an old shriveled up individual, toothless and almost gumless, piped: "Nonsense! There is nothing about it in Aristotle."

"But Marco Polo, Magister, claims— —"

"Who is Marco Polo? Who is anybody? Aristotle never said that the earth is round!"

"Cristóbal Colón is pledging his head and the heads of all his sailors— —"

"Nonsense!"

"They say that the Queen is willing to sell her jewels to finance his wild expedition."

"Women are always credulous."

"If it prove true, Spain will become the richest nation in the world, rivaling Rome in the days of her greatest glory."

"If—If—" the Magister repeated. "I have always taught my pupils to detest that word! The earth is flat. Aristotle— —"

A Jew entered. He was short, stout, and breathed heavily through his mouth. His beard, the color of carrots, sprinkled with threads of white, did not hide his heavy sensuous lips. His eyes, small and deeply set, shone like beads which supplant the lost luminaries of stuffed birds. His kaftan was threadbare and covered with grease spots.

"The Jew! The Jew!" a few called out.

"Make him eat pork."

"Give him the cross to kiss—the circumcised dog!"

"Put him on the rack!"

One of the soldiers pulled the Jew's beard. The other spat in his face. The Jew wiped himself and remained unperturbed.

The Innkeeper seemed unusually cordial to him.

"Give me another month's time, Abraham. I could not get the money together. What with the wars, and my wife's sickness— —"

Abraham waved his hand. "I know. I know. I have not come for that. I am looking for two merchants that have recently arrived in Granada."

"Two merchants?"

Abraham espied us.

"They look like foreigners, do they not?" he asked the Inn keeper.

The Innkeeper nodded. "Yes. With all the crowd here, I did not notice them."

"Will you ask them to be good enough to meet me outside?"

Abraham walked out.

The Innkeeper came over. "Señores," he whispered, "the Jew who has just been here—he is the richest merchant in Granada—begs to speak to you. He is waiting outside."

"Very well."

Abraham bowed several times, his small stubby hands upon his belly.

"Welcome, señores, to Granada. Welcome! Welcome!"

He reminded me of Don Juan's parrot.

"The gentlemen come from a long journey, do they not?"

"Yes, a very long journey."

He rubbed his hands. They produced no noise, as if they had been oiled.

"India?" he asked, smiling obsequiously.

"Yes."

"Ah, how fortunate am I to have the honor of speaking to gentlemen who come from India! Was the trip very long?"

"Very long."

"And dangerous too, I presume."

I nodded.

He clicked his tongue. "How much courage is required to travel! How many are lost on the way!"

I nodded.

"Marco Polo tells such terrible things, señor—but such marvels, too."

"I have not read his book."

"No? Is it possible? *'Mirabilia Mundi'* he calls it. I have not read it either. It is written in Latin. We are allowed to read only the holy language, señor. But a friend of mine, a bishop——" he grinned, "he owes me some money—related Marco Polo's adventures to me."

I looked at his boots, torn and muddy up to his knees. He smiled, raising his palm. "We must not judge by appearances, señor. But ask about Abraham in Granada, and outside of Granada—and you will hear what you will hear." He pulled my sleeve. "I do business even with Her Majesty, the Queen." He walked away a step or two, and bowed. He approached again. "With Her Majesty."

"Indeed?"

"I do not mean that I go to the palace or that I am invited to the royal banquets." He laughed. His teeth were yellow and long as wisps of hay. "But I supply the money. I am not such a rich man. But I can manage. It is not easy, but I can manage. A nobleman transacts the affairs with Her Majesty and I supply the money."

The snow ceased falling. The sun shone like a newly gilded platter. Soldiers and civilians, arm in arm, vociferated their joy, now considerably augmented by Bacchus.

"Señor," Abraham said suddenly, "come with me. Away from the crowd. I have a proposition which I am sure will interest you. Only who can speak in this noise? Will you come, señor? I know a small wine-shop where we can speak at leisure."

"I am not particularly interested in the business."

"Of course, señor. But if something wonderful is presented to you."

I deliberated for a few moments. "All right, let us go."

He tried to keep pace with me; his large flat feet kept at a wide angle, stamped the ground like the flapping of a giant bird's wings.

The wine-shop was a dingy place in a cellar. The proprietor, a Jew whose face was overshadowed by his enormous nose, bowed so low to us that I feared he would strike his head against the stone floor.

We entered a small room. Abraham ordered wine and instructed the proprietor not to permit anyone to disturb us.

Abraham filled the cups.

"You will like the wine, señor. It is very old. You cannot find a better vintage in Granada. The scoundrel charges me enough good money for it."

Abraham smacked his lips and rubbed his hands. "So! Now we can talk better."

"What, in short, is the business in which you would like to interest me, Abraham?"

"A gentleman's time is very valuable, I know, and life is too short to spend in such company as mine. I shall come to the point at once."

I nodded.

"I do not know whether the earth is round or flat. What has Abraham to do with such matters? That he leaves to sailors and queens and wise people. Abraham must provide money—isn't it so?"

I nodded.

"But he does not live in Zipangu where the chamber-pots—forgive the expression—are made of gold. He lives in Spain where even Her Majesty finds a lack of that beautiful metal. And if she finds a lack of it, why should not Abraham?"

I nodded.

"Well, your time is precious, señor, and I am jabbering away. Well —this is the business: Her Majesty—may she prosper forever— wishes to sell her jewels that a certain sailor or admiral, Cristóbal Colón, an Italian or a Portuguese, may buy enough boats and hire enough men to go to India by water."

"By water?"

"He says that the earth is round and if a man travels far enough on the sea, he will reach the other side of the world. I do not understand it, but I know that the Queen's jewels are worth many times the money asked for them. But there is not a man in Granada who has the required gold. The wars have impoverished everyone, señor —everyone."

"What makes Cristóbal Colón think that the earth is round?"

"Who knows, señor? The Queen is convinced. That is sufficient. Besides, for more information about the matter, I can refer you to Don Ricardo in whose care the jewels are at present—provided, of course, you are really interested in the business and are able to furnish the funds."

"What made you believe that I might be interested or that I might possess such funds?"

"Ah, señor, I have an eye that sees, an ear that hears, and a nose that smells."

"Take me to Don Ricardo."

Don Ricardo's castle, situated upon a hill, was smothered by pine trees. He had suffered from lung trouble in his youth, Abraham explained, and the physicians had advised him to breathe the pure air of the pine.

"You could never tell now that he had ever been ill. He is stronger than one of his trees."

Don Ricardo received us in his study. He was tall, straight as a tree indeed, and wore a short pointed beard, black as ink.

Abraham kissed his hand and remained bent during his entire stay.

"Don Ricardo, this is the señor, the foreign nobleman who is desirous to see Her Majesty's jewels."

I introduced myself.

Don Ricardo asked me how I liked Spain and Granada in particular; what I thought of one thing or another. We spoke at random for some time. Don Ricardo made a sign to Abraham who walked out, his back to the door.

Don Ricardo showed me a map and a plan of the trip. I was delighted to see to what extent my mathematical calculations coincided with the new conception of the earth's geography.

Don Ricardo continued. "The Queen is convinced, and the Admiral certain of the outcome of the enterprise. Besides, he who buys the jewels has nothing to risk. They are worth much more than the sum demanded."

He unlocked an iron box and took out two cases of jewels—diamonds, pearls, emeralds, sapphires, rubies. Among them, I recognized a necklace and a pair of earrings that I had sold some centuries previously to the mistress of a Cardinal.

Don Ricardo mentioned a price. I raised my hands and laughed a little. "Don Ricardo," I said, "thinks me Midas himself."

He praised the jewels, bade me examine them closely, related the history of some, including the necklace which he attributed to a Moorish Empress.

"Señor," he said, "I am not capable of bargaining. Abraham, the Jew, will conduct the negotiations."

"Very well, señor. I need at least a week or two to dispose of certain properties before I can even propose a sum."

We exchanged greetings.

For three weeks, Abraham pitted his wits against mine. He sweated, breathed heavily, swore in Hebrew and in Spanish, cringed and threatened. I was determined to vanquish him.

"Señor, you are cleverer than a hundred Jews combined!" he exclaimed.

I smiled. "The cleverness of the Jew is largely an illusion and a Christian superstition. By the way, Abraham, is it true that the Queen intends to drive all Jews out of her dominions?"

"Her Majesty knows best what is just."

"Where could the Jews go if they are driven out?"

He sighed. His small eyes glistened with tears. "The Lord of Israel will discover new lands for His People. Perhaps India—if Colón is right."

'This is still another reason why I must buy these jewels,' I thought.

"The country which drives out her Jews does not fare well, señor. Egypt perished, and other nations too. We may be hated and made slaves. We have sinned in the sight of God, but to be driven out——" He sighed. "Her Majesty knows best."

'And I shall know still better,' I thought. 'I shall see whether in truth a country can prosper without its Jews.'

The negotiations were finally terminated and Cristóbal Colón was provided with funds.

"Meanwhile, Kotikokura, we must continue our travels. We shall hear of the Admiral's success or his failure when the time is ripe."

LVI

GILLES DE RETZ IN PARIS—TREVISAN DOES A MIRACLE —I DISCUSS THE ELIXIR OF LIFE WITH GILLES DE RETZ—"YOU ARE MY BROTHER"—BLUEBEARD'S WIFE—MY PUPIL ANNE

CHARLES VI was no longer seated precariously upon the edge of his throne, the English no longer menaced France with an invasion, and the ashes of the Maid of Arc were cold and sparkless. The Parisians could devote themselves to the brewing of the elixir which would give them eternal youth and the Philosopher's Stone. Everybody toyed with magic. Thirty thousand sorcerers were reputed to be in Paris.

Every morning someone whispered into someone's ear that by nightfall, his formula would be perfected, that the last and thinnest veil that separated mankind from the Great Truth would be pierced.

Meanwhile, the Seine flowed on.— At night, the stars slumbered upon it; at noon, the sun sprawled upon it; and from time to time, barges and boats cut across its breast, like long blunt knives.

Riding on a black charger, Monsieur Gilles de Laval, Lord of Retz and Maréchal de France, arrived in Paris. Two hundred horsemen followed him. A bishop, a dean, vicars, arch-deacons, and chaplains preceded. They were dressed luxuriously in robes of scarlet and furs, according to rank, and carried crucifixes of gold and silver, encrusted with jewels. Twenty-five choristers sang litanies and triumphant marches.

The snow fell steadily, and Gilles de Retz, either unwilling to wet his face, or deep in meditation, kept his head upon his chest. Only his beard was visible,—a magnificent growth of hair, metallic in its blueness and combed like an Assyrian monarch's.

Bernard Trevisan, of Padua, magician and alchemist, had invited the Lord to his castle, on the outskirts of the capital, situated so close to the shore of the Seine, that its shadow head downward forever bathed in its waters.

Gilles de Retz came to Paris to sell the seignory of Ingrande, in spite of the protest of his presumptive heirs, to obtain funds for his experiments and his household. But perhaps more important to the Maréchal was the promise of Trevisan to perform the famous miracle of Albertus Magnus—the change of seasons; also his desire to meet me. I had introduced myself to Trevisan, to Nicholas Flamel, whose real age no one knew, and to Francis Prelati, a countryman of Trevisan, deeply versed in black magic, as an adept from India.

The guests were invited into the garden where the table was set for the banquet. The snow had stopped falling, but the ground and the trees were thickly covered with it. The Count of Raymond was indignant and threatened to leave.

Trevisan smiled. "Everything will be well, Count. May I ask you for a little patience?"

The guests, shivering, seated themselves,—the Maréchal at the head of the table, Trevisan at his right, and I at his left.

Gilles de Retz was sad. His face, pale and devastated by thought and debauchery, retained traces of an almost unearthly beauty, and his eyes still possessed a child-like wonderment. At moments, they darted a curious, almost maniacal light. His proximity pleased me. Was it his animal magnetism or was it some forlorn memory of the past? He had not uttered a word. His voice might have solved the riddle for me. The voice revealed to me at times, like lightning, the whole personality.

Bernard Trevisan rose, closed his eyes in meditation, and stretched slowly his right arm. Suddenly a scepter, studded at intervals with rubies and emeralds, rose from the depths of the earth, balancing itself gently, until his hand grasped it.

He opened his eyes, and smiled enigmatically. The guests applauded, whispering words of admiration to one another.

Trevisan raised the staff above his head and waved it three times to each of the cardinal points of the compass. Then he stamped the ground with it nine times in measured beats, uttering words of the Kabala mingled with sounds whose origin I could not guess for the moment.

The guests riveted their attention upon his movements, breathless.

'A little hypnotism,' I thought, 'is always a serviceable thing.'

Bernard Trevisan exclaimed in a commanding voice, that seemed to come from the depths of a barrel: "Retire, Winter! Release thy grip! Retire! Let it be Summer!"

The snow disappeared. The trees grew heavy with green leaves. Birds perched upon the bushes. A breeze charged with perfume floated about our faces.

The guests rose, applauded vehemently, and shouted: "Long live Bernard Trevisan! Long live Bernard Trevisan!"

Gilles de Retz embraced the magician. "Bernard Trevisan, you are indeed the Supreme Master of the greatest Art!"

The voice of the Maréchal was mellow and gentle, tinged a little with sorrow.

Nicholas Flamel congratulated the host. "But, master, I notice that not one bird either chirps or sings. In the summer, the birds are pleasantly noisy."

Bernard was nonplussed. He pulled at his short beard, and waved nervously his staff. The guests became impatient. A few coughed significantly.

I moved away from the rest, clapped my hands several times and commanded—"Birds, sing! Birds, sing!"

The birds began to chirp and sing. The guests stared at me in astonishment. Gilles de Retz grasped my hands and looked intently into my eyes, as if seeking something within them that he had lost or forgotten.

Bernard bowed before me. "Prince, *you* are the master of us all." Turning to the rest, he extolled the esoteric wisdom of India, compared to which all Occidental knowledge was child's play. He drank to my health. The banquet became a celebration in my honor.

The next day, at the side of Gilles de Retz I rode triumphantly through the city of Paris.

To prevent Kotikokura from inadvertently betraying his ignorance of India, I introduced him as a Buddhist high priest under an oath of silence for a twelvemonth. He walked amid the priests as an honored guest.

"Prince," Gilles addressed me, "your ability to make the birds sing proves the superiority of your magic."

"My lord exaggerates. Bernard Trevisan is world-famous. One of his former disciples at Marseilles recounted to me marvels performed by the master that I cannot hope to equal."

"Fame increases in proportion to distance, Prince. Bernard's most striking accomplishment is the change of seasons, which we witnessed last night, and you added the final, the supreme magic ingredient from the treasure trove of the East."

"And Nicholas Flamel, Monsieur le Maréchal? I hear he has discovered the Philosopher's Stone. . ."

Gilles de Retz laughed. "He is an old scoundrel, and his Philosopher's Stone is a charming fiction."

"Fiction?"

"He acquired immense wealth by exorbitant usury, and to account for it, that the courts might not prosecute him, he spread the rumor that he possessed the Philosopher's Stone."

"That was ingenious. And what they say about his great age—is it also fiction, monsieur?"

"That I do not know." Gilles looked at me, his eyes darting the strange light.

"And what of Francis Prelati?"

The Maréchal's eyes darkened and blazed, but he made no answer. We rode in silence.

"Prince, have your wise men discovered the Philosopher's Stone?"

"Our wise men are not interested in wealth. Poverty, they say, is the crown of truth."

"I don't agree with them. Poverty is colorless and breeds monotony. I love luxury and joy and constant change. I must hear the clatter of horses' hoofs preceding me. I must see the glitter of jewels and gold. I must hear delectable music. My fingers must be thrilled with the smoothness of silk and velvet. I seek not only truth but pleasure—unendurable pleasure indefinitely prolonged. . ."

"Monsieur le Maréchal," I said, "beauty and truth are one. . . ."

His face lit up with joy.

"There must be," he said a little later, "somewhere a magic formula that renews our youth. The Philosopher's Stone, which at a touch turns base metals to gold, is but a means, not an end. I need vast fortunes to procure—Eternal Youth. . ."

His face clouded again and the two long premature wrinkles deepened.

"Is it possible to discover the formula, Prince?"

"Perhaps."

"Perhaps," he repeated sadly, "it is always perhaps. And meanwhile, life slips by and youth withers. I am already thirty-four years old, Prince."

"I am thirty."

"We must hurry, Prince, and discover the secret."

We passed out of the last gate of the city and entered into the Bois de Boulogne. The naked branches of the trees formed a wide canopy over which the reflection of the sun made embroideries in red gold.

"I am glad you are not a Christian, Prince. I love the Church, for it has beauty and legend, but I hate her for her fear of the Ultimate Truth."

I made a gesture that I did not comprehend.

"The Church," he whispered into my ear, "fears the power of Satan."

"Satan?"

He scrutinized my face. Suddenly he drew from his coat an ıvory cross, with the image of a crucified rose. "Prince, from the first moment I saw you, I recognized in you a Rosicrucian. You are not merely a Hindu Prince. You are a seeker as I am,—a seeker of Beauty which is Truth. . . ."

I made a sign of assent.

"I am a Rosicrucian, Count," I remarked, "but I belong to the Eastern rite. Our Grandmaster dwells in the Himalayas inaccessible behind his veil of mystery and of snow."

He bowed ceremoniously.

"The seeker after the ultimate truth," he continued, "fears neither King nor Pope, neither God nor Devil." He lifted his fist, delicate and thin, almost a woman's, and dropped it vigoroŭsly at his side.

"Prince," he asked, " is there anything in heaven or on earth that you fear?"

"Yes, ugliness and stupidity."

"You are my brother, Prince," Gilles exclaimed.

He approached me until the heads of our horses touched. "Are we brothers, Cartaphilus?"

I pressed his arm.

Our approach to the Castle of Champtoce was greeted by trumpets and chimes. At the gate, a hundred children, boys and girls dressed in white, showered us with roses and sang "bergerettes."

Two servants helped us descend from our steeds. The Maréchal patted the heads and cheeks of the children.

"You shall be rewarded according to your deserts, my little ones," he said tenderly, his voice somewhat husky.

I was installed in the right wing of the castle which overlooked the garden. Kotikokura, the Hindu High Priest, under vows of silence, shared my suite.

The next morning the Maréchal invited me to hunt with him.

His retainers wore sumptuous attire. The horses were bedecked with gorgeous trappings. Two dozen hounds pulled impatiently at their leashes. Gilles de Retz, resplendent in his uniform, greeted me cordially and bade me ride at his side.

He waved his hand. The trumpets blew. Our black steeds galloped away.

As we reached the middle of the forest, the Maréchal and I dashed away from the rest. We leaped from our horses. The Maréchal took my arm and we walked slowly.

"It is not the actual hunting that pleases me," he said, "but the beauty of the horses and the men, the impatience of the dogs, the flourishes of the trumpets—and the captured animals, still alive, breathing their last, scarlet with their own blood." My eyes tried to delve into his soul.

He pressed my arm. "Do you love the sight of blood, Cartaphilus?"

"The mystery of life is the mystery of the blood."

"Cartaphilus, my brother, to you I may with impunity reveal the unrevealable."

"Speak!"

"I do not worship God. I find His work mediocre. The pleasures He offers are like bones, left over at the end of a feast. He is like an archbishop, always admonishing, always warning. Besides, He prefers innocence to experience, stupidity to intelligence, dullness to wit."

He looked at me, smiling ironically, intent upon seeing the effect of his words.

"My lord, what you say is too evident to require demonstration. Alas, there is no other God but God. . ."

He stamped his sword and exclaimed. "To the illuminati, we may drop all pretenses. You know there is another God—surpassing the God of Heaven . . . the god who honors the rebel. . ."

"Who?"

"Satan."

"If he is a god, Monsieur le Maréchal, he is also tyrant, and enslaves the soul. We in the East emancipate ourselves from both God and the Devil. . ."

"Perhaps you have no need of Lucifer. We need his light. He is the essence of intelligence and wit. He is the spirit of investigation. He teaches us to drink, drink deep, from the Cup of Pleasure and Beauty. . . ."

"You have merely reversed the order, my lord. You have only changed names. God has become the Devil, and the Devil God."

"Having reversed the order, we have changed the entire conception of life. Yahweh has become the Black One, horny and monstrous, and his virtues abhorrent. Satan is luminous and beautiful and Sin the Supreme Good."

Two servants approached, carrying upon their shoulders on a pole a young deer. The blood made a thin zigzag line according to the movements of the men. Several dogs followed, barking and stopping from time to time to lap the blood. Their muzzles were red like the noses of drunkards.

"My lord," one of the servants addressed Gilles de Retz, "the first trophy."

"Good!" His eyes dazzled with a light such as I had seen darting from the eyes of a demon in a temple of Egypt,—a phosphorescent light, a light that resembled the whiteness of knives and swords

They placed their burden upon the ground. The animal's body shivered. The Maréchal jerked out the arrow which protruded half way from the deer's belly. The animal raised himself and fell back, his legs slightly in the air. Blood splashed the Maréchal's boots. He breathed heavily and tightened his fists. For a moment his pupils were glazed, his limbs stiffened. Then he relaxed. He patted the dogs beating lightly their sides with his palm. The dogs wagged their tails.

The Maréchal's conception of Satan pleased me. His intellectual diabolism was a new weapon in my warfare against Jesus.

Gilles had not yet spoken to me about women. Weird scandals about his affairs were gathering about him like a flock of birds. He had recently wedded Catherine of the House of Thouars.

Who was Catherine? I never caught even a glimpse of her garments. Was it true that he kept her a prisoner in the tower that rose above the castle, like an immense mitre?

I walked through the garden. The smoke of roasting oxen and sheep curled above the trees. The Maréchal, despite financial difficulties, would not close his gates to the hundreds of people that came from all parts of the country, and his generosity would not allow any curtailment in food and drinks.

I heard footsteps in back of me, and turned around. Two women, arm in arm, walked slowly. When they became aware of my presence, they stopped almost frightened. I bowed.

"Prince Cartaphilus!" one of them exclaimed. "My brother-in-law often speaks to us about you." Turning to the other woman, "You remember, Catherine, what Gilles— —"

"Yes, I remember, Anne," she sighed.

Her voice had an uncommon sadness about it, and her face seemed almost unearthly.

Catherine was dressed in a black velvet dress whose high collar touched the chin, and her blond hair was surrounded by a thin gold band, studded with a large emerald.

"We are taking a walk in the garden, Prince. Will you accompany us?" Anne asked.

The only resemblance to her sister was her height and her aquiline nose. She was more heavily built; her hair was black; her lips sensuous, and her eyes gray and languorous, had nothing spiritual about them. She was dressed in a gown of white silk. About her throat was a necklace of pearls.

"I have read that the women of India possess unusual beauty. Is that true, Prince?" asked Anne.

I answered, "My memory of the women of India has been eclipsed, madame, since I have had the pleasure of seeing the women of France."

Anne blushed and her eyes closed a little.

'The eyes of Flower-of-the-Evening,' I thought. They stirred my slumbering senses.

Catherine sighed. "Sister, I am weary. I must go back."

"Very well, dear. I shall accompany you."

"No, no, I beg you. Remain a while longer with the Prince. You need air . . . and conversation." She smiled.

She kissed Anne, bent a little her knee before me, and left. I was not displeased. The matter that interested me most at the moment could not be discussed in the presence of so ethereal a being. . . .

"Shall we take that road, Madame? It seems to lead away from the smoke and the noisy merrymaking that takes place in the castle."

"My brother-in-law will never be persuaded to abandon his whim of being the provider of the riff-raff of the world."

"Riff-raff?"

"Alchemists, charlatans, visionaries, gypsies, what not. Is it well for a Maréchal of France to associate with such people?"

I did not answer.

"My poor sister is distressed. She occupies the tower to escape the din. Even there she finds little rest. All night she is awakened by red lights moving about in the castle and by huge shadows behind curtained windows. In her condition the excitement is most untimely."

"Is she ill?"

"No, but she expects a baby. . ."

"She could pose for the Madonna. . ."

"She is worthy of the comparison. There was never a purer soul than hers. She was intended for a nun."

"Why should not exquisite delicacy dedicate itself to love?"

"The Maréchal is too busy with other things. Men of his type should not marry."

"Your sister loves the Maréchal?"

"She loves him too well. . ."

Anne bent over a bud and smelled it. I caught a glimpse of the magnificent valley that separated her breasts. An irresistible impulse to grasp and crush them in my hands possessed me. I tightened my fists until my nails cut into the flesh. I remembered the Bath of Beauty. I remembered Ulrica and Asi-ma and Flower-of-the-Evening, —round breasts and pear-shaped, tiny and full. Why should I tremble before the invisible breasts of this woman? Was it merely Youth and Spring? Or was it because I could only see the valley that divided their loveliness? . . .

Anne looked up. "Smell this bud, Prince. It is intoxicating, as if the whole spring were encased in its tiny body."

I bent. My face almost touched hers. I breathed deeply, but not of the bud. I moved my head, until my lips met hers. I pressed into them. She did not withdraw. I lowered my face until it touched her breast. Anne uttered a stifled cry. She straightened up. I grasped her in my arms. "Anne," I whispered, "Anne, I love you." Her face was flushed. She breathed heavily, her eyes nearly shut.

I placed my arm around her waist and we walked in silence to a bench hidden among the bushes. She stretched out upon it. Her white gown and her immobility gave her the appearance of a statue.

"Anne," I whispered. "Anne." Her name thrilled me. My heart beat violently against my chest. "Anne." I covered her body with kisses.

"It is time for me to go to the tower," she whispered. "Catherine is waiting for me."

"We must meet again, Anne."

"Yes."

LVII

THE LABORATORY OF GILLES DE RETZ—GILLES CHAL-
LENGES GOD—BIRTH PANGS OF HOMUNCULUS—
THE FEARS OF CATHERINE—THE SECRET LOVE OF
GILLES DE RETZ

THE Maréchal invited me into his laboratory. Francis Prelati of
Padua, assisted by six apprentices, was engaged over ill-smelling
crucibles. The laboratory, except that it was much larger, resembled
very closely that of Trevisan.

Prelati greeted me cordially, but somewhat pompously. It was our
first meeting since Master Bernard had coaxed roses out of the
snow. Prelati was still a young man, clean-shaven and tall. He talked
about alchemy and physics with the same tricks of language as
his friend Trevisan.

He convinced the Maréchal that before long fabulous riches would
leap at his command out of the crucible.

Gazing out of the window I saw Kotikokura, followed by several
dogs, dash by.

"Your friend the High Priest," Gilles remarked, "prefers the
company of my animals to mine."

"His vow not to speak for a year, upon which depends the expia-
tion of a great sin, makes him fear the company of man. If he utters
one word before the time, he will have to resume his penance from
the beginning."

"Cartaphilus," he said suddenly, "in your company I have a curious sensation. I feel," he placed his palm upon his forehead, "I feel
. . . as if all the ages were surging about me. Have we lived once
before, and were you then my friend. . . ?"

"It is possible."

"Are we born or reborn, Cartaphilus?"

"We are links in a chain. . ."

"I want to destroy—that chain, to begin life anew, without the
superstitions of our ancestors, without inevitable decay and old age

and death. I want to create new life . . . that owes nothing to progenitors."

He grasped my arm tightly and looked at me intently. His eyes rolled a little backward. His beard seemed so blue, I almost believed he dyed it in some strange chemical.

"You are competing with God. . ."

"Why not?"

He raised his forefinger upon which shone an amethyst the shape of a serpent. "Within ten more days Homunculus will be ready for the arcanum. The spagyric substances I imprisoned in a glass phial are beginning to pulsate. Come!"

He unlocked a door which led into a small room like a monk's cell. Upon one of the walls was a crucifix upside down; upon another, the signs of the Zodiac. In a corner, a heap of dung over which large flies buzzed. The air was stifling like that of a stable.

"My Homunculus," he said proudly, "is prospering within it."
He pointed to the heap of manure.

"How can man be born out of dung?"

"Why not? It is the womb of the earth. But heat and manure are not sufficient, Cartaphilus. That is true. For forty days I shall feed him on the arcanum of . . . human blood. I have discovered the perfect combination. Maimonides failed because he could not obtain the pristine, the virginal blood of children. . . I, Gilles de Retz, Maréchal de France, obtain from God or the Devil whatever is needed. . ."

What did he mean by the virginal blood of children?

We walked out. I breathed deeply, many times.

"Cartaphilus, who are you?" the Maréchal asked again suddenly.

"I am—He Who Seeks."

"Seeks what?"

"What the Lord de Retz seeks—a newer and more beautiful life, only I seek more slowly . . . I wait."

"I am impatient, Cartaphilus. I cannot wait."

He looked at me perturbed.

That was the difference between us. We were brothers in spirit. But I could develop slowly, remaining sane and balanced. The Maréchal's feverish endeavors must inevitably prove futile. His ideas burst the bands of reason. A thousand generations of alchemists might discover the Philosopher's Stone, and create a new humanity . . . I could wait and see. Poor Gilles must hasten, he must force the lock of mystery or perish without baring the secret. Whatever of truth there might be in each generation, I could learn. Whatever of falsehood, I could unlearn in the next.

We reached the bench upon which Anne had stretched out in all her beauty. Gilles bade me sit. I was as thrilled as if Anne lay under my touch again. The Maréchal patted my hand and pressed it. His face at that moment, if shaven, would have looked almost like a boy's.

"Cartaphilus," he whispered, "you are he whom I have sought—he who understands—he who knows."

He knelt, and taking both my hands, pressed them to his lips. "Stay with me always. Be my brother. Let us take the blood bond between us. Call me Gilles."

"Gilles."

In the tower, a shadow moved from one window to another, slowly, ceaselessly.

Gilles looked up. "It is Lady de Retz, Cartaphilus. She is very restless. Frequently, the whole night through, she walks as she does now."

"Perhaps she fears you, Gilles."

"She fears my beard." He laughed a little. "Everybody fears it. I know they call me Bluebeard when my back is turned."

"Your beard is characteristic of you."

"I think so too. A black or a blond beard would not be compatible with my temperament. Perhaps my beard determines my life! Demosthenes became the greatest orator because he stammered. Caesar became the most fearless of generals because he was an epileptic. The maid Joan saved France—because—because—she was not really a woman."

"Not really a woman?" I asked.

"She never paid the bloody sacrifice that nature exacts every month from woman. She was not a slave to the moon. . ."

His brows contracted. From his eyes darted the curious fire that bespoke the strangeness of his mind. He stroked his beard, and combed it with the tips of his delicate fingers, covered with jewels of fantastic designs.

"She was a witch, a white witch, but a witch, Cartaphilus!—She confessed that she was!" he exclaimed suddenly. "Afterwards she recanted and lied, but once I caught her performing magic rites. She made the spirits speak and obey. . ." He covered his face with his hands and placed his elbows upon his knees.

I had heard of the Maid. People spoke of her indifferently or as some half-crazed girl, who claimed to hear voices.

He placed his palm upon my shoulder. "Cartaphilus, you have loved much. Your very name bespeaks it. Have you not discovered that a man yearns always to recapture again and again the thrill of his first infatuation?"

"It is true, Gilles."

"I love Catherine my wife. . . . She's beautiful and charming, a delicate bud. But my heart seeks the boy-girl, the witch, Joan of Arc. . . ."

At the windows of the tower, the shadow continued to pass to and fro. What fear, what anxiety made Catherine so restless? Did she guess the secret of Bluebeard's love? Had she heard the whispered rumors about his pact with the Evil One? Did she understand the duality of his motives? Was she really afraid of his beard? Were fear and love bedfellows in her heart?

"I love Joan of Arc, and I, by Hermes, shall snatch her out of heaven or hell."

I sympathized with Gilles. His unhappiness resembled mine— Salome, though, not dead, like the Maid, was equally unattainable.

Gilles de Retz stood up suddenly. He seemed even taller than he was. His beard against the background of his black velvet dazzled like amethysts.

"She will be mine, Cartaphilus! I shall conquer death. . . !"

I looked at him inquiringly.

"I shall invoke her spirit and capture it. She will be mine! She was too proud to accept me in life. She must accept me in death. Her spirit," he continued, "is obstinate. It is the counterpart of her body. But I am stronger. Francis Prelati, the greatest magus will assist me. We have made our pact with the Prince of Darkness. . ."

"I shall be with you, my brother."

He grasped my hands and pressed them to his lips.

I determined to expose the charlatans who had deluded the Maréchal and who devoured his substance.

"Cartaphilus, I know you are more powerful than my magicians. If they fail, you will not. . . Meanwhile, I must prepare for the tournament. The Count of Dorsay has challenged me this day to a bout. . . ."

He smiled. His face assumed a boyish expression. His eyes twinkled mischievously. Which was his true personality? Was his strangeness due to his thwarted love for the Maid? If Joan had

reciprocated his affections would he be merely the charming philosopher, the elegant knight? . . .

I begged to be left alone to meditate. My meditations were most
uplifting.

I expected Anne.

LVIII

I BREAK THE MAGIC CIRCLE—THE WHITE WITCH JOAN OF ARC—I CRASH A MIRROR—I WITNESS A MIRACLE —THE FLIGHT OF THE FALSE MAGICIANS

THE vault was hung round with black curtains. There was no light, save a torch fixed in a high candelabrum. A triangular tripod in the center was surmounted by a bowl out of which a thin smoke, like a line drawn with a hair, arose, filling the air with a strange odor. An altar of white marble supported by four columns terminating in bulls' feet stood at the left. It was surmounted by a cross upside down, placed upon a serpent in the shape of a triangle.

Master Prelati was dressed in an ephod of white linen clasped with a single emerald. About his waist was tied a consecrated girdle, embroidered with strange names; upon his breast the talisman of Venus hanging from a thread of azure silk. He wore a high cap of sable. His assistant was dressed in a priestly robe of black bombazine. Gilles de Retz, handsome and defiant, was resplendent in his uniform of Maréchal de France.

We remained at the vault's mouth. The magus walked to the altar, knelt and prayed in silence. Then he walked to the tripod and stirred the smoke with a fan of swan's feathers.

He motioned to us to approach. He described three circles, one within the other, with his long ebony staff.

"Remain within the circle. Never budge no matter what you see or hear. He who breaks the circle breaks the bond that unites his body to his soul."

He waved his staff to the four cardinal points of the earth, calling out four names, then remained silent, his head upon his chest, his eyes closed.

Slowly, he lifted his right fist within which he held a bundle of fagots snatched from the flames.

"Joan of Arc! Joan of Arc! Joan of Arc!"

There was no answer.

"Joan, this wood has fed the flame that consumed your body.

Your ashes dropped upon it and impregnated it. I am holding your body! Joan, I command you, in the All-Powerful Name, to appear before us!"

There was no motion.

He stamped his staff. "Joan! Joan! Joan!"

Again no response.

"Do not disobey my command. You know the torment of the spirit who disregards the summons compelling alike the living and the dead! Joan! Joan! Joan!"

The light of the torch flickered a little and the smoke broke in two.

"Joan, tarry not. I command you to appear at once!"

There was a rumbling noise, like the roar of a lion which gradually increased and became a hideous mixture of sounds. The smoke in the tripod turned a thick black, and a sulphurous stench filled the place.

The smoke dispersed. The torch was blown out, and against one of the curtains appeared the shape of a young woman, white and trembling like a light.

"Joan!" the Maréchal called out. "Joan!"

The apparition made no answer.

"Joan, you have come to me!" He started toward the apparition, but the magician's assistant restrained him.

"Joan, I may not come near to you. I may not touch the hem of your robe. Listen to me, Joan. I love you. I can love no other woman, Joan. You scorned me in the flesh—give me your love in the spirit!"

The apparition did not stir. Her lips tightened as if in defiance.

"Joan, by the gods we both adore, my spirit may join yours without leaving its earthly bondage. Speak! Tell me you desire this union."

The apparition shivered a little as a light shivers in the wind.

The Maréchal grew indignant. He rose. "I command you to speak! I, Gilles, Lord of Retz, Maréchal de France!"

He drew his sword from its scabbard.

Fearing he would do himself some injury, I determined to put an end to the trick. Deliberately I walked out of the magic circles. Before the magician realized my intention, I was beyond the reach of his hocus-pocus.

The three men within the circle uttered a cry of horror. The roaring of the wild beasts commenced again, and out of the tripod rose a choking smoke. I continued my steps undaunted. I had seen too many invocations of spirits. I knew that the apparition of Joan of Arc was merely a play of light and shade upon mirrors. I walked to the spot where, according to my calculation, the magic mirrors were hidden, and crashed them with the hilt of my sword.

"Bunglers!" I exclaimed. "If you wish to invoke spirits, learn to improve your art."

The magicians rushed out of the vault, the Maréchal following them with his bare sword.

"Gilles!" I called out. "Do not pursue them."

He continued his pursuit of the tricksters.

Suddenly, against the white curtains, the spectral image of the Maid appeared. I had smashed the mirror but the apparition remained! I bent my neck forward until it ached and opened wide my eyes. The Maid lingered on. . .

"Joan," I called, my voice trembling with awe, "Joan, speak to me!"

Joan tightened her face in pain or abhorrence, made the sign of the cross and vanished, slowly like a light that is carried away. . .

Had I labored under an illusion? Was this more than a trick? Had I left intact one mirror which now mothered the mirage of Joan, boy-maid, witch woman and saint? . . .

I drew the curtains aside. Every mirror was crashed!

Gilles returned.

"Cartaphilus," he said, placing his sword in its scabbard, "I am grateful to you beyond words, for more than all things else, I seek truth. I want no happiness based upon fraud and illusion."

He grasped my arm. "Come out, this place oppresses me."

But my thoughts still revolved around the pale wraith of the Maid.

By an irony of the fateful goddess, the Maréchal had missed the only genuine miracle of the evening, inexplicable to me then as it is today.

Kotikokura was looking out of the window of my room.

"What? Not asleep yet, my friend?"

He shook his head.

"You were watching for Ca-ta-pha, were you not?"

He nodded.

"Does it matter so much to you if he is in danger or not?"

He took my hand and kissed it.

"But now you must go to your room and rest. Ca-ta-pha has returned. The universe is saved."

"Look!" he said.

I looked where his forefinger indicated. The shadow in the tower walked to and fro, rhythmically, accurately like a pendulum.

He was about to tell me something when the door opened slowly and a figure in white appeared. She entered and placed her finger to her lips.

"Anne!" I whispered.

Kotikokura discreetly bowed himself out.

Anne approached me. I clasped her to me with the joy of one who has suddenly recovered a long lost treasure.

"Cartaphilus," she whispered, "my sister is very much perturbed."

"More than usually?"

"Yes. She has seen strange sights in the garden and in the forest this evening,—men with enormous lamps that blinded the eyes."

'The mirrors,' I thought.

"Why should lamps perturb her so?"

"Lamps and torches and black-gowned people and one who looked like a ghost. . ."

'The reflections,' I thought.

"Gilles has not entered her room for days. She is consumed more than ever with longing and with fears. . . ."

I laughed. "Does she fear him or his beard?"

"Have you not noticed," she said trembling, "how much bluer it is of late . . . ?"

I seated myself upon the edge of the bed and drew her upon my knees.

I smiled. "Color, my dear, depends upon the sun. The sun may be stronger these days. We are in the midst of Spring, as those who love should know."

"No, no! There is something more significant in it all. His beard was almost black when I first saw him. It is becoming bluer every day."

"Even if true—what could it mean, except that it changes as he grows older?"

"Older . . . and— —" she opened her eyes wide, "more terrible."

"What do you mean?"

"Ah, you do not know, Cartaphilus. There are horrible rumors about. I overheard many people. They say . . . he is in league . . . with . . . you know whom."

I laughed. "People always spread false rumors, particularly about men who like Gilles de Retz, are daring and rich and unusual."

"Cartaphilus, you are his friend. He says you are the wisest of all men."

"He exaggerates, dear."

"No, no—he does not. I know you are. It is not as if I had really met you for the first time some days previously. I feel that I have known you always."

"You have known me, Anne. Centuries ago we were lovers."

She looked scared.

"The Hindu religion teaches that the souls of people are reincarnated and true lovers meet again and again."

"It is beautiful—but is it God or the Other One—who teaches this?"

"God, Anne. Why suspect the Other One of all good things?"

"This place . . . this castle and forests and gardens . . . it is uncanny. My poor sister! She is as white as a ghost. I think she knows many things but she will not utter a word against Gilles. She defends him always. Love is terrible."

"Love is beautiful."

I embraced her. Her lips tasted like fresh honey, and her breath was the perfume of the bud over which we had bent the first time.

"In the morning we shall speak to Catherine and convince her that she has nothing to fear. This night you are my bride."

She pressed me against her, trembling a little. "Am I not a wicked woman, Cartaphilus? I have come to you of my own free will—and yet I am not your wife, nor even your betrothed."

"You are as pure as the rose is, Anne."

"You said that we were lovers in centuries past."

"And shall be again and again. . ."

Anne crossed herself and went to bed. Her body dazzled like a lake over which the moon shines. Her breasts rose and sank like the gentle flutter of doves' wings. Her eyes were thin black lines underneath the long lashes which nearly touched.

I taught her the divers ways of love which I had acquired from Flower-of-the-Evening and from others. Anne learned readily the tender secrets of many lands.

"Cartaphilus, how strong you are!" she murmured, as she stretched to the tips of her toes.

LIX

SULLEN PEASANTS—A DROP OF BLOOD GLISTENING IN
THE BLUE—THE NEEDS OF HOMUNCULUS—THE
DREAM OF GILLES DE RETZ—KOTIKOKURA MAKES
A DISCOVERY

I walked beyond the garden into the field. The peasants—men, women and children—were working feverishly. The scythes glittered ominously in the sun like scimitars, and the heavy pitchforks ripped into the hay like bayonets.

I approached one of the men who was wiping his forehead with his large horny hand, and bade him the time of the day. He glared at me and turned away, making the sign of the cross. Two women, becoming aware of my presence, uttered a stifled cry, then crossed themselves. Others looked up from their labor, and glared and pointed at me in silence.

Why were the farmers so enraged against the Maréchal and his guests?

I knew it was not a question of wages. Gilles de Retz was very generous, nor did he demand the right of the *prima nox*. Was it the lord's dabbling into alchemy? Hardly. It was the universal passion. The peasants themselves would have crossed their chests with their right hand while the left tightened over the gold produced by a Midas-fingered adept.

I arrived at the gate that led to the left wing of the castle. A girl of about ten was knocking at it with her small fists. She looked at me, her eyes filled with tears.

"What is the trouble, my dear?"

"My little brother went inside a long while ago and he has not come out yet."

I raised my hand to pat her. She withdrew her face and shoulders.

From within, a child's sharp cry—the cry of an animal that is pierced by a knife— —

"It's my brother, monsieur, my brother!" the girl sobbed. "My brother! My brother!"

The gate opened and the Maréchal emerged. His eyes were wide open and bloodshot. His hands trembled. He breathed heavily.

"Ah! My friend!" he exclaimed. His voice was husky.

The little girl screamed.

Gilles smiled. "They are all afraid of my beard—these little brats."

"My brother," she implored.

"Your brother? What about him?"

"He cried a while ago . . . I heard him."

"Foolish child," the Maréchal said tenderly. "He is probably playing and laughing with the rest of the children. Would you not like to accompany them?"

"No, no!" she screamed.

"Oh, very well. Here, take this gold coin and tell your mother to buy you a beautiful dress."

Gilles looked after her. "A very pretty child," he said slowly. "Very pretty." He took my arm. From his mustache, a drop of blood trickled into his beard. I shivered.

He spoke quickly and enthusiastically about a book he had just read. I knew that he endeavored to make me forget the child. Gradually his eyes resumed their usual clarity. His lips lengthened into a smile. He looked like a boy again—a boy who has pasted on his chin a blue beard to scare his comrades.

"I am a little tired," he said. "Would you care to drive with me?"

I nodded.

He ordered one of the coachmen to get a carriage ready.

We drove slowly through the garden and forest. He spoke of the beauty of nature, discussed Plato and Aristotle, and quoted poetry, including verses he had written himself.

Suddenly, placing his hand upon my leg, he said: "Cartaphilus. I am happy today, for I have discovered the secret."

"What secret, Gilles?"

"My Homunculus lives!"

"Ah?"

"A few days ago, I paid him a visit. He stirred!"

I looked at him, incredulous.

"He stirred for a second, then remained still again. The virginal blood was not virginal enough. There is always some impurity, even in the youngest blood once it has coursed through the body. What is needed is the blood of an unborn child, snatched from the womb. . ."

His eyes glinted. I thought of two knives. I heard a sharp cry and a little girl sobbing.

"Not a full-fledged one. The air must not enter its lungs. A child which has just received life, into whom the soul has stirred for the first time. . ."

"What woman would be willing to consent to this sacrifice?"

"What difference does it make whether she is willing or not? We cannot allow truth to be sacrificed for a woman. We must be strong, Cartaphilus. We must—if needs be—trample on human sentiments and emotions."

He pulled the corners of his beard. Was it the influence of Anne's words or reality? His beard was much bluer than when I had first seen it in Paris.

"Truth is beyond man and God and . . . Satan!" he exclaimed.

His brows knit and his fists tightened.

"Cartaphilus, I have observed your High Priest. There is something about him that symbolizes the earth. He is Pan—the reflection of the Earth, which is the magnificent palace of Him who rebelled against Adonai. God is in His Heaven. What is Heaven to us? We are the lovers of the earth. The earth is beautiful; the earth is joyous."

His face, in contrast with his words seemed tortured, as if a powerful fist had pressed against it.

"I should like to have the High Priest appear as Lucifer at the Black Mass which must precede the birth of Homunculus. I dare not address him for fear of tempting him to answer in violation of his vow. He understands you, however, by a mere look or gesture."

"Your hospitality is so generous that he will not refuse your wish."

He pressed my hand. "Brother."

"Does not the Black Mass mean, Maréchal, that you have decided to make final your covenant with Satan?"

He nodded. "There is no other way, Cartaphilus. One cannot serve two masters at once. Sooner or later, one must burn one's boats. . ."

"Do you think the sacrifice will be efficacious?"

"I am convinced of it. The child created by passion is weaker than the child created by reason, just as a base metal is weaker than gold. Besides, with the High Priest present, Satan himself will come to baptize his son."

Satan as godfather seemed so ludicrous that I could not refrain from laughing a little.

"And the godmother, Gilles? Who shall it be?"

"The godmother," he answered solemnly, "is the woman whose womb will deliver the base metal which will be transformed into gold."

"Have you found her?"

"The sacrifice will be ready when required."

He closed his eyes and breathed quietly as a man asleep. His face had the dull placidity of old age. One long white hair glistened among the blue of his beard. Was it the drop of blood which had changed its original color? How much pain was Gilles destined to inflict? How many children would shriek before he discovered the secret of life or more likely, the futility of his efforts? Was truth really worth such sacrifices? Was Homunculus a boon great enough to justify the murder of a child ripped from his mother's womb? Had not Yahweh discovered a simpler process to reproduce life? Had he not, also, perhaps, experimented for æons, to find at last nothing more beautiful, nothing more efficacious than the embrace of the male and the female? Perhaps it would be better if man, instead of attempting to create life himself, matched his ingenuity against God's to frustrate creation. . .

Could I permit this monster to live? Yet Gilles de Retz was my intellectual kinsman. In his inhuman fashion, he loved me.

I sheathed the dagger that, for a moment, twitched in my hand.

Gilles opened his eyes, startled, and laughed. "I actually fell asleep, Prince, and dreamt—how silly and false dreams are!— that you stabbed me. But instead I see you placed your hand upon my heart in symbol of friendship. And now I shall place my hand upon your faithful heart, Cartaphilus, my brother, and swear eternal allegiance."

'How much truer a dream may be,' I thought, 'than reality!'

"Gilles, since you have granted me your friendship, may I speak freely to you?"

"Speak, Cartaphilus. Nothing you say can offend me since the purpose of your words springs from your heart."

"Gilles, it is not possible to obtain truth in a lifetime. It is better to catch a glimpse of it and guess the rest, or to leave it unfathomed. You are endeavoring to compress eternity into one existence. It cannot lead to your happiness or the happiness of those about you. . ."

"Happiness? What matters happiness, Cartaphilus? What matter those about me? What matter I?"

"You are treading a dangerous path."

He laughed and, placing his palm upon my knee, said: "I destroy to build a newer and better world. I am the negation of the Creator who made a mess of creation. The world will never forget Gilles, the Lord of Retz, Maréchal of France who dared to face truth unflinchingly, and to rebel against God."

"People forget the great and courageous things a man accomplishes. They remember his peculiarities. They remember that Nero fiddled while Rome burned. They may forget your philosophy and remember—your beard!"

He remained pensive. His eyes clouded as if someone had drawn a film over them. Only the perverse glitter pierced through like the sharp fine edges of stilettos.

Kotikokura pulled at my sleeve. "Ca-ta-pha! Ca-ta-pha!" His nostrils shivered, and his teeth chattered.

"What is the trouble, my friend? What has happened?"

A dog that followed him was munching a large bone, tearing the shreds of flesh that clung to it.

"Look, Ca-ta-pha!" He pointed to the animal.

The bone was the arm of a child! I was seized with nausea.

"Ca-ta-pha—come!" He pulled my arm and preceded me. From time to time, he looked back to see if we were observed. He led me to a trap-door hidden behind a rock. He opened it. We descended several steps. He opened another door. An intolerable stench struck my nostrils like a fist.

"Look, Ca-ta-pha!"

When my eyes became accustomed to the dark, I saw strewn about piles of bones, skulls in which an eye still persisted to glare like a bit of porcelain, legs torn from their sockets, arms placed upon each other in the shape of crosses, flesh over which enormous flies buzzed and rats munched. In phials, blood coagulated like frozen cherries.

"Come, Kotikokura. This is too horrible! Too horrible!"

I breathed many times deeply, as if to smother the memory of what I had seen.

"How did you discover this, Kotikokura?"

He told me how for days he had been smelling something strange; how the dogs, their muzzles to the earth, discovered the rock. His curiosity was greater than his prudence. He opened the door and discovered the holocaust of children.

"We have seen much death and we are not pure-handed ourselves, Kotikokura—but have you ever seen such a loathsome thing?"

He shook his head vigorously.

"During the Crusades, we splashed through blood, but the deeds of the followers of Christ never were half so monstrous as the work of Anti-Christ . . . !"

I rubbed my heart as if to remove all traces of the hand that had been placed upon it in sign of friendship and allegiance. This must stop! No friendship could survive this! No promise could bind!

LX

THE LOVE OF ANNE—ANNE PROPOSES—I BETRAY A FRIEND—POWDERS AND MASKS

ANNE entered,—an exquisite phantom in white.

"Catherine is happy today."

"Happy?"

"She has felt life! She says that never—not even when Gilles thrilled her with his first kiss—did she experience such joy. Besides, my brother-in-law told her that he would show her his laboratory, initiate her into his great secret,—and ever after she would have nothing to fear."

I stood up with a jerk.

"He would show her the true meaning of life and birth."

"Anne!" I exclaimed, "don't let her go to him! Never, do you hear? She must not."

"What is the matter, dear?"

No friendship could endure this! No brother could be forgiven for such a crime! It was Catherine, then—the beautiful, the exquisite Catherine whom he meant to sacrifice to his insane illusion. When it was an abstract idea, woman in general, I could tolerate it,— but Catherine whose face was like Spring and whose body like a young tree!

"It shall not take place!" I shouted.

"What is the trouble, Cartaphilus? I beg you to tell me!"

I related to Anne the Maréchal's insane obsession, omitting, however, the gruesome things I had witnessed.

She buried her head into the pillow and sobbed, "Poor Catherine! Poor Catherine! Cartaphilus, can you imagine what she has been suffering? She pretends to believe nothing—the rumors, the cries, the complaints of mothers. Even the strange lights and shadows at midnight did not convince her. 'Gossip, sister,' she says, trembling the while. I am sure she will not believe or pretend not to believe what you have told me, Cartaphilus. Even if she saw the glittering knife in his fiendish hands, she would continue to love and trust him. She may even allow herself to be sacrificed."

"We must not let her, Anne! She is too beautiful. . . ."

"The monster! The monster!" she shouted.

"Not a monster, Anne. Gilles is a remarkable man. His face, at times—have you not noticed?—is like a child's. But he is mad. He does not mean to do a murderous deed. He thinks he is serving God —his God—in his own fashion."

"The monster! The monster!" she continued. "He denies God and man and murders innocent children. He allies himself with the powers of evil against our Lord. Cartaphilus, how can you deny he is a monster?"

She knelt before the painting of the Holy Virgin that hung upon the wall. "Holy Mother, help us save my sister from the clutches of the fiend! Mother Mary, help us save her unborn. Mother of us all, protect us! Amen!"

She rose and seated herself next to me. "Cartaphilus, what shall we do? How shall we proceed to stop this foul deed? How escape?"

"You have spoken to me of your brothers, Anne. Can we not implore their help?"

"They are strong and courageous. They would do anything for Catherine, but he will not permit them to enter his castle."

"So great a castle must have some secret gate."

She knit her white smooth brow. She placed her mouth to my ear, as if fearing that someone was overhearing. "There is a gate, dilapidated and hidden by bushes to the left of the field. One man can pass through it at a time. No one watches it."

"That is good. And how many men can your brothers muster?"

"I do not know—a thousand fighting men, if needs be, who would fight to the death to save Catherine."

"They will not have to fight once in the castle if we explain their mission to the Maréchal's soldiers. They come on a peaceful errand."

"On God's own errand," she added, looking at the Madonna.

"Have you a trusted servant who could carry our message to your brothers?"

"I think so, Cartaphilus. A young man who is in love with Madeleine, my chambermaid. He would go into the fires of hell for her and she would do as much for me."

"Send him; but one messenger is not enough. Something may happen to him on the way. He may miscarry our orders. . . ."

"I have a carrier pigeon, Cartaphilus—a most beautiful and intelligent bird. My mother gave us several at our departure. The monster permitted the birds to escape. One returned. He can carry a message under his wings."

"Splendid!"

She pressed my hands, her eyes filled with tears. "Cartaphilus, the Lord Jesus has sent you to us."

'He will always get the credit,' I thought.

"Cartaphilus, supposing the man loses his way and the pigeon is slain? Perhaps my brothers may not be able to come at once. They may be at war with their neighbors. What—what will become of Catherine?" Her despair heightened her loveliness.

"Then—Anne," I said, caressing her head, "then, Cartaphilus will save her single-handed."

She stared at me. "Single-handed?"

I nodded.

"Who are you?" she asked, breathing heavily.

"Cartaphilus, my dear," I smiled.

"You are a messenger from Heaven, Cartaphilus. I know it." She looked at the crucifix on the wall.

"Anne, I am betraying my friend."

She placed her head between my knees.

"Promise me one thing, Anne."

"Yes, Cartaphilus—anything."

"Gilles must not be subjected to torture. He must not be abandoned to the rabble which, hound-like, tears its victims to pieces."

"The Church can deal with her erring children, Cartaphilus," she added. "You will recognize her beneficence and her wisdom if you accept baptism! Let my love persuade you."

She crossed herself three times.

I raised her and with my lips I made the sign of the cross on her body.

"We might marry then, Cartaphilus, and remain together forever."

'The eternal woman!'

I seated her upon my knee and caressed her. She sobbed lightly. Gradually, her sobbing subsided. She placed her arms around my neck. The perfume of their pits delighted me like the deep drinking of an old wine. I laid her gently upon the bed. She offered her treasures as gracefully and as beautifully as flowers open their petals.

At dawn, she left the bed. Shivering a little from the morning chill, she returned once more.

"Love me again, Cartaphilus. I have a premonition that this is our last embrace. Love me!"

"We shall meet again, Anne."

"You will go away. Your eyes are restless. They are seeking a far-off gate."

'Asi-ma,' I thought.

"How shall I live without you, Cartaphilus? How can another man's embrace delight me after this?"

"One forgets."

"Man forgets—but not woman—not Anne."

The sun made a lake of gold upon the bed.

"Kotikokura, you play the Devil."

He grinned.

"Play your part well, but above all keep the mask I gave you."

He touched his belt.

"If the brothers do not come and if I cannot dissuade him from slaughtering his lovely wife, I shall throw the powder into the air. One breath of it will paralyze all except us if we wear the masks. We can then carry the victim away and escape. Remember the sign, Kotikokura. Put your mask on and I shall do likewise, or else we shall suffer the general fate."

Kotikokura nodded.

"Meanwhile, cause no suspicion. Obey whatever the Maréchal commands."

LXI

WHITE MASS—BLACK MASS—BLACK PRAYER—RITES OF
SATAN—BEAST OR GOD—THE SACRIFICE—THE BAP-
TISM OF HOMUNCULUS—JUDAS—I SEND A PRESENT
TO ANNE

THE people entered, dipping their fingers into the holy water, and
bending their knees before the altar. Those of rank seated themselves in the front pews, the peasants in the rear. A box in the manner of the theaters was reserved for the Maréchal and his guests of
honor.

The chapel was like an enormous jewel, carved and chiseled into
the shape of a room. The altar was of gold and lapis-lazuli, the pillars
of red-veined marble. The walls and ceiling were frescoed with
magnificent paintings.

The organ played and an invisible choir chanted a beautiful
litany. The Bishop, accompanied by two priests, entered slowly. The
canopy which covered them was of white silk, embroidered with
gold. The Bishop held in his hand a crucifix—a mass of precious
stones. Six young boys, dressed in black velvet, scattered incense
from censers of jade.

The Bishop mounted the steps of the altar and knelt. He rose
and with his back to the worshipers chanted short verses, at the end
of which he shook a tiny gold bell. The people responded: "Ora pro
nobis." "Ora pro nobis." The organ played a melody so low, it
floated about the place like the vague perfume of a god.

The Maréchal and Catherine knelt, pressing their heads against
the balustrade of the box. Anne closed her eyes. Her hand clasped
mine tightly.

"They have not come, Cartaphilus," she whispered.

"Do not fear, Anne."

"My messenger has not returned. Do you think he has reached
my brothers?"

"If not he, the pigeon."

"I tremble lest— —"

"Fear not, I am ready."

She knelt and in kneeling, kissed my hand.

The Bishop uncovered the ciborium. The worshipers approached one by one, in silence, took a tiny wafer—the body of Jesus—and bending their knee, left.

The music ceased. The priests removed the ciborium and the bell. The Maréchal rose and whispered into Catherine's ear. She rose also and bowing, said: "Whatever my lord desires."

He kissed her forehead and descended to speak with the Bishop.

"Do not go, sister!" Anne implored. "Do not go!"

Catherine looked at her reproachfully. "Anne, is he not my husband? Should not a wife obey her husband?"

"He is a — —"

I pressed her arm. Anne stopped short.

"Catherine, in the name of our Lord Jesus, do not go today."

"Anne, shall I be false to my vow?"

"He is false to his."

"Do not speak thus, sister."

The Maréchal took my arm and bade me descend the steps. "Contrasts thrill me, Cartaphilus. To go immediately from the worship of Adonai into the Temple of Lucifer, from the White Mass to the Black Mass, to pray fervently in both places!"

The steps turned in a spiral. When we reached half way, I listened intently. It seemed to me that I heard hoofbeats in the distance. But the noise died out and there was a deep silence. There was still time to dissuade him from the hideous deed he was contemplating.

"Gilles, why should man seek truth since truth is infinite and man is finite?"

"You are younger than I, Cartaphilus, and yet you consider me in the light of your junior. You need not fear for me. Adam ate of the Tree of Knowledge but only one apple. I shall wrest from God the seed!"

"Mortal eye cannot gaze at truth full-faced. Be content if you lift a corner of the veil . . . !"

"One glance—and death—I am satisfied."

The Maréchal knit his brow.

"Cartaphilus, you speak like a Christian. We are now in the house of him who is greater than Adonai. The ignorant call him the Prince of Darkness, but he is Lucifer, the bearer of Light."

From the middle of the ceiling hung a large candelabrum whose shape was a phallic caricature of the one in the Temple of Solomon and which spread a yellowish light, resembling the pallor of a jaundiced eye.

The walls were painted with grotesque figures,—goats with the heads of men, bulls with bodies of goats, elephants whose trunks and legs suggested colossal organs of procreation, snakes, stallions, bats revolving about naked figures that were partially women and partially beasts.

In the center of the Temple glowered a large marble statue of Pan: a giant priapus protruding from his belly, like a strangely shaped arrow hurled by an insane hunter.

The altar, marble encrusted with gold and jewels, was partially surrounded by a velvet curtain of a deep scarlet embroidered with the triangle of Astarte.

The worshipers were assembled. Their faces were painted with phallic symbols or covered with masks of animals.

The Maréchal's face acquired a beatitude which was incongruous with his eyes, wide open as an owl's in the dark and as ominous. His beard glittered like a cataract of amethysts.

The organ played a strange hymn, a co-mingling of solemn notes and a dancing medley. A hooded person, whose sex was difficult to determine, shook a censer, scattering an incense which resembled a decayed perfume mixed with human excretions.

Gilles de Retz invited me to sit with him.

"We need not take part in the common prayers. For us is reserved the Great Moment." He looked at me triumphantly, his gray eyes assuming their demoniac glitter.

I waited for a sign from Catherine's brothers, but I heard no sound. While I trusted my magic powder, I did not desire to display my power. I was already too conspicuous as the friend of Bluebeard. I did not wish to be compelled to explain the scientific device which produced a gas that paralyzed every muscle.

The priest entered, gorgeously attired. Upon his chest he wore upside down, an immense crucifix, studded with many diamonds which glittered like lamps.

He knelt before the altar and chanted. "Our Father which art in Hell, hallowed be Thy Name."

The worshipers responded: "Amen."

"Thy Kingdom come."

"Amen."

"Thy Will be done on Earth as in Hell."

"Amen."

"Bring us this day our daily light."

"Amen."

"Lead us into temptation."

"Amen."

"That we may be free from desire."

"Amen."

"Deliver us from good."

"Amen."

"Which maketh men weak."

"Amen."

"Which bringeth pain and falsehood into the world."

"Amen."

"For Thine is the Kingdom and power and glory forever."

"Amen."

The priest uncovered the ciborium. The worshipers approached, one by one, forming a circle.

"Partake of the body of the Enemy," the priest repeated at intervals. Each person took a wafer, desecrated it, and cast it upon the floor.

"Partake of the body of the Enemy."

Was it a bugle in the distance or the triumphant note of the organ? I listened, my eyes wide open.

There was perfect silence again.

The circle of worshipers was completed. A black-draped acolyte filled the large cup which each one drank and turned upside down to prove that nothing had remained within it.

"Drink the sacred blood of our Lord Lucifer," the priests chanted.

Three times the circle turned. Three times they drank the full cup. Their legs became unsteady and their eyes glistened. Many laughed.

The organ played: *Gloria in Excelsis* backward.

The worshipers began to dance about Pan, swaying, contortioning, moaning, howling.

I became more and more impatient. Would Kotikokura remember the sign? Would he have the mask with him? I touched my cloak. Mine was safely hidden.

The worshipers danced on. Their clothing hung from their bodies. Their mouths were covered with foam, like galloping horses.

A stench which was more than mortal struck my nostrils. Human excreta mingled with a strange odor that seemed to be a permanent exhalation of Lucifer's Temple. Was this the ultimate corruption? Was it the stench of Second Death . . . ?

The choir sang a beautiful litany in a minor key. The dance degenerated into obscene gestures. The worshipers tore their clothing, exhibiting their nakedness. Some inflicted wounds upon themselves with tiny spears and knives. They screamed, whether in pleasure or pain, I could not tell.

"How is the worship of Satan superior to that of Jesus?" I asked.

The Maréchal looked at me, one eyebrow lifted. "Lucifer releases the primal forces throttled by Adonai."

"They are beastly, not human."

"By releasing the Beast we discover the God," he said mysteriously, raising his forefinger which glittered with jewels.

Once more I heard a noise that seemed the call of a distant bugle. I rose and bent my head in the direction. The Maréchal looked at me intently. Had he heard it also?

"Tomorrow," he said, "these men and women will walk the earth free. Freed from passion, they will see the light."

"What light?"

"The true light."

"All religions speak of the true light. Meanwhile, man gropes in the dark. . ."

The priests struck a cauldron seven times, with a staff in the shape of a pitchfork whose sharp points darted thin blue flames. A sulphurous vapor jetted out and darkened the temple for a few moments.

"He is with us," the priest announced.

"He is with us," the people responded.

"He who has conquered Adonai."

"He who has conquered Adonai."

"Lucifer, the Light-bearer."

"Lucifer, the Light-bearer."

The Maréchal took my arm and bade me approach the altar.

The priest blew a silver horn three times to the East, to the West, to the North and to the South. The curtain was drawn aside. Upon the altar, Kotikokura stood disguised as the Prince of Darkness. From his temples rose two tall horns, priapic shaped. His face dazzled. A blue stream of smoke curled from his nostrils. About his chest was a breastplate of gold, studded with one large ruby. His feet were encased in black hoofs, his hands in black gauntlets which shone with tiny jewels. In his right fist, he held an ebony staff, terminating in two gold prongs.

The worshipers threw themselves upon their faces. The priest knelt. "Blessed be the Lord of Life."

"Amen!" the people responded.

"May His Kingdom come."

"Amen."

"Ahriman shall conquer Ahura-mazda."

"Amen."

"Ahriman shall stand upon the crest of the universe and rule it forever."

"Amen."

The organ played. The choir sang an ancient Persian litany.

The Maréchal approached the altar and knelt. "Has the Great Moment arrived, O Prince of Light?"

Kotikokura nodded. Two long streams of smoke curled out of his nostrils.

"Thy Name be glorified forever, Lucifer!"

"Amen."

The choir burst into a triumphant song.

The Maréchal rose. "Bring in the sacrifice!" he commanded.

I listened intently. It seemed to me I heard the hoofs of horses, but they might be merely the peasants or the Maréchal's own men passing by. I looked at Kotikokura. His hearing was acuter than mine, but he did not seem to hear anything. Perhaps they had already arrived, but planned to enter noiselessly, to avert useless slaughter.

Catherine, veiled in black, entered, preceded by the priest.

"Prepare!"

The priests uncovered the victim. Catherine, white-faced, her eyes tightly shut, tottered. The priests supported her.

"Woman, rejoice, for the Lord of Light has chosen you to bring truth into the world!"

The priests began disrobing Catherine, exposing the delicate curves of her motherhood to the gaze of the Satanists. She recoiled.

"Woman, do not hinder us!"

Catherine looked at Gilles, her eyes dimmed with tears. Her chest heaved a little, as if stifling a sob. Her lips moved. I knew she endeavored to pronounce his name.

But Gilles did not hear. His face looked like the ruin of some magnificent castle.

I made a sign to Kotikokura. He nodded almost imperceptibly.

Catherine bent her head upon her chest, as if to cover her lovely nakedness. She raised the corners of her eyes a little and looked at me. I was on the point of calling out: "Fear not! Cartaphilus will not allow him to mutilate your body and to slaughter your child!"

She was stretched out upon a bench. The priest brought a gold basin and a long knife whose edge was sharpened to the thinness of a hair.

"Bring in the Child of Reason!" Gilles ordered.

The priest pushed forcibly the wall on the left which opened like a door. Now I understood the true geography of the place. The temple was adjacent to the cellar where I had seen the corpses of the children.

Meanwhile, the person whose sex was difficult to determine and who had scattered the strange incense, helped the Maréchal cover his head with a tallith upon which were embroidered formulæ from the Kabala and wound seven times about his waist a red girdle.

Would help come too late? Even if the hoofbeats that I now distinctly heard were those of our horsemen, it was doubtful whether they could reach us in time.

The priest brought a large glass jar in which a strange creature lay huddled together—something that resembled a human fœtus or the embryo of a monkey.

Was this the Child of Reason? I had long discovered that reason could not rule the universe, but I had never suspected the misshapen form of her progeny!

The Maréchal raised the knife and made an inverted cross upon his chest. The reflection glittered upon Catherine's face.

The hoofbeats approached. If I could only delay the madman a little longer!

"Gilles," I whispered, "the cross must be made three times or the result is frustrated."

He looked at me. His eyes were two coals aflame.

He made the cross three times and bent over the body.

I heard drums and sharp words of command at a distance.

"Gilles! From left to right, not from right to left!"

Gilles repeated the gesture as I had told him.

"Gilles!" I said.

"Stop!" he shouted. "Do not delay me now!"

It was no longer Gilles who spoke. His voice was raucous and strained.

He touched the body with the point of the knife. One moment more, and it would have been too late!

I grasped his hand and threw the knife to the floor. My fingers closed on the mechanism releasing the poisonous vapor, when suddenly trumpets resounded and doors were broken in from all sides.

A thousand fighting men flooded the Black Temple.

Gilles stared at me. "Judas!" he shouted.

He was surrounded by soldiers. Two soldiers grasped the Maréchal's arm.

"I am Gilles de Retz, Maréchal of France."

"You are the Devil! You shall burn in your own hell-fire!" one of the brothers shouted, hewing his way to the altar.

Catherine jumped up, covered herself with a black veil, and kneeling before her brother, she sobbed.

"Spare him. He knew not what he was doing."

I motioned to Kotikokura. In the fracas that ensued, we made our escape.

"Whatever happens, must, Kotikokura. From all eternity to all eternity things are destined to happen, but however exciting these escapades may be, we cannot afford to wait and see their dénouement. A hundred years from now they shall all be dust,—the good and the wicked, the beautiful and the ugly, the true and the false, Bluebeard and Catherine—and Anne. At most, a legend may sprout out of the dung of Time."

Kotikokura nodded.

"Before we leave, however, I must send Anne a present."

I stopped at the next town and hired a messenger to deliver to Anne a box in which I placed a ruby as large as a pigeon's egg and a letter.

"Wear this, my beautiful one, in the cool valley that separates the two hillocks of passion. Farewell. Cartaphilus."

"Kotikokura," I said, "I will have none of God, and I will have none of the Devil. Gods and Devils get along capitally for the reason that the existence of the one depends upon the other. Wherever heaven is, hell is not far off. The Prince of Darkness is also Lucifer, the Lord of Light. Man, however, is destined to suffer whether gods or devils rule. He is the sacrificial goat. From whatever tree he plucks the fruit—whether it grows in the Garden of Eden or in the Garden of the Other One—the taste is always ashes."

LXII

THE CITY OF FLOWERS—LA FESTA DEL GRILLO—THE SANITARY EXPERT—THE INTOXICATION OF KOTI-KOKURA—THE ADVENTURE OF TWO YOUTHS

FLOWERS hanging over the tall stone and iron fences; flowers at the windows; flowers in the hair of women, between the lips of merchants selling fish or fruit in the narrow tortuous streets; flowers over the ears of little boys and girls playing in the yards; flowers around the necks of donkeys and horses; flowers sailing over the yellowish waters of the Arno,—a carnival of flowers, an orgy of perfume!

"What an appropriate name for the city, Kotikokura,—Fiorenze —Florence, the City of Flowers."

Kotikokura plucked several roses and placed them in the ribbon around his headgear.

"Kotikokura, you are the god of Spring."

He grinned and began to dance.

"And the High Priest of the great god Ca-ta-pha."

He bowed solemnly before me.

The sun barely showed above the hills, and a grayish fog, thin almost to extinction, rose slowly from the ground. A young shepherd urged his flock to cross the Arno, now almost dry, from one bank to another. An old woman beat a large hog that would not leave his puddle. A few dogs barked and their echoes, like small rocks, beat against the sides of the hills. Two crows dashed by, large worms in their beaks. Several sparrows bathed in the dust, chirping violently.

"Kotikokura, nothing changes. I saw these sparrows and crows and sheep and this old woman more than a thousand years ago. Here they are again! We are all enchanted. Every few centuries, we wake up for a moment, then fall asleep again. Things seem different only because our eyes are unaccustomed to the light."

Kotikokura offered me a rosebud.

Wagons began to rumble and horses and donkeys and oxen to trot, each producing a different and peculiar harmony. The wagons

were bedecked with flowers and ribbons, and filled with tiny cages
of all materials—wood, iron, tin, porcelain. Within each cage, a
grasshopper, still and motionless, and a small leaf of cabbage or
lettuce.

The merchants descended, tied their animals to iron posts, and
arranged their merchandise. Other merchants with various goods
drove into the square and all along both banks of the Arno, sellers
of spice breads, of sweets, of toys, of confetti; a merry-go-round
with grotesque animals, turned by a small donkey as sad as a clown;
games of chance, cards, dice, hoops to be thrown over iron spikes,
wheels that stopped at lucky numbers, here and there an old man
or woman selling crosses, candles, and amulets. Beggars led by dogs
and playing on flutes or accordions or singing obscene parodies of
current, sentimental ditties.

Inn keepers raised the iron shutters of their shops and placed
tables and chairs on the sidewalks, shouting all the time to the
merchants not to crowd too near their doors.

People, pedestrians, or in carriages, were coming from all directions, singing, laughing, imitating the music of grasshoppers. The
sellers shouted the names of their wares, embellished by delectable
adjectives, at the top of their voices.

"Buy a grasshopper here! He sings like a bird."

"Grasshoppers in golden cages."

"Rare song-birds."

"Get your spice bread."

"Confetti! Confetti! Confetti for your sweetheart."

Children pulling their elders toward the cages; girls in mock
refusal to accept the arms of youths; men and women laughing uproariously, blowing horns, shouting the names of friends.

Long before noon, each person was carrying a cage with a grasshopper, coaxing it to sing. But always the animal remained motionless and still.

"Kotikokura, shall I buy you a 'grillo'?"

He nodded.

I bought him a cage. He hung it around his neck. We seated
ourselves at a table and ordered sweet wine. Kotikokura emptied
cup after cup. His eyes glistened and darted to and fro like mechanical things.

A tall man of regal bearing with long blond hair and a flowing
beard, dressed in a cloak of red velvet, stood near our table, watching the crowd.

'Thus Apollonius must have looked in his youth,' I thought. 'This is no ordinary son of Adam.'

I rose. "There is a vacant chair at our table. May I ask you to join us, signor?"

He looked at me. His eyes were blue with a glint of gold.

"Thank you."

He seated himself. Kotikokura filled a cup of wine and offered it to him.

"We are strangers in the city. Could you tell us in what saint's honor this holiday is given?"

He smiled. "The Florentines are not religious enough to honor a saint. They would rather honor a pagan god—or a grasshopper."

"Perhaps one ought not to ask the reason for any merrymaking. It is a reason in itself. But it is a human weakness to ask always why."

"This is 'la Festa del Grillo'—the Feast of the Grasshopper, for the grasshopper is considered the emblem of summer."

"It seems to me that the rose or some bird would be a more appropriate symbol."

"I disagree with you there. The grasshopper is the most fortunate and the most rational of animals. The gods were merry when they created him . . . !"

Kotikokura refilled our cups.

"Is not man's life illogical?" the stranger continued. "He spends his youth and early manhood in learning an art or a trade. And when he has at last acquired knowledge and wisdom and perhaps wealth, he is old and undesirable. The young wenches that laugh so gaily and throw confetti into our cups, pass him by or mock him.

"How different is the life of the grasshopper! He begins by being old, so to say, for his early life is devoted to the accumulation of food for his descendants, eating and digesting.

"But what a magnificent dénouement! His last few weeks—corresponding to years in human calculation—are a carnival of love! No food, no cares! Nothing but song, merrymaking and mating! That is why the Florentines, true descendants of the Athenians, make this apparently humble creature the symbol of the richness of summer."

"Are you a student of nature or a philosopher?" I asked.

"I dabble in many things. My chief interests are scientific. The problem of sewerage engages my attention primarily, but I am also intensely devoted to the study of military machinery."

"Military machinery?" I must have looked startled.

"Is that so surprising?" the stranger asked, while a gentle smile crept from the corners of his mouth to his eyes.

"Rather. You have the bearings of an artist. I would take you for one of the masters who have made this city a shrine of beauty."

"I toy with art as well as with science. Man is a fighting animal primarily and man interests me supremely. But his instruments of destruction are always antiquated. I should like to fashion weapons that raise fire and strike the enemy a hundred miles away. I like to build bridges, channels and impenetrable defenses. . ."

He stroked his beard leisurely.

'Is it possible?' I thought. 'Can Apollonius change thus?'

"Can you conceive of anything more fascinating than a steel bridge that can span a sea, and yet may be folded and carried upon the back of a donkey; or a projectile the shape of an apple which, cast by a small mechanical device, strikes a distant palace and crashes it like a child's toy?"

"You are an artist, even though you employ metals and motors in place of words. You have a painter's eye and a poet's illusion. . ."

"The illusion of one generation," the stranger replied affably, "is the commonplace of the next."

Kotikokura tried to persuade his grasshopper to sing. He stood up and danced. "Sing, sing!" he shouted.

Several people stopped and kept tune to his dancing by clapping and stamping their feet.

"It is useless, my friend," the stranger said a little sadly. "He never sings when imprisoned."

Kotikokura reseated himself. The stranger continued to speak for some time on military problems and engineering. "Some day," he said, "I shall construct a machine that can lift me up to the skies like an eagle. . ."

He rose. Pressing matters, he explained, compelled his attention. Perhaps his disposition was too restless to permit him to linger. Had he stayed a while longer, I might have confided to him matters that would have changed his life and the history of the human race. However the fateful moment flew away like a careless bird.

"I thank you very much for your hospitality, gentlemen. I would gladly remain longer with you, but I am leaving tomorrow for a long trip, and I must prepare many things."

"A long trip?" I asked.

"Yes, to Constantinople, perhaps to Asia."

"You will not regret it."

"Have you been there?"

"On several occasions."

"I always refrain from asking questions about places I expect to visit. I prefer to be unbiased and uninformed."

"An artist— —"

He smiled. "You insist upon considering me an artist, signore."

"An artist or a philosopher. . . But will you refresh yourself with another cup before we part?"

Kotikokura filled the cups.

He drained the cup without resuming his seat.

"If I had the time, I should like to make a statue of your friend," he whispered. "He is the very incarnation of Pan. . ."

He smiled politely and made a gesture of farewell. I should not have permitted him to go out of my life like a cloud that leaves no trace.

"I hope we shall meet again," I mumbled politely, instead of startling him into staying. "I am Count de Cartaphile."

"A descendant of the Crusader?"

"Yes. How well informed you are!"

"I am interested in all things human."

"And all things mechanical."

"Yes."

"And also, I take it, in all things divine?"

"No. The earth is sufficient for me. . ."

"May I know to whom I have the honor of speaking?"

"I am Leonardo da Vinci."

Kotikokura was laughing. He had drunk a little beyond measure, and his eyelids looked heavy.

"Human pleasures are pathetic, Kotikokura. Look at those poor people trying to be happy."

Kotikokura opened his eyes wide and nodded.

"They throw confetti at one another; they sing; they blow horns; they dance; they laugh—but beyond it all, do you not feel a great emptiness, and a great fear, Kotikokura? Do you not hear invisible wings like the winds that whistle through cemeteries . . . ?"

Kotikokura nodded, his eyes closed.

"Can you not see Death, the Giant, riding his Phantom Horse, grinning to himself as he surveys his harvest?"

Kotikokura placed his head upon the table.

"No, no . . . you must not fall asleep. Come!"

He blinked several times, rose and steadied himself on my arm.

Two youths, dressed in green cloaks, were walking in front of us, arm in arm. Their caps, surmounted by red plumes, were slightly tilted. Their black curls, barely covering half of their napes, were ruffled by a light wind that had just risen. Kotikokura, a little unsteady, was hanging on my arm.

"Do not these youths remind you of exquisite music? I fear to see their faces. I do not want to be disappointed. . ."

Three men, slightly unsteady on their feet, turned the corner, and approached the youths. The latter tried to avoid the encounter, but the men stopped them.

"You shan't go any farther, my little chicks," one of them shouted. The others laughed.

"You will come along with us."

"Stand aside!" one of the youths commanded. "Let us pass."

The men looked at him from head to foot, and laughed.

"Just look at him! Why, my little midget, I can swallow you at a gulp," one man, tall, muscular, and heavy-bearded, shouted gaily.

"It's a girl," another said.

"They are both girls . . . can't you see?" the third one added, scrutinizing their faces.

"It is fortunate for you that we have left our swords at home . . . or we should give you proof of our manhood!"

"There are other ways of determining that problem," one of the three remarked with an obscene leer.

"They are boys!" the first of three exclaimed.

"It does not matter what you are, my little ones. Come with us . . . !"

"Take your foul hands away! Stand aside, let us pass or tomorrow your bodies shall swing from the gibbet," exclaimed one of the two, his voice raised in a boyish treble.

"Ha, ha! Ha, ha! The fellow has courage," cried the bearded roysterer, clumsily embracing the child.

"Tomorrow takes care of itself. When we come across delicious fruit, we pluck it," shouted the second, a red-faced youth with Spanish mustachios.

"And we pluck it tonight," added the tallest of the three, a dark, clean-shaven villain.

A little hand descended upon his cheek with enough force to make him hear the angels sing. Fury and desire outstripped his pain. He seized the combative little figure and pressed the humid ardor of drunken kisses upon the child's mouth.

The other two men grasped the second youth by the arms and pulled him into the thicket.

I approached. "Why do you molest these young people?"

"Mind your own business!"

The youths looked at me. Their faces were almost exactly alike and of singular beauty.

"I shall not interfere with you, if you will not interfere with them."

"Stand off or——"

One of them placed his hand upon the hilt of his knife. Kotikokura, who was standing in back of me, jumped at his throat.

The others drew their swords. Kotikokura loosened his grip on the first one who coughed violently, then struck the second roysterer a blow over the face which upset him. I gripped the third, and with one delicate twist which I had learned in the East, dislocated his arm. His sword dropped and he bent in two, howling with pain.

"These drunken ruffians will no longer annoy you," I said to the youths who were holding each other's arms, trembling.

"We are grateful to you, signor," one of them answered manfully.

"May we accompany you to where you desire to go, seeing that it is not safe for two young people like you to be out on such a night unaccompanied and unarmed?"

"We are going home, and if you will be good enough to accompany us, we shall be beholden to you."

We stopped at the gate of a palace, situated near the Duomo.

"It is here that we live, signore," one of the youths informed me. "Should you care to come in, our uncle will be delighted to make your acquaintance and thank you for your chivalrous aid."

I made a few evasive excuses.

"Do come!" he insisted.

"Are you certain that you are not inviting—the Devil and his —valet?"

They laughed.

We accepted.

LXIII

ANTONIO AND ANTONIA—BOY OR GIRL—I BLUSH—I
TELL A STORY—BEAUTY IS A FLAME—TWO RINGS
FOR ONE

BARON DI MARTINI, a distant relative of the Prince—or if the
rumor was true, a half-brother—greeted us cordially.

"Can you imagine, signore, two young scatterbrains going about
the city unattended? I did not know about it until half an hour
ago, and I have just sent some servants in search of them. I am
really grateful to you, signore, for having saved them from much
unpleasantness."

A lackey removed the cloaks of the youths. One of them embraced the Baron.

"What!" he exclaimed, "dressed as a boy, Antonia? What does
this mean?"

"It is la Festa del Grillo, uncle! Summer! On such a day surely
I may have a fling at life . . ."

The Baron laughed.

How had I been so unobservant? The handsome youth was a
girl! The scoundrels that accosted them suspected aright. Nevertheless, there was in the slim, graceful figure, a touch of something
that justified the boyish mummery.

"Uncle," said the other, "we have invited these gentlemen to be
our guests."

"Splendid, Antonio," the uncle remarked.

Antonio, slim and impetuous, was evidently a boy. However it
imposed no strain upon the imagination to regard him as a girl in
disguise. Without being effeminate he still had that first bloom
of childhood, which is either sexless or epicene.

"Is it proper really," I asked, "to intrude upon you in this
fashion?"

"I insist, signor, you must be my guests," the Baron replied.

"I asked the young gentlemen—or as I notice now—the signor

339

and the signorina, whether they were quite certain they were not
inviting . . . most sinister characters."

"Sinister characters!" the uncle laughed. "I do not think a
gentleman can ever disguise himself."

"It was easy for the signorina to masquerade as a lad."

Antonia clapped her hands. "I am so glad I deceived you."

"You ought to see me dressed as a woman," Antonio interjected.

"Oh yes, he is wonderful!" exclaimed Antonia. "He should have
been a woman . . . and I a man, really."

"Silence, woman," the boy commanded gravely, "or I shall
presently chastise you."

Antonia laughed. "You should have heard him threaten the three
scoundrels that were annoying us, Uncle. 'It is fortunate for you
that we left our swords at home. Stand aside, let us pass, or tomorrow you shall swing from the gibbet.' "

Everybody laughed.

"Really, signor, these young scatterbrains are keen at reading
faces. They take after their mother, my sister, a remarkable woman.
May her soul rest in peace!"

"We hesitated to accept your invitation because we are strangers
in Florence and have no wish to transgress upon your kindness. I
am Count de Cartaphile of Provence."

"Count de Cartaphile!" the Baron exclaimed. "A descendant of
Count de Cartaphile who single-handed slew a regiment of infidels
and captured the Holy Sepulchre almost alone?"

I nodded.

"What a fortunate coincidence, children!"

Antonio and Antonia looked at me with new interest.

"What an honor, Count . . . and what a delightful surprise! I
am writing the history of the Crusades. How often I have spoken
to my nephew and to my niece about the exploits of your ancestor,
and his companion, the Red Knight! I once wrote to you to Provence
but evidently my message, entrusted to a wandering scholar, failed
to reach its destination. You must be our guest, Count—as long as
you remain in Florence."

"Yes, yes," the children insisted.

I promised to stay overnight.

Baron di Martini showed me the garden and orchard which surrounded the castle. Kotikokura walked behind us between two large
dogs, black as charcoal.

"The more I read about the chivalrous deeds of Count de Carta-phile and the Red Knight, the more fascinating those two characters become."

We walked in silence for a while in a deluge of flowers.

"Do you think it really possible, Baron, for two knights such as the Count de Cartaphile and the Red Knight—single-handed—to capture the Holy Sepulchre from a thousand defenders?"

I looked at him quizzically.

He nodded. "Sheer physical strength is not enough. Your ancestor may have known the secret word that enlists invisible powers. Both he and the Red Knight, too, undoubtedly called angels in armor to help. The hosts of Heaven were their retinue."

"I am familiar with these legends. Our family chronicle tells that the Red Knight appeared in several places at once. . ."

"Space and time," the Baron replied, "are not subject to immutable laws. Their limitations are more elastic. . ."

"Are you," I asked, "a mathematician as well as a historian?"

"Why?"

"In my youth, I had a friend—a distinguished Arabian mathematician—who resembled you very much, Baron, and I often noticed that those who resemble each other physically have much in common mentally."

"Our thoughts shape our features, no doubt."

"Or, perhaps, our features shape our thoughts. . ."

"Truth," the Baron replied, "is an equation permitting of many solutions and it is sometimes difficult to draw a clear line of division. Even sex and personality are not always defined. Human character, too, may be a double equation. The unknown quantity may stand for both good *and* evil."

"You are indeed a philosopher."

"My nephew and niece," the Baron continued, "are a double equation. They look alike and they think the same thoughts. You can substitute one for the other. . ."

"Remarkable children," I added.

"And very lovely. But there they are, whispering to each other. I am quite certain they are conspiring to keep you with us beyond tomorrow."

Antonio and Antonia advanced toward us.

"How delicate is youth!" I said.

"Nothing," the Baron added, "surpasses the loveliness of spring. I wish I could keep them from growing older! Before long I shall lose them. Each will go and lose himself in the labyrinth of love and life. . ."

"Worse still, perhaps . . . they will lose each other!"

Antonia and Antonio raced toward us. Each offered me a rose. The boy's rose was white, hers red. My face flushed. I was a little embarrassed, a pleasurable sensation. 'How many centuries have passed Cartaphilus,' I thought, 'since you have last blushed! You are still young. . . It is well.'

"You are too kind," I said, at loss for words.

"Without you, Count, we might be dead . . ." Antonia remarked archly.

"You exaggerate your peril."

"No, no, Count," the Baron interposed. "You do not know the Florentines. Art and crime both flourish within our walls."

"Count," said the girl, "you must know many stories. . ."

"Tell us one," said the boy.

"A story!" the girl repeated.

"They still are children," the Baron remarked, "even if they pretend to be grown up."

Kotikokura ran, the dogs after him, barking lustily.

"It is strange, Count—those two dogs, ordinarily ferocious toward strangers, have become from the first moment inseparable companions of your man."

"He is a lover of animals, Baron, and animals, no doubt, scent his affection at once."

Antonio and Antonia, on either side of me, we walked slowly through the garden. The delicate pressure of their arms—one barely heavier than the other—delighted me. It was like the warm pulsation of the heart of a bird.

The Baron, summoned by the Prince on business of state, apologized for his absence and asked the scatterbrains—as he was pleased to call the children whenever he was most affectionate—to entertain me.

We were sitting in a corner of the enormous reception hall, whose walls had been frescoed by the old masters of Florence, Antonio on my right, Antonia on my left. Kotikokura sat opposite us, a dog on either side of him.

I raised the chin of Antonio with my forefinger, then that of Antonia, and looked into their eyes.

"Who are you?" I asked.

They smiled.

"Who are you?" I repeated.

"We are Toni," Antonia answered.

"Both Toni?"

They nodded.

"Are you one or two?"

"We are one and two."

"Where did I meet you before?"

"You met me . . . far, far away," said Antonia, speaking like a child that is telling a fairy tale.

"And me still farther," added Antonio with boyish eagerness.

"He always tries to outdo me, Count. It is the vanity of the male. . ."

"Silence, woman!" the boy commanded. "Man is the master."

"No!" she exclaimed.

"Woman must remain the inferior of man—always," the boy insisted.

"Toni!" she exclaimed. "How can you say that?"

"Except you, my dear. But you are not a woman."

"Well, I shall be one."

"Never!"

"Yes . . . and I shall be the queen of a great nation where women rule over men."

"Do you not think that woman is the equal of man, Count?" Antonia asked.

"Some women are the equal of goddesses."

"See?"

"Then some men are the equal of gods, Count."

"They are."

"And is not a god greater than a goddess?"

"Sex distinctions are not important among the gods. . ."

"See, Toni? But Count, tell us the story you promised!"

They pulled their chairs nearer to me.

"Ready!" they both exclaimed.

"Once upon a time, there were two children—a boy and a girl——"

"No, no, Count."

"We are no longer children."

"Are you sure?"

"Of course."

"Some of the things I shall tell, you may not understand."

They laughed.

"Count," Antonio whispered, "we have read Aretino and Boccaccio."

Antonia blushed a little and nodded.

"What!" I exclaimed in mock reproof.

For a moment, they were nonplussed but, catching a faint smile about my lips, they burst into laughter. Each placed an arm upon my shoulders, and their voices mingling into one, said: "You cannot deceive us, Count. You too believe that the beautiful is the good. Uncle sometimes tries to appear severe on moral questions. Dear uncle—he considers himself responsible for our welfare. But you are like an older brother. You can afford to be candid with us. . ."

"You are right, little sister and brother."

"Don't call us little," Antonia reprimanded me. "Call us sister and brother."

I placed my arms about their waists. "Brother and sister, you are supremely good, because you are supremely beautiful . . . and as long as you will be beautiful, you will be good. Ugliness is the only sin. . ."

"Tediousness is the only evil," Antonia added sagely.

I related divers experiences. By merely calling the centuries years and the years months, I discovered that, after all, one could squeeze upon a tiny canvas what had been spread leisurely upon an enormous wall. Although I used various names to hide my identity, they knew perfectly well that I was telling my own experiences.

Salome and Ulrica intrigued Antonia, Flower of the Evening and Damis fascinated Antonio. They asked questions, apparently very innocently and merely for the sake of elucidation, but in reality they showed that uncanny prescience of sex which sometimes startles us in the very young.

I thought of the white rose, symbol of purity, whose perfume and pollen are but sexual allurement to entice the bee and the butterfly. Under the petal of their youth, the children's senses were stirred, and the perfume of their desire was wafted to me.

They snuggled against me. Suddenly, Antonia stood up. "Why, my dear, the Count must be thirsty and hungry too."

Antonio clapped his hands. "Why, of course! You will never be a woman, sister. You will never think of important trifles."

She smiled. Was her smile irony? Was it wisdom? Was it pity? Was she a daughter of the Sphinx?

A servant entered. Antonia ordered wine and cakes and fruits in such abundance that I burst out laughing.

"You overestimate my capacity."

Antonia filled our cups. We drank to beauty, which is truth, and to truth which is beauty.

"Oh," she exclaimed suddenly, "we have forgotten him." She pointed to Kotikokura who was smiling, his eyes half-closed. "He is such a queer and dear fellow," she whispered.

She filled a cup for him and brought him some cakes and fruit.

I told them anecdotes about Africa and India. Cheered by the wine, they laughed uproariously.

"What a strange ring you have, Count. Is it from India?"

"No, Toni—this ring belonged to one of Mohammed's nephews . . . it brings good luck to its wearer."

"Has it brought good luck to you?"

"I have had the good fortune of meeting you."

"It is rather the other way, then, Count. He who wears it brings good luck to those with whom he comes in contact."

"Do you really think it beautiful?"

"Very."

"Well, then, I shall have it cut and made into two rings, and if you will allow me, I shall present each of you with one, so that you may always have good luck or bring good luck to others."

"Oh, Count, you are too good to us, really!" they exclaimed, their fingers pecking at my sleeves like small birds.

"We shall remember you—always," Antonio said.

"Whenever we are unaccountably happy, we shall think of you." Antonia added.

"Will you think of us, too?" the boy asked.

"I shall think of you—long after you have forgotten me."

"Count, would you like to see the rings our mother gave us before she died?"

"Oh, yes, Toni, bring the little box."

Antonio went out. Antonia placed her small hand in mine and leaned her head against my shoulder.

"Count . . . who are you?"

I was startled.

"Who are you?"

I kissed her dark tresses gently, and equally gently removed my hand from hers. This bud was too tender, too beautiful, to be plucked.

Antonio returned. He opened a small gold box, with two rings livid with exquisite rubies. Centuries of mystery and of passion seemed to slumber in the depths of the stones.

"How beautiful!" I exclaimed.

"Mother told us to wear them when we are happy. Shall we not wear them tonight, brother?"

And the two rings blazed on the hands of the children, flaming like rose leaves, scarlet like drops of blood.

Kotikokura snored, his head resting upon one of the dogs, their shadow mingling and forming a bulky elephant whose trunk made a semicircle.

We talked, intoxicated by something that was not wine. At last nature demanded her toll. The sandman strewed his ware into the golden eyes of the two children. Antonio yawned. Antonia blinked.

"It is time to retire," I said.

They were reluctant, but finally yielded.

At the door, Antonia threw me a kiss. Antonio raised his hand half-way, checked himself, and blushed.

I was about to draw the curtains of my bed, when I heard footsteps, hardly heavier than those of a cat, approach. I strained my eyes, but I could see nothing. The hall was very long, and I had time to conjecture.

A soft-tipped finger pressed against my lips. "Sh. . ." I moved slowly toward the wall. The bed hardly felt the weight of her.— She pressed her lips on mine.—My hands were many mouths, drinking nectar.—A long kiss.—A pressure of breast against breast, a mingling of lips, a moan. . .

Like some white weightless feather which a zephyr wafts about a garden, she rose and disappeared in the blackness of the room.— —

Thoughts like many-colored confetti fell softly upon my brain, making beautiful patterns which bore no names.— —

Suddenly, I heard the soft footsteps again. Was she returning? Did her lips ache for another kiss . . . ? Again the pressure of a finger against my lips. "Sh . . ." Again a kiss, tender and impetuous. Did my hands deceive me? Was not beauty a flame? Was not joy a slow swooning?

I awoke. I rubbed my eyes and forehead trying to remember something—something incredibly beautiful and delicious. What was it? When did I . . . ? Was it a dream? I felt a pressure against my thigh. The ruby—a frozen drop of flame—on the head of the serpent.

"Antonia," I whispered.

I placed the ring upon my small finger. It fitted perfectly. I rose. Something fell to the floor.

"The other ring! Antonio?" I placed the ring on top of the other. They melted into one.

'Who are you?'

'We are Toni.'

'Both Toni?'

'Yes.'

'Are you one or two?'

'We are one and two.'

'Both one?'

'Yes.'

How incredibly beautiful!

The Double Blossom of Passion—the almost impossible loveliness of John and Mary in one!

A courier arrived with a letter from Baron di Martini. Affairs of state compelled him to prolong his absence for a few weeks. Unfortunately, the presence of the "scatterbrains" was also essential. Meanwhile, he would consider it a special favor if I remained his guest.

"Are the children gone?" I asked.

"Yes, Count. Early this morning, a messenger from the Duke came to fetch them."

"Kotikokura, we must go."

He sighed. His eye caught my hand. He grinned. I felt a little uneasy.

"It is the gift of the children."

Then, discreetly as ever, Kotikokura made preparations for our departure.

"Before I go I must see a goldsmith who will make two rings of this one—one for Antonio and one for Antonia. Alas, Kotikokura, we shall never see the children again—at least, never as they were . . . last night . . . never. Ah, the perfect hour of youth is more frail than the outer rim of the moon when the dawn kisses her lips!"

LXIV

MAN A RHEUMATIC TORTOISE—I TAKE STOCK OF MY-
SELF—I BRING THE HOLY GRAIL TO ALEXANDER VI
—I DISCUSS THEOLOGY WITH THE POPE—THE HOLY
FATHER AND HIS UNHOLY FAMILY—I AM TALKA-
TIVE—ALEXANDER ASKS A QUESTION—TRAPPED

KOTIKOKURA and I walked along the shore of the Tiber which, heavy
with recent rain, moved ponderously like a man newly enriched.
Lonesomeness made me shiver with a sudden chill. I took Kotikokura's arm and felt comforted a little. Strange that this queer being
—captured almost like a wild animal in the African jungle—was
my only companion.

Fourteen centuries! What profound change had occurred in me?
I remained bewildered among my thoughts. I had learned divers
magics, sciences, languages and philosophies. I had witnessed the
rise and fall of emperors and civilizations. I had seen the colossal
growth of Christianity—its physical power and its spiritual weakness. I had learned the meaning of history and the meaning of
legend, and how truth and fiction mingled irrevocably together. I
had experienced innumerable shades of love from grossest sensuality
to a touch so vague that it would hardly graze the tip of a butterfly's wing. Beggar, saint, prince, monk, god and devil, I had lived
a thousand lives.

What new paths had I discovered? How was I different from
Cartaphilus, the young captain in the Roman army of occupation
in Jerusalem at the time when the young Jewish carpenter was
condemned to die on the cross? Under changing masks I remained
myself. In spite of all, I was still Cartaphilus!

What, then, was the purpose of traversing so long a road? Would
sixty or seventy years have sufficed? Was everything relative in a
world that would not or could not remain still for a fraction of a
second?

Yes, that was my discovery: things only seemed, there was
neither truth nor lie, neither good nor evil, neither God nor Devil.

"There is neither life nor death," said Apollonius. "The feet that tread upon the dust and the trodden dust are not as different as they seem. Life and death are one!"

Progress? There was no progress. For every step forward humanity takes one step back. Man hurls his ideas far ahead of him, like golden discs, but he himself crawls onward like a rheumatic tortoise.

"Kotikokura, have I changed much since you first met me—you remember, in Africa—long, long ago?"

He shook his head.

"Am I still the same?"

"Ca-ta-pha god always."

"Perhaps you are right, Kotikokura. Does not a tree, once grown to maturity, remain unchanged, even if it lives two thousand years? Time merely draws circles about its trunk to indicate that he has forgotten nothing and no one, that he still is the punctilious slave of Eternity, who sits unmoved upon the peak of the universe, and within whose shadow all things are."

Kotikokura nodded.

"You, however, have changed considerably, Kotikokura. You are hardly recognizable. They even mistook you once or twice for my younger brother."

Kotikokura grinned.

"When you reach maturity, will you become Ca-ta-pha?"

He laughed.

"Would that please you greatly?"

He nodded vigorously.

"Is Ca-ta-pha the highest peak to which man may aspire?"

He nodded.

"Then has Ca-ta-pha simply turned about himself, when he believed that he was climbing the staircase to the stars?"

"Ca-ta-pha god."

"So be it then! Let Ca-ta-pha turn and turn, like the sun—and by turning, radiate light! Kotikokura shall be his moon—the reflection of Ca-ta-pha and"—Kotikokura grinned—"grin as a moon should."

His Holiness Alexander VI, was financially embarrassed. The money received from the sale of indulgences fell far below expectations. Italy was overtaxed. Beyond the Alps, the people groaned and grumbled. Still, he had made a vow to finish the inner buildings of the Vatican during his lifetime. Who could tell how suddenly the Scissors of Time would snap the thread? Bricks and marble and cement remained like hills of debris in the yard of the Vatican, while the walls gaped and the rain splashed upon the foundation.

Rome felt the tension of her master.

Alexander intrigued me. He wore his sins—incest, sodomy, murder —gracefully like a cloak. His extraordinary political sagacity, his love for the arts, were woven into the pattern. I was anxious to meet the vicar of Christ and Priapus!

"Kotikokura, having gathered fame, let us profit thereby."

Kotikokura looked at me, a thousand questions dancing in his eyes.

"The great-grandson of Count de Cartaphile shall profit by the exploits of his ancestor."

Dressed in ancient armor, inlaid with crosses, and accompanied by Kotikokura, I rode solemnly upon a tall white horse through the main streets of Rome.

People gathered in clusters whispering, or followed us at a respectable distance. Some knelt, many crossed themselves, or bowed deeply. For three days, I repeated my silent and peaceful conquest of the city. On the fourth morning, I stopped at the gate of the Vatican, and begged admittance to the Holy Father. Meeting some resistance, I bribed my way to his door.

Kotikokura remained outside with our horses.

The Pope's study overlooked his gardens, and from the open window came the delightful perfume of violets and lilacs. His Holiness was sitting at a long table whose massive legs were carved in the shape of young bulls, the coat of arms of the Borgias. A large copy of the Decameron, illuminated and encrusted, occupied the center of the table. His Holiness was dressed in white from head to foot. There was devouring curiosity in his eyes, but also irony played like lightning about his lips and chin, and his large wide forehead radiated intelligence.

I knelt. He lifted slightly his foot encased in a gold-embroidered white slipper. I kissed the sharp point. He made the sign of the cross over me and bade me rise.

"Are you indeed the great-grandson of Count de Cartaphile?"

"I am, Your Holiness—this is the very armor he wore when he delivered the Holy Tomb from the hands of the Infidels."

The Pope nodded. But something about his lips told me that

he was skeptical. I liked him for it, foreseeing an interesting mental skirmish, such as I had not enjoyed for a century.

"I have brought with me the Holy Grail, the cup out of which our Saviour drank at the Last Supper. My ancestor kept it hidden in a secret vault, which no one could unlock save he who lived a life that was truly Christ-like. Seven years, Holy Father, I spent in prayer and fasting. One morning, the vault miraculously opened by itself. The glory of it made me swoon. When I regained consciousness, the Holy Cup, filled to the brim with red wine, was in my hand. I drank it, and my body which had been emaciated from starvation, suddenly felt lithe and powerful as a youth's."

Alexander continued to smile enigmatically. "It is well to live a Christian life, and the rewards are many and great. May I see the Holy Grail, Count?"

The cup was a fine piece of Eastern workmanship—jade studded with emeralds. The Pope fondled it in his plump hands. He closed his eyes a little. I could not help thinking that he compared the sensation to the touch of a woman's breast.

"It is indeed beautiful, Count, and he who made it was an artist."

"The Lord Himself inspired his hands."

He raised his left brow and smacked his lips, as Nero was in the habit of doing.

"Every true artist, Count, is inspired by the Lord, even if he paints the manhood of a faun or the breasts of a Diana."

I yearned to tell him: "Magnificent Pagan!" but for the time being, my rôle was that of a perfect Christian. I smiled, pained a little.

He laughed. "Count, you must not take words too literally. I mean that all art is divine."

"Yes, Holy Father."

He placed the Holy Grail upon the Decameron.

"Beauty is beauty everywhere."

"Your Holiness, the Holy Grail is not only beautiful. It possesses miraculous power. Anyone drinking a drop of wine out of it, or merely touching it with his lips, regains youth and strength."

The Pope raised the cup to his lips.

"Provided," I continued, "his life be as pure and undefiled as a child's."

"Of course," he smiled, replacing the cup upon the table.

"Holy Father, it would be selfish for me to keep so precious a thing for myself."

He looked at me, closing his left eye.

"It belongs to all Christendom."

The Pope meditated, one palm upon the table, the other upon his leg.

"How can the religion of our Lord Jesus flourish unless all believers pay Peter's pence to Saint Peter?"

He continued to remain pensive.

"Holy Father, if the world hears of the cup which works miracles, sacrifices will roll like a flood into the Papal exchequer."

The Pope stood up. His weight did not diminish his stature. He was taller than Nero, but shorter than Charlemagne. He walked over to the window, breathed deeply, caressed his robe.

"Count, are you the only one who knows of the story of the Holy Grail?"

"Yes, Your Holiness, but by this time, Rome certainly knows of my existence. Rome and the world will listen to my tale."

"How so?"

"For three days, Your Holiness, clad in this armor, I rode through the city upon a white charger. The people are much intrigued. If it becomes known that a descendant of Count de Cartaphile has come to the Eternal City to bring to the Father of Christendom the Lord's Cup at the Last Supper, the four corners of the earth will reverberate with thanksgiving."

He interrupted me.

"So be it!"

We remained silent for a while.

"And what reward do you expect, Count?"

"Reward?"

"It is in the nature of man to demand payment."

"Your blessing, Holy Father, is the only reward I crave."

He scrutinized me. "You make yourself suspicious, my son."

"Suspicious?"

"You ride through the city on a white charger, dressed in armor. You bring me a precious cup of splendid oriental workmanship. You insist upon its miraculous power. No, it can hardly be that you desire no other reward save my blessing."

"I am the true descendant of Count de Cartaphile who saved the Tomb."

"That is a fairy-tale, and I am inclined to think that you are aware of it, Count."

His perspicacity pleased and astonished me.

"Count, it is better to make the people believe than to believe oneself. An actor who really feels his part is not half the artist, nor half as effective as one who has learned his rôle perfectly, and gives the illusion of feeling. I prefer to deal with an intelligent scoundrel rather than with a zealot. The scoundrel, at least, has his price.

"Zealots are a great source of danger and infernal bores. Only recently, I was constrained to order the burning of Savonarola, Prior of San Marco in Florence. He was a scholar and a pious man, but lacking in humor as a man upon the rack. I was sorry to consign him to the flames, but he was undermining the structure of our Church. Besides his implacable hatred of life revenged itself upon beauty. One statue is worth more than a hundred priors. . ."

He reseated himself. "Well?" he asked.

"Your Holiness, I am not a zealot nor do I bequeath the Holy Grail for any other purpose except that of enriching the Church. I am satisfied to bask in her glory. I should also like to bequeath to your Holiness the ancient armor worn by my sire——"

The Pope laughed. "I hope sincerely that you are merely acting. A man capable of such jests delights me immensely. Who are you?"

His eyes, hidden a little in the heavy bags of flesh, darted sharp short rays. He was certainly keener than Nero, taught in all the delicate nuances of the sophistry of the Church, and accustomed, like the rest of his family to subtle intrigues. It would not be so easy to extricate myself from his suspicion, but the elements of danger added zest to the conversation. I was prepared for everything. The Borgias were famous for the poisons they administered to their prisoners and to their guests—candarella, a mixture of arsenic, quicksilver and opium. I had hidden a powerful antidote in the gold cross on my chest.

"Who are you?" Alexander reiterated.

"I am Count de Cartaphile, Your Holiness."

He shook his head. "I know the genealogy of the Holy Roman Empire. There never was a Count de Cartaphile except, of course, in the legends of the Church."

I smiled. "It certainly would be neither proper nor indeed prudent to contradict Your Holiness."

"Fear nothing. You are my guest. Accept at least this much in return for your precious gifts."

"Holy Father, no greater honor has ever been mine."

"You bribed my officer, did you not, Count?"

This time I was really startled.

He laughed. "Am I not right?"

"Holy Father, I— —"

"Do not fear, my son. I am your Father Confessor."

"I bribed him, Your Holiness."

"Of course. I know he is very faithful. He allows no visitors to disturb me, except for a consideration. A saint who fasts and prays for seven years lacks the knowledge of human nature and the sense of humor to bribe an officer of Christ's Vicar on Earth."

I smiled.

"And do you think that Pope Alexander the Sixth, a Borgia, would allow a knight in full armor to ride through the streets of Rome for three days in succession, without investigating?"

"It was for the very purpose of attracting your attention, Holy Father, that I rode through the city. Even a man who fasts for seven years knows— —"

He shook his head. "A man who fasts for seven years and prays incessantly as—Count de Cartaphile—would not offer the Holy Grail to Alexander the Sixth. He would declaim hoarsely against a Pope who neither fasts nor prays. He would not understand at all the difference between a religious faith and a gigantic government."

"Is not faith the supreme tenet of the Church?"

He struck the table with his fist. "No!"

I was uneasy. Was the Holy father always so frank? Did he single me out because I was a stranger? Was he attempting to draw me out? What was his ulterior motive?

"No!" he repeated. "The Roman Empire prospered without a special religion. Greece flourished on skepticism. What is needed is a strong hand and a cool head. Life is not an affair of prayer and fasting, Count. If we followed the example of the Saints we would be barefooted, ragged and ignorant."

"It is not a question of this world, Your Holiness, but of the next. 'What shall it profit a man if he gain the whole world and lose his soul?' "

"Tut, tut! The soul? What is the soul?"

I remembered suddenly Pilate. 'Truth? What is truth?'

"Is there no soul, Your Holiness?"

"The soul is an illusion engendered by man's fear of death. The sane man squeezes out of the earth all the pleasures it is capable of offering. *Carpe diem!*"

I remained silent.

"What is the soul, Count, compared to the senses—to the ex-

quisite intelligent senses? You ought to know what I mean. You
have traveled much and if your name belies you not—loved much."
How much of my history did he know? This man was truly
uncanny.

"I have traveled a little, it is true."

He laughed. "Is it a little to travel through China and India?"

I smiled. "It is not possible to dissimulate before you, Your
Holiness."

"The cup comes from China. Of course, no one save you and I
must know it. You speak to your valet sometimes in an African
dialect. And a man like you would not miss India—the home of all
cults and plagues."

A Cardinal entered, red-faced and important.

"Well?" Alexander asked.

"The royal ambassadors are impatient, Your Holiness."

"That is well, Monseigneur. They will accept our terms. Bring
me the map."

The Cardinal bowed and walked out.

"The Chinese understand life and know how to turn excruciating
pain into exquisite pleasure. You certainly," he leered lewdly, "must
know the secret of unendurable pleasure indefinitely prolonged . . . ?"

Each word rolled upon his tongue like a delicate morsel.

I stared, amazed. Did there exist, perhaps, some organization or
brotherhood of voluptuaries throughout the world, which initiated its
members into the secret of unendurable pleasure indefinitely prolonged . . . ? Was Alexander VI a member of this fraternity?

The Cardinal returned with a large map. The Pope bent over it,
then taking his goose-quill, drew several bold lines, dividing the
world between Spain and Portugal.

"Summon the ambassadors."

The ambassadors appeared. His Holiness showed them the map.
Pointing his stubby forefinger to the map, he said: "Henceforth,
these lands and these seas belong to His Majesty, the most Catholic
King of Spain, and these to His Majesty, the most Christian King
of Portugal."

The ambassadors looked startled.

"Whatever new or old lands Colón and his followers may discover, I likewise allot to Spain."

"But Your Holiness," the Portuguese Ambassador ventured, "my
exalted sovereign— —"

Alexander continued, without heeding the interruption: "Except these islands, which by right of conquest appertain to His Majesty, the King of Portugal and his descendants forever."

The Ambassador repeated timidly, "Your Holiness. . ."

Alexander raised his finger. "Peace! Peace! The Vicar of Christ has spoken. Neither the word nor the sword shall erase the faintest line that his hand has drawn."

His Holiness extended his hand. The two ambassadors kissed the ring obsequiously and walked out, their backs to the door.

"God speed," Alexander pronounced, making the sign of the cross.

The Pope rang a small gold bell. An officer entered.

"Captain, relieve the Count of his armor."

The Pope caressed the Holy Grail.

"Captain, place the armor in the corner."

The officer obeyed, waited a moment, and left.

"Sit down, Count."

I seated myself.

"Clothes shape our personality. In that armor, you were Count de Cartaphile who fasted for seven years that he might possess the Holy Grail which his ancestor had obtained from the hands of our Lord." He looked at me, and smiled. "Now you are a gentleman, relieved of the burden of piety and sanctity—a scholar, a master of wit."

I nodded.

"And my guest."

What was the sinister meaning of the word "guest"?

"This cup is too exquisite for the coarse lips of the multitude, but the Church needs money. We shall remember your deed and weave a beautiful legend about the myth of your ancestor. Posterity could do no more—even for Jesus."

"But Jesus was not a myth, Your Holiness!"

"You believe in the historical existence of Jesus?" the Pope asked with unconcealed amazement.

"Of course, Holy Father."

He laughed. "Have you never heard of the Hindu god Krishna? Is not Krishna—Christ?"

"But Jesus, Holy Father, actually existed. He was crucified and— —"

"And resurrected too?"

I gazed open-mouthed at the Vicar of Christ, refusing to be entrapped.

"His birth and his existence," the Pope calmly continued, "are as true as his death and resurrection. The cross itself is a priapic symbol worshiped hundreds of years before Jesus. What warrant have we of Christ's life? The gospels, written centuries after his supposed death, are a compilation of preposterous nonsense that even a child, allowed to think freely, could puncture and ridicule with ease.

"The Roman writers of the period, addicted to gossip and exaggeration as they were, and ready to pounce upon any picturesque incident, never allude to Jesus. Jozephus, the most meticulous of historians, ignores him entirely. Whatever mention of him is found in the later editions of his books, is a clumsy and all too evident interpolation."

"Your Holiness, can a legend subsist without basis of fact?"

"Imagination is a great architect. The flimsiest material suffices for a magnificent structure. How can a philosopher accept the multitudinous contradictions of the Holy Book? How can he accept an absurdity as colossal as the Trinity?"

He laughed. "There is a tribe in the jungle of Africa, with a triune divinity. The father is a man, the mother a camel, the son a parrot. Their religion is as rational as ours. . ."

"What is the name of this strange divinity, Holy Father?" I asked, laughing.

"I do not remember. Something like Pha-ta-pha—Yes, it must be that. The words read the same backwards as forwards. That proves the god's perfection, does it not?"

We laughed.

"Such flimsy pretexts are the foundation of all religions, Count."

We remained silent.

"How," the Pope asked suddenly, "could Satan with his poor bag of tricks tempt the Son of God? Why must the Only Begotten Son remind his Father, omniscient and omnipotent, that He is forsaken at the critical moment? 'My God, my God, why hast Thou forsaken me!' I could wring the neck of the idiotic monk who, transcribing the Bible, did not have sense enough to erase from it this unpardonable offense, both against Jesus and Yahweh! The whimpering son of an absent-minded father!"

He struck the table with his fist. The Holy Grail tottered on the Decameron.

"Is a legend strong enough to uphold the Church?"

"The Church is an organization, Count—a vast Empire, composed largely of children. The average man is always a child. For his good, we invent fables and legends and promises, ridiculous and vain. Thus the favorite few may cultivate in peace and ease the fine arts and philosophies. The Church is the guardian of civilization. . ."

His logic was invincible. I would have gladly agreed with him. Alas, I knew differently! Once more reason failed. The irrational was the truth! Like the sudden flash of lightning which rends a clear sky, I saw before me Jesus, his trial, his crucifixion. And like the thunderclap which follows, I heard: 'Tarry until I return.' I closed my eyes. My head turned.

Alexander, proud of his eloquence, continued, but his words seemed to come from a great distance. My ears were smitten by the thunderclaps that frightened me in Jerusalem.

"Jesus is a Hindu divinity. Mary is a less imaginative conception of Venus. The very name of the goddess, risen from the foam of the sea, thrills and intoxicates! Venus—goddess of joy, goddess of beauty! Venus— —" He closed his eyes. His nostrils shivered. He reopened his eyes, and smiled. 'Venus has become a mother—a virgin mother!'"

The thunderclaps died in the distance. The Pope's voice sounded clear and convincing.

"Jesus would have fared much better if infidels had presided over the Council of Nicæa! What a mess they made of it, Count! The bigoted Bishops disputed and wrangled and fought, and in their blind passion, they never realized that they included two contradictory genealogies of Jesus in the gospels! They should have edited either Luke's or Mark's. Besides, the attempt to trace the descent of Jesus to David, through Joseph, makes the immaculate conception preposterous. Jesus is either the Son of God, or the descendant of David. How can He be both at the same time?"

It amazed me not to be able to crush the shrewd and subtle Pope with powerful arguments.

"You are surprised, Count, that the Vicar of Christ does not believe in Him? Why shouldn't a Pope rise superior to his profession?"

'I must make a dent in the armor of his conceit. I must defeat his logic by facts!' I thought. 'Besides, what subtle triumph for me if I, of all men, prove the existence of Jesus to the Bishop of Rome!'

Was it a racial trait which made me anxious to prevail in an argument? Was it vanity? Was it my passion for truth? I cannot tell, but "Your Holiness is mistaken," I blurted out suddenly. "Jesus lived! I saw him! I spoke to him."

Alexander laughed. "Many have spoken to Him."

I shook my head.

"Many have seen Jesus. Our nunneries are crowded with brides of Christ. . ."

Whatever the consequences of my confession, I would confute and confuse this son of the Borgias.

"If Your Holiness will permit, I shall recount the truth about Jesus."

He seated himself deeply in his chair, and playing with a diamond studded cross that hung around his neck, listened without interrupting me. Avoiding unnecessary details and sentimental reflections, I told him of my quarrel with Jesus. I described his trial and crucifixion, and in bold strokes, related the major incidents of my life, omitting only my excursion into Africa, Salome and Kotikokura.

When I had finished, he smiled. "In the archives of the Vatican, there is an account by a Bishop——"

"An Armenian Bishop?" I asked.

"Yes! You have read it, Count." He laughed, slapping his thighs.

"No, Your Holiness. It was I who confessed to the holy man, on the promise that he would not divulge my secrets."

"He speaks about this promise, it is true, and he does not disclose the man's history. He only recounts what was permissible for him to reveal," the Pope said thoughtfully.

It pleased me that the Armenian Bishop had kept faith with me. I tried to recollect his face, but his features wavered in my mind like a torch in the wind. The face of Apollonius emerged, luminous and superb, instead.

"Ever since the story has become known," His Holiness resumed, "we are pestered by Wandering Jews. Ordinarily, they are either ranting charlatans or dupes of their fancy. But truly, Count, a man like you—a thinker and a wit—should not indulge in so stale a farce. . ."

"I am telling the truth, Your Holiness."

"What is truth?" Alexander yawned. "And how can you prove it?"

"Holy Father, it is difficult to prove the simplest proposition. Mathematics, even, must accept certain premises and axioms, must accept the possibility of drawing a triangle or a circle in a universe which permits neither circles nor triangles to limit its endless flow. . ."

"You have not mentioned the shoes, Cartaphilus!" His Holiness laughed.

"Shoes?"

"Did you not leave a pair of shoes with the Bishop?"

I searched my memory. "True, Your Holiness, a pair of sandals. My valet forgot them. I had to buy another pair as soon as I reached the first town."

He laughed uproariously. "Of course. What is the Wandering Jew without the shoes? He must always leave behind him shoes— symbol of his wanderings and of his father's profession."

'His father's profession,' I mused. 'Can we never extricate ourselves from our ancestors?'

An officer entered, whispered something into Alexander's ear, and left.

"Ah, you are fortunate indeed! Come to the window, and we shall witness a magnificent spectacle."

The sun was setting; its rays like delicate long fingers bedecked with many jewels, lay languidly upon the garden, making it glitter.

A soldier opened the large brass gate to the west of the garden. Four stallions, two black, two white, dashed in. They galloped about for a few moments, then trotted quietly, their fine heads erect, their step elastic.

The Pope nodded. At one of the open windows of the Vatican, a young man and woman, holding hands, were smiling at the spectacle.

They were nearly of the same height, had the same raven-black hair, large dark-brown eyes, which they squinted a little, due to the light or to myopia. Their noses were strongly aquiline, rapacious as the beaks of birds of prey. Their lips, leavy and shapeless, pouted in perennial mockery. Debauchery was beginning to erase the more delicate lines of their chins. Their foreheads, rising above their heads like superimposed structures, radiated remarkable intelligence and unsavory subtlety.

Cæsar and Lucretia Borgia were undeniably their father's children.

His Holiness waved his hand. Cæsar answered the greeting by a similar gesture. Lucretia threw him a kiss. The young woman glanced at her incestuous companion,—a significant glance, pregnant with meaning. Cæsar crushed her hand violently. She closed her eyes, and clenched her teeth.

'Poppaea!' I thought.

His Holiness opened a little his mouth, and breathed deeply. I no longer doubted the rumor of the libidinous ties which united the Holy Father with his unholy family.

Meanwhile, the gate opened once more and two mares, as vigorous and proud as the stallions, rushed in. The latter stopped in their easy perambulation, sniffed and neighed noisily.

The mares ran to a corner of the garden as if seeking shelter. The stallions approached them. They ran away a short distance, and stopped again. The stallions dashed toward them. One of them touched a mare with the tip of his muzzle. The others rushed at him and bit him. He turned upon them, biting, kicking.

A terrific battle ensued. Blood and thick foam streamed to the ground. The hoofs, striking the earth, scattered sparks. The mares looked on tranquilly, chewing the sparse blades of grass, that grew between the crevices of stones.

A white stallion fell, his legs in the air. His enormous belly was ripped. The other three continued their warfare, neighing and snorting and stamping their hoofs. A black stallion looked up. Realizing, suddenly, the reason of the battle, he dashed toward the mares. His head was covered with blood and muddy foam, and his wet mane hung in clusters over his eyes. He pawed the ground and neighed vociferously.

One of the mares ran away. The other faced him for a while, then ran in a circle. He followed her, but not too closely for at every few steps, she made a threatening gesture.

The circles, however, became smaller and the kicking less vigorous. Suddenly the stallion reared into the air. The mare remained still accepting the virile tribute of her conqueror.

The two remaining stallions were struggling wearily until, exhausted, one fell, his large tongue licking the great red wound from which oozed a thin stream of blood. The other breathed deeply, shaking his head violently to relieve himself of a heavy mass of foam. The second mare passed by. He neighed, lowered his head as if tossing an imaginary horn intended to pierce a foe. She turned as if attempting to dash away. His teeth caught her mane. . .

Pope Alexander and his children observed with glistening eyes the performance of the most ancient of cosmic rites. Alexander remained at the casement for some time, then turning to me said, his voice hoarse and trembling, "How beautiful! Alas, the gods have not made man to enjoy himself!"

Tall and grim, the Pope's secretary entered. "Your Holiness, it is time for Mass."

"Tell the Cardinal to celebrate Mass today. I am not well."

"Saint Peter's is filled with people."

"I have spoken. Go!"

The secretary retired slowly, lips tightened in a gesture of disgust. At the door, he turned once more and made the sign of the cross.

Alexander smiled sardonically, more Pan than Pope.

I looked at his feet, half expecting to see hoofs under the white satin shoes!

"What strength!" he continued, as if he had never been interrupted. "What a magnificent motion! And the charming coquetry of the mares! How many women are as capable of arousing such passion? What sustaining power! For how many women would we sacrifice our lives . . . ?"

He walked up and down for a few minutes, as if to regain his composure.

"Is what you told me the truth, Count?" he asked suddenly.

"Yes, Your Holiness."

"Then—you are now nearly fifteen centuries old."

"Yes, Your Holiness."

He smiled cynically. "Do you feel the burden of the years?"

"No, Your Holiness."

He remained silent.

"How could you live so long without being seriously ill; without being wounded or scarred?"

"I have been ill, and wounded and scarred, Your Holiness."

"But you always recuperate?"

"Yes, Your Holiness."

His tone had changed considerably. He seemed annoyed at me, either because he was unable to prove that my statements were lies or because if what I said was the truth, I was incomparably his superior. Alexander VI knew he was mortal.

His silence perturbed me. In order to break it, I said: "Your Holiness, once by accident, I cut off part of my small finger. A hundred years later the finger, healing almost imperceptibly, was restored to its former size. I imagine, therefore, that all severed parts would grow back again, if man lived as long as the crocodile and the tortoise, who are well-nigh immortal."

"You were circumcised as a boy, I take it?" the Pope asked, raising his left eyebrow, and screwing his lips into a cynical smile.

"Yes, Your Holiness."

"Well, has beneficent Nature restored that whereof you were deprived?"

I was startled. It had never occurred to me to think of it.

"No, Your Holiness."

He laughed.

I smiled.

"I am, after all, the Wandering Jew. . ."

"This is ingenious, Cartaphilus, but it is not the truth."

I did not answer.

"Not the truth!" he exclaimed. "Acknowledge it!"

I remained silent.

He rang the bell three times. Almost instantly, three officers stood at the doors with drawn swords.

"Tomorrow, we shall see whether you are telling the truth or a lie. The rack will make you speak if I cannot. Besides, it will prove to you most emphatically whether in reality the beneficent forces of Nature can mend your broken limbs, whether you are indeed the equal of the Crustaceans and the Olympians. . ."

I rose.

"Holy Father, you are jesting. What will the world say if the Vicar of Christ violates the sanctity of the confessional?"

He rose in his turn and placed his hand upon the diamond studded hilt of a small dagger concealed under his robe. He spoke almost gently. "Alexander VI is not a simpleton like your Armenian Bishop. You know too much for the welfare of Christendom. . ."

"Holy Father, is this the reward for— —?" I pointed to the Holy Grail.

"For that we shall make you a beautiful legend. Cardinals shall read masses to your soul when you are dead—if you are dead— for ninety-nine years. No one may live who has listened to all I have told you."

"I have learned to forget, Your Holiness."

"Only the dead forget. . . . Besides," he continued almost caressingly, "you cannot die." Turning to the officer: "Surrender this man to the Fathers of the Inquisition. Order them to postpone all other trials until they have wrung a confession from him. My secretary will prepare the details of the indictment at once."

"Holy Father— —" I pleaded.

"Silence, Jew! You ought not to complain. The Inquisition is an instrument perfected by one of your co-religionists—Thomas de Torquemada."

The officers approached and surrounded me.

"And by the way," His Holiness added, "he has a valet who is waiting outside. Tickle him also a little to make him speak."

The officers smiled.

"But first this man—a Jew and an infidel."

He motioned with his head and reseated himself. I was pulled away unceremoniously. His Holiness fondled the Holy Grail.

LXV

THE HOLY INQUISITION—UNTAPPED RESERVOIRS—A NUN VISITS ME—"DANCE!"—THE ABBESS OF THE CONVENT OF THE SACRED HEART—SALOME BATTLES AGAINST THE MOON

A LONG room. In the center, upon a platform, a round table. In an angle, a bench, the length of a tall man, at one end a pole, at the other a windlass—a simple thing, almost a toy.

A soldier in back of me, the tip of his sword touching my body. At the rack, a colossal individual stricken with elephantiasis—an enormous face, the color of mud, a nose wrinkled like an elephant's trunk, crossed with heavy red and blue veins, and ears like two open palms. At the table, three stout individuals dressed in black.

The man in the center reading, reading accusations against me. Jew, blasphemer, mocker of Jesus, the Pope and the Holy Church, enemy of all Christian institutions, false claimant to the French nobility, plunderer of holy relics—reading, reading—

What would be the final judgment? Would I be burned at the stake? Would I become a mass of blisters and raw flesh, unable to live, incapable of death? Would I be ordered to the rack, my members torn from their sockets, my flesh cut into shreds, while consciousness persisted in each writhing nerve? Would I be buried alive, to feed, living, the worm that dieth not?

Should I confess or refute the crimes and sins attributed to me? Which meant less torture?

Never had I been in such imminent danger, not even when the cenaculum of Charlemagne tried me for heresy and bribery. Then, I had a flicker of hope,—the Emperor might remember my services, he needed my drugs to relieve his pain. The Borgias knew neither mercy nor gratitude.

Meanwhile, the man continued reading, reading a strange and and new version of the life of Cartaphilus, Wandering Jew, Anti-Christ.

Where was Kotikokura? Was he tried separately? Had he escaped? Had he, like some wild animal, scented the danger awaiting him?

The man read on. Soon he would stop—and then—no, Cartaphilus must not surrender without a struggle! But the soldier's sword touched my back, and the monstrous individual stood erect beside the rack.

The ring of Antonio and Antonia! The ring! The ring! Why did this word reverberate in my mind?

The ring!

I turned it on my finger. A ray of the sun played upon it. It glittered like a small lamp in a dark cellar.

One of the three judges looked at it, fascinated.

The ring!

The word rose from a great depth, as a bucket rises from a well —heavy and overbrimming.

The ring!

He continued to look at it, his lids motionless.

"Save yourself, Cartaphilus! Save yourself!" Was it my own voice? Was it the voice of another? A fierce determination took possession of me. The desire to live, to rescue my body from the claws of the Inquisition, flared up with primordial intensity. Fear vanished. My strength multiplied. I was no longer a man, but an army.

"These," the voice—this time clearly within me—cried, "are mortals, Cartaphilus. You are the stuff of which the stars are made . . . !"

I stretched forth my arms and fastened my look upon the Inquisitor at the left. The man blinked and tried to turn his head. He struggled. The tension was plainly tangible. I continued to concentrate upon him. The rays of the ring pierced his eyes. Suddenly he succumbed. His head dropped like a toy and he began to breathe with the regularity of a sleeper.

The man in the center droned on, without raising his head.

The Inquisitor on his right rose suddenly, and raised his arm to utter a malediction. I could almost hear the words: "Demon! Jew!" His fiery eyes sank into mine for a moment. In spite of the most desperate resistance, I held him. 'Cartaphilus' I shouted within myself, 'Hold him! Hold fast.' I summoned new reserves out of the depths of myself, as one wrenches a root deeply buried in the earth. An irresistible power, an overwhelming will-to-be, raw, invincible, like life itself, rose from its hiding place in the last layer of my being.

"Sleep!" I commanded. "Sleep! Sleep!" My eyes burned into his. The ring splashed him with fire. Suddenly, no longer a man but an automaton, he breathed deeply, reseated himself, placed his head upon his arm, and snored.

The Chief Inquisitor looked up, astounded. I waved my hands. I recited a passage from the Vedas to distract his attention from his two colleagues. Catching his eyes, I sucked them into mine. His self disappeared in the whirlpool. He struggled like a drowning man, but the waves of energy emanating from me robbed him of his senses. His eyes became as glass.

"Order the soldier who stands behind me to drop his sword and leave," I whispered.

"Leave!" he commanded. The soldier obeyed.

"Order the Executioner to depart!"

"Depart!" he reiterated.

The executioner departed.

"Now sleep! Sleep!"

He closed his eyes and reclined in his chair.

I breathed heavily through my mouth, like a man who climbs a steep hill, a load upon his back. But I was not exhausted. New strength had flowed into me from the untapped reservoirs of my life—the life of centuries.

The three men, snoring mechanically, looked like crows, their heads half-hidden between their wings.

For the moment I was safe. The bayonet did not pierce my back, nor did the monster in red glare at me, his enormous nose shivering and creasing like an elephant's trunk. But I was still within the chamber of the Holy Inquisition and outside, doubtless, were the sentinels of the Pope. Maybe Alexander himself, preceded by silver trumpets, was on his way to the court-room! I had to decide upon immediate means of escape.

As I was weighing one thing and another, half accepting, half rejecting, the door opened. A nun, heavily hooded so that hardly more than the lashes of her eyes and the tip of her nose were visible, entered. She looked about furtively.

Where had I seen her, and when? That gait . . . that carriage! Who was she? The nun approached me and lifted her veil.

"Kotikokura!" I exclaimed. I opened my eyes so wide that they hurt me. "Kotikokura, my friend! Is it possible?" I embraced him.

He kissed my hands. "Ca-ta-pha! Ca-ta-pha, my master!" His eyes filled with tears.

"What is the meaning of this attire?" I asked.

He placed his forefinger to his lips and gave me a bundle. I opened it. Within it was a nun's attire.

In a few minutes, I was as orthodox a nun as walked the streets of Rome. Kotikokura made a gesture of admiration.

"Oh, wait a minute, Kotikokura! One must not run away so unceremoniously from one's host—if one's host is the Pope."

Upon the back of the scroll which contained the indictment for high crimes against me, I wrote in large letters: "To His Holiness, Pope Alexander VI from the Wandering Jew." I put the scroll into one of my shoes which I carefully placed on the rack.

I looked at my judges. Suddenly the word "dance" reverberated through my mind.

I approached the table. "Dance!" I commanded. "Dance! Dance!" I repeated.

The Holy Inquisitors lifted their heads slowly, opened their eyes, and descended from the platform.

"Dance, dance!"

They raised their robes in the manner of elegant ladies and began to dance—a weird, disjointed, savage dance. In Kotikokura the dance aroused tribal reminiscences. He looked bewildered. His legs shivered.

The Convent of the Flaming Heart was situated upon a hillock, a few miles to the west of the Eternal City—a beautiful white building, surrounded by vineyards.

The driver urged the horses upward the narrow path that led to the stone gate.

"Is Salome here?" I whispered to Kotikokura.

He nodded.

'Salome a nun—in a convent,' I mused, smiling. 'But not half so strange as the fact that Cartaphilus and Kotikokura are nuns!' I looked at Kotikokura and it was with the utmost difficulty that I restrained myself from bursting into hilarious laughter.

We descended from the carriage. The driver opened the gate. A nun approached.

"The Mother Superior awaits you."

We walked in silence in the large garden and were led into a waiting-room.

"The Reverend Lady will be here presently."

A small door, almost that of a cell, opened to our right and Salome appeared. She raised her eyes and made the sign of the cross.

"Salome!" I exclaimed.

She placed her forefinger to her lips.

"In my cell, we shall be able to speak without being overheard. Follow me!"

Her cell was a large room whose window faced the Tiber. A crucifix of excellent workmanship hung from one of the walls. Underneath it, several shelves crowded with books and manuscripts. At an angle, test tubes and other delicate instruments. Here and there, a flower vase, a statuette, a painting.

She closed the door behind us.

"Salome!" I exclaimed again. I pressed her to my heart.

"I am an Abbess, Cartaphilus, and you a nun. We should be colder and more distant in our dealings."

She laughed a little.

"Salome an Abbess!" I laughed in my turn.

"It is not so strange, Cartaphilus. Since I cannot be Pope and rule mankind, I can at least rule my nuns and pursue my studies. The nuns are obedient. Unlike the Pope's subjects they do not rebel. Many are intelligent and beautiful. Unsoiled by the rude hand of man, they tremble at my touch. Their cheeks blossom at a glance. If Eros visits their dreams, they consider themselves wicked sinners. They kneel before me, place their heads upon my knees, and weep. My hand comforts them. . ."

Salome closed a little her eyes, and remained silent for a while. "Besides," she said smiling, "Holy Orders enabled me to reciprocate your courtesy. Without my assistance, you would have suffered some unpleasant experience."

"How did you know of my presence in Rome?"

"How did you not know of mine?"

"Salome is incomparable always."

"You ascribe my knowledge to feminine intuition, Cartaphilus?"

I smiled, for such a thought had flitted through my brain.

"If intuition knows more than reason, it is superior to reason," I remarked.

"It was not intuition, but reason. You are incorrigible and unchangeable, Cartaphilus! You still consider woman only a little higher than the animals. Feminine intuition seems to you an impersonal, unreasoned thing, akin to animal instincts."

I was about to object, but she raised her forefinger to her lips. 'An Abbess,' I thought, 'but a remarkably charming one, nevertheless.'

"What you call feminine intuition is a more sublime form of reason. Woman omits several intermediary steps in the chain of reasoning and arrives at her conclusion more rapidly than man with his clumsy masculine intellect. Bewildered and piqued, man dubs the swift processes of her logical mind—intuition."

"Salome is subtler than the Holy Father."

"If the Holy Father had been a woman, he would not have excluded from his reasoning the possibility of your escape. His 'intuition' would have been disastrous for you."

"How well for me, Madre Perfetta, that he is merely a man!"

Salome smiled and caressed my hands. "You must be hungry and thirsty."

She offered me wines and sweets.

"But tell me explicitly, Salome, what happened? How were you able to rescue me?"

"There is less mystery in this than it seems and much more reason than instinct. I saw you ride through the city as an ancient knight, and if I had not seen you, I would have heard about it. Every one spoke of the strange visitor. . ."

I rubbed my hands, pleased at my prank, in spite of its aftermath.

"Cartaphilus is a child always, delighted with toys. I understood you desired to attract the attention of His Holiness. I knew a visit to Alexander would not pass without some unpleasantness. Your masculine conceit, intensified by your Jewish propensity for argumentation, would, I was certain, make you boast of matters whose secret only a woman knows how to keep."

I smiled. "That's contrary to the world's opinion. A woman's tongue— —"

Salome, irritated, interrupted me. "Well, I watched and listened closely. When I saw Kotikokura waiting for you at the gate of the Vatican, I knew that the moment for immediate action had arrived. Bribery discovered for me that you were to be tried as a Jew and a blasphemer. Bribery made it possible for Sister Kotikokura to visit you. Bribery allowed you to escape. Bribery will induce forgetfulness. . ."

"And the Pope? How is it that he was not present at the trial?"

"He was detained by a French Ambassador who recounted some magnificent anecdotes of intrigue and murder, but Alexander VJ would have witnessed your torture. That would have interested him more than the Ambassador's tales."

"Salome, you are the Goddess of Wisdom and Beauty!" I knelt before her. She made the sign of the cross above my head.

"Salome, has not the time come for us to travel together? We can protect and comfort each other. Infinity is in sight. The parallel lines of our lives must join at last. . ."

She shook her head. "I must remain here for years, perhaps for centuries, under one guise or another. This place affords me silence and a sanctuary for meditation and for my experiments. I shall not be free until I liberate my sex from the slavery of the moon. . ."

I looked, not understanding, although I dimly remembered the remark of Gilles de Retz that Joan of Arc was not a slave of the moon.

"It is the moon's tyranny that makes woman man's inferior—the scarlet sacrifice the chaste goddess demands of every woman, whoever she may be—peasant, princess, or abbess. She accepts no scapegoat, she admits no ransom—save age. In pain and discomfiture, every daughter of Eve must pay bloody tribute to the moon's cold and virginal majesty. Yes, before woman can be man's equal—or his superior—we must overthrow the governance of the moon . . . !"

Her voice had an unusual pathos. For the first time, I realized to the full the tragedy of being a woman—the tragedy and the courage. I looked at Salome. Her face had the tenderness of a madonna.

"I understand," I said.

"What?" Salome asked.

"I had not grasped your image at first, nor its profound significance."

"Always the ponderous slowness of the male."

"And . . . have your experiments been successful?"

"Partially only. I must combat not only a biological law, but woman's ignorance and her fear. In spite of all I shall conquer! Woman shall be free! Woman shall be man's equal! Then only will their union be beautiful and perfect; then only shall the love of Cartaphilus and Salome be consummated. No, my friend, I must remain. You, however, must go—and at once."

"At once?"

She nodded. "This painting of the virgin hides a secret iron door. When it is opened, you will step into a boat always anchored there. Salome is a good general. She plans her retreat as carefully as her advance. The man who drove you here—deaf and dumb, and faithful as a dog—will row you across the Tiber. He will have food and clothing for you. You will be two small merchants traveling through the country. Disappear as quickly as possible from Rome and Italy. The Pope's spies are already instructed to capture you. You have hurt the vanity of a Borgia, but we shall outwit him. The Borgias are, after all, mere children. Could they live as long as we—what prodigious monsters they might become, or who knows—what prodigious saints! However, we have no time to lose."

She raised the painting and unlocked the secret door.

"Farewell, Cartaphilus."

"Since it must be—farewell, Salome."

We embraced. She opened the door. Was it the setting sun or the magnificence of Salome's hair which cast the golden reflection upon the water?

We stepped into the boat. Salome made the sign of the cross over us. "God speed."

The Tiber beat lazily against our boat. The hills opposite were masses of clouds nailed against the sky.

LXVI

DARLINGS OF THE GODS—STIRRING THE ASHES—BIRDS ON THE WING

"Kotikokura, we are indeed the darlings of the gods. I do not know whether we are shielded from torture because of the love they bear us, or more likely—for some sinister ulterior purpose."

Kotikokura's eyes glowed with green fire, like an animal's in the dark.

"Maybe the high gods reward me because I defended my Enemy before his own vicar. I must insist upon his existence, for if he does not exist, I am not even a wraith!"

I remained silent. My last sentence reverberated in my brain and rolled upon my tongue.

"Kotikokura, how strange that I never considered this! If he does not exist, I do not exist either . . . and you are but the shadow of my dream. . . ."

Kotikokura knitted his brow, not understanding.

"He must exist!"

Kotikokura nodded, unconvinced.

"We are, perhaps, two sides of the same medal," I remarked, musingly, "and perhaps, for this very reason, we never see eye to eye . . . but must remain forever incomprehensible to each other."

Kotikokura rubbed his nose, perplexed. He had never quite grasped my relationship to Jesus.

"Some day, perhaps, the metal will melt in the alembic of love or disaster. Some day the two may be one. . ."

Kotikokura's eyes darted to and fro.

"But this is mere poetry, no doubt, my friend, induced by my happiness of having escaped from the clutches of the amiable Vicar of Christ. I shall never tempt the Devil—or a Pope—again!"

Kotikokura grinned.

"I yearn to be once more a tranquil water, running securely between its two banks. Let us go beyond the Danube, Kotikokura.

Let us see what the Barbarians have accomplished. Do you remember Ulrica, Kotikokura?"

He nodded.

"What a delightful creature she was! Where is she today? Less than a pinchful of the dust we tread upon; less than the foam that dots the sharp point of a wave in mid-sea; less than the echo of one word uttered between two hills; less than the wind stirred by a butterfly's wing. . ."

Kotikokura's eyes were covered with a thin film.

"The Pope was right: the soul is the daughter of fear. Man disappears utterly like a bird in flight. . ."

Kotikokura nodded.

"We, too, are transitory, Kotikokura. However long we endure, we shall seem to Eternity only as birds on the wing, lingering awhile over the tops of trees or describing a few wide circles over the surface of a lake, the tips of our wings barely scratching the water. . ."

Kotikokura wiped his eyes.

LXVII

THE JOY OF LIVING—THE FRIAR OF WITTENBERG TALKS ABOUT LOVE—CHRIST AND ANTI-CHRIST—KOTIKOKURA'S ADVENTURE—A FINE NOSE FOR SULPHUR—I RAISE A STORM

Two gentlemen, traveling unostentatiously at random, wherever a boat might sail or a coach drive, squandering months and years with the prodigality of early youth. Ah, the joy of locomotion! The delight of being unrooted!

"Once I bewailed the fact that I had neither a country nor a speech nor a name. Once I mourned the length of my days. Man should live a man's span of years, I argued—then sink into eternal sleep. Ah, the joy of living on and on!"

Kotikokura grinned.

"I am happy, Kotikokura! I am happy that I have neither country nor name. I am happy to be alive. . ."

K tikokura began to dance.

"Dance, my friend, dance upon the tombs of a million generations! We are Li̇ʳ -all else is Death!"

Kotikokura tooᴋ my hand and whirled me about.

Out of breath, we seated ourselves upon a rock.

"Listen, Kotikokura! Listen to the tinkling of the sheep's bells! Listen to the shepherds' call! We are in Arcady, Kotikokura!"

He slapped his thighs.

A man, carrying a long cane, stopped before us.

"Do the gentlemen require a guide to climb the Jungfrau this morning?"

I shook my head.

"Every traveler likes to make the ascent. . . ."

"Has he whose shoes I saw this morning in your museum climbed to the top?"

He seemed not to understand for a while, then grinned, raising his upper lip.

"The Wandering Jew? They say he came from the other side of the mountain."

"Does he really have such enormous feet? Why, they seem to be three times as large as mine."

"Why not, sir? Think of his travels!"

His seriousness unarmed me.

"Have you seen him?" I cried.

"My grandfather heard his voice one night. He howled like a wolf whose leg has been caught in a trap: 'I am the Cursed One! I am the Cursed One!' In the morning they found his shoes in front of the Church door. They seemed nailed to the ground. The Lord would not permit him to desecrate His House."

"Did he continue his journey barefooted?"

"The Devil must have given him another pair of shoes. The Devil always takes care of his own."

I was about to ask whether God did likewise with His own, but I desisted.

We reached a little inn, set snugly between the rocks. The innkeeper invited us into the garden. At a table opposite ours a young Augustine monk, his arm about the waist of the waitress, sang, waving his cup in tune.

Upon seeing us, the girl blushed, and rushed into the house. The friar raised his cup and addressed us.

"To your health, gentlemen!"

We raised ours. "To yours, frater!"

I begged him to sit at our table. He brought his cup. I filled it. We drank to each other's health once more.

"They have splendid beer here," I said in Latin.

"And a waitress who would delight Gambrinus himself," he remarked.

"For a friar," I said, "your frankness is most engaging."

"Jesus nowhere forbids love," the monk insisted.

"He did not. That is so. Nor did he prohibit drink, I can assure you of that."

He looked at me, a little uncertain. His eyes were blue and candid as a child's.

"You speak a perfect Latin. Are you a cleric?"

I smiled. "No, I am a retired gentleman with a hankering for scholarship."

"Many a nobleman nowadays takes to learning. The new invention of Gutenberg— —"

"Gutenberg?" I queried.

"The printing press, sir, the printing press. It makes it possible to obtain a hundred copies of a book at a small cost. It enables everybody to judge for himself the works of the masters."

"Are you referring to the movable type?"

"Exactly. I was certain you knew. . . ."

"Why, in China, hundreds of years ago, I saw a machine of this nature."

"My dear sir—not hundreds of years ago!"

"Yes, yes."

He laughed heartily. "You saw—hundreds of years ago—in China— —?"

"Did I say 'I saw?' "

He nodded.

I laughed in my turn. "I meant that I saw the drawing of a printing press invented hundreds of years ago in China. I am by no means certain that to spread knowledge indiscriminately is a benefit to mankind."

He wiped his finely curved lips with the back of his palm and looked at me, his brow knit.

"Am I speaking to an enemy or to a spy?"

"I have not even had the pleasure of knowing your name, frater."

"I am Martin Luther. In Germany, the mention of my name causes a storm."

"Your scholarly attainments, I am certain, deserve— —"

"No! Martin Luther is the enemy of the Pope!"

"Ah?"

"Do you know who I am now?"

"A man of great courage and of great mind," I answered quietly. "You need not fear me."

He remained silent.

"It is not a simple matter, however, to fight the Vatican, frater."

"David slew Goliath."

I nodded, unconvinced.

"I will translate the Bible into German. Every Christian shall read the words of Jesus. The words of Jesus will blast Anti-Christ in the Vatican. . ."

"To the Pope the Church is an empire—not a religion."

Luther waved his fist many times. "If it is that, then we have the right to dethrone the monarch. We have the right to secede from the empire. Germany for the Germans!"

'Mohammed' rang in my ears. 'If Martin Luther finds his Abu Bekr,' I thought, 'no Pope can withstand him.'

"If Germany disclaims the Vatican, will she build a Vatican of her own?" I asked.

"The Pope needs Christ, but Christ needs no Pope."

I was not thrilled. Why did I not offer my gold and my services? This German monk could be a powerful weapon in my immemorial battle with Jesus. What could destroy the Nazarene more effectively than a schism? A house divided against itself must crumble. I could awaken Mohammedanism from its lethargy. I could remind it of Allah and his Prophet. I could stir up racial memories in Mecca and in Medina.

Alas! The salt of victory had lost its savor. The sword was placed into my hand, but I had not the desire to wield it. Vainly I endeavored to discover clearly the origin of my quarrel with Jesus. Vainly I tried to revive the ancient anger of my heart. My memory was a heap of ashes. Of the great conflagration that once surged within me, a few sparks only dim and cold, rose wearily out of the ashes. . .

Was Jesus my enemy? Had He ever been my enemy? Was the Armenian Bishop right, perhaps, that his apparent vindictiveness was love in disguise. . . ?

But even as a man who, weary from much walking, finds it difficult to sit at once, so the ancient impetus, the ancient gesture persisted. 'Even' I said to myself, 'if my quarrel with Christ no longer envenoms my life, let Christianity perish. Encourage the fist that strikes against its walls!'

I rose and raised my cup. "To Germany and to freedom from the bondage of Anti-Christ!"

Luther rose in his turn, and clinked my cup.

Several peasants, men and women, entered, laughing and singing. They shouted into the shop: "Beer! Beer!"

The Inn keeper and the waitress ran in and began counting the people.

"A barrel! A barrel!" they demanded.

The Proprietor rolled in a barrel.

A tall middle-aged man approached our table.

"We are celebrating my son's return from the army. Will the gentlemen join us?"

The merrymaking lasted until dawn. Luther danced and sang and discoursed on the beauty of women. Whenever the waitress appeared, he pinched her cheeks and congratulated her on her manifold delectable parts.

"Frater, is concupiscence a sin?" I asked.

He laughed, and immediately after grew angry. "Having made sex a sin, the Church created the orgy. Concupiscence is no sin, my friend. Sex is God's blessing. Jesus forgave Magdalene but he drove the money-lenders from His Father's House."

Mary Magdalen—Mary, my great, my beautiful love! It was so long since I had pronounced her name. It rang in my ear, more mellow than the sheep's bells I had heard in the morning.

> *"In der Woche zwier im Jahr hundertvier,*
> *Schadet weder dir noch mir,"*

declaimed Luther robustly.

Everybody laughed, repeating the verses again and again, and promising to tell them to every one.

I became aware suddenly that Kotikokura had disappeared with the buxom waitress. I had noticed that Kotikokura and she had eyed each other. I rose and walked quietly into the rear of the garden. Suddenly, I heard a stifled cry. I waited motionless.

"My bear! My lion!"

'Doña Cristina,' I thought, and could not refrain from laughing.

There was a quick scurrying of feet. The waitress ran into the house, somewhat disarranged. Kotikokura walked directly into me.

"Whither, my lion? My bear? Why the hurry?"

His eyes glittered like a beast's of the forest and as he grinned, his teeth looked ominous. But walking back to our table, he assumed a crestfallen appearance.

"Why so sheepish, my bear?" I asked.

"Woman!" he grumbled, as he drank several cups of beer in succession.

"Post coitum omne animal triste," I said.

Luther did not hear me. Still declaiming the virtues of the daughters of Eve, he hiccoughed:

> *"In der Woche zwier im Jahr hundertvier,*
> *Schadet weder dir noch mir."*

Kotikokura snored majestically as a lion should. I went into the garden. Luther was writing at a table. I walked on tiptoes anxious not to disturb him. Suddenly, he raised his head and glared at me, shouting: *"Apage satanas!"* I was too startled to stir.

"Get thee behind me, Satan!" he shouted again, his blue eyes glittering. Raising the wooden inkstand, the shape of a soup bowl, he hurled it at me. I bent quickly, escaping with a scratch upon my cheek.

"Frater," I asked, "why this violence?"

He squinted and rose with a jerk.

"Forgive me, I beg of you, my friend. I thought . . . I saw Satan." He crossed himself. "He often comes to tempt me."

'Mohammed,' I mused, 'heard angels and Luther sees devils.'

Luther was crestfallen.

"Did I harm you, sir?" He looked at my cheek. "The Lord be praised! Only a tiny scratch! Will you forgive me?"

I extended my hand which he shook several times.

"It is terrible, sir. He pursues me everywhere."

"Who?"

"The Evil One! Sometimes, he comes in the shape of a cleric. Once, even, he appeared as the Pope, wearing upon his tonsured head the triple crown of Alexander the Sixth. When it suits his whim, he approaches in the shape of a large black cat or dog. One night he stood over my bed as a vampire with long sharp teeth, and a blue beard, dipped in blood; at dawn he comes to me as a young witch, with tempting lips and inviting thighs."

"And this time . . .?"

"I thought I saw him *in persona*—two large horns like a goat's, a long tail that twirled about his legs, and flames dashing out of his nostrils. Forgive me—it must have been the beer I consumed last night . . . and the waitress."

"The waitress?"

"Yes. The whole night through she tantalized me in my sleep, singing the couplet I recited last evening."

"If you had yielded to the temptation, master, she would not have tortured you in your sleep!"

He laughed, and bade me sit at his table. I made a gesture, indicating that I did not desire to disturb him. He insisted. "I have just finished an essay. You are a much traveled man whose opinion I value."

He sprinkled a fistful of sand over the paper and shook it.

"Do incubi, succubi and devils really visit human beings?" I asked.

He looked at me in childish wonderment. "Is it possible that you doubt it?"

"I have never seen any."

"It is because you have not recognized them. They are the subtlest of creatures. I can smell sulphur a mile away. . . ."

"Really?"

"It is only on rare occasions, such as today, that I err."

"Perhaps not even today, frater," I smiled.

He laughed. "The Devil is not quite so subtle." Nevertheless, he threw a rapid glance at my feet.

"Not cloven," I remarked.

He laughed heartily, rubbing his forehead with vigor.

"This essay," he said, "is a sort of summary of what I intend to write in the near future. May I read it to you?"

"I am much honored."

He declaimed the vices, the cruelties, the injustices, the sins of the Pope. I had never listened to a more vivid invective.

"He who dares proclaim this," I said, "is a man of history."

"I dare proclaim it and I shall make history!" he exclaimed, raising his right arm. "The Lord Jesus is on my side against the Enemy. *Hier stehe ich. Gott helfe mir. Ich kann nicht anders.*"

Should I goad him on with offers of material help? I must—once more! If I failed this time, I should consider myself vanquished. And if I win—if I win—what indeed should I win? Who knows what new and bloody idol will usurp Heaven, if Christianity dies!

Luther, his right arm in the air, continued, "I am going back to Wittenberg, and upon the gate of the *Schlosskirche* I shall nail my ultimatum to Anti-Christ. I shall challenge the Fiend to answer my theses!"

"You may divide Christendom. . ."

"There is more joy in heaven over a handful of real Christians than over a million sellers and buyers of Popish indulgences. . . ."

I remembered the words of Alexander VI. "It is better to deal with scoundrels than with zealots. Zealots have no sense of humor." This man was a zealot, but he could be merry. He loved woman and wine. 'To test once more the truth of logic or its utter bankruptcy, I shall help him!'

"Every man will read for himself the Sacred Word of the Lord. I shall translate the Holy Scriptures into the beloved and simple tongue of my fathers. There shall be no more secrecy or mystery. . ."

"Is it not dangerous to allow the uninitiated to interpret the Scriptures?"

"Far less dangerous than to allow a set of men, many of whom are more ignorant and more stupid than laymen, to misinterpret. The priests have robbed my poor countrymen until they are on the point of starvation. They have browbeaten us until we dare not raise our heads. They have stultified the intelligence of our peasants until· they have become more brutish than the beasts of the field."

The waitress appeared on the threshold. Luther rose and, stretching out his arms, called to her, "My beauty, my dove, come hither!"

A man who could change so rapidly from divine to mundane affairs was destined to achieve greatness—if no accident intervened. Thus, I imagined Mohammed must have dismissed Gabriel the Archangel, to embrace his buxom wives.

"Father, you should be more respectful to the cloth you wear," the waitress admonished.

"Would you want me to remain a fool my lifelong?"

"What do you mean?"

> *"Wer nicht liebt Wein, Weib und Gesang,*
> *Der bleibt ein Narr sein Leben lang."*

The waitress laughed. The proprietor, who appeared at the moment, applauded. "Bravo! Bravo!"

> *"Wer nicht liebt Wein, Weib und Gesang,*
> *Der bleibt ein Narr sein Leben lang."*

"Splendid! You must allow me to offer you some wine—half a century old—which my father brought with him from Cologne."

Luther walked over to him, shook his hand, and made the sign of the cross over his head.

The bottles were brought and emptied. Luther and I told anecdotes. The proprietor laughed uproariously, slapping his belly.

"Don't tell me any more, gentlemen! No more, or I shall die laughing."

"In a few hours, I leave for Wittenberg," Luther said suddenly, grown pensive, "but whether I shall reach it the Lord knows."

"Are the roads so dangerous?"

"For Martin Luther."

"Would you allow me and my friend to accompany you?"

He looked at me. His eyes had the vision of far-away places, as Mohammed's had of the desert. He placed his hands upon my shoulders, making the sign of the cross over me.

"It is the will of Jesus."

Long before we reached Germany, we heard the name of Martin Luther, either whispered in praise and hope, or hissed with a curse.

"You are already history, frater."

He sighed. "I should have preferred to devote my life to writing quietly in my cell."

"From the clash of desire and disillusion, bursts forth the conflagration of genius."

We were walking between two rows of immense poplars. Their tops shivered like the plumes on the helmets of warriors, marching in triumph. The rays of the sun, undaunted soldiers, tried to pierce the massive barricade, to crawl between the barbed wire of the leaves, to lasso the forest like a galloping stallion. In vain! The cool shadow stretched peacefully and unconcerned, like a black god, deaf to the futile clamor of the universe.

Luther wiped his forehead with a large kerchief and breathed deeply.

"Should a new Christianity arise from the ashes of the old, would man be allowed in truth to speak his thought?" I asked.

"Even so."

"Would you abolish the celibacy of the clergy?"

"Nothing in the Holy Bible commands man to live alone. The Lord created all good things for the joy of his children."

'This in itself,' I thought, 'is worth the effort. Fighting to purify religion, this monk may restore paganism. Perhaps Athens and Rome will be born again in their glory. If it is true that man appears again and again in slightly different guises and incarnations, why cannot whole civilizations return from the grave? Life, the gigantic snake, constantly sheds and re-dons its coat!'

"Frater, I believe in you and in your power."

He pressed my hand.

"You will purify Christianity and make Europe more habitable. You will bring love and intelligence and freedom."

"For the glory of Jesus, amen."

"Will you permit me to have a share in this regeneration? Your struggle will be greater than you suspect."

He smiled. "There will be such a storm, my friend, as when Lucifer with his host was driven out of Heaven."

My resolution was made. 'Ahasuerus is the harbinger of storms. So the legend has it. Let there be storm!'

"Frater, however spiritual and divine our ideas may be, gold is always essential for their execution. . . I have gold, frater, very much gold."

He withdrew a little.

I smiled. "Does Martin Luther fear my money? I will donate fifty thousand guilders to equip the Army of Truth and Freedom at Armageddon."

Luther did not answer. He bent his head. The breeze ruffled his thick curls. Suddenly, he began to make very short, deliberate steps, as if counting them.

"It is God's will, else He would not permit you to cross my path."

"I shall give you my gold, on one condition——"

He raised his eyebrows.

"That this transaction remain a secret forever between us."

He seemed reluctant.

"It is my penance for an ancient sin."

"Very well. You shall explain when we meet Lord Jesus face to face."

It was dawn. Luther slept peacefully, as a child, his fists closed.

"Kotikokura," I whispered, "come!"

We walked away on tiptoes. At a sufficient distance, I said, "Kotikokura, we are now in sight of Wittenberg. It is safer for us not to be in the company of a man who will make history. We must change our direction."

He nodded.

"Whither shall we wend our enormous feet, Kotikokura?"

He scratched his nose.

"Italy—Spain—France?"

He shook his head.

"We might go to the new countries to the east of us, but they say the inhabitants are still savage."

I meditated for a while. "I have it, Kotikokura!"

He grinned.

"We have never been across the channel."

He did not comprehend.

"The channel, my friend, separates Europe from England, and permits the latter to enjoy peace while the former is in the throes of

endless conflicts. They have a great university in England—Oxford.
I shall drain the paps of wisdom for a while."

He grinned.

"I am serious, Kotikokura. I know more than Dr. Faust who sold
his soul to the Devil, but I must organize my knowledge. I have
been neglectful of late—these several centuries. I have not read
enough what the sages have written. I must learn their opinion of
man and the universe. And you—it is about time you learned how
to read and write, Kotikokura."

He made a grimace.

"You must! You heard Luther say that knights are becoming
scholars. You have reached the age——"

"No! No!"

"What? You prefer to remain ignorant and illiterate?"

He shrugged his shoulders.

"You think life is sufficient."

He nodded.

LXVIII

KOTIKOKURA SUCKS A LEMON — WE CROSS THE CHANNEL—KOTIKOKURA LEARNS TO WRITE

KOTIKOKURA, yellower than the lemon he was sucking, bent over the boat's railing, not precisely for the purpose of watching the tumult of the waves.

"Come, Kotikokura, it is better for us to walk briskly up and down the deck, inhaling the strong air than to shake like melancholy willow trees at the edges of lakes."

He looked at me, and endeavored, but in vain, to grin. His upper lip shivered a little and the edges of his front teeth glittered like white lights immediately extinguished.

I took his arm and we made long strides—ten forward, ten backward.

"Count, Kotikokura—one—two—three—four, and you will forget the crazy tossing of the boat."

He mumbled, "One—two—three."

"One—two—three—four—five," he grumbled.

"The gods invented seasickness to protect the English. Don't stop counting or your nausea will seize you again."

"Six—seven—eight—nine—ten."

"It is more difficult to conquer that corner of the earth than all Europe combined."

"One—two—three—four—five—"

"One—two—three—"

Kotikokura pulled his arm away and bent over the railing. Then he leaned against me, placing his head wearily upon my shoulder. I caressed it. "Only a while longer, Kotikokura. We who have seen centuries pass can laugh at the discomfort of hours!"

He grinned weakly.

"Hold my arm, Kotikokura, or we may lose each other in this artificial night."

We made small careful steps, our hands in front of us, as if descending into a dark cellar.

"Are those mountains or houses that we are approaching? Is that a horse ripping his form through the gray veil, or two elephants riding on top of each other? Are those torches or stars moving in space? This is a fairyland, Kotikokura, and the people must be strange dreamers. Indeed, they say that there are great poets and philosophers here."

The fog thinned and ripped in various places. It crawled out of the branches of the trees; it rose from the hats of people like smoke out of chimneys; it swept the ground like a phantom broom. Some obstinate shreds, laboring under the illusion of weight, clung to a fence or a wall, diminishing, thinning.

Suddenly, the sun—like the standard of a conquering army—rose triumphantly over the peak of the citadel of the world.

The Thames, crowded with barges and small sailboats, flowed tranquilly under the bridge. A few patches of the fog, the size of kerchiefs, still floated on its surface.

We entered a coffee house. The people were drinking jugs of dark beer, discussing the future of the lands discovered by Christopher Columbus. Several boats had recently left England. Wherever Her Majesty's flag was planted, that was English ground. Some foretold trouble with Spain; other predicted inconceivable wealth from the New World.

"Kotikokura, let us clink cups to our success. Without my gold, Columbus would have been unable to equip his ships."

Kotikokura clinked.

"If these lands are really another continent and not merely India, man can drown the errors, the stupidities, the cruelties of his ancestors in the sea, and begin anew, Kotikokura! In life's comedy man must improvise, rhyme at random, strutting about from one part of the stage to the other. The discovery of Columbus enables him to rehearse his part—to improve his acting. For once the gods are merciful! And yet, Kotikokura, I suspect their kindness. . ."

Kotikokura drank his beer and wiped his mouth.

"To start afresh! That is man's cry through the ages. Destroy the tree of life, plant a new seed! Poor Bluebeard,—that was the meaning of his gory hocus-pocus. What a horrible seed he planted! Can man tear the roots that bind him to Adam? New lands, Kotikokura —but where are the new people? A New World—but the same race of men!"

We walked out arm in arm.

"Kotikokura, tomorrow we leave London for Oxford, to learn the wisdom of the ages. Your infancy is over. You must learn to read and write."

Kotikokura grumbled.

"But my friend, even the Queen of this land knows how to read and write."

"Queen—woman."

"If necessary, Kotikokura, I shall have to use the birch on you."

He looked at me, uncertain whether to take me seriously or not.

"Don't grasp your pen as if it were an implement of murder, Kotikokura. Take it gently—thus. It is only the delicate feather that once flourished upon a goose."

Kotikokura held the pen between the tips of his forefinger and thumb.

"Nor so daintily, Kotikokura. The most delicate of ladies requires a little pressure. Does not Aristotle exhort us to seek always the middle course?"

He threw the pen on the floor and started to run away. I held his arm tightly.

"Kotikokura, for shame! You are worse than a five-year old urchin. What is the meaning of this irritability?"

He grumbled.

"Pick up your pen and start your page again. You shall have no beer today."

He shrugged his shoulders.

"Pick up your pen!" I ordered.

He glared at me, but obeyed.

I raised my arms in despair. "Oh that the High Priest of Ca-ta-pha should disobey his god! Oh, that in my old age—"

He kissed my hand.

LXIX

I MEET "THE WANDERING JEW"—I AM MALIGNED—
A CROSS-EXAMINATION—BOOTS

"By Jove, he is confounding the Bishop!" exclaimed a young man,
his black gown flowing about him like an enraged sea.

"He is an impostor, Arthur, I tell you. He——"

"Impostor?" A third youth interposed.

"An impostor, I say!" the second insisted.

Several more students gathered about them, vociferating in Latin
and in English.

"He is the Wandering Jew as truly as I am Arthur Blackmore."

I pressed Kotikokura's arm. "Are they speaking of me, Kotikokura?" I whispered.

He rubbed his nose.

Arthur Blackmore touched my elbow. "Milord, do you not believe
with me that he is the Wandering Jew?"

"I regret to say that I have not seen him."

"What! Is it possible? For the last three days, the university, the
whole town indeed, has been in turmoil."

"Where is the man who claims to be the Wandering Jew?" I asked.

"He will be here shortly. At present, he is in secret conclave with
the Bishop. He will be examined publicly today. Will you not come,
Milord, and convince yourself?"

"I shall be delighted to witness the trial," I said.

"Here he is now!"

A man of about fifty, long-bearded, long-haired and sharp-eyed
as an eagle, walked between the Bishop and two professors toward
the Main Hall.

The Hall, constructed like a chapel, was crowded with students
and professors. Upon the platform, sat the Bishop and the two
professors, one a young man, fair-haired and blue-eyed, who spoke
with a slight Irish brogue, the other a huge middle-aged man whose
huge bones bore evidence of his Saxon extraction. His head was

almost completely bald. The Bishop had the appearance of a man of much culture and kindliness. His face was rubicund, his hair, such as the shears had left, gray.

The Bishop rose, blessed the congregation, and ordered the Wandering Jew to enter.

Humble, stooping, the latter appeared and faced the three judges. The small hump on his back was unconvincing to me. His shoes were larger than needed. His grizzly beard covered his face too thickly to allow the study of lips and chin. His nose, very thin and hooked, cast a triangular shadow upon his right cheek.

"Isaac," the Bishop said in a voice that suggested the coolness of high hills, "relate publicly what you have told us in private: the story of your quarrel with our Lord Jesus."

Isaac bowed. His cavernous voice seemed to rise from a tomb.

His story was a travesty of mine. He was the son of a shoemaker who, having joined the Roman army, was singled out by Pilate for promotion. At the trial of Jesus he mocked and shouted with the rest: "Crucify Him! Crucify Him!"

Isaac sighed deeply, as if in great contrition. He followed the sorry procession to the Place of Skulls. On the way, as Jesus fell, the cross having become too heavy, Isaac shouted angrily: "Go to your doom! Hurry!" Jesus looked at him. No mortal had such eyes. They were like two burning spears.

Isaac covered his face with his hands. The audience was breathless. His arms dropped slowly to his side. Jesus hurled his curse: "I shall hurry but thou must tarry until I return."

The audience sighed. I shivered. The impostor had resuscitated my tragic experience. I saw the eyes of Jesus. I heard his voice. The storm of my own emotion howled about me.

Isaac continued. Ever since, he had wandered from one end of the earth to the other, praying for the return of Jesus. Every seventy years, he fell into a trance out of which he awoke as a man of thirty—his age at the time of the crucifixion.

The Bishop asked him his present age, based on his last transformation. He was only forty, but he looked much older. Alas, the burden of his guilt!

The judges asked him questions about his experiences, about his health, the manner of earning a livelihood, to all of which he answered very plausibly. They spoke in a dozen languages to him. He understood each. The Bishop seemed convinced.

The young professor wished to know if he had made any friends, and how it felt to see them die while he continued to live. Isaac wiped his eyes and sighed deeply.

The older professor continued to be skeptical. He cross-examined him again and again. But Isaac had rehearsed his part perfectly.

I felt indignant. I was maligned! Was this the man who fought Jesus? Was this whimpering, melancholy actor the symbol of my race? Had he enacted his part proudly; had he hurled back an anathema,—I would have restrained my tongue. What other nation, scattered and hounded, had resisted annihilation? Greece, Rome, Egypt—all had disappeared from the map. The Jew might needs pretend humility in his daily life. But when brought to court against his Enemy . . .!

The trial was nearing its end.

I stood up with a jerk. "Is it permissible, Your Reverence," I asked the Bishop, "to put a question to the Jew?"

"Yes."

"Isaac," I said, "what was your father's name?"

Isaac looked at me. The suddenness of my question disconcerted him. He shivered a little and remained perplexed.

"Well, have you forgotten it?" I asked.

"Abraham," he answered. "I had not forgotten it; only the memory upset me."

"It's a lie! Your father's name was Joseph."

"Joseph! True, true! I was thinking of my brother."

"The Wandering Jew was an only son!"

The Hall changed into a hive of bees, buzzing noisily. The Bishop stood up. The two professors bent over the pulpit.

"And your mother's name—have you forgotten that also?"

"It is so long ago, sir," he whimpered.

"Your mother's name!" I insisted.

"Esther," he answered.

"It's a lie! Her name was Ruth, as any one can find out by consulting the secret history of Pilate in the library of the Vatican, as I did. You have read diligently the confessions of the Wandering Jew to the Armenian Bishop. You have listened to the rumors and gossip, but over these trifles you trip!

"Ahasuerus never cringed as you do. That is fable. He was proud and dignified. Nor did he pretend poverty. He was wealthier than kings. You are a fraud, seeking sympathy, notoriety, and a purse."

"Impostor! Fraud!" rang through the hall.

"Besides, was it necessary to stuff your back with a cushion?"

Several people rushed up to Isaac and tapped his back. I had guessed rightly.

Isaac knelt before the judges and begged forgiveness.

"Jesus may pardon you when you tremble before him at the Last Judgment. We, however, cannot forgive the insult to ourselves and the mockery to our Lord," the Bishop said, and turning to an attendant, he ordered, "Take him out and await our decision."

Isaac, beaten and spat upon by the audience, was dragged out.

My familiarity with the story of the Wandering Jew aroused suspicion. The Oxford professors attempted to entrap me in divers discussions. It tested my ingenuity to escape from the meshes of their cross-examination. I was not in a mood to play with danger, and shook the dust of Oxford off my heels leaving behind me a pair of boots.

LXX

QUEEN ELIZABETH PASSES—DUST TO DUST— I DISCOVER MYSELF IN A BOOK

AFTER our departure from Oxford we spent a generation or two in Ireland. Under the name of Baron de Martini I bought an estate, where life flowed on as a small river hidden between two valleys.

One day a rock was hurled into the quiet waters. An heir of the man from whom I had bought my estate discovered a flaw in the title.

I determined to go to London to seek justice at the fountain head.

London fluttered like a young bride. Flags, music, confetti, laughter, and colors—a hundred nuances of red, green, blue, yellow —as if a rainbow had been crumbled and scattered by some absent-minded divinity, or one awaiting nervously the verdict of a goddess he courted.

London expected the Virgin Queen.

"Kotikokura, we are fortunate. We have arrived on time. It is a good omen. We shall win our case."

Trumpets announced the arrival of Queen Elizabeth. Soldiers urged and pushed the crowds to the two sides of the streets, making room for the procession. A regiment of cavalry preceded the landau all gilded and dazzling like a setting sun, drawn by six milk-white steeds, arrogant, as if the applause and the hurrahs were intended for them.

The Queen sat erect as a statue, a coronet upon her head and masses of jewels upon her chest and arms. In her right hand, she held a scepter, in her left a large fan of peacock feathers. It was not possible to tell whether she was thin or stout, for her dress, hoop-like and stiff from the whalebones, occupied nearly the entire carriage, which moved very slowly to allow the people to gaze upon their monarch. From time to time, she nodded slightly to one side or the other.

The people shouted: "Long live the Queen! Long live the Queen!"

393

Many in the front lines knelt; others threw flowers and confetti on the horses or against the wheels, careful not to strike the august occupant.

For a fraction of a second, her eyes met mine. The procession seemed to whirl about me. I closed my eyes tightly as if to lock within them the impression they had received. When I opened them again, the landau had already passed by, leaving behind it a small hillock of dust.

"Did you see her eyes, Kotikokura?" I asked nervously.

Kotikokura shook his head. He had noticed her fan, the largest he had ever seen.

"They resemble Salome's, Kotikokura!"

He shrugged his shoulders.

The royal carriage was followed by less magnificent ones, occupied by officers of the army and navy and ladies of the highest nobility. The people exclaimed from time to time the names of an occupant, and waved their hats.

I was too perturbed to be interested. Hatred and love, pleasure and disgust, mingled within me, making curious patterns.

"Her hair,—did you notice, Kotikokura?—also resembled Salome's, but it was faded, despite the sheen of the oil, and tended to grayness."

Kotikokura watched the people throw flowers and ribbons and hats into the air.

"She has a ruler's face, Kotikokura. There is no doubt of that,— majestic, serene, wise. But what does she lack? What ingredient in her make-up repels rather than attracts?"

Kotikokura was busy removing the wet confetti which a girl had thrown at him, and dotted his entire face, like colored smallpox.

"It is not a question of homeliness, Kotikokura. Homely women have pleased me. She is not homely."

Kotikokura grumbled, "Woman," waving his fist at the invisible perpetrator of the jest.

"She is neither man nor woman! Have you noticed that?" I said a little irritably.

Kotikokura nodded, fearing to disagree.

Another regiment approached in a tumult of trumpets.

"She is like the sphinxes we saw in Egypt, Kotikokura. Impenetrable as stone. No wonder she is a virgin!"

Kotikokura grinned.

"Ah, if Salome were queen! If she drove in a golden chariot

through the streets of her capital! Man would grow mad with
beauty! Ah, Salome!"

The last horseman galloped past us. The people began pushing in
all directions, shouting to one another, exclaiming their last hurrahs.

"And yet, she does resemble Salome,—and that is what angers me,
that is what saddens me, Kotikokura."

Kotikokura, holding his elbows at right angles, cleared the passage.
Now and then, some one swore at us, shouting ugly epithets.

"Fool, you nearly cut through me!"

"Draw your sword, rascal!"

"The caricature of a thing we love is distressing, Kotikokura.
This is what Salome might have been, had the gods been in a less
joyous mood. A twist here, a wrench there,—a passion extinguished,
a feminine charm removed. . . And yet, she must be a great
queen. But a woman, alas, she is not!"

Kotikokura continued to clear the way unperturbed.

"But I must forget this woman. I must obliterate her image, that
the image of the greater queen may not become distorted in my
mind."

"By Jove, will you not cease pushing?"

"Villain!"

"Scoundrel!"

"Low-bred!"

"Come, Kotikokura, let us not get into useless trouble. Here is a
bookshop. Let us enter for a while."

The owner, a very small man, clean-shaven, red-checked, approached us, limping a little, and bowing deeply.

"Have you seen the Queen, gentlemen?"

"Yes."

"Alas, I could not go. My rheumatism did spite me just on this
day! Is Her Majesty as beautiful as our poets claim?"

"She is," I answered.

He raised his eyes, so vague a blue that they appeared nearly
white, and sighed profoundly. "Who knows if I shall ever have the
joy of gazing upon my Queen?" he exclaimed.

"No doubt you will," I consoled him.

"Is the gentleman interested in the new edition of Master Shakespeare's plays?"

"No."

"In Ben Jonson's then, assuredly."

"Why assuredly?"

He smiled, raising his upper lip and keeping it pasted against his gum. "The purchasers of my books seem to be divided into two camps nowadays."

"Ah!" I answered, resolved to care for neither one. "What I should like, if you permit it, is to look about and perhaps discover something that might interest me."

"The classics, no doubt. The gentleman is a classicist."

"Hm, hm!"

"I have Cicero and Aristotle and Plato and Marcus Aurelius."

"Marcus Aurelius?" I asked.

"A fine old edition."

He climbed on the ladder quickly, like a squirrel, forgetting, evidently, the rheumatism in his leg, and descended, a heavy folio in his arm which he presented to me tenderly, as if it had been an infant on its way to the baptismal font.

I examined the book, seeking the passages which I had heard the Emperor read while his beautiful wife toyed with her slave.

"Ah!" I exclaimed, as I read: 'Be thou erect or be made erect.' The eyes of the Empress had closed a little and the fan of the youth had grazed her face. . .

I seated myself on a bench and continued reading, recalling the while the Emperor, the visitors, the old whispering artist. Kotikokura, seated himself on a rung of the ladder and read, moving his lips, a child's book with letters almost as tall as fingers.

"Nothing is true!" I shouted rising. "Nothing is true save dust!"

The bookseller, taken by surprise, shivered and retreated, grasping his rheumatic leg. Kotikokura dropped his book to the floor.

"Nothing, I tell you! What is Marcus Aurelius but dust? And his wife who betrayed him under his nose, while he preached virtue —dust? And all the lords and ladies that flattered him while he droned monotonously? Dust—dust! Does it not choke you, as it chokes me?"

"Yes, Milord!" he groaned, "all dust. Ouch! What a leg, sir, what a leg!"

"In this you have an illustrious predecessor," I remarked, "Charlemagne—Charles the Great, Emperor of the West, suffered from rheumatism."

"Is it true, milord?" he asked, dazed.

"But for a long, long time now, he has been relieved of the torture. Dust does not pain, my friend. Keep that in mind and it will help you greatly."

"It has already, a little. Will your lordship buy the book?"

"Yes."

He rubbed his hands whose hard hooked nails gave the appearance of eagles' claws.

As I was about to leave the place, I spied a pamphlet whose covers were black from spots of grease. The title, in Latin, read: "The Wandering Jew—His Trial at Oxford University. His remarks, Opinions and Ideas Expounded, Commented Upon and Analyzed by the Reverend Bishop of Canterbury with annotations by Master Aubrey and Master Battermann, Doctors of Sacred Theology."

I jerked the book out of the shelf and turned the pages rapidly. No doubt about it! It was the record of my examination by the Bishop in Oxford.

LXXI

FRANCIS BACON, LORD VERULAM—I GO TO THE THEATER—I MEET "MR. W. H."—THE JEALOUSY OF KOTIKOKURA—ANTONIO-ANTONIA—I LIFT A CURTAIN—THE MASTER THIEF

THE London solicitors were more garrulous than the Irish and their more meticulous knowledge of the law made it less possible for them to reach a conclusion. My plan was to receive a favorable judgment without appearing before the courts in person. What judge was both powerful enough and susceptible enough to gifts to accomplish this? For the time being, it was uncertain. Queen Elizabeth died unexpectedly and the favorites of the new King were as yet unknown.

"It is best to wait, Kotikokura. Are you not of my opinion?"

Kotikokura nodded.

"Meanwhile, let us travel about the country, learn its customs and habits. When we are away from here, we may find it necessary to call ourselves Englishmen. We must not arouse any doubt."

Upon our return, I discovered that Francis Bacon, Lord Verulam, a philosopher whose work I had read and admired, had been appointed Chief Solicitor of the Crown.

I wrote him a long letter in which I praised his great contribution to philosophy, and begged him to accept, as a token of my profound appreciation, a watch, the shape of a little book, studded with precious stones, the work of a Florentine artist.

The Lord's reply was an epistolary masterpiece. He invited me to Gray's Inn where, despite his position, he was still constrained to live.

The Lord's kindliness and simplicity were equal to his greatness. He thanked me profusely for my gift, the most appropriate and opportune conceivable, and particularly agreeable since it came from Florence, the most beautiful of cities which he had visited in his youth. I thanked him for the praises he had accorded my city which my ancestor, a man of the same name as I, Baron di Martini, had helped to enrich by his remarkable work in history and by his love for art.

"The Florentines, like the Athenians of old," Bacon said, sighing a little, "are the only true patriots. We do not understand the meaning of patriotism. Mere allegiance to King and Flag is not patriotism. A man should identify himself with his country, should merge into it as a tiny stream merges into a river. Greater still is the patriotism which flows beyond the frontier of one nation, uniting with the limitless sea of mankind."

He twisted his short red beard and bit its tip. His eyes, round almost as an owl's, stared into the distance.

"I discard all philosophies which consider the world *ex analogia hominis* and not *ex analogia mundi*. Philosophers even Aristotle at times, prefer to proclaim their own abstract notions as truth. They never take the trouble to observe. They prefer to close their eyes tightly and speak of light in terms of the darkness in which they live. I consider philosophy a human and a practical thing."

His round eyes seemed to grow rounder still.

His words thrilled me. Had man at last awakened from the lethargy of futile scholastic argumentations? Was he endeavoring to see truth, to love reality?

"Man," he continued, "can do and understand so much and so much only as he has observed in fact or in thought of the course of Nature; beyond this, he neither knows anything nor can do anything."

Who was this man, this oracle of truth? Apollonius? No! Apollonius partook of divinity. This man was mortal, of the earth. One after another I passed in review the great men I had known. No— he was a new pattern—destined, perhaps, to re-create the mind of man. Francis Bacon—I must remember him—and see how future generations would assay his philosophy.

"In my main work, '*The Novum Organum*,' he said, "I elucidate the questions we are discussing."

"I am most anxious to see the work."

"Alas, who knows whether I shall ever complete it? I have been laboring at it nearly all my life but——" he stopped, sighed, and pulled one hair out of his beard.

"Is it a matter of health, my Lord?"

"Health, too, but mainly duties that occupy my time—duties and debts. I beg your pardon, Baron. I have no right to burden you with my troubles."

"On the contrary, my Lord. You honor me greatly. Perhaps, too, if it is merely a matter of money— —"

"Merely a matter of money, Baron? Money! People speak so glibly about it. Money—is it not the basis of all reality?"

"The lack of money," I answered, "is a greater reality than its possession."

He smiled.

I considered this the most favorable moment of broaching the matter of my suit.

Lord Verulam listened attentively and meditated. "Give me a few days' time to consider this, Baron. I believe it can be adjusted—not so easily, perhaps, but it can be."

He looked at me, his round eyes blinking a little. We understood each other.

He glanced at his watch which hung around his neck by a golden chain, also my gift.

Then, once more philosopher and man of the world, Bacon directed the conversation into other channels.

"Ah, it is time for the play. Is the Baron interested in the theater?"

"Life's distorted reflection in the mirror of art always amuses me."

"Will Shakespeare of the Globe Theater is putting on 'Romeo and Juliet' today, a charming play, though too sentimental. Master Willie Hewes is positively enchanting as Juliet. So consummate is his acting one can hardly believe he's a boy. Would you care to see the performance?"

I accepted the invitation.

The play pleased me mildly. The plot which I had read in several Italian stories, was hackneyed, the end decidedly stupid. But Master Willie Hewes was exquisite.

When had I seen a youth so handsome, so delicately fashioned? Where had I heard so musical a voice? Who in my memory compared with him? Walhallath? John? Damis? He was as beautiful as they, but more piquant. Perhaps it was the rôle he was playing or the glamor of the lights that enhanced his fascination.

Who was Willie Hewes? Suddenly some one or something tugged at my sleeve and whispered into my ear: "Toni."

"Toni!" I repeated aloud. But Toni's hair had been black. He was a Toni whose hair had turned to gold.

His Lordship looked at me, chafing a little in the stiff ruffle about his neck. He noticed my agitation.

"How do you like the lad, Baron?" he asked with a smile.

"Willie Hewes, my Lord, resembles a younger brother of mine who died years ago."

"Should you desire it, Baron, I shall ask Willie to join us over the punch bowl. He is quite a manly fellow, swears, drinks, fences, and makes love to the wenches. If the lad were less enamored of Shakespeare, he could choose a titled lady for his bride. But his strange passion— —"

"A youth's whim, my lord. Besides, is not this Shakespeare the playwright?"

"Yes, of course. Willie's love may be a reflex of his admiration. Meanwhile, however, the scandal sears his character. I told him so, but he would not listen to me. He recited the sonnets Shakespeare dedicated to him. They are not shocking to a classical scholar, but they make ribald tongues wag in London. However," Bacon laughed, "I nearly fell in love with the lad myself."

"The youth intrigues me, my Lord."

Lord Verulam called Willie. He jestingly admonished the youth about his morals, pinched his cheek and prophesied the gallows for him.

"There is more romance and less pain upon the gallows, my Lord, than in a lingering death upon a bed,—the fate of great magistrates."

"Wretch!" the Lord exclaimed. "I shall tie the noose around your neck myself."

"What, my Lord, could be sweeter! The honor robs death of its sting."

The Lord laughed, pinched Willie's cheek again, shook my hand and left.

"Your acting was inimitable," I said.

Willie smiled and thanked me.

"I have not seen your equal on the stage."

The lad blushed a little, closed and opened his eyes slowly. I looked intently at him. Was it Antonio or Antonia? Had they mingled at last into one?

"You will forgive me, my 'ad," I said, "if I scrutinize your face. You resemble most strangely a brother of mine whom I loved exceedingly."

Willie looked at me. "Your eyes are like mine."

"My brother—Antonio—resembled me."

"Antonio! What a pretty name!"

"Will you allow me to call you by that name?" I asked. "It thrills me—the memory."

"Do please call me Antonio. It's delicious. And since you are my brother, how shall I call you?"

"Cartaphilus."

"Cartaphilus? What a strange and beautiful name!"

"It means the Much Beloved in Greek, Antonio."

He winked slightly. "Is it merited?"

"You are wicked, Antonio. His lordship tells me that your reputation is scandalous. The other Antonio," I added jestingly, "was a good and virtuous youth."

The boy looked at me sadly.

"Forgive me, Antonio. I did not mean to hurt you." I pressed his hand, small and white, almost a child's.

"I thought that being my brother, you would know me better, Cartaphilus."

I remained silent.

"Why do people misinterpret everything, Cartaphilus? Even so wise a man as Lord Verulam. Only Master Will knows the soul. He knows— —"

Piqued by a sudden sense of jealousy, I said, "Cartaphilus knows his brother better than Master Will."

He shook his head.

"Yes!" I insisted. "And to make amends for his awkwardness and folly, he will buy his brother the finest cloak in London—a silver sword, and a bracelet of gold."

The lad clapped his hands gleefully.

'Antonia,' I thought.

His face clouded suddenly. "My brother is mocking my poverty. Yes, I am but an actor—an outcast from respectability, and my cloak is neither over-beautiful nor over-new." He made a step away from me.

"Antonio!" I exclaimed. I looked deeply into his eyes, as if piercing his very soul.

"What is the meaning of this?"

He returned the look, the long lashes of his black eyes touching and parting slowly. He sighed.

"Why do you wish to buy presents for me?"

"Are you not my brother? Shall I not celebrate our reunion after such a long absence? Give me your hand and tell me that you too rejoice that we have found each other again."

He squeezed my hand.

We walked arm in arm, discussing the theater, morals, life. I had never met so precocious a youth. Antonio? Yes, but more still. Antonia? Yes, but more still. The two combined,—boy and girl, man and woman. Thus must Salome have been in the first bloom of her loveliness! Thus she must be again, if she overcomes the moon!

Behind us, two boys carried the things I had bought for my new friend.

"But I have known you only a few hours, Cartaphilus."

"Really? Do you believe in your heart that you have known me only a few hours?"

"I do not know. Just now, I had the feeling that you were indeed my brother—What do I say? Dearer than a brother—one I had known not only from the moment I drew breath, but from some distant endless past, from the beginning of all things."

"You are right. You have known me always, for always I thought of you, Antonio,—always—and in my mind you were born centuries before you drew your first breath."

What strange emotion indeed drew me to this boy? He seemed dearer to me than Damis, more lovable than John. I pressed his arm which, though firm, had the soft contours of a girl's.

"Who are you, Cartaphilus?" he asked me, almost in a whisper.

"Your brother, Antonio."

"My brother is the strangest man I have ever laid my eyes upon. He is more beautiful than the moon which lies upon the crystal pillow of the lake. His language is as sugared as Shakespeare's."

"Do not speak of Shakespeare, Antonio!"

"You are jealous, Cartaphilus," he laughed.

"I am."

"I am happy that you are jealous! I see that you are, after all, a man."

"And you, Antonio?"

"I am . . . a . . . woman."

"What did you say, Antonio?"

He laughed uproariously. "Should it not be so—a man—a woman? Always that. All plays, comedies, tragedies—what are they but a man and a woman, seeking or avoiding each other?"

"You are an actor always."

"And you, Cartaphilus, are you not an actor?"

"Yes. You have guessed my nature. I am an actor, with many parts."

"And your latest—the brother of Antonio. Is it not so?"

"Is it a comedy or a tragedy, Antonio?"

"The difference between the two is very slight. Shakespeare often turns his tragedies into comedies. By a slight twist here, a change there—presto, a comedy has become a tragedy and vice versa. Romeo and Juliet he first conceived as a comedy. Romeo marries his sweetheart. And there was an epilogue too in which—" Willie smiled sadly. "No, that was really too gruesome. The epilogue showed them as husband and wife, quarreling and hating each other. It was Shakespeare's own life. He could not endure it. It was too horrible."

"Is Shakespeare very unhappy?"

"Very."

"This is why you love him."

"Perhaps."

"I wish I were unhappy, Antonio. . ."

"You will never be unhappy, Cartaphilus. You have the temperament of an actor. You will always be able to change your part if it becomes too unpleasant."

This youth's intuition was uncanny. He knew me as well as I knew myself after centuries of meditation!

Upon seeing Willie, Kotikokura became gloomy. I detected a murderous twitch in his hands. Willie sensed his animosity and straightway began to placate him. He called him a hundred endearing names. He wrestled with him, patted his face, ruffled his hair. Kotikokura, bewildered, began to grin.

"I have brought you a toy—a little dog in the shape of a youth, to play with, Kotikokura. Have you seen anything or any one more delicious than this creature?"

Kotikokura relented.

"Besides, do you not recognize him? He is Antonio, Kotikokura. Look at him."

Kotikokura stared, surprised.

"Antonio resurrected. He is our little friend of Florence."

"Kotikokura!" Willie exclaimed. "Kotikokura! What a name! What a strange, beautiful, funny, ridiculous, charming, gorgeous, fantastic, terrible, devilish, divine, uproarious, sad, merry name! Kotikokura! Kotikokura!" Willie jumped upon his neck. "You are the dearest, best, most horrible creature in the world! You are Pan, Caliban, Ariel."

Kotikokura began to dance. Antonio joined him.

"Come, Cartaphilus, dance! What is life but a dance,—grotesque and magnificent at the same time? Dance!"

Carried away by the merriment, we danced until out of breath, we fell in a heap upon the floor.

"I am thirsty, Cartaphilus," Antonio whispered.

"Kotikokura, wine!"

Kotikokura filled our cups. We drank to beauty that is truth, as Toni had drunk—so long ago. Was this a dream, a play by Master Will Shakespeare or reality?

"Oh, I forget," Antonio rose with a jerk. "My new garments! I must try them on."

"By all means, little brother."

"I do not like to be naked in the presence of other people," he said seriously.

"Not even in mine?"

"Please— —"

"We shall not embarrass you then, Antonio. Dress in that room behind the curtain while Kotikokura and I drink another cup together."

"No peeping," Antonio warned.

"I swear it."

Kotikokura poured himself a cup of wine, emptied it at one gulp, and repeated the process three times. He wished to forget something, to drown some emotion. Was it love for the youth or hatred or jealousy? Very likely, a mingling of all these emotions, too entangled and irritating. He stretched out upon the floor and snored promptly.

Sleep is a yearning to disappear from the earth, a temporary death without which man could not continue to live. That was why I, deathless, could endure life. I died every day for a while.

Willie Hewes was still dressing himself. I could hear now and then a movement, a creaking of the floor. A desire to see the youth naked possessed me. Was he as handsome as the other Antonio? Was his skin as white? Was his body as exquisitely shaped? And there was something else too,—something I could not explain, a curious uneasiness. Did he really feel embarrassed? How unusual for an actor! Did not Bacon say that the youth was known for his escapades with wenches, that his reputation at the Globe Theater was not that of a modest youth?

I promised I would not "peep." I might arouse his displeasure. It would be a pity. At the beginning of friendship, it might prove disastrous.

But even while these ideas crossed and recrossed my brain, my hand lifted carefully a corner of the curtain.

The long Venetian mirror reflected in gorgeous nakedness—not Antonio, but Antonia—the most beautiful of girls—two small breasts round as apples, a throat as firm and smooth as marble, hips and arms and a torso dazzling like the morning sun. The body was firmly knit as a boy's, but rounded delicately, giving the illusion of softness. The hair, curled and cut at the nape of the neck, resembled that of a Grecian statue.

"Antonia," I whispered.

Willie turned around and caught her breath. By an ancient instinct, she covered with one arm her breasts, with the other her femininity. Her face flushed, her lips parted.

"Cartaphilus! Did you not swear——?"

I entered the room. "I swore, but I am happy I perjured myself. Antonia, my dearest, my loveliest maiden!"

She hid her head upon her bosom and sobbed quietly.

I embraced her. "Is it not infinitely more delectable to find that Antonio is Antonia?"

"Everybody will hear of it now and I shall have to leave the theater. I shall have to be merely a woman. No more for me the joy and the recklessness of a boy!"

"How can you think that, my love? If Antonia desires to be Antonio, shall Cartaphilus frustrate her wish? How much more poignant her beauty, vacillating between boy and girl. . ."

She raised her head, and wiped one tear that hung midway between the eyelash and the cheek.

She clasped my head and looked into my eyes.

"Is it right for Cartaphilus to love his sister?"

I seated her on my knee upon the edge of the bed and as I fondled her delicately with my lips and fingers, I recounted my experience with the two Florentine children.

"Cartaphilus is not your brother, Antonia. He was never your brother. He was always your lover. Antonia desired to be Antonio. She said she had been intended for a man. And now, at last, she is —and yet is not—a man. Is there anything more exquisite in all the world than Antonia-Antonio—Toni—both in one?"

She pressed my lips against hers, biting them a little with the edges of her teeth.

I continued to enlarge upon the episode of the twins. Before I finished my tale, she had fallen asleep in my arms. I placed her gently upon the bed. I undressed and joined her.

My first passionate caress awakened her.

"Will," she whispered. She looked at me. "Forgive me, Cartaphilus —I love you."

"And not Shakespeare?"

"When I am with Cartaphilus—no."

"Toni!"

She stood up suddenly. "Where is Kotikokura?"

"Do not fear, my love. He is fast asleep. Besides, he never intrudes."

"He is a dear fellow. I like him greatly. There is something of the wild forests about him. If Will saw him he would put him into a play."

"Tell me what prompted you to disguise yourself as a boy?"

"It was the only way I could be near him, since the law does not permit our sex to appear on the stage."

"But Shakespeare knew your sex?"

"Not at first. . ."

"He loved you. . ."

"Yes. . . He was completely bewildered . . . at first, but in his heart of hearts he suspected my secret."

"How do you know?"

She pouted. "Because he poured his soul into his sonnets." Her lips moved, caressing each word affectionately.

> "And for a woman wert thou first created,
> Till Nature, as she wrought thee, fell a-doting
> And by addition me of thee defeated
> By adding something to my purpose nothing."

"And when he discovered that nature had not been so cruel? . . ."

"He was overjoyed. It remained a sweet, shameful secret between us. If my true sex were known, I would be banished from the stage, and the Lord Chamberlain would punish Will. In the eyes of the law we are no better than vagabonds."

"Do you like to play the boy, to be his play-boy?"

She hesitated a minute. Then she said shyly, "Yes." She blushed "He called me master-mistress of his passion. . ."

We spent the rest of the day and the night in the exquisite pleasure-pain of amorous dalliance. At one moment, she reminded me of Antonia, at another of Antonio, and as I fell asleep, she was Salome in the desert.

When I awoke, the sun glared into the room and Kotikokura raised slowly the curtain.

I stood up.

"Where is she, Kotikokura? Where is she?"

Kotikokura grinned, thinking that I was dreaming. I realized that he had probably never guessed the delectable gender of Willie Hewes.

"Where is the youth?" I asked, jumping off the bed.

Kotikokura handed me a letter.

"Dearest Cartaphilus,

"If I remained another night with you, I should never be able to go back. I must tear myself away as one tears an arm out of its socket. But it must be done, my love, my brother.

"Will Shakespeare is the saddest of men and his life is a torture. Without me, what would become of him? He would nevermore write. He needs me.

"As for me—what does it matter, Cartaphilus? How long more can I be Willie Hewes, or Antonio without suspicion? How long more before—no matter, dearest—my heart breaks! A thousand kisses— and one for Kotikokura.

"P.S. Forgive me if I do not accept your gifts, save the little chain. I must return to Will Shakespeare as I was before I met and before I loved too much the Much-Beloved. . . .   Toni."

I turned my face to the wall and wept. Kotikokura wept also.

LXXII

ENGLAND SMOKES—MERMAID'S TAVERN—WILLIE HEWES GIGGLES

LORD VERULAM sent a messenger to fetch me. He was very cheerful. He had studied my question carefully. There was a way to silence those preposterous heirs.

"I found it for you, because your case is just. Never in all my career, did I pronounce judgment in favor of him whom I considered guilty. I have received payments and gifts for my labors, it is true, but never—I swear it by my God and country—have I betrayed truth and justice."

There was a strange pathos in his voice.

"By the way, Baron, do you smoke?"

"I have noticed the popularity of the pipe in England. What is it you smoke?" I asked.

"Tobacco. A plant recently introduced from America. It is the best thing that has come out of the New World."

He offered me a pipe. We seated ourselves deeply into our chairs, and blew the smoke upward like chimneys of homes where abundance reigns.

I thought of Salome and the desert and Flower-of-the-Evening, and as I closed my eyes, the image of Willie Hewes reappeared before me in the glory of her epicene youth.

Why had she left me for Shakespeare? "Another night with you and I should never be able to go back."

"My Lord," I said suddenly, "what can you tell me about this Master Will Shakespeare?"

"You have seen his 'Romeo and Juliet.' "

"Yes, I know. But is he really a genius?"

Bacon smiled. "The age of geniuses is past, Baron. We must resign ourselves to be people of talent. Master Will is a clever craftsman, but he is a thief. He steals with the unconcern of a child whose conscience has been untutored. 'Mine,' he calls out gaily, whenever he comes across something that pleases him. He has done me the honor to borrow from me."

"Do you allow this, my Lord?"

"It amuses me. I hear people praise him: 'What depth of thought and emotion!' They really praise me unwittingly. Besides, I have enough ideas to spare for a poor fellow who is hungry for fame as a cat is for mice. If only he would not be so anxious for the applause of the groundlings and torture my ideas and the charming fancy of the Italians into such barbarous forms!

"My gracious sovereign, Queen Elizabeth—may her soul rest in peace—had a fancy for him and his work. She used to go to his theater masked, and she established his reputation."

"Do you believe, my Lord, that his fame will be enduring?"

"No. He will die with his generation. The only man who may outlast his contemporaries is Ben Jonson. He is a scholar and a thinker, but his daily broils are intolerable."

"Is he handsome?"

"Who?"

"Shakespeare."

His Lordship laughed uproariously. "Handsome? A face like a bag-pipe the Scots use for serenading their lasses, a head bald to the neck with a fringe of red that looks like the scrapings of carrots."

"How does it happen, then, that Willie Hewes is so obsessed with Shakespeare?"

"I do not understand it, Baron. It is scandalous on Will's part to parade his emotions so brazenly. The boy does not know better. His age is his excuse. You and I are men of the world. We understand classic vagaries. But the world condemns them, even in its more liberal moods, with an obscene smirk. I have spoken to Shakespeare about the boy and his own reputation on several occasions. He looked at me bewildered and tears rolled down his puffed cheeks. He is intolerably sentimental. I turned away."

"Willie Hewes is a strange youth."

"I like him immensely. No shepherd in Virgil's Eclogues is more delightful. The stage will spoil him, I fear, and his association with Shakespeare is unfortunate. I do not approve of the new movement, headed by people nicknamed the Puritans, for purging a man's soul by destroying it, which seems to gain a firm foothold in England. But there are limits beyond which freedom is license. Shakespeare has been accused of being a panderer. His treatment of his poor wife almost exhausts my patience."

"Is he married?"

"He married at the age of seventeen, I believe, forsook his wife, leaving her to support his two or three children. He still refuses to return to her bed, preferring to play Jupiter to his Ganymede," Bacon snorted indignantly.

We remained silent, puffing at our pipes slowly. How could Antonia-Antonio love such a man? What hidden charm or beauty did he possess which made him attractive to her?

I determined to seek Shakespeare and his master-mistress in their nightly haunt.

"Where," I asked, "is the Mermaid's Tavern, whither I am told the immortals of England foregather?"

Bacon laughed.

"Have a jug of ale with me and the literary cutthroats of England tonight!"

We entered the Mermaid, arm in arm. A long narrow room, crowded with vociferating people. A heavy smell of stale tobacco, ale and frying foods. We remained standing and looked about.

"There is Master Shakespeare, Baron," the lord whispered.

I had already espied him. Bacon's description was admirable. Willie Hewes, her face still besmudged from theatrical paint, held one arm around his neck while with the other she raised a cup to her lips. She saw me. Her arm remained stiffened for a moment, then proceeded quietly its way.

"Antonia," I said, without sound, merely moving my lips. She looked at me, utterly unconcerned, as if I had been a stranger.

Shakespeare, tears rolling down his cheeks, was reciting at the top of his voice, with false pathos:

> "Goode friend, for Jesus' sake forbeare
> To dig the dust enclosed heare;
> Bleste be the man that spares these stones,
> And curst be he that moves my bones."

No one paid attention to his bibulous whine of the epitaph he proposed for his tomb. Tearfully he repeated the verses again and again. Willie Hewes stopped him. Shakespeare placed his head upon her shoulder and sobbed.

"Antonia," I repeated.

She raised her head a little and I saw the small golden chain I gave her glitter about her neck. She raised her cup again and swallowed the contents quickly. Her lips were covered with foam which she wiped with the back of her hand.

A man, not very tall, but enormously stout, rose suddenly from a table and cup in hand, began to dance about, spilling the ale upon his great stomach which shook like half-frozen jelly. The rest applauded and shouted compliments and vulgarities.

"This is Ben Jonson, Baron," Bacon laughed.

"If these are gods, what are men?" I asked.

"The reflection of their gods," he answered.

Ben Jonson whirled about and upset, with the sweep of his arms, the cups upon the table. The guests rose, swearing and challenging one another to duels.

I looked once more at Willie Hewes. She was giggling drunkenly.

LXXIII

A LETTER FROM SALOME—I RETURN TO AFRICA—I AM DETHRONED—FLAMES

THE memory of Willie Hewes tortured me. Was it love? Was it disillusion, jealousy, pity?

"Kotikokura, I am tormented."

Kotikokura made a wry face.

"This place bores me and it bores you too, I notice."

He nodded.

"Where shall we go? What shall we do?"

He scratched his nose.

"If Salome— —"

A servant interrupted my sentence. He brought me a letter.

"From Salome!" I shouted to Kotikokura.

Kotikokura shrugged his shoulders.

The letter was written in Chinese interspersed with Hebrew and Arabic. She scolded me for having risked my liberty at the Oxford Trial. She called me an irrational child. She upbraided me also for the assistance I gave Luther. He hated the Jews, and favored the burning of witches. Europe had become a cauldron of controversy, stupidity, cruelty and confusion. Why could I not discover something worthier of my age and knowledge than religious wars? But then I was a man, too restless, too impulsive, too romantic to grasp the eternal verities. She loved me, nevertheless, or perhaps because of it. She was still a woman and therefore a mother.

As for herself, she had not yet conquered the Moon, which being feminine, was too clever and too subtle. But in time she would ensnare the reluctant goddess.

The new generation of nuns was less beautiful and less intelligent. At any rate, they no longer interested her and being an Abbess, a century old, demanded certain proprieties which displeased her.

This letter was to inform me that she had set out on a journey. Where? Well,—could not Cartaphilus guess as Salome guessed his whereabouts?

413

A few more admonitions, some critical remarks about Man, regards to Kotikokura, her arch-enemy, and a kiss for me— —.

"Kotikokura, Salome sends you regards."

He shrugged his shoulders, but I detected a twinkle of delight in his eyes.

"You must acknowledge that no woman approaches her in beauty and wisdom, Kotikokura."

He shrugged his shoulders.

"Be truthful, my friend."

He turned his face to the wall.

"You are like the ostrich, Kotikokura,—or at least as the ostrich of the proverb. You will not face reality. How human! Does man ever struggle for truth? No, he struggles, sacrifices his life and happiness for his opinions, which in his heart of hearts he knows to be false."

Kotikokura drew with his finger the alphabet upon the wall.

"Kotikokura, where is Salome?"

He continued his invisible writing.

"If I only knew!"

I walked up and down the room, thinking, debating.

"Kotikokura, I have it! I have it! She has gone to Africa."

Kotikokura looked at me.

"She is weary of Europe. Where would she go if not Africa?"

Kotikokura's eyes darted to and fro.

"At any rate, what place can you imagine more appropriate for us two, Kotikokura?"

He bent almost in two.

"Be erect, or be made erect, Kotikokura! What does this atavistic gesture mean?"

He straightened up.

"Let us go back to Africa,—the cradle of the Universe! Come, High Priest of Ca-ta-pha!"

He bowed three times to the ground and made the sign of the Camel, the Parrot and Ca-ta-pha by dividing his body into three cardinal points.

"Kotikokura, look!" I gave him my telescope, a recent invention of a Hollander.

"Do you see that church surmounted by a cross?"

He nodded.

"Is it not on the spot where the temple of Ca-ta-pha stood?"

He returned my telescope.

Our camels trudged slowly forward.

"Do you know what this means, my ancient friend?"

He looked at me, his face drawn.

"It means that our enemy has conquered. I am a god no longer; you no longer a high priest."

"Ca-ta-pha god always!" he exclaimed, half sobbing.

"And Kotikokura, his high priest. But where are the people who worship us?"

Kotikokura began to weep. His tears fell, darkening the sand.

"Be brave, my friend! This is the history of all things. They blossom for a while, then wither, and other things usurp their place."

He continued to weep.

"I have more reason to weep than you. For was I not a god feared and worshiped? Was I not he who made the universe? Did not people tremble at my name?"

"Ca-ta-pha god always."

"Only in your memory and in the dim subconsciousness of my people."

Kotikokura waved his fist.

"It was not their fault, I am certain. The eloquence of the sword and the whip persuaded them. What are gods, after all, Kotiko-kura? Frail blossoms upon the Tree of Life, they succeed one an-other always. The Tree remains."

He wept on.

"Kotikokura, you will soon turn the desert into a garden by your tears."

He endeavored to grin but could not.

Two natives, dressed as priests and blacker than their garments, carrying a tall wooden cross, were followed by men and women singing and beating tom-toms.

"Hearken, Kotikokura! The song is the self-same song they intoned for me. The words are altered. The melody has remained intact. We are not dead! Our souls live in the new body!"

Kotikokura was about to jump off the camel. His hands twitched.

"No, no, my friend! You must learn to lose gallantly and accept the inevitable. This is the meaning of intelligence and the secret of happiness."

The procession disappeared in the woods. We approached a tree.

"Wait a minute, Kotikokura. There is something carved upon this tree."

I read: "No matter, Cartaphilus! Other gods have died before you. Other queens have been dethroned. Other high priests have been defrocked. Farewell. Salome."

"She always precedes us, Kotikokura, and always knows our paths and our emotions. I am afraid of her."

Kotikokura pouted.

"But the fear of her, Kotikokura, is more exquisite than all other love, all other joy."

Kotikokura descended from the camel and carved upon a tree next to one on which Salome had carved her message:

"Wicked people—die—god Ca-ta-pha lives—lightning—broil you —devour you—cursed—high priest—Kotikokura."

"Let us rest, Kotikokura, before we turn back for we have nothing more to do here. Give me my pipe and some opium, not tobacco."

In the fumes that rose and curled gracefully, I saw—who was it —Willie or Salome? My eyes closed slowly. The smoke, white and dazzling like a lake beneath the rising sun, descended upon me.— "Salome, Salome!" Her lips pressed into my lips—her body mingled with mine.

I woke with a start.

"Ca-ta-pha! Ca-ta-pha!"

"What is the trouble, Kotikokura?"

"Look, look!"

The church was in flames. The cross upon it blackened and fell. Bells rang, tom-toms beat, people screamed.

"You set fire to the church, Kotikokura, did you not?"

He shook his head.

"Who then?"

"Ca-ta-pha—god—lightning."

"It is a lie, Kotikokura. You set fire to it. You smell of smoke."

"Ca-ta-pha god always."

"We have no time to discuss this matter, however. Let us flee."

We mounted the animals and galloped away.

The flames rose high and in the dawn appeared, like a setting sun overtaken suddenly by day.

Kotikokura took his flute and began to play.

"Nero!" I exclaimed.

LXXIV

THE BROKEN VESSEL—EUROPE IS SICK—THE NEW PROPHET

WE continued our journey, sadly, silently. Now and then, Kotiko-kura grumbled menaces and anathemas, waving his fists.

The camel-drivers whom we had left some miles away from our destination, to await our possible arrival within three days, were jubilant at our unexpected return. They kissed our hands, patted our animals, and blessed Allah and Mohammed, his true Prophet.

A snake showed his head out of the sand and vanished again.

"Look, Kotikokura! Do you remember?"

He knit his brows.

"Was it not the snake that perpetuated our friendship? Had he not bitten me, you would not have partaken of my blood. By this time, you would be less tangible than the sand our camels tread upon, leaving their zigzag imprints. As for me, I should have missed the most faithful of all companions."

He pulled my hand to his lips and kissed it.

"There is neither absolute evil nor absolute good, Kotikokura. Venom may become divine ichor, and nectar cut the entrails like the sharpest of vinegars."

He nodded.

"Let us make the snake the coat of arms of the noble and ancient house of Kotikokura."

He rubbed his hands.

"Kotikokura, once Christianity was a vase too strong for any hammer. That the vase was not beautifully fashioned or acceptable to logic, is another matter. At least, it stood erect and motionless in a world of storms and hurricanes. But the vessel has been shattered to bits. Whatever essence it contained has been spilled and mingled with the mud. Each country, city, and petty community has placed upon its altar a fragment, shapeless, meaningless, and worships it, calling it the full vessel, the only true one. Whoever speaks of another fragment or recalls the full vesel, risks excommunication and the rack."

Kotikokura nodded.

"It is more difficult to travel through Europe than to pirouette among eggs. We must be extremely wary, Kotikokura. We must imitate with utmost precision, every word and every gesture. Christianity has become more intricate than the Chinese language, and a sound placed slightly higher or lower on the Chromatic scale is an unpardonable blasphemy."

Kotikokura nodded sadly.

"Jesus, my ancient countryman, is it not distressing to be god? Jesus, if I do not believe in you, at least I do not mock you as your believers mock you. If I do not worship you, I do not blaspheme you as your followers blaspheme you. You should not be the god of these barbarians, who love the sword more than they love you. You should have remained among your own or, better still, gone among the gentle Chinese or Hindus. They would not have mutilated your words.

"The Lamb has strayed among the wolves who worship him, but they worship him in their own fashion!"

Kotikokura listened, his eyes darting to and fro.

We traveled slowly and cautiously, adopting the dress, the religion, the customs of the various countries. We shouted hurrah with the people on the public square upon the passing of soldiers or royalties. We crossed ourselves properly in the churches and upon general religious festivities. Our names and our appearances changed with the changing countries. We were clean-shaven. We wore pointed beards, full beards, mustachios.

"Each nation is clamoring for justice, Kotikokura. Do you know what it means by justice? It means a sharper sword. It means the ability to crush its neighbors. Each one prays to the Lamb. Do you know what the prayer is? 'Make us more ferocious than tigers; more powerful than lions! Let our teeth be sharper than the teeth of all others, that we may tear our enemies to bits! Grant us victory, O Lord! We shall bring as sacrifice to Your Holy Name, O Perfect Lamb, the bleeding flesh of the vanquished!'"

Kotikokura nodded.

"Do not imagine, however, Kotikokura, that Europe will die because of its iniquities. Only in legends, such as the Bible, iniquity kills. In reality, only a grain of justice, of love, of intelligence, of freedom is required for existence, and that grain always exists by force of circumstances and despite religions or the volition of man. Europe will not die, for that would imply a logic which life does not possess."

Kotikokura nodded.

"But if it will not die, it is nevertheless covered with ugly ulcers like a leper and the stench is unbearable,—particularly here in Germany. This poor country, once the seat of strength and robustness, has become the pleasure-ground of wild beasts and birds of prey. Let us not linger too long."

Kotikokura nodded sadly.

"They say that there is still one country in Europe which has retained civilization and freedom."

He looked at me inquiringly.

"Holland. I overheard, while you were engaged in fondling a kitten, two students who believed themselves safe since they spoke in Latin in an inn frequented by coachmen and soldiers, that in the capital of that country, there lives a man whose work in philosophy is beautiful and illuminating. They say he is a Jew, a polisher of lenses, who has refused to become a professor at the University or accept money from the prince. On the crest of a hill of dung, now and then a rose blossoms. Such is the strange way of life. The glory of a civilization is but the achievement of a few rare souls. The rest is manure.

"Let us seek out this new prophet."

LXXV

I DISCUSS GOD WITH SPINOZA—NEW VISION—APOL-
LONIUS WALKS WITH US—I MAKE MY PEACE WITH
JESUS

HOLLAND seemed, in truth, a more comfortable place than the rest
of Europe. The inhabitants had recently proved their personal
prowess and the advantage of their geographical situation to an
astounded world. If it was not characteristic of their stolid nature
to show much enthusiasm and exuberance, one breathed, at any
rate, an air of confidence and quiet happiness. The small houses,
white wood or brick, were spotless in their cleanliness. The men
sat upon the thresholds, raised sufficiently to allow a comfortable
posture and smoked enormous pipes in silence. The women spun at
the open windows. In the distance, at every angle of the compass,
the mills turned ceaselessly, glittering in the sun like dull mirrors.

People of a dozen religions lived if not lovingly together,—something which could hardly be expected—at least without murdering
one another.

Nevertheless, being a foreigner and therefore naturally suspected
—for man has this in common with the dog that strangeness in-
timidates and enrages him—I preferred not to ask freely for the
whereabouts of a philosopher once excommunicated by his own
people and generally considered, if not an atheist, at least a vague
and indifferent believer.

From an old bookseller, I discovered that Benedictus Spinoza,
finding Amsterdam unsuitable to his health, had for some time now
been living at The Hague, if indeed he was still living.

"We must not linger too long, Kotikokura. Our sage seems to
be of a very delicate constitution. It would be a pity to reach him
after his departure from this troubled, superstition-devoured earth."

At The Hague, a lens polisher informed me that the renegade
lived on the outskirts of the city, taking greater care of his lungs
than of his lenses.

An old woman, clean as if she too had been whitewashed and scrubbed like the houses, scrutinized me for a long minute.

"The master is in his room," she said, pointing to the attic. "He has been writing for the last two days steadily. He should not do it. He is not feeling very well."

"It is true, then," I said, "that his lungs are not strong."

She sighed. "It is, sir. And it is a pity. He is the best man in the world, whatever the others may say. He has lived with us for two years and never have I heard an unkindly word. And as for religion, whenever I beg him to come along to church, he accompanies us. He does not blaspheme or mock. It is not true, sir. He— —"

The stairs creaked.

"He is coming down, sir."

Spinoza appeared,—a middle-aged man, his face drawn, his eyes large and brilliant as if they had just looked at a newly-discovered star.

"Master," the old woman said quietly, "are you feeling well?"

He smiled, coughed drily, and answered, "I am feeling well. . . Thank you, little mother."

"You are working too hard. It is not right," she admonished. "Young people never understand that—"

He placed his hand, long and thin and nearly transparent, upon her shoulder. "Am I young?"

"Of course. But here I am chattering while this gentleman is waiting to see you, master."

She walked out of the room. Spinoza gave me his hand.

"Master, I come from the end of the earth to see you."

He smiled. His finely shaped lips curled a little. His eyes closed half-way. "I do not deserve this honor, sir, I am certain."

"To see a man free from the superstitions that ravage the world is worth a trip from the moon."

Spinoza played with one of the long black curls that fell over his cheek. "Experience has taught me that all the usual surroundings of social life are vain and futile, seeing that none of the objects of my fears contained in themselves anything either good or bad, except in so far as the mind is affected by them." He coughed. "But forgive me. I have just quoted a passage from my work. It may be totally irrelevant."

"On the contrary, master. It is quite relevant and like a precious jewel, has many facets."

"I wonder, my friend," he said gently, "if you would care to walk with me along the shore? I love the sea. We come from the sea and shall eventually return to the sea. She is the Mother."

We walked silently, leaving imprints upon the sand which the low tide endeavored, but in vain, to reach and fill. Spinoza stopped from time to time to breathe deeply or cough, bending upon his cane. His face was smooth and the two red spots upon his cheeks, the symbol of the fire that consumed his lungs, gave him a youthful appearance. His broad forehead, however, cut by three profound wrinkles, running almost parallel, refuted his youth and if judged by itself gave the impression of great age. His nose, long and sensitive, was Greek rather than Jewish, and his smooth chin, in contrast with the rest of the face, showed that determination essential to one who would remain unperturbed amid the malignity of the people about him.

"Master, have you read of Apollonius?"

"Only here and there. He was one of the few who understood God."

"God?" I asked, a little ironically. "I thought there were gods but no God."

He looked at me sadly and nodded. "The many gods do not refute God, my friend."

"I am older than I seem, master," I said, "and I have traveled the world over but I have never discovered God."

"It is not necessary to live very long nor is it essential to travel the world over to discover God. God is everywhere and eternal. Neither time nor space bind Him and the foolishness of the people does not destroy Him. The world is one, and all things in it are parts of one self-evident, self-producing order, one nature which is the Substance, which is God. In it are we all; it makes us what we are; it does what its own nature determines; it explains itself and all of us. It is uncreated, supreme, omnipresent, unchangeable, the law of laws, the nature of natures."

He coughed.

'Apollonius,' I whispered.

"The Substance is eternal bearing no relation to time. No temporal view of time can exhaust its nature. All things, even those that happened a million years ago are eternally present. There is no before and no after."

"Is God, an inanimate force or a living intelligence, master?"

He stopped, planted his cane in front of him, and answered:

"God must have infinite ways of expressing Himself,—each perfect, self-determined. We know but two—body and mind, equally real, equally true,—constituting as far as we can judge, the whole Substance. From the faintest line to our own bodies, every visible or tangible thing is an expression of the extended or corporeal aspect of God. In the same manner, our minds are but the extended or mental aspect of God. Mind—body—two parallel lines and both the expression of divinity. God is therefore both the animate and inanimate, the living and the dead,—everything that is or ever was or ever can be."

He straightened up and looked into the distance as if all space had been eliminated and infinitely stretched out before his enraptured gaze.

I could make no remark, ask no questions. His words thrilled me as if the sea in front of us had suddenly changed into a majestic orchestral composition; as if the sky had burst into a luminous white light.

'Apollonius,' I thought, 'Apollonius come to life again. There is no past and no future.'

"Jesus," he said softly, "claimed to be the Son of God, and so He was, and so was Mohammed and Moses, and so is everyone, every man, every creature, however humble, however powerful, each partaking of the divinity to the extent of his ability and nature. God is everywhere, always. We are not only His sons, we are He. Our finiteness is lost within His infinity, even as the thin stream that trickles down a mountain into a rivulet which flows into the large river, which in turn mingles and becomes the salty depths of this sea."

We resumed our walk. For a long time, neither of us spoke. Apollonius, his long beard shivering in the breeze, accompanied us, and enveloped us with his white silken robe. 'Whenever you desire me intensely, I shall be with you.' He was with me. Life was eternal. There was no death. Jesus, too, was not far off, walking over the waters, perhaps, as his disciples claimed. He had returned but not to destroy me. He was the Son of God, even as all men, even as the birds that flew above our heads.

Spinoza coughed and closed his eyes.

"Master, were it not wiser to return home? The air is very strong here."

He looked at me and smiled, placing his hand upon my shoulder. "We must die sooner or later. The fool alone fears that which is inevitable. The wise man looks upon death as a soft cool bed wherein he may rest after the fever of the day."

"Is it not a pity that man's life must be so short that he hardly has time to learn how to walk unscathed among the thorns that surround him?"

"Life—death—are synonymous and interchangeable terms. The sun which is setting now in front of us and will soon disappear— does it die because it is no longer visible?"

"Is it possible, master, for a man to live for centuries?"

"Why not? He would partake of the body of God in a greater measure than the rest of humanity."

"Would you consider endless life a blessing or a curse?"

"I would consider it useless, but not a curse. God inflicts no penalties. The true mind knows nothing of the bondage of time, thinks of no before and no after, has no future, dreads nothing, laments nothing; but enjoys its own endlessness, its own complete- ness, has all things in all things."

"Then, Master, the Wandering Jew may not be a myth."

"The Wandering Jew is truth whether considered as a living entity or a personification of his race. He is the symbol of restless- ness and search. Some day, he will find what he seeks, and will no longer wander."

"What does he seek?"

"God. Everyone, everything seeks God as every drop of rain seeks and, ultimately finds, the sea."

I pressed his hand. "It is true!"

"The wise man, my friend loves God with a fragment of that very love wherewith God loves Himself and his meditation is not of death but of life, of the Eternal Life whereof he is a part and has ever been and ever will be a part. He is bound as a nut in a shell, but he is the monarch of infinite space. The nightmare of his phantom life has ceased to trouble him."

The air became chilly. Spinoza wrapped himself tightly in his black cotton robe.

We turned our steps homeward. He quoted parts of his Ethics and explained them by mathematical formulæ. Never since Ali Hasan did mathematics contain so much beauty and wisdom. I did not dare interrupt the flow of his words lest the cup slip from the hand and the precious draft spill upon the sand.

We reached his door. He looked at me for a long time.

"If the way to God seems exceedingly hard, it can nevertheless be reached. All things excellent are as difficult as they are rare."

"Master," I said, almost in a whisper, "you are weary today. May I come in a day or two again and listen to your words once more?"

He sighed. "Yes, certainly."

He pressed my hand and entered the house.

I did not wish to be importunate, and let a few days pass before I visited Spinoza again.

"Come, Kotikokura, this time you will accompany me. You, too, must hear the master's words, limpid as the waters that tumble from a mountain."

He combed his hair and arranged his cloak.

"True, in his presence, we must be annointed and beautiful. He holds communion with God. We are his priests."

We walked slowly, rhythmically. The sun had passed the meridian and like a vase over-brimming, bent a little, to pour his libation upon the earth, the cupped hands of the universe.

A calm and delicious joy possessed me.

"Kotikokura, we no longer wander strangers in an inimical country. We are the children of God—God Himself."

"Ca-ta-pha god."

"Yes, he is god. Kotikokura god also. The sun is god. This butterfly that perches upon the window sill, mistaking it for a meadow, is god. The air we breathe, the water we drink—everything! Life is a perpetual eucharist! Ah, Kotikokura, the curtain of night has been lifted, and the truth is beautiful."

Kotikokura's eyes closed half-way, voluptuously.

"I sought logic but found instead irrationality. I sought beauty but found ugliness. I sought life and discovered death. The master, in his few years of existence, without hurry, without despair, sought what every man should seek—God—and found Him infinitely more beautiful than any priest or saint had ever imagined Him. People speak glibly of God's omniscience and omnipotence, but think of Him as dying upon the cross, as shouting through bushes, as riding upon a camel, as howling across the thunder. Spinoza, out of his own magnificent brain, discovered the true nature of God—timeless, spaceless, all-inclusive. No one is a stranger, no one is homeless. The gates have been thrown wide open, all are welcome, all are within the limitless castle. No Heaven, Hell, Purgatory, no angry judge, no sycophantic angels, no merciless devils. We are all one. An infinite circle embraces us like the white perfumed arms of a new love."

Kotikokura raised his arms ecstatically to the sun.

"This God requires neither prayer nor bribing. No hosannahs must be sung to His Holy Name. The knees need not bend before Him, or His mercy be invoked. He is not merely a human king a thousandfold enlarged. He is that which is. He is ourselves. He is Ca-ta-pha. He is Kotikokura."

Kotikokura grasped my arm. We quickened our pace. Our hearts beat like triumphant drums.

On the threshold of Spinoza's home, the old woman sat, knitting slowly. She was not aware of our arrival. Kotikokura scraped his foot. She looked up. I greeted her. She answered vaguely.

"The Master," I said, almost in a whisper, "is he in his room? May I see him?"

"The Master," she answered, "is dead."

The universe, so beautiful, so vast, so perfect a few minutes previously, shrank to the size of a coffin and God assumed the shape of a worm.

"He was buried yesterday," and lowering her head, she proceeded to knit, tears trickling upon her hands.

I remained standing, silent for a long while. Then I seated myself next to her.

"The Master called you Little Mother. He loved you."

She looked at me, her face wrinkled as if a nervous hand had crumpled it.

"I loved him too. He was the gentlest man that ever lived. He did not know the meaning of hate. Even the spiders in his room he would not kill." She wiped her heavily-rimmed spectacles, wet from tears. "He made these, the Master, and I can see through them as if I still had the eyes of my youth."

"What has become of the Master's papers?"

"They are locked in the drawer of his table. His printer will take care of them. So the Master ordered."

"Did he suffer much before he died?"

"It was during the night that he began to feel ill. I went up. He smiled and motioned me to approach. 'Master, shall I bring the priest?' 'No,' he said, 'it is not necessary. God knows every-thing.' I began to weep. 'Foolish Little Mother,' he said. 'Why do you weep? Must not everyone die?' 'You are too young, Master.' 'There is no time, no past, no future. There is neither death nor life.' I did not understand him. I am not learned. I am an ignorant woman. I see life and I see death, but I felt what he meant. It was his great goodness that made him say what he said. 'Sit here near me,' he said, 'and knit, Little Mother.' The whole night I sat up. Towards morning, I fell asleep. When I awoke, he was dead. The doctor came but it was too late."

"For the Master's sake, I wish you would do me a favor, Little Mother."

"What favor can a poor old woman like me do?"

"I want you to take this purse that your last days may not weigh too heavily upon you."

I placed the purse in her lap.

"No, no, sir. I cannot accept it."

"For his sake, Little Mother."

"But I have done nothing to deserve this money."

"You have indeed. You have been good to the wisest and best of men while others misunderstood and maligned him."

"No, sir. I cannot— —"

"Had he had money, would he not have given it to you?"

"Yes, he would, I am sure."

"This is his money. You must take it."

I rose. She was about to rise also. I pressed her down gently.

"I beg of you, Little Mother."

She looked at me for a long minute, kissed my hand, and made the sign of the cross.

"May Jesus repay you for this, sir."

"Jesus has paid me in advance. It is because of him that I had the good fortune of meeting the Master."

I took Kotikokura's arm and we walked slowly homeward. "Jesus, Spinoza, Ca-ta-pha,—all Jews and all denied by their people! Strange race giving birth to gods whom they do not recognize, whom they crucify, stone and stab. Stranger still that Spinoza whom I only saw once should have made me realize that I no longer hate Jesus, that he is of my blood, that he is my friend! Who, indeed, should know him and love him if not Ca-ta-pha?"

A dove, white as a handful of snow, descended from one of the houses and settled at our feet.

"Kotikokura!" I exclaimed, "Jesus lives."

"He lives and Spinoza lives and Apollonius and all those who thought beautiful thoughts, whose hearts beat in harmony with the universe, with God."

Kotikokura raised his arms toward the sun and uttered the prayer of his tribe.

"The sun is the Father, the Earth his beloved Daughter, conceived immaculate, by His eternal wisdom. Hail Sun, Father of us all!" I exclaimed.

"Ca-ta-pha . . . Ca-ta-pha . . . Ca-ta-pha." Kotikokura uttered, facing the sun.

I communed in silence with the World Spirit. My soul was one with the universe.

LXXVI

AT THE DOCK OF SAARDAM—THE HUMOR OF THE TSAR —KOTIKOKURA FORGETS—I BUILD A CITY—THE EMPIRE OF GOLD

WE were standing at the dock of Saardam, watching the work of the shipbuilders.

Suddenly, one of them, a man of gigantic proportions, waved his arm and spoke to the rest in a strange jargon, a mixture of German, Dutch and Russian, but quite comprehensible nevertheless.

"Who of you wants to go to Russia? The Tsar will pay you ten times your wages here. He will give you full protection, will let you keep your religion, and your customs."

The rest looked up, some smiling, a few waving their fingers about their temples to indicate that he was raving.

"He has been saying this since he came to work a week ago," said one.

"Yes, every day he says the same thing."

"Is he crazy, do you think?"

"Maybe he is a spy."

"But if a spy, the government would have been after him."

"Yes, that's true. He is just a little off."

"Those of you who are unmarried will find beautiful and strong women there. Those of you who have wives and children will get extra wages. Who wants to go to Russia?"

Several laughed.

One shouted, "You better go on with your work or I'll tell the boss."

"Who dares to speak to me in that manner?" He raised an enormous log and was about to strike. The people retreated. He dropped the log which rebounded several times.

"In Russia, your head would have rolled at my feet."

"And he wants us to go to Russia," one laughed.

The others joined him.

"Slave on here! You would have become rich in Russia. Fools!"

He turned his back upon them.

"Kotikokura, who is this man? Look! We knew him. We saw him."

Kotikokura nodded and knit his brow.

The man walked toward us.

"Who, Kotikokura?"

Kotikokura rubbed his chin.

"Those eyes—that chin—his stature—his strength—who?" Just as he was about to turn the corner, I called out: "Attila! Attila!"

Kotikokura nodded vehemently. The man heard me, stopped in front of us, scrutinized me, and smiled broadly.

"I am a descendant of Attila. Wherever I pass, I conquer."

"You are not a descendant merely, Sire, but Attila himself," I said, bowing low.

His eyes, sharp as the points of knives, tried to pierce through me.

"Is it so difficult to recognize a king, Sire?"

"Who are you?" he thundered.

"I am Your Majesty's servant," I answered.

He threw his arms about me and kissed me on both cheeks noisily like the clapping of hands.

"Peter Romanoff is your friend. Will you come with me to Russia?"

"Wherever Your Majesty commands?"

"Who is that man?" He pointed to Kotikokura.

"My companion, Sire."

Kotikokura made a profound obeisance.

"I like his face. He looks like one of my people."

Kotikokura kissed his hands.

Peter walked between us, holding our arms.

"Can you imagine, the fools not willing to go where fortune awaits them? Could they not recognize me? Do I look like a common laborer?"

"Your Majesty, the sun shines in vain for the blind."

"Splendid! You will teach my ministers the art of courtesy. I want to turn my court into a more magnificent palace than that of Versailles. Louis the Fourteenth is splendid. He has taste and manners. He treated me discourteously but—" he raised his arm and waved his fist,—"I shall be the emperor of the world!"

"Attila!" I exclaimed.

"I need men. I need a navy. These fools will not come."

"They will come, Sire. I shall persuade them."

"How can you persuade them when I found it impossible?" he scowled.

"Your Majesty, the people are accustomed to respect the uniform. I shall talk to them dressed as a high officer of your army. They will come."

"You are my friend, my joy, my hope!" he exclaimed, and kissed my cheek.

He looked at his boots and laughed heartily. "I do not blame the poor devils. Does a great emperor wear muddy boots and a torn coat? Promise them everything, my friend. We need boats and sailors and shipbuilders. Russia shall become the mightiest of nations! She shall conquer the world!"

The tip of his boot struck a horseshoe. He picked it up.

"What other monarch can bend this iron?"

He grasped the shoe with his enormous hands, closed his eyes, and pressed until the points met.

He threw the shoe away. Kotikokura picked it up and with one movement, unbent the iron until it became a straight line.

Peter glared at him. "You are a strong man———"

Kotikokura grinned.

"But a poor courtier. Don't you know that it is dangerous to excel the Tsar?"

Kotikokura's chin dropped.

Peter flung his arms about him and kissed him. "Do not fear. You shall be the commander-in-chief of my bodyguard."

Kotikokura bowed to the ground.

We entered a wine-shop.

"Wine!" Peter ordered.

We seated ourselves at a table. Kotikokura filled very tall cups. Peter raised his cup. "To Russia!"

We drank the contents at one gulp. Kotikokura refilled the cups.

"To Peter, Tsar of Russia!" I toasted.

Kotikokura raised his cup. "To Ca-ta-pha, god!"

Peter drank but looked at me for an explanation.

"My friend invokes God to bless the Tsar and his country."

Peter crossed himself and drank another cup. His face flushed, twitched, as if a fly were pestering it.

"What is your name, my friend, and what is your nationality?"

"Once my name was of great consequence and people trembled

at it. Now I have none. I await Your Majesty's baptismal. And my nationality? I am a Russian!"

He looked at me, his fine lips pouting, his small mustache shivering.

"You are of royal blood."

He rose, poured some wine over my head. "In the name of Jesus Christ, Our Saviour, and His servant, Peter Romanoff, Tsar of Russia, I baptize you Prince Daniel Petrovich,—for you are as wise as the prophet Daniel and I make you my son. You shall be my chief minister."

I kissed his hand over which a few drops of the wine trickled. "Permit me, Sire, to be your shadow, rather than your minister."

"So be it."

His Majesty poured some wine over Kotikokura's head.

"In the name of Jesus Christ, our Saviour, and His servant, Peter Romanoff, Tsar of Russia, I baptize you Duke Samson Romanovich,—for you are as strong as Samson and the adopted son of the House of Romanoff. You are the commander-in-chief of the Tsar's bodyguard."

Kotikokura kissed his hand.

The Inn keeper laughed, considering it all the farce of drunken men.

"Chop his head off, Duke!" the Tsar commanded.

Kotikokura rose, drew his knife, and was about to jump at the man's throat.

"Stop!" I shouted, and turning to the Tsar, I continued, "Sire, we are on foreign soil."

Peter kissed us both.

"I merely wished to test your fidelity. Samson, you acted as you should. It is not for you to question my orders. You are my strength. And you, Daniel, have done your duty well. You are my wisdom. You must not allow anger to overcome your master. I am proud of both of you. The Lord Jesus has sent me the two men needed for my country."

We all crossed ourselves and proceeded with our drinks.

Peter's eyes closed and he began to snore.

"Is there a bed here?" I asked the Inn keeper.

"Yes, upstairs."

"Samson, let us take His Majesty to bed. It is not well for an emperor to expose himself to the ridicule of the rabble."

Kotikokura lifted the colossal body of the emperor and carried

him up the stairs, placing him gently on the bed. He removed his
boots and smoothed his pillow. Peter opened his eyes and stood
up.

"Once more have I tested you, my dear friends. I only pretended
to sleep. Your wisdom, Daniel, is incomparable, and so are your
strength and faithfulness, Samson. Approach, that I may kiss you
both."

He kissed us.

"Bring me a woman, Samson. It is not well for a monarch to
sleep alone."

Kotikokura made a movement to go.

"Where are you going, Samson?" I asked. "Do you forget the
fate of monarchs in the hands of strange women?"

"Splendid, Daniel! Splendid, Samson!"

Peter rose, stretched, and yawned.

"I no longer doubt you. I needed three signs of your wisdom and
fidelity and I obtained them. We cannot remain here overnight. My
royal guard is in revolt at Moscow. They have allied themselves
with the nobles and churchmen who are horrified at my new ideas.
They call them German ideas."

"They are your ideas, Sire. Ideas have no validity unless they
take root in a strong man's soul."

"Splendid, Daniel! Those traitors hate me because I wished to
civilize them; they hate me because I ordered their beards shaved,—
their beards full of lice and vermin. They hate me because I introduced tobacco, good manners, and sensible clothing. They call me
Anti-Christ!"

"Anti-Christ!" I laughed.

"We go back at once! And oh, the revenge!" He stretched himself. "The sweet revenge! Samson, you will be busy."

Kotikokura grinned and danced.

"But you must not let me forget myself entirely, Daniel, even if
I get so exasperated at your words of prudence that I order Samson
to chop your head off."

The arrival of Peter at Moscow occasioned a universal panic.
The conspirators so vociferous, so arrogant, during his absence,
scurried off like frightened mice. This dismay was largely due to a
rumor that I had caused to be spread from town to town as we
were reaching the Capital, that the Emperor was returning with
a vast army of German, Dutch, and English mercenaries whose new

guns and cannons were capable of bombarding places from a distance of many miles.

The Kremlin was empty, save for some old serfs who, uncertain of what was transpiring, and unconcerned, continued to tend the gardens and to scrape slowly, drearily, the mud which the boots of the noblemen had left behind.

The Emperor seated himself upon the throne, Kotikokura in the garb of a general, heavily medaled on his left, and myself at his right. At the various entrances, officers stood at attention, their swords drawn.

"There must be no mercy, Prince," Peter thundered. "We are in Russia now. My people understand only the knout and the sword."

"We shall respect the customs of the land."

"Samson, I have given you your medals in advance of your deeds. See that I am not compelled to tear them off your chest, skin and all."

Kotikokura stiffened up and stamped his enormous sword.

I almost regretted having accompanied this strange and terrible Monarch. The affair, however, promised to be a huge comedy, and I could not refrain from taking a part in it. Kotikokura was superb in his new attire. Did he take his new position seriously? Would he deny Ca-ta-pha, preferring the mastership of a mortal monarch? Could he serve two masters? Sooner or later, there would be a crisis, I was certain. Despots weary of their favorites. I must warn Kotikokura. He was but a child.

The Patriarch, the chief of the Strelitzes and several Boyars, appeared. They formed a semicircle about the throne.

Peter glared at them in silence for a long while, then stood up and pointing his forefinger at them, exclaimed, "Traitors to your God, your Emperor, and your Country!"

They fell upon their faces, grumbling words of mercy.

"Grunting hogs, bearded and dirty! You thought you could outwit and outpower Peter Romanoff. In his absence, you turned his palace and his country into puddles of mud in which you wallowed, planning the while to rid yourself of your lawful master, divinely appointed!"

"Mercy, Little Father," several grumbled.

"How dare you ask for mercy?"

The Patriarch raised his head. "Be unto us like Jesus, Master of all of us, Little Father!"

"Judas!" the Emperor shouted, and unsheathing his sword,

severed the priest's head with one blow. The blood jutted out of his neck like some fantastic fountain.

"Duke!" he commanded Kotikokura, "let this scoundrel's head be placed upon a spike over the roof of the palace as a warning to others whose hearts may harbor treachery. Do the same to the rest of these wretches! Throw their carcasses to my dogs!"

"Little Father! Mercy! Mercy! We are not guilty! We were misled! Little Father!"

"Take them out! They stink like a litter of hogs."

Kotikokura waved his sword. A bugle sounded. A company of soldiers appeared. They dragged the corpse and the bodies of the rest who were too limp to move.

Kotikokura followed gravely, his sword and medals dazzling in the sun, which shone calmly through the stained glass.

I summoned an officer.

"Perfume!" I commanded.

He brought a large bottle of perfume.

"Your Majesty," I said, "Pilate who could not endure the smell of the rabble, washed his hands with perfume at the trial of Jesus; and Nero—the lover of the beautiful—maligned and misunderstood by vulgar historians, found the essence of flowers invigorating and delightful."

Peter cupped his hands, which I filled to the brim. He washed his face, and breathed deeply through his mouth. "Daniel Petrovich! You will civilize us! Ah! Ah!"

He smelt the tips of his fingers for a long while.

"I am pleased to hear you say that Nero was not a monster, but a man who loved the beautiful. Great emperors are always misunderstood."

"The shriveled blade of grass complains against the splendor of the sun. The descendants of the men whom you have ordered beheaded, may proclaim their great Emperor a monster."

Peter smiled. "The descendants of these men will not gossip about me. They will not live long enough for that.

"My people do not respect me, Daniel Petrovich, if I do not chop their heads off."

Kotikokura entered, followed by two officers, immensely tall. They remained at attention.

"Duke, have you carried out my instructions?"

Kotikokura nodded.

"Are the heads of the scoundrels upon the roof of my palace?"

Kotikokura nodded.

"Let us go and see them, Prince."

Kotikokura and the officers preceded. His Majesty took my arm. The coagulated blood of the setting sun mingled with the slowly dripping blood of the severed heads which garlanded the roof of the Kremlin, like a grotesque and horrible wreath. There was something alive in the glaring eyes which had not yet closed and in the heavy beards, shivering like ferns gray, red, and black, in the breeze.

The Tsar slapped his thighs and laughed uproariously. "Look at the Patriarch, Daniel Petrovich! There he is in the center, his mouth is wide open as if he wanted to swallow a sheep. He was always greedy. Look at the chief Strelitz! Ha, ha, ha! His left eye seems to wink—the panderer! Look at that fellow,—who is he? Let me see —yes, he is Gabriel Gabrilovich, stupid and obstinate as a jackass. Doesn't he seem to bray! He-haw! He-haw! Ha, ha, ha! Look at the red-bearded fellow. He is positively laughing, Prince. Watch! Laugh on, you damned wretch,—and may the devils tickle your soles forever!"

The two officers laughed. Kotikokura grinned. I tried in vain to feel the horror of the situation. It seemed so theatrical and unreal.

"Are you amused, Daniel Petrovich?"

"A little."

"You are squeamish. The West has an effeminate sense of humor. We Russians can laugh at anything which is really funny. And aren't they funny? Ha, ha, ha, ha!"

I smiled drearily.

"Do you pity them, Daniel Petrovich?"

"It is ridiculous to pity the dead, Your Majesty."

"I pity the dead, Daniel Petrovich. They cannot eat, they cannot drink, they cannot laugh, they cannot kiss women."

"Life—death—there is no difference, Sire. All things are within the Great Substance, all things partake of it."

"I do not understand."

I was treading on dangerous ground.

"What I meant, Your Majesty, is that after all, you have not robbed them of so much. Tomorrow, in one year, or ten, they would have died without Your Majesty's gracious assistance. Decapitation may be a boon, a deed of mercy."

"How?"

"You have relieved them, perhaps, of some terrible malady—a canker, leprosy,—who knows what fate had in store for them?"

"That is right and you speak most wisely, Daniel Petrovich. From now on, decapitation shall be reserved for those whose crime is excusable. Real traitors shall suffer deaths infinitely more lingering. I do not wish to be charitable. I do not mean to relieve them from greater pain. Peter Romanoff is not a doctor or a saint. He is the Tsar of Russia!"

His voice was so imperious and so final in its intonation that I dared not object to his interpretation of my words. I bowed, my right hand upon my chest.

For three days and three nights Peter gave a feast in the Kremlin.

Even at the orgies of Nero, I had never seen such abandon— voluptuaries without refinement—mighty drinkers and eaters— Homeric heroes resurrected. The day was for food and wines, the night for endless and promiscuous embraces.

The grass and flower beds were crushed and destroyed as if Attila's horsemen had galloped by, and the feathers of torn pillows flew about like a heaven of deplumed angels.

Never since my Bath of Beauty and Salome's feast in Persia had I witnessed such unlimited sensuality. The men vied with one another in capacity, the women in endurance. Wagers in gold and slaves and mistresses were made for what seemed incredible prowess of mere human beings.

Kotikokura outdid three Russians in their feats of endurance. The women gazed at him with terrified desire. He was supremely happy.

"Kotikokura," I whispered, as he passed by. For the first time in centuries he did not hear.

Pathetically sober and disgruntled I watched the fretful pageant. Had Kotikokura transferred his affection to a new master? Was he unfaithful to Ca-ta-pha?

I drank much to forget this indignity, but the wine did not go to my head.

Two of Kotikokura's competitors died from heart failure. One was carried out on a stretcher. The festivities ended with the decapitation of ten of the guests. Five were quartered to boil in oil and six women immured in nunneries for having made in their drunkenness remarks disrespectful to the majesty of the Tsar.

Peter sedulously endeavored to paint upon Russia the coating of Western civilization.

Recognizing that clothes and manners determined the mental attitude, Peter was merciless to those who refused to dress in the "German fashion," clip their beards, refrain from expectorating in the presence of women, or wipe their boots before entering places of worship or offices of the government.

Nevertheless, we progressed slowly.

"Your Majesty," I said one day, "however sedulously a man endeavors to repair a house that is fallen into ruins, he will find always walls crumbling, the ceiling leaking, the cellar infested with vermin and rats. It is wiser to build anew. . ."

Peter was in the habit of thinking quickly.

"Where shall I build my new house?"

"On the Baltic, sire."

He undid one of his medals, a cross studded with diamonds, which he wore upon his chest, and pinned it upon mine.

"Let us drink to St. Petersburg, the new capital of Holy Russia."

The insight I gained into world politics through the wars and the treaties of Peter made me realize that Europe would be ruled, in the future, neither by armies and navies nor, before very long, by monarchs, but by wealth. The bankers were becoming the potentates of the world. The Tsar, influenced by courtesans and monks, considered my idea visionary and derogatory to his divinely appointed authority.

I founded banks at my own risk. With the aid of a few men of affairs, chiefly Jews of Spanish and Portuguese descent, I established wide financial ramifications. The credit and the currency of the Emperor were weapons in my hands. Peter never dreamed that I, not he, was the real master of Russia!

Russia alone, however, was unsafe. I needed expansion,—a great net to capture all nations. If I controlled the world's money, I could never lose. No one could win without me. Life was a lottery in which I held all numbers!

Peter grown stout, gouty and tormented by pains in the groin, drowned his troubles in vast quantities of vodka. He proclaimed himself the Patriarch of the Holy Synod. The slightest deviation from his whims was not alone an insult to the crown, but to God the Father, the Son, and the Holy Ghost. About his neck he wore an immense black cross of wood. He counted rosaries until he fell asleep.

The symptoms indicated too clearly the end of his reign. His successors would not relish the favorite of a predecessor. The moment for my departure had come.

"Kotikokura," I said one day, "we have been estranged for too long a time. Your love for the Tsar has snapped the golden band that united us two. I never could imagine a blow powerful enough for that. I was mistaken!"

He shook his head.

"What! Did you only pretend a greater loyalty to the Emperor than to Ca-ta-pha?"

He nodded.

I looked into his eyes. "Kotikokura, are you still my ancient friend? Do medals and swords and position mean less to you than my love?"

He threw himself at my feet. I raised him and embraced him.

"Kotikokura!" I exclaimed, shaking his shoulders. "You have returned to your friend! Never was Ca-ta-pha happier!"

"Kotikokura—happy—" he grumbled, tears streaming down his cheeks. "Ca-ta-pha—god!"

"Well, we shall forget all about it. What are a few years in a life as long as ours? An hour of unpleasantness—that is all."

He nodded.

"Now, however, it is time for us to leave this half-barbarous nation to her fate. Our Tsar is no longer the charming man who won our hearts in Holland. Tomorrow, dressed as two ordinary noblemen, we leave for the West."

Our departure was hardly noticed. My shadowy position had become more shadowy for some time. Indeed, it was difficult to know who was in power and who merely wore the trappings of officers. My banks, however, were firmly established. They were owned by myself under many names,—a much safer way.

As we crossed the frontier into Sweden, I raised my arms and breathed deeply.

"Let us thank the Eternal God, the God of Spinoza, that we escaped whole from the jaws of the Bear. Few have accomplished that feat!"

Kotikokura doubled up and made the sign of my godhood.

LXXVII

THE THRONE OF THE GOLDEN CALF—I MAKE A DEAL WITH MAYER-ANSELM ROTHSCHILD

"Kotikokura, Ca-ta-pha shall rule man more truly than all the other gods for he shall be the master of his bread and of his roof. Ca-ta-pha shall be worshiped by every man, woman, and child. For as soon as he is able to articulate words and until he utters his last sound, man worships money. Ca-ta-pha shall be the god of money!"

"Ca-ta-pha god always."

"You were right, Kotikokura. You guessed the true nature of your master. What if his worshipers supplanted him by the cross? The whole world shall bend the knee and pray—oh, how fervently! They shall worship the Golden Calf, but the Golden Calf shall be my puppet. I am its master!

"Where are your medals, Kotikokura?"

Kotikokura lowered his head.

"I did not mean to reprimand you, my friend. I need your medals. They will serve as passports for us, and open many doors. For a long time to come, we shall be Russian noblemen. Russia is still a land of mystery and legend. Anything I may care to tell, will be believed—not because I am Ca-ta-pha, the oldest man in the world, he who has seen empires rise and fall and religions in their cradles and in their coffins—but because I am a Russian."

Kotikokura undid his belt which was closely lined with medals of all shapes.

"You were indeed the favorite of the Tsar, Samson Romanovich."

Kotikokura grinned.

"From now on, you will play a less gorgeous but very much safer part. It is better, I assure you, to stand firmly upon the ground than to balance yourself on the tip of the highest branch of a tall tree."

We laughed heartily and our laughter soldered together once more firmly the band that united us.

I was walking along the River Main in Frankfort, meditating on the words of Spinoza and the meaning of life when someone tapped me gently on the arm. I turned around. A little man with a sharp nose, sharp eyes, sharp pointed beard and a sharp protruding belly, bowed deeply.

"*Ich bitte um Verzeihung,*" he said in a sharp voice.

'Porcupine,' I thought. 'One must not touch this man.'

"By whom have I the honor of being addressed?" I asked.

"I am Mayer-Anselm Rothschild, the banker."

"I am Prince Daniel Petrovich."

"I know."

He reminded me of Abraham with whom I had done business in the matter of the jewels of Queen Isabella. But gone was the old humility. He was, unwittingly perhaps, the first of the new dynasty— the dynasty of money.

There was something so poignant, so dynamic in this little man, that I withdrew a little.

He smiled. "People are generally afraid of me. My friends call me the Living Sword. But Prince Daniel Petrovich certainly does not fear Mayer-Anselm Rothschild."

"On the contrary, sir, he is pleased to make your acquaintance." I gave him my hand which he kissed. His chapped lip, or his beard, pricked me like a needle.

"Prince, I have a proposition which may interest you."

"What is it?"

"We cannot speak freely here. Would His Highness care to take the trouble of visiting me at my office?"

I hesitated a moment.

"Really, Prince, it is worth while."

His voice had become soft and oily, as if he had withdrawn his needles.

"Very well. I shall come."

He rubbed his hands vigorously, standing on tiptoe. He hailed a carriage and we drove to a shop over which a red sign with the word banker swung lightly.

"I am not more than twenty-five, Prince, although I look much older," Rothschild said, as soon as we were seated at a table. "But this is because I have thought and worked so hard. I know you are not against youth. Indeed, I understand that most of the men you engage are young."

"It is true."

"The older generation does not understand the new world which is growing in front of their noses."

He lowered his voice. "You are not prejudiced against Jews. Many of your best men are Jews."

"I find the Jews cleverer, readier to accept new conditions, and contrary to current opinion, honest."

Rothschild nodded and sighed. "How we Jews have been maligned, Your Highness! There are, of course, dishonest men among us as there are among all nations, but is it conceivable that a people persecuted and hated as the Jews could have long continued to do business with the Gentiles, if they had not been at least as honest as the latter?"

"The Jew was not originally as clever as he is now, Rothschild. The persecution that you bemoan sharpened his wits."

"Perhaps. But it really is unbearable at times," he answered sadly.

"No matter. The Jew will conquer and dominate!" I exclaimed.

"Is that a jest, Prince?"

"It is the truth and a fine piece of irony besides. The Jew will control the money of the world. He who controls a man's money, controls his life. While the Jew will be persecuted and hounded, he will rule the destiny of mankind."

He remained silent, looking at me furtively. He was endeavoring to understand why I was interested in the Jews and whether I was sincere. Unable to reach a conclusion, he sighed.

"Do not fear, Rothschild. I conceal no trap."

"I do not fear, Your Highness. A Jew must have courage to live."

We spent several days discussing plans and measures for gigantic investments. This young man's mind was as sharp as his physique. I entrusted him with a large sum of money.

"Rothschild, I have confidence in you."

"Thank you, Your Highness."

"You will succeed. Your descendants, if they are as intelligent as you——"

"I am married to a woman of character and intelligence, Prince."

"Good! Your descendants will be wealthier than kings." He bowed.

"Rothschild, we may or may not meet again. You will feel my influence. I shall work in silence, invisible. Let it seem always that you are the sole master. Never let my name cross your lips."

"Never, Prince."

"Extend our business to the end of the earth, Rothschild. Consider the world an angry steed which we must ride. Underneath our yoke, he may foam and fret but will obey nevertheless."

Rothschild grinned, his teeth set.

"They say that King Frederick of Prussia is amenable to humor and wisdom."

"So they say."

"I must visit him then."

Rothschild sighed.

I smiled. "You cannot overcome your Jewish instinct. You would like to mingle with the great of the earth while your wife struts about, smothered in jewels."

Rothschild closed his eyes. "Prince, I cannot deceive you. It was this I sighed for."

"Well, my friend, it will happen—to you, or to your descendants. But whether this will help the Jews or not, I cannot tell."

"The Jew is bound to be misunderstood, Your Highness. If he is humble, he is kicked about. If he is vain, he is despised. If he is poor, he is beaten; if he is rich, he is menaced. It is better to be rich and vain. Menace and hate do not hurt as much as the tip of a boot and a whip."

LXXVIII

FREDERICK PLAYS CHESS—THE TABACKS COLLEGIUM —THE KING'S MONKEY—I QUARREL WITH VOLTAIRE—VOLTAIRE'S FAUX PAS

"KOTIKOKURA, this is Sans-Souci. Sans-Souci may be but a bit of irony for which His Majesty is famous. However, it is interesting that he refused to admit me on the strength of my Russian title, but invites me most cordially because I speak all the languages of Europe and because I studied philosophy at Oxford."

Kotikokura scratched his nose.

Frederick the Second was playing chess. He glanced out of the corner of his eye at me, nodded vaguely, and continued his game. Suddenly, he struck the table and shouted. "General, you have forgotten your rules of war. This move is inadmissible."

The general, an elderly man, bald to the neck but making up for his lack of hair by two long side beards which reached to his chest, replied in a bass voice, contrasting comically with the King's falsetto: "As Your Majesty commands."

"Not as I command, general, but as the ancient law of chess commands."

Turning to the others who were sitting around, smoking long porcelain pipes, the new vogue, or snuffing, Frederick continued: "Gentlemen, was not the general's move inadmissible?"

Several whispered, "Yes, certainly, Your Majesty."

The King frowned. "Prince," he said, addressing me, "do you play chess?"

"Yes, Your Majesty, and you were wrong."

Frederick stood up full length and stared at me.

"How do you know I was wrong, Prince, since you entered after the general had made his move? Besides, you are too far away from the table to see the board. . ."

"Your Majesty, had you been right, there would have been a

444

vociferous reply to that effect from all these gentlemen, not merely a hardly audible 'yes, certainly, Your Majesty.' "

Frederick laughed. "Prince, you have a sense of humor and an independence of mind which I try to foster in all my friends."

He stretched out his hand, large but too delicate for his frame. I kissed it.

"Prince Daniel Petrovich of Russia," he called out to the rest who rose and bowed.

One thin man of uncertain age, yellow and wrinkled, with eyes that darted long rays, sitting apart from the others, chuckled.

His Majesty glanced at him. "Monsieur de Voltaire wants to be noticed, gentlemen. Well, monsieur, why do you laugh?"

Monsieur de Voltaire tightened his thin lips until they vanished and gave him the appearance of an old toothless woman.

"Who can help noticing—the monkey, Your Majesty?" he asked.

The others laughed. His Majesty smiled ironically.

"Monsieur de Voltaire thinks himself very handsome. His good fortune with the ladies tends to strengthen his opinion."

Voltaire continued to grin.

"Why are you laughing?"

"His Majesty spoke of the independence of mind which he tries to foster in his friends, *n'est-ce-pas?*"

"Yes."

"Well, that is why I laughed, Sire."

"Gentlemen," Frederick addressed the rest, "are you not permitted independence of mind and speech in my company?"

The reply was a long acclamation.

"Voyez-vous, monsieur?"

"Non, Sire, j'entends."

His Majesty's nostrils shivered, his fists stiffened over his heavy cane.

"Prince, have you ever heard a citizen speak thus to a monarch?"

I smiled inconclusively.

"But do not forget, Prince, that the citizen is Monsieur de Voltaire whose pen is sharper than a monarch's sword," remarked the thin-lipped philosopher.

Several emotions crossed the face of the King.

"Shall we try it, monsieur?" Frederick made believe he was unsheathing his sword.

There was general laughter. His Majesty clapped his hands. An officer entered.

"Beer!" he commanded.

We seated ourselves around the enormous fireplace in which crackled and glowed a heavy log whose resin perfumed the place. Two great greyhounds curled themselves around the King's feet. From the painted bowls of the pipes resting comfortably upon the stomachs of the men, rose grayish smoke, curling into weird patterns.

We emptied many steins of beer and general gaiety prevailed. Monsieur de Voltaire who abstained from drinking, grinned at intervals.

"Gentlemen, Prince Petrovich can speak every language of Europe."

"And of Asia, Your Majesty," I added.

"What! Is that possible?"

"Yes, Your Majesty."

"Gentlemen," Fredericus Rex addressed the rest,—three officers, two scholars, one cleric, and several noblemen, "you are all learned and masters of many tongues. Can any of you compete with the Prince?"

Turning to me, he said, "Not as a test, Your Highness, but merely *de curiosité, vous comprenez.*"

"*Oui, Sire.*"

I was addressed in Greek, Latin, Hebrew, the Western European languages. One spoke to me in Sanskrit, another in Chinese, a third one in Japanese.

I understood that these men were assembled for the purpose of examining me. I answered each one, and every now and then, I turned to the Monarch and related in German or in French, curious customs prevailing in those countries.

Frederick applauded. "You are a marvel, Prince. I do not understand how so young a man could acquire so much knowledge. It is incredible. *Inouï, Monsieur de Voltaire, n'est-ce-pas?*"

Voltaire grumbled. "Mere memory, Your Majesty."

Frederick laughed. "Do not mind Monsieur de Voltaire, Prince. He scorns every art in which he is not proficient. He says 'mere king' with equal glibness."

Voltaire grinned.

"The great Rousseau he calls—"

"A jackass," Voltaire interposed.

"The incomparable Shakespeare—"

"A barbarian."

"The perfect Boileau—"

"A grocer."

"Virgil—"

"A burly peasant."

"Homer—"

"A blind nurse woman putting her grandchildren to sleep with childish and monotonous stories."

"Corneille—"

"A pompous ass dragging a hearse."

"Racine—"

"A nun."

"Bossuet—"

"An empty drum."

"Michael Angelo—"

"The wooden horse of Troy.—Your Majesty, has your monkey performed well today?"

There was much laughter and spilling of beer, the tall grenadiers never forgetting that this was *"das Tabaks-Collegium"* filled and refilled their pipes ceaselessly.

The conversation turned to religion. I described the ceremonies of the African tribe. My auditors laughed. Frederick chuckled, now and then stroking his graceful hounds or looking into their eyes as if to find there the affection and understanding that he did not find among men.

"The trinity of the Africans is more intelligible than that of the Christians," Voltaire said, his face screwed to the size of a fist. "No Christian has the remotest conception of God. A poor Jewish lens grinder, Baruch Spinoza, excommunicated by Jews and Gentiles alike, discovered Him by mathematics."

The cleric laughed.

"It is the truth!" Voltaire shouted, his voice cracking like a whip. "Spinoza whom people call an atheist was the only man who loved God,—Spinoza and Voltaire, also called an atheist by the ignorant, which means by all."

"Monsieur de Voltaire," the cleric admonished, "you are blaspheming the Lord. A newer Dante some day shall recount the tortures of one whose vain name upon Earth was François Marie Arouet de Voltaire."

"The Lord, Reverend Father, will pardon me."

"What makes you think that God will pardon you?"

"Because that is his business."

The churchman rose incensed, waving his cup. *"Monsieur, vous êtes impertinent!"*

"Monsieur," Voltaire answered calmly, *"votre nez est couvert de tabac. Mouchez-vous!"*

The ecclesiastic reseated himself, drew a red kerchief out of his pocket, and wiped his nose.

The King slapped his thighs, his lean frame shaking with laughter. There was a long silence. Suddenly, Frederick grasped his knee. "Ouch!"

Voltaire laughed. The others glared at him.

"Monsieur, is it proper to laugh at a Monarch's predicament?"

"I am laughing at rheumatism which does not seem to discriminate between a royal knee and an old washerwoman's, Your Majesty."

"Monsieur would spend his life in the Bastille rather than avoid a witticism."

"The King allows freedom of mind and speech, *n'est-ce-pas?"*

Voltaire rose and walked out, beating his leg with a short whip.

"If you are not careful, monsieur, the whip shall be in the hands of another, and the part struck shall be somewhat higher than your calf."

Voltaire remained at the door for a moment. "Your Majesty, here is the whip and here the part higher than my calf."

He turned his back to the King, bending forward.

"Cochon!" Frederick shouted, his voice a thin thread, *"Ne te montre plus ici!"*

Voltaire walked out.

Frederick reseated himself. No one dared to utter a sound or make a comment.

"Let us have another drink and forget that French buffoon. His work will not outlive him a day."

All agreed.

"It lives now only because monarchs are too kindly disposed."

Everybody chimed in. They had found him a monkey in truth. His philosophy was mere antics. His Majesty should command a good horsewhipping for the scoundrel.

"If I did it, all Europe would rise in arms against me. His influence is tremendous and his tongue stings like a lash. Besides, somehow I like him. I do not know what attracts me to him. And he likes me too. Tomorrow, I shall get a letter from him,—such a letter as no one but a witty Frenchman can write. He will tell me things that will split my sides with laughter. But this time, he must really go. He has been for nearly three years with me. Besides, that man has seduced half of the court women, including the servants and the coachmen's wives. *Cochon!* He faints every day, and every evening he is resurrected. He will live to be a hundred. He is the personification of France,—hog, nightingale, and peacock. There is no country like France, gentlemen. I would give half my wealth if we could produce a Voltaire."

An officer entered and informed His Majesty that it was time for the council, also incidentally, that Monsieur Voltaire had left.

"The fool!" His Majesty shouted.

My stay at the Court of Frederick the Great was of a short duration. I had no intention to amuse His Majesty by my ability to speak many languages, tell anecdotes, or cure his rheumatism. My experience with Charlemagne, was too painful to be forgotten.

Elections in Poland were more turbulent than ever. The nobles could not decide upon a ruler. Frederick wished to reduce the noise and the danger by cutting a slice of the Polish kingdom. He needed money. His experiments in alchemy had proved futile and costly. My banks, less gaudy, but more substantial, supplied his needs.

Thenceforth Europe was firmly in my grasp.

I was the secret monarch of the world.

"Kotikokura, we must leave Sans-Souci. Before long swords will rattle and cannons boom. Our ears are too sensitive for such noise."

Kotikokura grinned.

"There are still a few countries which I must capture. Then, I shall retire and watch the comedy. Do not imagine, however, that I mean to bring war and devastation upon the world. On the contrary. Ca-ta-pha is a gentle and peace-loving god. He will endeavor, whenever allowed by the cupidity and cruelty of man, to spread art and joy and wealth. It is probable, my friend, that his desire will be frustrated. It is also probable that people will blame him for their wars, and deny his peaceful pursuits. But that is unavoidable. Every crown is a crown of thorns. However, I shall be as cautious as possible, and the thorns shall not pierce too deeply."

Kotikokura grinned.

LXXIX

ROTHSCHILD MOVES TO PARIS—A FASHIONABLE SALON
—THE GOD ENNUI—KOTIKOKURA'S NEW LANGUAGE
—ROUSSEAU MAKES A FOOL OF HIMSELF—I RECEIVE
A MYSTERIOUS INVITATION—THE GOLDEN BOY—
HERMA—A GLIMPSE OF LILITH

ROTHSCHILD transferred his main office to Paris. Quietly, subtly, like a spider, he was weaving the intricate web to capture all Europe for me.

France was a wise and fortunate choice. The king and nobles were deeply in debt and ready to pay exorbitant interest for ready cash. The banks were in a dilapidated condition, requiring the hand of a genius for reconstruction.

Meanwhile, Mayer-Anselm proved as honest as he had promised to be. My money, nearly tripled, awaited me wherever I ordered, while my many names were never associated with that of Prince Daniel Petrovich, Member of Russian Royalty, scholar, linguist, traveler, and lover.

Kotikokura and I walked arm in arm along the shore of the Seine. The stars dipped their long fingernails into the cool waters of the river. One flat-bottomed barge emerged silently from under the bridge. A couple, their arms wound about each other's waists, bent over the rail and laughed.

"Spinoza was right, Kotikokura. The sea is our Mother. From the sea we come. Into the sea we go. Everything changes. The water remains. Where is the Paris through which we rode triumphantly with that strange man whose beard was a frozen cataract of amethysts? There is hardly a pile of stones, a bit of iron which is still intact. The Seine, however, flows on unconcerned. The Seine is like us, Kotikokura. All things about us decay and turn to dust. We remain."

Kotikokura nodded.

"And yet, is there so colossal a change? Are there not now as then houses, streets, men, women? Now as then, people live by illusion. Then it was the Philosopher's Stone. Now it is Reason. Always the futile search for happiness."

Kotikokura nodded.

"Then as now, a handful of people ruled the rest of the nation. Then as now, a few managed to live in luxury, while the rest tried to squeeze out of the hard and stony earth the milk of existence. Then as now, the poor hoped to become rich and the rich fought to retain their wealth. Nothing really changes, Kotikokura. Nothing is ever born. Nothing dies."

I looked at my watch.

"But we are late, Kotikokura. The Marquise is awaiting us. Her food will become unpalatable. A dinner is more important to a hostess than all the truths of life and death. She is right. We live by food and not by melancholy meditation, watching the stars dip their fingertips into rivers."

Madame la Marquise du Deffand bade me sit next to her. She placed her small ivory fan upon her lap and felt my face with both hands. They were delicate and white, but the knuckles had begun to assert themselves. She touched every part of my face and throat, lingering over my lips and forehead.

"Since I am blind, Prince, I have really begun to see faces. You are very handsome."

"Madame forces me to acknowledge the truth which I prefer to hear rather than to express."

She laughed a low guttural sound not unpleasant, but cheerless.

"You Russians learn the art of words so readily. You have much in common with us although it is not evident on the surface. But then, you have been in France before?"

"Long ago, Madame, in my youth."

The Marquise laughed. "Long ago! How can you know the meaning of long ago, monsieur? But youth, of course, will draw voluptuous pleasure even out of such a thought, however distasteful it may be to those really afflicted with age."

"How should Madame know the distastefulness of age?"

She struck me lightly with her fan. "Flattery is always delicious— at my age."

"I insist, madame. You can have no conception of the meaning of age."

"Let me feel your lips, Prince."

She felt my lips with the tips of her fingers, perfumed with lavender.

"No," she said, "you do not grin. You are sincere."

Her face, half-hidden in her velvet bonnet trimmed with lace, had, if not beauty, at least a daintiness and charm peculiar to so many French women. A few, thinly-drawn, almost imperceptible wrinkles danced about her eyes, tightly shut, and about her lips.

"I do not know what you may have heard about me, Prince. A blind person suspects every whisper."

"I have heard only praises— —"

"I have not always done what I should have done—that is true. But monsieur, I was bored. I strove to evade the great God Ennui."

I sighed. "Who has not been smothered by his terrible shadow, madame?"

"Your voice seems different, Prince. I should almost have believed it another man's. Strange! It sounded far, far off, thousands of miles —or perhaps, thousands of years. I was frightened."

"I spoke of the god Ennui, madame. One should be realistic."

She bade me give her my hand which she pressed. "Let me whisper something into your ear."

I bent until her lips touched and pressed my ear.

"*Je vous adore.*"

I kissed her fingers.

Meanwhile, the Salon became crowded with ladies and gentlemen. The hearing of Madame la Marquise was very acute.

"The man who is laughing now," she said, "is Monsieur d'Alembert, a fine genius but rather effeminate. Once," she sighed, "I thought I loved him. Youth—you know. The lady who speaks now is Madame d'Epinay. Beware of her, Prince! She smiles always, I remember, but it is a false smile, I assure you. But then, it was a man's fault, as usual. Her husband, Monsieur de la Live, has hardened her heart. Had he only been a little more careful in his faithlessness,—for it is not expected of a man to be a model of virtue. It is enough if one can betray with tact, and charm, and wit."

"Madame, every country has its own customs. Virtue is a matter of time and space. It partakes neither of infinity nor eternity. Charm, however, seems to prefer France for her habitation."

She whispered, "The lady who has just sneezed—she takes too much snuff at one time—is Madame Geoffrin, a splendid woman and as virtuous as it is compatible with politeness and humor."

The Marquise laughed a little. *"Mon ami,"* come nearer, and I shall tell you a comical story about Madame Geoffrin." I approached until our legs touched. I understood she desired more the proximity of my thigh than that of my ear. It amused me although the posture was slightly uncomfortable.

Mlle. de Lespinasse, tall, angular, with magnificent eyes and hair, bent and whispered into the ear of the Marquise. One or two other ladies approached. I took the opportunity to rise and walk away. Madame du Deffand motioned to me with her hand to remain, but I made believe I did not see. A little later, I saw her lips stretch into a painful grin. I, too, had disappointed her, I understood, and life was a bore.

Kotikokura, in a corner, wearing his Russian uniform and all his medals, was smothered by the attentions of three ladies, chattering incessantly. I approached and bowed. Kotikokura rose.

"Please do not disturb yourself, Duke, I beg you."

"Monsieur le Duc is most fascinating," one of the ladies observed.

"I have long ago discovered it, madame," I said.

"It is strange. He knows so little French but makes himself understood splendidly."

"He never uses a verb."

"That is marvelous, Prince. I must speak to Monsieur Diderot about it. He says that the verbs are the life of a language."

"Medals—Tsar—Russia," Kotikokura whispered to one of the ladies who played with his decorations.

"Now isn't that just charming? Le Duc means these medals have been given him by the Tsar of Russia."

Kotikokura nodded.

"Splendid!" another lady ejaculated.

"The Duke will reform our language, Monsieur le Prince. I think I shall stop using verbs myself. Duke charming—medals beautiful," she addressed Kotikokura.

Kotikokura was flustered and uncomfortable. To avoid bursting out into laughter, I snuffed a large quantity of tobacco and sneezed several times.

Kotikokura started to rise again. The ladies pulled him back. "Monsieur le Duc—*ici*—with us."

I walked away, leaving him to his delightful discomfort.

The conversation became very noisy, the remarks fragmentary. A fellow, his face besmirched with tobacco and mud, wild-eyed, half toothless, shouted back, waving his fist, while his moth-eaten wig toppled to one side like an uncomfortable crown: "Back to Nature, all you wicked and godless creatures!"

"But Monsieur Rousseau, what does it mean?" the first man insisted.

"It means that you throw away all your false books, false habits, false words, false arts."

"Everything is false, naturally, save *le Contrat Social* by Jean Jacques Rousseau."

There was general laughter.

"Jean Jacques is charming, *n'est-ce-pas?*" one woman observed.

"I think he is the rudest man in the world," another answered.

"Go back to God!" Rousseau shouted.

"It is too great a journey from Earth to Heaven, and I have a touch of the gout, monsieur," some one said, and turning to a man who was sitting near the window, "What say you, Monsieur Saint-Lambert, to a visit to God?"

"I say that belief in God is the origin of all follies."

Rousseau, exasperated, unable to speak, danced about waving his fists.

"Jean Jacques has the St. Vitus dance again," Madame la Marquise du Deffand remarked, fanning herself.

"The idea of God is necessary to happiness," Rousseau blurted out.

"Only beauty is necessary to happiness," Saint-Lambert answered. A lady next to him kissed his cheek.

"Happiness," Madame du Deffand said, "is the Philosopher's Stone which ruins those who seek it."

"There is a God!" Rousseau shouted, "There is a God! Messieurs, there is a God. If any one contradicts me, I go!"

"I contradict!" several voices answered.

"*Cochons!*" Rousseau blurted out, as if his mouth had been filled with pebbles, and dashed out of the room, his wig upon his neck.

"He is a fool!" Saint-Lambert remarked.

"Voltaire is right about him," another added.

"He is disagreeable," Madame du Deffand declared. "His '*Emile*' is contrary to good sense, his '*Héloise*' is contrary to good manners, and nothing in the world is quite so dull and obscure as his '*Contrat Social.*' "

There was general applause.

"Monsieur le Duc, do you believe in God?" one of the three ladies asked.

"Ca-ta-pha god," Kotikokura answered.

"Magnificent!" they shouted.

"Ca-ta-pha god! Ca-ta-pha god!"

The words became contagious. Everybody repeated and laughed.

"Ca-ta-pha god."

Kotikokura, indignant at the general merriment, rose and exclaimed, making the sign of my godhead, "Ca-ta-pha god!"

The three women kissed his face at the same time. Bewildered, he reseated himself.

The conversation drifted to politics. "Liberty—canaille—the king —equality—la France—treason" bombarded the room like a cannonade.

Madame Geoffrin walked among the people. "I beg you, gentlemen, no politics! Please, I beg you."

It was becoming very warm. The ladies nibbled at biscuits and fanned themselves, scattering about the scent of many perfumes and stale powder. The gentlemen consumed ices and wines.

"Your husband is a monster, madame, and you are an adorable creature," one man whispered to a woman. She struck him very gently over the mouth with the tip of her finger and after consulting her calendar, she breathed a date.

Other gentlemen whispered into other ladies' ears variations of the eternal formula.

I was bored. I suddenly felt my age. What had I to do among these children?

Some one pulled gently at the lace of my sleeve. I turned around. A young woman whom I had not noticed until then, whispered to me, *"Monsieur le Prince s'ennuie, n'est-ce-pas?"*

I nodded.

"Moi aussi."

I bowed politely.

"I am Herma," she said. "How shall I call you?"

"Call me Lucifer."

Her voice was deep and unsuited for her frail body. Her features were irregular but not unpleasant. Almost breastless and hipless in an age which insisted upon exposing its feminine charms, she appeared a pleasurable anomaly.

"Since monsieur is bored and since I am bored, would monsieur care to accompany me to my salon where he may find things and people to interest him?"

I looked at her, knitting my brow a little.

She smiled. "Monsieur need not fear. I do not mean to seduce him."

I smiled in my turn. "Mademoiselle would have no difficulty."

"The remark is a trifle banal."

"It is. Pardon." I gave her my arm. "I beg you to take me to your salon."

"We can leave here à l'anglaise," she said.

"But my friend, the Duke——?"

"Do not worry about him, Prince. The ladies will take care of him and return him to you when no longer needed. He is perfectly safe."

"As mademoiselle commands."

Mademoiselle awoke the coachman who was fast asleep.

"Home," she ordered.

Our journey was made in silence. I was grateful to the young woman. Every now and then, I glanced at her. There was something strange about her. A curve about her mouth and a soft down upon her upper lip reminded me of some one I could not name.

She had never been introduced to me and I was not certain whether she knew more about me than the fact that I was a Russian Prince who appeared bored.

The horses slackened their pace. We turned into the Boulevard du Temple.

"Mademoiselle," I said, as we alighted, "I am grateful to you for your silence. I was much in need of it, after the noise made by so many chatterboxes of either sex at Madame du Deffand's."

She smiled and nodded.

"My friend, Contessa di Rosacroce, who I hope will visit us tonight, believes that the male is the more garrulous of the species. Among animals and birds, she has discovered the same tendency."

"La Contessa is very observant, mademoiselle."

"She is a marvelous woman, Prince. She has traveled the world over, knows many languages, and is remarkably beautiful." She sighed. "Ah, so beautiful, Prince!"

We had already climbed the steps that led to the door of the house. Mademoiselle raised the knocker, the shape of a coiled snake, and struck three times, slowly, then three times in quick succession

The door opened.

"Has anybody arrived?" she asked the butler, a tall negro dressed like an admiral.

"Not yet, mademoiselle."

"So much the better."

"Prince, are you interested in paintings?"

"Certainly."

"I have some canvases which will please you, I hope."

We walked slowly from one painting to another, praising their merits, discussing the artists. My eye was arrested suddenly by a painting, hanging in an adjoining room.

"Mademoiselle, may I examine that work—_là bas?_"

"Of course. An ancestor of mine. On my mother's side, I am Italian. It is for this reason, perhaps, that I have been attracted to Lilith."

"Who is Lilith?"

"La Contessa. I call her Lilith. I imagine Lilith must have been like her,—so beautiful, so wise, and. . ."

"So wicked, may I add?"

"Wicked!" she exclaimed. "Prince!"

"Pardon. How otherwise could Lilith be but beautiful, wise,—and wicked?"

"Perhaps you are right, Prince. At least, she is very dangerous. I would not advise you to fall in love with her."

"I could not."

"Why not?"

I kissed her hand.

"That is banal," she answered.

"All truths are truisms and all emotions banal, mademoiselle. It cannot be helped. We live in a world which flows on forever, and forever repeats itself."

"You speak just like Lilith."

"May I be—Lucifer, then, for you, mademoiselle?"

She smiled. Her eyes closed a trifle. We approached the painting which had allured me so strangely.

"Who is this lady?" I asked.

"Her name, Prince, is—Mona Lisa, La Joconde."

"I knew her!" I exclaimed.

"It is hardly possible, Monsieur—Lucifer. She has been dead for centuries."

"No matter. I knew her or one who resembled her phenomenally."

"She resembles me, they say."

I looked at her. "Exactly. Your smile. Your lips. Now I remember!"

"Have you also seen me, like Lilith, in a dream?"

"No, no. This was not a dream. I knew her. I loved her. Who is the painter?"

"Leonardo da Vinci."

"Leonardo da Vinci!"

"Why the surprise? Everybody knows that he painted the Mona Lisa."

"But where is the ring?"

"What ring?"

"Pardon. My mind was wandering."

"You are as whimsical as Lilith, monsieur. She ought to like you immensely."

"Did Mona Lisa have a brother who looked like her? And did Leonardo paint him too?"

"She had a brother who was painted by Leonardo, but he did not transfix his beauty upon a canvas. It was his skin that he painted with gold. The boy died from suffocation. Leonardo's love unwittingly killed him."

"What was his name?"

"Antonio."

"How was Mona Lisa called as a girl?"

"Antonia—Antonia Lisa, but when the boy died in agony, her uncle, who brought her up, called her Mona—the only one. He could not bear to be reminded of the dead boy."

"It seems strange that I have never heard the story."

"You have never," she said astonished, "read the 'Ballad of the Golden Boy'? The poem relates accurately, except for minor details, the fate of Mona Lisa's brother."

"I shall surely read it," I said absent-mindedly.

Antonio—Antonia—I could see each luminous body walk through the long hall, and approach my bed. I could feel again the delicate texture of their skins. I could hear their stifled moans and the delicate imprint of their kisses.

But Herma, living, distracted me from my reveries. The ghosts disappeared.

In a distant corner of the salon, I saw gleaming in the soft candle-light, a marble statue.

"The God of Love," she sighed, "— Hermaphroditus."

I gazed musingly at the statue. Was this the goal of my long search, the double flower of passion, Mary and John, Antonio and Antonia, man and woman, in one?

I felt some one breathing deeply in back of me. I turned around.

Mademoiselle gazed raptly at me. In the chiaroscuro of the place, she was no longer a woman. The delicate down upon her lip had grown darker. Her body assumed a man's contours. . .

"Who are you, mademoiselle?" I asked, bewildered.

"I am Herma, Lucifer, Hermaphrodita. . ."

She pressed my hand.

"The statue is the gift of Lilith. It represents— —"

"You, Herma!"

"At times. . ."

A dozen emotions assailed me—hate, love, passion, disgust, disillusion, desire.

"Are you disappointed, Prince, to meet the sister of the Son of Hermes and Aphrodite?"

"I am—*bouleversé.*"

"Lilith also— —"

"Let me see you, Herma—in the light—here."

She had changed. Once more, she was a girl; once more Mona Lisa!

I grasped her head and pressed my lips against hers.

"Be careful, Prince," she admonished. "Lilith is jealous. . . ."

"What does she love in you, Hermes or Aphrodite?"

"Both."

"And you— —?"

"I love Lilith and Lucifer."

She rushed out of the room.

I seated myself on a chair, breathless. My head ached, nearly as it did upon my return to Jerusalem. My eyes burned as if hot sand had been thrown into them.

LXXX

ASSORTED LOVERS—THE TRANSVESTITE—NARCISSUS-
NARCISSA—LOVE IS A SHOE—THE ESOTERIC BAR-
ONESS—THE LOVER OF DREAMS—L'HOMME SER-
PENT—SHIFTING SEXES—QUEEN LILITH AND KING
LUCIFER—GODS FOR A NIGHT—A MISSIVE FROM
SALOME—I LAUGH

HERMA tapped my shoulder.

"Lucifer, the salon is already filled. You must come in."

I stood up. "If you knew the multitude of memories that galloped
through my brain, Herma, you would forgive my inattention."

"Lilith too speaks of memories—memories, always. Both of you
live in the past and yet you are still so young. Does not the present
exist for you at all?"

"It exists now that I have discovered you."

"So she said," Herma sighed.

"Who?"

"Lilith."

"Who is Lilith?" I asked, a little uneasy.

"You will see her. She has sent word she will be here later in the
night. If only—" she looked at me sadly, her lips trembling.

"If only what, my dear?"

"If only I could have you both in one! Lilith—Lucifer! Ah, how
much more fortunate you are! . . ."

"Why?"

"I am—" she smiled, —"both in one."

The salon was immense. The smell of incense, perfume, and
tobacco gave a strange sensation of sensuality mingled with religious
exaltation. It was as if kneeling at an altar, one thought of naked
women or if while embracing a woman, one had a vision of Jesus
upon the cross.

The paintings on the wall, even the furniture, suggested something
hovering between the two sexes.

Herma introduced me to the guests.

Monsieur le Chef de Police, attired as a lady in a scarlet dress embroidered with silk, lisped compliments to my beauty.

"He lisps only when he visits me," Herma whispered into my ear. "You ought to see him on horseback in parades. He is magnificent."

"Mademoiselle Fifi," Herma said, pointing to a young dandy who was leaning against a column, "allow me to introduce you to Prince Lucifer."

Mademoiselle Fifi combed her heavy black beard with her fine sensitive fingers, whose long nails reminded me of a mandaıin's.

"She was a charming girl. She has transformed herself into a man. I think she erred. As a man, she is too effeminate. . ."

"Effeminate, Herma! With that beard?"

A pale youth, dressed in the height of fashion, gazed at himself lovelorn in a tall mirror. He played with his locks, turning now to the right, now to the left, but always absorbed in himself.

"Whom do you love?" I asked.

"Myself," he said. "It is the oldest and the deepest of passions."

Near him a young girl threw kisses at herself in a glass. She never looked at the boy. He never looked at her. Each was too absorbed in the image cast back by the mirror. The girl did not look up when I addressed her. Her heavy-ringed eyes were fastened hungrily only upon her own reflection.

"Who is she?" I asked.

"I do not know," Herma answered. "We call her Narcissa."

We approached an elderly gentleman who knelt and kissed my shoes.

"How beautiful are feet encased in shoes!" he exclaimed. He rose. "Do you not think, Monsieur le Prince, that Eros had the shape of a shoe? *Le tout ensemble*, I mean. Not the particular. I have studied the nature of love, monsieur, all my life. Mademoiselle, would the Prince be interested in my book?"

Herma looked at me.

"*Nihil humanum— —*"

He knelt again and kissed my feet.

"May I present monsieur with my shoes in exchange for his book?"

"I shall place them in a golden case, monsieur. I shall worship them as one worships a god."

"*Monsieur le Comte, vous vous trompez.* Eros is not a shoe but a flame," said a rosy-faced figure whose sex I could not determine.

"A flame in the shape of a shoe, monsieur."

"No monsieur. A flame in the shape of——"

We passed on.

"Baroness de Boncourt," Herma bowed. Even in her sitting posture, she was taller than I. Her hair was a deep violet. It seemed to me that I was standing in front of a pole surmounted by strangely colored hay.

"Baroness de Boncourt," Herma confided, "knows all the ways of love except one."

"Which is that?"

"The way in which Adam knew Eve."

Herma whispered, "That enormous man who sits upon the floor, Turkish fashion, is Baron de Patrin. You understand, that all these names are fictitious. I do not know who these people really are. I don't want to know."

I nodded.

"Well, Baron de Patrin preferred to be neither man nor woman in order to love mentally, undisturbed by the flesh or the whim of a partner, some pale wraith of his fancy. He is a capon. Some call him Fra Abelard. I call him the lover of ghosts."

"In what respect does he differ from young Narcissus?"

"He loves not himself but his dream."

"Has he succeeded?"

"Alas, he has forgotten love entirely. He has grown, as you see, terribly stout and now he grumbles continually something about the meaning of life."

"What is the meaning of life?"

"Listen!"

Baron de Patrin muttered to himself: "Life is a wind circular and spiral and all things are specks of dust, square or triangular."

"He repeats that ceaselessly."

"Perhaps he is right, Herma."

"*Lucifer, vous êtes adorable.* You do not laugh at these people. You do not look at them superciliously. I love you."

"I have lived long enough to know that life is a comedy too profound for laughter."

"And for tears."

"Yes, my child."

"Lilith calls me a child, too, but I feel as old as the universe."

"Only youth is capable of such an adorable arrogance."

"Lilith, too."

"Do not speak of Lilith."

"Ah, you are jealous, that makes me happy!"

In the center of the room, upon a platform, was a wide armchair, gilded and surmounted by a crown.

Herma seated herself upon it and asked me to sit at her right. She raised a long ebony scepter, and majestically struck the floor three times.

"Mesdames et Messieurs, the early part of this night we shall devote to the Muse! Monsieur Michel Jean Sedaine, incomparable poet and playwright, will read his new masterpiece."

Her voice had become deep and slightly cracked like a young adolescent's. She had assumed her masculine expression. When was she woman, when man? What emotions stirred one being or the other into life?

Monsieur Sedaine's poem was long and declamatory and his voice one-toned as the weary beating of a drum. He strutted about, waved his arms, struck his chest.

"How ridiculous is the Muse, Herma!" I whispered.

She looked at me reproachfully.

Monsieur Sedaine was applauded. He was followed by other men and women who recited madrigals and sonnets about love, sentimental and lachrymose, and passion.

Suddenly, Herma jumped off the throne. "La Reine Lilith, mesdames et messieurs!"

Like a resurrected queen of Egypt, dazzling with rare jewels, her eyes half-shut, her mouth slightly pouting, her fingers outstretched and arms pressed against her sides, entered, making small rhythmic steps—Salome!

I jumped up. "Salome!"

She opened her eyes wide, looked at me, and drooped her lids again. Behind her, two immense negroes, naked to the waist, carried her train.

Herma knelt and kissed the hands of Salome.

"Rise!" Salome ordered.

Herma rose and helped Queen Lilith to the throne. A harp, invisible, played one of the compositions that I had heard in the enchanted palace in Persia.

Salome seated herself.

"Dim the lights!" Herma commanded.

We remained in semi-obscurity and for a long time there was perfect silence.

"Your Majesty," Herma asked, "shall the inspired ones continue their reading?"

"Yes."

Herma called upon another poet. She seated herself upon a golden stool at the feet of the queen. I remained standing.

"Salome," I whispered while the recitation proceeded, "my supreme, my incomparable love, have you forgotten Cartaphilus?"

She made no answer but patted the head of Herma who assumed, under her touch, a masculine personality.

"Salome," I continued, "do not torture Cartaphilus as you tortured him in the Palace of Pilate."

"Herma," Salome whispered, "you are very beautiful tonight."

"Lilith, my queen!"

"Salome, magnificent and wise beyond compare, spurn not Cartaphilus!"

"Herma, I dreamed of you last night. You were he who— —"

The poet finished his verses. The audience exclaimed: "Bravo! Bravo! Bravissimo!"

Herma called upon another poet to recite.

"Salome, what have we in common with these people? Are they not mere dust? We are the Eternal Flame that the stars are made of."

Salome's eyes were riveted upon the slim body of Herma.

"Herma," she chanted, "you are not of the earth. You are the daughter-son of Hermes and Aphrodite. The nymph Salmacis is united with you, making one. . . ."

I touched Herma's small breasts with my arm. Under my touch Herma assumed a feminine aspect. Her breast buds swelled and throbbed.

Salome looked at her, and her breast blossoms withered. Herma was a boy.

Herma looked at both of us. One side of her face was a woman's, the other a man's. She took both our hands and said: "Queen Lilith —King Lucifer—one—eternally one."

Had she guessed our relationship? I looked at Salome imploringly. She smiled vaguely and pressed my hand.

I knelt.

Salome stood up. "King Lucifer shall improvise a dialogue in verse with Queen Lilith."

I was startled. I had always considered poetry the consolation of those who were incapable of living intensely.

"Life is a greater poem than mere sounds, dexterously arranged, Your Majesty," I said. "King Lucifer has lived."
Salome exclaimed: "The Queen has spoken, Sire."
"So be it, then! The King obeys provided the Queen responds."
"The Queen shall respond."
"A crown, Herma!" I commanded.
Herma clapped her hands. The butler brought a small golden coronet, studded with a few jewels, some relic of royalty.
"Let the lyre play!" I ordered.
I knelt upon one knee and began to improvise a poem in the somewhat theatrical mood of Herma and her guests. Salome as Lilith, responded in the same mood.

LUCIFER

"Lady of mystery, what is thy history?
Where is the rose God gave to thee,
Where is thy soul's virginity?"

LILITH

"Lord, my Lord, is thy speech a sword?
What is it thou wouldst have of me?"

LUCIFER

"There are pleasant passes of tender grasses
Where the kine may browse and the wild she-asses,
Between the hills and the deep salt sea,
But where is the spot that is branded not
With the sign of the Beast on thy fair body?"

LILITH

"Lord, my Lord, ask thy Scarlet Horde!
Who spilt my love and my life like wine?
Who threw my body as bread to swine?
If my sins in heaven be seventy times seven,
What between heaven and hell are thine?"

LUCIFER

"Lady, where is it thy fancies hover,
With wolves' eyes prying restlessly
For some naked thing that they might discover,
Some strange new sin or some strange new lover,
Beyond the lover who lies with thee?"

LILITH

"Lord, my Lord, who has struck the chord
That holds my heart in a spider's mesh?
Prince of the soul's satiety,
Whence springs that hunger beyond the flesh,
That only the flesh can appease in me?"

LUCIFER

"By the love of a love that is strange as myrrh,
    By the kiss that kills and the doom that smileth,
By thy cloven hoof and my fiery spur,
    Thou art my sister, the Lady Lilith,
I am ———"

LILITH

"My brother—Lucifer!"

LUCIFER

"I am thy lover, I am thy brother,
    Time cannot prison us, space cannot smother,
    Proudest of Jahveh's kindred we,
Whom Chaos, the terrific mother,
    Begot from stark Eternity.

"I am the cry of the earth that beguileth
    God's trembling hosts though they loathe my name,
    The dauntless foe of His loaded game!
But where is the tomb that had hidden Lilith,
    Of the Deathless Worm and the Quenchless Flame?

"I hunted thee where the Ibis nods,
    From the Brocken's crag to the Upas Tree,
My lonesomeness was as great as God's
    When He cast us out from His Holy See,
But now at the last thou art come to me!

"Let Mary of Bethlehem lord it in Heaven,
    While stringèd beads her seraphs tell,
    (How art thou fallen, Gabriel!)
Thy bridesmaids shall be the Deadly Seven,
    And I will make thee a queen in Hell!"

When we finished, Herma wept.

Salome kissed her upon one cheek, and I upon the other.

"You are gods. I am but a mortal," she sighed.

She stood up with a jerk. "No matter! Tonight we shall be gods. Mesdames et messieurs, we are all gods tonight! . . ."

The people applauded.

"Dust shall burst into flame," Herma continued.

"Bravo! Bravo!"

Herma rang a large gold bell that hung against the wall. Servants appeared with drinks and pipes filled with hashish.

"Drink and smoke, mesdames et messieurs. Man becomes a god only by intoxication."

Baron de Patrin grumbled: "Life is a wind circular and spiral and all things are specks of dust square or triangular."

"Come nearer me, Lucifer," Herma asked. "Let my body be your pillow this night. This night I too shall be a goddess. Tomorrow I am dust and you will desert me. . ."

"Hermaphroditus—Hermaphrodita—eternal god-goddess!" I exclaimed.

"Dance!" Herma commanded.

An invisible orchestra played.

The guests began to dance—strange unrhythmical dances. In the smoke that rose from their pipes, they assumed grotesque and unhuman shapes. One man whom I had not seen until then, dressed in a red veil, turned about himself, twisted, rolled upon the floor.

"The human serpent," Herma informed me. "He knows the love of all animals and birds and even insects. He has discovered sixty-seven new ways of love, possible, alas, only to one who, like him, can twist himself like a serpent."

"Does he also know," I inquired tantalizingly, "the secret of unendurable pleasure indefinitely prolonged . . .?"

Herma looked at me startled. She pressed my hand in a curious way which I assumed to be the secret grip of a strange lodge.

"Salome, am I once more in Persia? Are you deluding me again? Are these phantoms cast against mirrors? . . ."

"Cartaphilus is a child always and always bewildered," Salome answered in Greek.

"You speak the language of the gods," Herma said wearily, her eyes closed. Her lips assumed the smile of La Joconda.

The human serpent twisted about the violet-haired Baroness, forming with her a bizarre and lascivious pattern.

The shoe adorant convulsed at the feet of Salome.

"Life is a wind——" the voice drawled out in back of us.

"Greater love has no man," Narcissus whispered, making eyes at himself. Narcissa was still lost in the contemplation of her lilied loveliness.

Mademoiselle Fifi leaned languorously against the Chief of Police. The Chief of Police, in the scarlet dress embroidered with silk, with cushions to supply the breasts which nature denied him, ogled a lackey passing with a tray of cordials.

My eyes became dim. The lights danced among the dancers who seemed motionless. The music retreated—retreated—like the band of an army, passing by a window and continuing its march.

I felt warm flesh pressing against mine. Herma lay between Salome and me.

"Salome," I whispered, my words coming into my mouth from an immense distance, "Salome!"

"Cartaphilus!"

"Must always a dream or another human form, however lovely, interfere between Salome and Cartaphilus?"

"When Salome conquers the moon—Cartaphilus shall conquer Salome."

Something beat against my ear like a bass drum—bang, bang, bang! I could not open my eyes. Bang—bang—bang! I must see— I must! Bang—bang—bang! I must! Bang, bang! I opened my eyes wide, wide, for fear they would close again.

It was morning. The sun pierced vainly through the curtained windows. All about me, men and women snored and groaned or lay still, like dead. Herma slept, her face bloated, her lips frozen into an ironic grin. Salome was gone!

Bang, bang, bang! Some one was knocking furiously at the door. No one moved. The servants had disappeared. I rose, tottered to the door, and opened it.

Kotikokura, wild-eyed, his sword drawn, was ready to strike.

"Kotikokura!" I exclaimed.

"Ca-ta-pha!" His sword dropped. "Ca-ta-pha!" He embraced me.

"This is the enchanted palace of Persia, Kotikokura," I grumbled.

He took me in his arms like a child and placed me in a carriage. I fell asleep. When I awoke again, Kotikokura administered cognac and iced oranges.

"What has happened, Kotikokura? Where have I been?"

He explained that he suddenly became aware that I had disappeared from the salon of the Marquise. Nobody had seen me go. He shouted: Where is Ca-ta-pha, god Ca-ta-pha? Everybody laughed. He rushed out, upsetting several men and women. He looked for me at the hotel and at the cafés,—everywhere indeed where I was accustomed to go. He feared foul play. He had heard of spies and kidnappers. He rushed about the streets, calling out: "Ca-ta-pha! Ca-ta-pha!" He stopped carriages, peered into windows, and finally returned to the hotel. I had disappeared! Meanwhile, day was breaking. He was desperate and commenced to search once more.

Finally, a lady, heavily veiled, stopped him, and pointed out the house where I was.

"It was Salome!" I exclaimed.

His jaw dropped.

"Dear old Kotikokura, best of friends and companions! What would I do without you?"

Kotikokura began to dance.

A lackey brought in a letter.

"From Salome, Kotikokura."

"Mon cher Lucifer,
Kotikokura, the most faithful of creatures"—Do you hear that Kotikokura?

Kotikokura grinned, his eyes luminous like a cat's. ". . . must have taken care of you. Do you remember anything as grotesque as last night? *Mon ancien, mon ami!* Do not remain very long in Paris. The storm is rising. It is not safe.

"Before leaving, however, see Dr. Benjamin Franklin, inventor, publicist, statesman, and possessor of twenty-seven mistresses and several illegitimate children, which is not a mean record for a representative of a new country.

"Help him carry on the revolution. It may be that the New World will be a more habitable place than the old one. I doubt it. But let us try. Besides, you will lose nothing. Your banking system is splendidly organized. Rothschild is very clever. You have chosen well.

"Poor Herma! When she wakes up, she will find neither you nor me. A god-goddess for one night. But what a god—what a goddess, Cartaphilus!

"I am leaving for the Pampas, where I hope to create a more perfect being than Herma. I shall communicate with you as soon as I wish you to visit me. Meanwhile, take care of yourself and of your charming monster.   Lilith, Regina."

I remained pensive. I could not remember the embraces of Herma. Had I been enchanted by the ludicrous circus? Had I foregone godly pleasure? I tried to recollect. I remembered I protested against her —I called out: "This is not what I yearn for! You are neither Mary nor John! Go away!" I ran. Herma pursued me. "Help! Help! Monsieur le Chef de Police!" Suddenly, I noticed a tall pole with a yellow top. I climbed quickly. Herma fell and wept. I laughed.

"Kotikokura, oh that we may never find what we seek!"

He helped me descend from the bed.

"I am sick, Kotikokura."

"Sick of the wine?"

"Sick of the earth. . ."

"No, no!"

"Pan—you love the earth too much."

He gave me another cool drink into which he mixed cognac and orange juice.

"Bacchus!"

He began to dance.

I laughed heartily.

LXXXI

TWO PARALLEL LINES MEET—THE GARDEN OF SALOME
HOMUNCULA—A CENTURY IN RETROSPECT—AD-
VENTURES IN THE NEW WORLD—THE WOMB OF
CREATION—A SIMIAN ABELARD—I PLAY CHESS—
THE BLACK KING AND THE RED KING—THE LAST
INGREDIENT — ULTIMATE MEANINGS — KOTIKO-
KURA SNORES

SALOME was standing at the tall bronze gate, waving her hand. In the
reflection of the setting sun, she dazzled like a luminous body—a
lake on fire or a full moon surrounded by a magnificent aureole.
She was the snowy peak of a mountain, surmounted by a golden
crown, a cataract of white roses, the foam of a gigantic wave congealed, a dream carved in stone.

"Gallop faster, Kotikokura, or she will disappear. She is Fata
Morgana."

We whipped and urged our horses and in our haste, we drove past
her. Salome laughed, and ran a little to meet us. She embraced me,
pressing me tightly to her breast.

Kotikokura stood a little aside.

"Come here, you little monster!" Salome ordered.

He approached her like a boy who is guilty of a misdemeanor. She
embraced him.

"You are old enough, Kotikokura, to behave better."

Kotikokura kissed her hand.

She took our arms and led us back to the gate of her inaccessible
dominion. Meanwhile, a host of men and women whose faces were
hidden by their enormous sombreros, ran from all sides, took care of
our horses, and rushed to meet the long caravan which was approaching slowly.

"What is that, Cartaphilus?" Salome asked.

"My belongings and my gifts to the incomparable queen."

She looked at me a little perplexed.

"I have come to stay, Salome. The Wandering Jew must have a

spot to call his own. This is the twentieth century. He has exhausted all countries. The Zeppelin and the airplane make a jest of distance. I shall stay here for a century, perhaps forever. . ."

"Don't be too sanguine," she said, pressing my arm.

"Even in the most romantic novels or among the Anglo-Saxons, no hero waits more than two thousand years for his wedding night."

"Incorrigible as ever and as ever, arrogant."

"And more than ever in love with you."

"Kotikokura, you should have taught your master patience and modesty."

"Ca-ta-pha god."

"In a godless world, there is still one believer," she smiled.

"And in an unromantic world, there is still one lover," I added.

"You are Don Quijote and not the Wandering Jew."

"No, not Don Quijote," I protested. "I saw him wandering about with Sancho Panza and their donkeys. He was a charlatan, a reformer of the kind one meets in America. He derived much profit from his grotesque notions, and the blows he received were much exaggerated by Cervantes who desired to arouse pity in the hearts of his readers. Sancho Panza, poor fellow, lived in the world of illusions attributed to his master. He believed in chivalry and in his master and received as recompense, rebukes and sarcasm from the latter, and the ridicule of every succeeding generation that reads the book."

"Sancho Panza reminds me of Kotikokura. He too believes in his master and his master's illusions and as reward, he obtains— —"

"His master's love," I interrupted.

"Ca-ta-pha god," Kotikokura insisted.

Salome laughed and looked at me. Her eyes were like green stars.

"Salome is more beautiful than all illusions, more gorgeous than drug-begotten dreams."

I kissed her throat.

"Cartaphilus does not wait for his reward," she said.

The gate opened wide at our approach. A burly individual bowed to the ground.

In the center of the garden, a tall fountain rose and fell softly like a long whip that strikes caressingly the back of a cherished animal. In the basin, black swans glided shadow-like. Peacocks spread wide their tails and followed their mistress, reflections of her magnificence. Upon the tall palm trees, small monkeys rushed up and down, screaming. A gigantic tortoise whose back glittered as a strangely polished jewel, moved imperceptibly, its head shaking like a silent bell.

I looked about, bewildered.

"Child," Salome said, stroking gently my cheek, "you fear it is illusion again."

"You always guess my thoughts."

"No, this is not Persia—and what you see is reality."

"So it seemed to me then."

"This time you need not fear," she assured me.

We entered the palace, a building massive and yet graceful, practical, solid. Here and there, however, were touches of daintiness that bespoke the nature of the owner. A strange mixture of freshness and antiquity pervaded the place which, instead of giving the impression of incongruity, suggested a beautiful harmony, as if time had merely removed the glare and blatancy characteristic of newness, but left all the freshness. I thought of an aged tree whose leaves had the tender greenness of saplings.

Salome guessed my thought and smiled, pleased.

"Just like yourself, queen of queens."

"And like you too, Cartaphilus. And like this wild creature Kotikokura."

"Life is not an evil, Salome."

"Perhaps we are dead and that is why we are incorruptible. We live not in time but in eternity."

"Are you quoting Spinoza?"

"You were more fortunate than I. I came some months after his death. The old woman was dying also. She spoke to me of you."

"She never knew my name even."

"Your name? What name? If I were to discover your whereabouts by your name— —"

We laughed.

Salome ordered two servants to undress us and help us with our bath.

In a corner of the garden, shaded by willow trees and rose bushes, the cool soft waters of a lake splashed noiselessly their artificial banks.

After our ablution in the lake, we were anointed with oils and perfumes as in the time of the kings of Israel, and were offered silken robes and satin slippers, studded with jewels.

I thought of the glory of Salome rising out of the waters, more fragrant than the roses that hid her from view.

Dinner had meanwhile been prepared and the table spread in a ten column portico.

Kotikokura preferred to eat with the majordomo, the colossus who had opened the gate for us. I was not displeased for I wished to be alone with Salome.

A youth and a young girl whose skin was as smooth and as black as ebony, dressed in silken garments emphasizing the suppleness of their limbs, waited upon us.

We reclined on opposite sides of the table on couches, Roman-fashion, eating delicate but simple foods, and drinking out of exquisitely chiseled goblets, wines and liqueurs that sparkled like molten jewels.

At a distance, some one played the lute. The music mingled with the perfume of many flowers and the singing of birds.

"Salome, this is Paradise and only a god as cruel and as jealous as Yahweh shall drive me out of it."

Salome smiled. "Or a goddess as merciless as Princess Salome, daughter of King Herod."

"Fortunately, Yahweh is dead and Salome is no longer Princess of Judea."

"Who is she?"

"She is the Goddess of Reason, and Reason knows no cruelty."

She laughed. "Strange that Cartaphilus should accept a Goddess of Reason."

"Salome is the mother of Beauty."

"And Cartaphilus the father of flattery and chivalry."

We remained silent, eating the fruits which, like manna, tasted of all delicious things.

Salome smiled. "My servants believe that you are my bridegroom, come to wed me."

"Your servants are attentive and knowing."

"Only a month ago, their mistress died and her great granddaughter has inherited her wealth. . ."

I knit my brow.

"Cartaphilus, will you never be able to jump at a conclusion except by a slow and masculine process of ratiocination? I have lived here with few interruptions for a hundred and fifty years nearly, since our strange night at Herma's. How could that be accomplished save by calling myself my own descendant? To your right, there is a crypt in which are buried my great-grandmother, my grandmother, and my mother. I have raised statues to all of them."

"And the corpses?"

"Wax figures, of course, and a little magic. The black art is not dead. . ."

"Oh lovely great-granddaughter of Salome, more beautiful and more radiant, be indeed my bride!"

"Salome does not break her promise. The time is nearly ripe."

"Then Cartaphilus shall remain here forever."

"Shall the Wandering Jew forswear his wanderings?"

"He is not a Jew any more and he will no longer wander save in the company of the great-granddaughter of the incomparable queen."

"It will be the death of Cartaphilus."

"Then death shall be more welcome than life."

"Salome belongs to an old generation. She may not believe in divorce."

"Have not nearly two thousand years proved the constancy of Cartaphilus? Why, there are stars that are less— —"

"Persistent," she interrupted.

"The ancient order of geometry is overthrown by the new mathematics. Two parallel lines may meet long before infinity," I said, and raising my glass, I continued: "Here is to Einstein—greatest of mathematicians!"

We descended several steps. A gate opened and closed behind us automatically. We were surrounded at once by high stone walls, surmounted by an immense glass dome.

"Where are we, Salome?"

"The new Garden of Eden in which I fashion a different world."

I touched a rose. It curled its petals until it assumed the shape of a red-furred cat. Out of its pistil or muzzle—I could not tell which —jutted a thin stream of perfume. I retreated before what seemed a leopard, glaring at me. The leopard unfolded into a vast dahlia. Peacocks' tails were the leaves of a palm tree. A butterfly, waving its wings, was a carnation of the loveliest hue. A bud that Salome offered me assumed the shape of a bee, the tips of its leaves buzzing. Out of chalices of flowers, birds sang exquisite music. Out of birds' beaks hung branches, laden with fruit. Lizards, many-colored, grew like microscopic trees. The animal world merged with the plant; perfumes mingled with color; leaves were incipient wings; songs approached human voice.

"Taste of this, Cartaphilus."

Salome offered me an apple. I bit into it. A sensation of nakedness overcame me. I looked at myself.

She smiled. "This is my Tree of Knowledge."

"Does knowledge mean nakedness?" I asked.

"Life is overdressed. Knowledge is the tearing of veils."

"Salome! I am as a man who has been swung about many times and is set upon the ground suddenly. Everything turns. The earth is no longer solid. The sun whirls about my eyes. The universe rocks under my feet."

"Thus creation must have impressed Adam."

"Be good enough to explain things to me, O marvelous Queen!"

"It is very simple. I am weary of the earth. The earth is magnificent and interesting only to those whose lives are numbered by a few years. I have seen her too often. She is the most monotonous of mothers. Always she bears the same children. Her patterns are unvarying, like the knitting of a senile woman. I am the new mother! I shall create newer and more beautiful things! I shall change the dull face of life. . ."

I knelt before her. "Goddess of Reason and Beauty! Creatrice Supreme!"

She bade me rise. "But greater and more resplendent than all things created shall be my new humanity."

"New humanity?"

"My Homuncula is nearly completed."

My thoughts reverted to Bluebeard.

"No, not the Homunculus of that strange man whom I inspired, but whose masculine lack of creativeness shaped a ridiculous monster."

"Did you know Gilles de Retz?"

"Of course. I met him before you came to Paris. His genius was too great for him. It overflowed him as a stormy river overflows its banks."

"Salome, whom have you not seen and understood?"

"Are you surprised, Cartaphilus, that I experimented with life?"

"Tell me your experiences, Salome."

"Some day, I shall turn writer."

"What a poetess you will make!"

"It is so easy to write poetry,—an art for the very young. I shall write prose, lucid and clear,—ideas that will illuminate the mind of the reader. When I am too weary of life, I shall write about it, Cartaphilus, and you will see whether woman is inferior to man."

"And yet, Salome, how seldom did I discover a great mind in woman! What feminine Spinoza, what Bacon, what Apollonius have you encountered?"

"Woman considered herself the inspirer of man. She has preferred to remain behind the throne and whisper into his ear. She is forgotten. His name is carved in gold."

"Is it merely that, O beautiful Princess?"

"That and her biological tragedy. That and the tyranny of the moon and the greater tyranny of childbirth."

We walked silently between the rows of strange flowers and animals.

"Homuncula, however, overcomes both the moon and the horror of birth."

I looked at her, expecting to see the crazy glint of Bluebeard's eyes. But the eyes of Salome were as cool as the shadows of the roses.

"Is anyone interested in a new humanity in Europe or in America, Cartaphilus?"

"The last one who mentioned it was Goethe, the German poet. I visited him at the termination of the French Revolution, which broke out as you surmised, not long after your departure. Alas, he was as garrulous as an old woman and much more interested in the medal which Napoleon had pinned upon his chest and court intrigues than in Homunculus."

"Homuncula, Cartaphilus. It would be futile to create a man. . ."

"Goethe shared your opinion, Salome:

> *'Das Unbeschreibliche*
> *Hier ist's getan,*
> *Das Ewig Weibliche*
> *Zieht uns hinan.' '*

"Goethe understood," Salome remarked.

"He was blinded by his sexual nature. If he had been true to his own philosophy he would have concluded Faust:

> *'Das Unverkennliche*
> *Hier ist's getan,*
> *Das Ewig Maennliche*
> *Zieht uns hinan.'*

Man is the creative principle!"

"Man is critical, not creative! Woman is the dark, the terrible Mother!" Salome exclaimed proudly.

"Goethe anticipates this, though he senses the horror of the Dark Mother. . . *'Muetter—schreckliches Wort!'* "

" *'Schrecklich'* in the sense of 'tremendous.' He is right," Salome explained. "Over all mythologies hover the Norns, dark feminine creatures, mistresses of life and death. Goethe's mind caught a glimpse of the truth!"

"The truth, perhaps, is the union of the Eternal Feminine and the Eternal Masculine—Salome and Cartaphilus!"

She smiled. "Perhaps. What more did Goethe tell you?"

"He was too elated over Napoleon's colored ribbon which hung upon his chest to indulge in philosophy."

"Who is this Napoleon, seducer of poets?"

"It is true,—you have been here for a century and a half. . ."

"During which time I refused to remember the rest of the world," she interrupted.

"Napoleon became the emperor of France after the revolution proved a futile gesture."

"As it was bound to prove."

"We have seen so many revolutions, Salome, and so many emperors. . ."

I plucked a beetle which unfolded its hard wings, becoming a violet as blue as if a bit of Italian sky had been torn off and made more luminous by long polish.

"Napoleon, not taller than this shrub, galloped across Europe, his hand thrust into his uniform, his lips pouting, his brows knit, one curl—the last remnant of his hair—in disarray upon his forehead. Kings, princes, emperors, dismayed, dashed precipitously, leaving their thrones and their countries to the mercy of the Upstart. The vacant thrones he refilled with the members of his family; the treasures and museums he looted and transferred to Paris; the poets he corrupted by pinning medals on their chests. He passed through the world like a thunder-storm."

Salome smiled.

I laughed heartily. *"Il fait gémir le monde parce qu'il est incapable de faire gémir la paillasse.* This is what a Polish Countess related to me. Napoleon had taken a great fancy to this lady who at first snubbed him, preferring me. His Majesty was infuriated. The countess was pretty, but not unusually so. 'A splendid animal,' Napoleon had called her. I pleaded with her. It was madness to refuse an Emperor and it might prove disastrous to her country. She consented to share the imperial couch."

Salome smiled. "Cartaphilus must have felt thrilled to think of his own magnanimity, relinquishing his mistress to the emperor."

"After all, he was only a mortal! . . . Well, Madame la Comtesse reappeared the next day, shaking with laughter. *Mais, ma chère, qu'y a-t-il?* When she managed to restrain her convulsions, she said: *'Napoleon est un très grand empereur mais un très petit homme.'* "

"For two days and two nights, I had to quench the fires which His Majesty had kindled but was unable to quell."

"What happened to this *grand empereur?*"

"He was finally defeated by all the monarchs combined who imprisoned him upon an island where he died, poor fellow, devoured by vermin and vanity."

"Stupid mankind!" Salome exclaimed. "Is the New World different from Europe?"

"The New World, *ma très chère,* imitates the old. It has copied its vices perfectly and its virtues clumsily."

"Ah, by the way, did you see Dr. Benjamin Franklin, Cartaphilus, as I suggested in my letter?"

"I saw Franklin."

"What sort of man was he?"

"He looked like a debauched woman, was as practical as a Jewish peddler, had the imagination of a dray horse, uttered advices like a successful grocer—except once." I laughed. "He told me not to get married but choose an elderly lady for a companion. It was cheaper, safer, her body was generally much younger than her face, and above all, she was grateful!"

Salome laughed. "Rather clever. And did you give him the money?"

"Certainly. But it was a bad investment. The Americans were so inconceivably sentimental that they considered a debt incurred for the sake of their liberty in the nature of a gift. The politicians could not conceive that any man desired to recover his money after such a splendid victory and the establishment of a democracy. I did not insist. America appeared as too profitable a field for future investments. Indeed, at present, I rule the world from the world's new center—New York. . . ."

"*Le grand Empereur!*" Salome laughed ironically.

"*L'homme encore plus grand!*" I added.

"Vanity, thy name is Cartaphilus!" she exclaimed.

Kotikokura reclined underneath a palm tree. A half dozen monkeys were playing about him. One of them, perched upon his knee, shrieked. Kotikokura answered him. There was a general noise like a tumultuous laughter.

Kotikokura began to play on his flute. The monkeys made a circle about his feet and listened, enraptured. The peacocks approached, spreading their tails. Small birds alighted and remained motionless. The swans stretched their necks, opening and shutting their bills. A squirrel, his tail in the air, dropped the nut which he had held in his forepaws, and did not budge. The tortoise approached, its head in the air like a priest at prayer. Several servants emerged from various parts of the house, open-eyed and open-mouthed. The majordomo stood in the distance, his large hands upon his enormous belly, his flat feet beating time.

Salome appeared on the balcony.

I threw her a kiss. She threw me a rose.

"Today you shall see the Homuncula, Cartaphilus," Salome whispered. "Come."

Salome locked and unlocked several iron doors. We walked through corridors, halls, rooms, turned in strange mazes, climbed and descended stairs.

"Why the secrecy, *ma chère?*" I ventured to ask.

"Is it not self-evident, my friend? I have been at work for a century and a half. A stupid servant, an over-curious guest might annul my labors. You are the only person who will see the Homuncula."

"I am grateful for your confidence, Salome."

"You and I,—are we not the sole gods of the world, the sole survivors of the Tempest of Time?"

"We must never separate again, my love."

"Don't be mawkish, *mon cher.* The survivors of a tempest need not necessarily, as in romantic books, marry and live happy ever after."

"It is less ridiculous than walking each his own way among the débris."

"You are the Eternal Youth."

"My glands function perfectly, Salome. That is all. Steinach, a great Austrian scientist examined me not long ago. I think I could die in an accident. But my glands are extraordinary. The glands which, in the average person, secret the seed of new life, constantly pour new vitality into the stream of my blood like the fresh sap of a tree. Man is immortal through his progeny. I am my own progeny. I remain always young and always sterile."

"Glands— —" Salome meditated, placing the key into the door.

"It is not Jesus who gave me life, Salome. His eyes conveyed a powerful shock to my nervous system which, in some inexplicable way, altered the mechanism that controls my secretions. It may be possible, some day, by applying electricity or the X-ray, to produce the same result in all men. We shall have, then, a race of immortals."

"No, no!" Salome exclaimed. "I hope that will never occur, Cartaphilus! The people who are alive today are so ridiculously constituted, so slightly endowed with the capacity for pleasure or thought that a life beyond the ordinary one would change earth into hell."

"Let us impregnate with our own immortality only those who deserve it."

"A perilous venture! Besides, who deserves immortality?"

"There are a few men, Salome, whose personalities partake of the eternal flame. Alas, their glands age and die!"

"Only the descendants of my Homuncula will merit immortality and shall have it, Cartaphilus."

She opened the door to a vast room which, contrary to the habitation of Bluebeard's Homunculus, was scented with strange and delicious perfumes. A garden blossomed out of the walls and ceiling. In the center, a magnificent statue lay outstretched upon a couch.

"My Homuncula," Salome said proudly.

"Salome is greater than Phidias."

"Oh art, Cartaphilus—it is but child's play. Homuncula lives!"

"Of what material is she fashioned?"

"The essence of flesh."

I looked at her, perplexed.

"You cannot understand it, Cartaphilus. I have discovered strange things."

"Strange indeed, Incomparable One!"

I approached the Homuncula. Salome held my arm. "Do not stir, Cartaphilus. You must not go near her. Watch from a distance. Look,—is she not made for pleasure such as even you and I have not experienced?"

"She resembles Herma," I remarked.

"But Herma—poor human child—was neither man nor woman completely. My Homuncula is both perfectly. Every atom of her body is constructed for joy. Jahveh, in His hurry, created man for the purpose of living merely. Pleasure was only an impetus toward existence. It was not life's very purpose. Mind, too, was merely a substitute for deficient muscle. Man was mud electrified. My Homuncula is of the very essence of life. Death cannot overcome her. Therefore she will be able to devote herself to joy with abandon! . . ."

"Salome is a glorious artist!" I exclaimed.

"My Homuncula will not know the ugliness and travail of bearing children."

"How then——?"

"Why were the birds favored by Jahveh? Why cannot man be born like the bird?"

"Will the descendants of Homuncula be both man and woman?" I asked.

"Of course. 'Male *and* female created He them.' How can they know perfect joy save by being both man and woman? Jahveh reserved this double boon for the snail. I give it to the creature I have fashioned, not for my pleasure, but for her own. But we have remained here too long, Cartaphilus. We may disturb subtle bio-chemical processes. Homuncula is not yet entirely alive. She is still, as it were, in the womb of creation. . ."

Salome was feeding the swans. They placed their flat bills in her hand and wound their necks about her wrist.

"Cartaphilus, whom else did you see after the French Revolution who is worthy of memory?"

"In France, I met Heine, a Jewish poet, driven out of Germany by the intolerance of the princes and his very thrifty family, who insisted upon making him a banker. What a sharp mind Heine possessed and what a tender heart! A typical Jew, Salome. It is strange how that race persists."

"Has America produced any people worthy of consideration?"

"America!" I laughed. "I had a strange experience there."

"What was it, Cartaphilus? I am in a mood for gossip."

"The American women are the most beautiful in the world. Many of them partake of the epicene charm which the Greeks gave to their immortal statues. I fell in love—mildly, naturally. Always the vision of Salome eclipses all my amorous fancies. . ."

Salome smiled. "Cartaphilus speaks always with one objective in mind. And they say that Man can discuss impersonally!"

I smiled. "May I not wind my neck around your wrist like that fortunate swan?"

Salome placed her arm about me.

"Oh, that I were a swan and——"

"Come, come--tell me about your experience in America."

"Well, I fell in love with a young girl whose name was Jackie— in some ways more boy than girl."

"All beauty wavers between the two sexes," Salome interposed.

"In our perambulations, we crossed from one state into another— a nominal frontier, you understand. We registered at a Philadelphia hotel as Mr. and Mrs. Peterson. The night was spent in tepid pleasure. Mrs. Peterson was as sentimental as she was passionless. She had the intelligence of a gosling which was most incongruous with the splendid poise of her physique. But I had already discovered the frequency of this discrepancy and the surprise was not as great as the annoyance.

"In the morning, an officer of the police knocked at the door. I was accused of abduction. All explanation was futile. My offense consisted, not in seducing the girl, but in crossing the state line. If I had remained with her in New York, no minion of the law could have interfered with my pleasure. I had crossed into another state and the law allowed of no ignorance. Besides, it seemed that morality was becoming too lax of late. I had desecrated the sacredness of the American hearth. Americans utter their platitudes more eloquently than any other people of the globe. I was given the choice between marrying Jackie or going to prison for many years. Neither appealed to me. However, I knew of a positive antidote to morality, an antidote which, by the way, is far more efficient in America than anywhere else.

" 'How much?' I asked, with the characteristic brevity of the new land. The gentleman of the police mentioned a sum which he snatched out of my hand. Without even thanking me, he left, warning me that the next time I committed this dastardly crime, I should have to go to prison for years under the Federal statute or—'Double my money,' I said ironically.

"Jackie glared at me. 'What about me?' she demanded.

" 'How much?'

"Her price was exactly ten times his for she clamored that she was a decent girl misled by me. The swiftness with which she grasped the situation—for I am quite certain it was not a preconceived trap—was typical of her race. A child of ten in that country speaks in terms of capital and interest, and at seventy, he still retains this terminology. I gave her what she asked. She threw her arms about me. 'You are a brick, old man!' she shouted, which means in that country of eternal slang that I was generous and a man of principle.

" 'Why don't you marry me, Pete dear?' she asked, her feminine sentimentality reasserting itself.

" 'I shall return in a few centuries, Jackie, my love. Perhaps by that time, you will have developed a mentality compatible with your magnificent physique. . .'

"She did not wait for me to finish my sentence, gave me a violent blow on the chest and left me, shouting: 'You're a nut!'—which I learnt later was a man who had different views from the others, thought differently, or whose appearance suggested culture. 'You're a nut!' is as terrible an indictment in modern America as 'You are a witch' was during the time of the Puritans. Indeed, so fearful are the Americans of being 'nuts' that even the cultured and the learned vociferate: 'We are just like the rest; we are lowbrows; we are not "nuts"!'

"In a world of geese, can you conceive the hatred they would bear a swan who suddenly raised his graceful neck like the one who seeks your lovely hands, ma chère?"

Salome smiled.

"A week later, I left the New World. I shall return, as I promised, in a few centuries. . ."

"And the American man, Cartaphilus?"

"The American man," I laughed. "His history is divided into three chapters—he is successively the slave of his mother, of his wife, and of his daughter. The American man? Salome, even the most zealous feminist would be inspired with pity. The African Tribe over which you ruled, ma chère, has been transplanted to the New World. . ."

"I am right, Cartaphilus,—the earth must be populated with a new race. The descendants of Adam are intolerable in whatever continent we place them."

"There are still a few men here and there, Salome, whose existence compensates for the ugliness and stupidity and cruelty of the rest."

"You are the eternal optimist, Cartaphilus."

"In England, there is George Bernard Shaw, a white-headed Lucifer,—witty and wise. He believes that if man willed intensely to live, he could prolong his life indefinitely."

"Truly, I must hurry with my Homuncula before the children of Jahveh discover the secret of longevity," Salome interposed.

"In England, also, I met a man by the name of Havelock Ellis,—the purest intellect since Apollonius whom he resembles, physically even, save that the beautiful dark eyes of the Greek have become a magnificent blue. He lives as simply as Spinoza. He has written as no man before him of the delights of sex. If such a man lived for a thousand years— —"

"We cannot populate the earth with a handful of men."

"Then there are a few Jews who have revolutionized the torpid mind of man. Einstein has rediscovered and amplified my law of relativity, Freud has reinterpreted the meaning of immortality. . ."

"How?"

"Within our subconscious minds, we carry our own history and maybe the history of the race."

"That is not a new conception. In Greece, and in India, I knew several philosophers who held similar ideas."

"Freud has given life a new face. He teaches man to know himself without being ashamed of himself."

Salome shook off the particles of bread that clung to her fingertips and taking my arm, we walked slowly between the rows of palm trees.

"In Switzerland, I met a man by the name of Lenin,—a strange being, a Russian nobleman. He was a veritable volcano. If this man ever seizes the reins, the world will certainly accelerate its rotation."

"In what way?"

"There will be neither slaves nor masters, neither rich nor poor, neither— —"

Salome laughed. "It is inconceivable, Cartaphilus, how a man who has lived for nearly two thousand years can still harbor such youthful illusions. How many messiahs have we not seen and heard! Truly your glands must function with the accuracy of a clock."

We laughed.

"No, *caro mio*, only a new superhumanity deserves our consideration."

"I remember once some years ago, I met a scholar and a poet whose name was—let me see—Nietzsche, of course. A great poet and a great scholar. He lived alone upon the top of a hill—a thin, sickly individual with an enormous head. He spoke in ditherambs, like an Athenian god. 'Superman! Superman!—A new humanity!' I asked him: 'But master, if at last the superman appears in truth,

what joy will it be to us men? The superman will lock us in cages
and exhibit us to the youthful superman as we exhibit the monkeys.
What delight is there in being an inferior animal?'

"He rubbed his forehead and covered his eyes, which could not
withstand the light of the sun. 'Perpetually create new values, new
vistas, new heights! Let your purpose be a sword! Overcome yourself! Go beyond good and evil! Beyond life! Beyond death!' he
exclaimed.

"He grasped my arm. He was overcome with vertigo. I led him
back to his room and left shortly after."

"Nietzsche understood, Cartaphilus. He understood the meaning
of creation!" Salome exclaimed. "I should have met him. I shall
accomplish what he hoped. I shall mother the Superman and the
Superwoman."

"Salome, you are the Eternal Mother. This enables you to visualize your dream. You love the child before it is born. You create him
mentally before he is created in truth. But I am the Eternal Father.
I must learn to love my progeny. The child must exist before it
can gain my affection."

"Perhaps that is true, Cartaphilus," Salome said, thoughtfully.

"It is for this reason, no doubt, that I prefer the great men who
are already alive to the supermen who dwell in the poet's brain, or
the homunculae in the womb of creation. . ."

Kotikokura, arm in arm with the majordomo, passed us, followed
by the tortoise whose efforts at speed were a pity to behold, and
two monkeys who jumped like drunken grasshoppers. The procession made us laugh. I related Kotikokura's adventure in the salon
of Madame du Deffand.

"He is becoming more and more human," Salome remarked.

"Perhaps he is the superman of the future. Who knows to what
mental stature he will grow within the next ten thousand years?"

"It is not such a wild notion as it may seem, Cartaphilus. He
grows slowly. That is a good sign. We grew too rapidly. What difference is there really between Cartaphilus and Salome in the time of
Pilate and now? At most, a mellowing, a ripening, a tolerant
outlook."

"Is not all this a dream, Salome? Have we really lived as many
centuries as it seems to us? Have we not, by some strange mathematics, calculated days as years?"

Salome sighed a little.

"I have not visited the Garden of Eden today. Will you accompany me?" she asked.

"Cartaphilus does not exist for himself. He is but the shadow of his Love. . . ."

"And Salome is becoming so enamored of her shadow that she may feel as lonesome without him."

"How long will she drag her shadow after her as a futile train, O Queen?"

"Look, look! It is climbing the tree like a squirrel."

"Both shadows, Salome, interlaced like branches. Is it symbolic, *ma très chère?*"

She nodded.

"If I seem to walk Salome, it is an illusion. I am flying. My feet have turned into wings."

She pressed my arm. "Come, Cartaphilus."

The Garden of Eden had a different complexion. Colors, sounds, perfumes had changed.

"When at last my experiment proves successful," Salome exclaimed, "the earth shall not be the monotonous singsong of an old woman which it is today. It shall be the mad dance of a young girl who— —"

She was interrupted by a shrill cry.

"Let us see what has happened, Cartaphilus," she said anxiously.

In a corner of the garden, a small monkey was rolling in agony upon the ground. A gigantic carnivorous rose released its grip over the animal and resumed its normal posture. Blood dripping out of its chalice, reddened the long powerful stalk.

"A simian Abelard, paying his sanguine tribute to a floral Héloise." I suggested.

Salome wavered between indignation and amusement.

"There is no reason, *ma bien aimée,* why a monkey may not turn monk, and why a rose—possessor of a *relique précieuse*—may not compose immortal letters in the shape of magnificent perfume."

"It would be a delight to see Cartaphilus a monk," Salome said, her voice slightly irritable. "You are incorrigible! Pick up the little victim."

"He is immoral, Salome. I am surprised you pity him. The rose in her virginal purity— —"

"Stop chattering, Cartaphilus. Let us carry him out and see if we can save his life."

"Come, my poor little monk! What business did you have in the Garden of Eden anyway? Only snakes luxuriate in such places. Had you read the Bible faithfully, you— —"

"I do not understand how he got in here," Salome remarked.

"He must have strayed between your lovely feet, Salome. He is thoroughly wicked, I assure you—or at least, he was. For the sake of his immortal soul, nothing better could have happened to him, for nothing is half so productive of moral habits as the inability to be immoral."

We walked quickly out of the garden, the monkey groaned in my arms.

"Kotikokura!" I called. "Kotikokura!"

Kotikokura appeared in three leaps.

"Kotikokura, my ancient friend, I bring you a sinner permanently repentant."

He took the monkey in his arms. The animal stopped moaning, and licked Kotikokura's face. Kotikokura's eyes filled with tears.

"Kotikokura, watch closely this move. It is a most excellent one."

Kotikokura bent his head until he nearly touched the board. I raised slowly one of the pawns, carved out of amber, and painted red, and placed it a square forward.

"A simple move, Kotikokura, and apparently without consequences. Moreover, because of it, the red castle is lost to the Black Queen. Ah, but watch!"

Kotikokura knit his brow, his eyes darting to and fro.

"The Red Knight dashes to this side, captures this Black Knight. In three moves, well-calculated and infallible, he will appear galloping before the Black King; at the same time, from the top of this castle, we shall bombard the thick of the army; while from this angle, the Red Queen will emerge, in a blaze of light. The Black King will hear the deafening shout of victory—'Checkmate! Checkmate!' He will be swept off the board, and— —"

Salome, dressed in a Japanese kimono dazzling with many jewels, and carrying a parasol upon which was embroidered a magnificent eagle, wings outspread, approached, making tiny steps.

"The Queen! The Queen!" I exclaimed. "Kneel, Kotikokura!"

We knelt.

"For some reason or another I have never been able to master chess thoroughly, Cartaphilus."

"A patience, too great for a woman, is required for this game."

Salome smiled. "Of course, woman must create and accomplish. Man is a drone."

"Great destinies are shaped by his idleness."

"A consolation for a masculine weakness. Man is so busy finding excuses for his shortcomings, that he has no time to eradicate them."

Kotikokura offered her his seat. He remained standing behind her, holding the parasol over her head.

"Do not let me disturb you, Cartaphilus. Continue your game."

"This is more than a mere game of chess, *carissima*. I am planning in an objective manner, my last, my most daring, most comprehensive campaign."

"And what is this most daring, most comprehensive campaign, if I may ask?"

"The civilized world is divided sharply into two camps,—capital and labor. Labor, which you remember as a cringing slave, has risen to the grandeur of a monarch. The struggle between the two forces will be a grandiose spectacle, out of which Labor, the Red King, will emerge triumphant!"

"Why so enthusiastic, Cartaphilus? Are you a workman, anxious to increase your wages?" Salome asked ironically.

"I am weary of the old world, Salome. Besides, I wish to be the leader of the force which must conquer. I have become accustomed to lead,—to own the world. I prefer not to be the deposed sovereign."

"And should Labor, contrary to your expectation, be defeated?"

"Then I shall play with the Black King."

"Whatever happens, I win. My rule is permanent. There are not, as Disraeli, the most brilliant Jew of the last century, intimated to me, two hundred men who rule the world. There is only one! The two hundred men are my agents. Among them, there are representatives of all nations, but the majority are children of Israel. Many partnerships, many aliases and corporations conceal my identity."

I laughed.

"Salome, how curiously false is history! Not long ago, Europe and America were alarmed to the point of hysteria about certain documents discovered in Russia, known as the Protocol of Zion, which purported to be the secret plans of the Jews, trying to rule the world and destroy Christianity."

"Is it true?"

"Only in a sense,—for I am the Protocol. I am the Jew ruling the world! And I am no longer a Jew and do not desire to destroy Christianity."

"I cannot understand your interest in the old world, Cartaphilus, but I am not opposed to your campaign which will, no doubt, mean the depopulation of the Earth. It will make room for my new race,—the descendants of Homuncula."

"Such a war as I am planning is beyond man's imagination. You are right, Salome. Blood will rise in great billows like an ocean, whipped by a storm. I have already chosen my tools. Lenin, an aristocrat—this Red King—shall be the monarch of Labor. Mussolini, a man of the people—this Black King—the monarch of Capital. Both are Renegades. Renegades are the most passionate upholders of their new ideas. But first of all, another king,—the White King must be crushed!"

"Who is the White King?"

"The greatest potentate of Europe. Favoring neither capital nor labor, he aims to speak for both, and for his people. I must destroy him. I have no hatred against this scion of Charlemagne, but he threatens my rule."

"Why indulge in such childish notions of glory, Cartaphilus!" Salome exclaimed.

"But, O peerless woman, love me, and with one gesture—like this —I shall fling to the earth empires, emperors, continents!"

I swept with my palm the board, and knelt.

Kotikokura dropped the parasol and gathered the pieces.

Salome was sitting in the sun, drying her hair. I approached. Kotikokura in back of me, carrying a golden box, was followed by "Abelard" grown plump and pompous, a velvet cowl upon his head.

I knelt upon one knee. "Nymph celestial, your earthly lover has a gift for you. Accept it, I pray!"

Kotikokura placed the box upon her lap. Salome opened it and uttered an exclamation of joyous surprise.

"The crown and jewels, O Salome, that Isabella of Spain once wore. I bought them that America might be discovered. America has been discovered and inhabited—and corrupted. No other head in all the world save yours, O love, deserves to wear this precious ornament."

Salome's eyes closed half-way, her lips opened slightly and her chest filled.

"Aphrodite was never as delectable as Salome. Goddess of

Beauty, you are Eros and Aphrodite in one!" I exclaimed, rising and placing the crown upon her head.

The majordomo and all the servants came running from various parts of the garden.

I knelt again and all the rest followed suit. "Abelard" kept one paw in the air like a celebrant ecclesiastic. Salome rose, lifted me, and embraced me passionately. Her lips had the freshness of early morning.

"My love," she whispered.

She clapped her hands. The majordomo approached and lowered his head, pressing against his belly.

"A banquet in honor of my bridegroom!" she commanded.

The majordomo whistled. The servants scurried about like ants. Kotikokura, followed by "Abelard," walked away slowly. Was he downcast or too moved to congratulate me?

"Salome, you said 'bridegroom'—not husband. Was it intentional?" I asked.

"Yes, Cartaphilus. Today we shall celebrate our marriage, but we must postpone its consummation."

"Salome," I pleaded, "how long shall my lips parch in the desert of my desire?"

"Tomorrow or as soon as you can arrange it, you must leave, Cartaphilus."

"Impossible!" I exclaimed.

"Yes, you must leave for Europe again. Steinach, in Vienna, you tell me, has isolated the feminine hormone. I need this hormone. I need other endocrine products from his laboratory. Homuncula can never be truly born without perfectly balanced internal secretions. And there is one more ingredient which I lack to complete my conquest of the moon. . . ."

"I am stunned——"

"Think of my lonesomeness when you are gone!"

"Will you be lonesome, Princess?"

She pressed me to her heart. Her eyes glittered.

"It is well, beloved. I obey!"

"If I can achieve my end without the ingredient or if I can isolate the hormone in my own laboratory, I shall send you a message. You will know that I have emancipated myself and my sex completely from ancient biological fetters. When I am free I shall be yours. . . ."

"You are the creature predicted by Apollonius, the goal of man's passionate pilgrimage. I seek neither Mary nor John, but—you, the synthesis of all sex attraction, the perfect Double Blossom of Passion! Hermaphroditus and Hermaphrodita are monsters: you are the ultimate, the unimaginable ideal!"

"Homuncula's charms are more seductive than mine. . . ."

"Homuncula knows neither suffering nor struggle. Her perfection is a gift from you. You have wrung your perfection out of the hands of the gods. However marvelous she may be, you and I, though immortal, belong to the race of men. We are united by indissoluble memories, by immemorial ties."

Salome's eyes moistened.

"When I am ready I shall send my messenger. You will know by this token that the two parallel lines of our lives have intersected at last. Come back to me then, the only man who ever captured his dream."

"——After two thousand years!"

"Two thousand years is little time for man to discover himself; for woman to shake off the yoke imposed upon her by a biological accident when the first man and the first woman first crept up from the slime of the sea."

"I shall obey, most desirable of your sex, or rather, of the new sex for which the world has not yet invented a name!"

"When you are in Europe, execute your audacious game. Start your war, move your pawns, save the world, if you can! If the experiment ends in failure and confusion, come back to me. A new creation awaits you here."

The train dashed on noisily like a whipped animal. Kotikokura and I smoked cigarettes in silence.

"Kotikokura, do you bear me a grudge for being betrothed to the most perfect of women?"

He shook his head. I pressed his hand.

"Does not your master deserve a little rest after two thousand years of wandering and disillusion?"

He nodded sleepily.

"If only I can get those ingredients or if Salome can distill the elixir of life without them! I am once more a heart-hungry boy!"

Kotikokura yawned.

"We must try to understand her, Kotikokura. She is the eternal mother."

"Ca-ta-pha eternal god."

"And Kotikokura eternal friend. We are the perfect triangle, the meaning of ultimate truth. I have discovered nothing else in twenty centuries. . . ."

We lit fresh cigarettes.

"Life is so simple and its essence is love!"

Kotikokura dozed.

"I have sought wisdom and happiness in every corner of the world before I discovered this secret. But that digger of ditches who, for one fraction of a second, waved his red handkerchief to us, may have discovered it likewise. Wisdom and happiness are attitudes, not realities. This is a truism and a platitude, Kotikokura. But no truth has reached perfection unless it has become a truism and a platitude, an axiom incontrovertible and beyond explanation. Before that, truth is an epigram, the *tour de force* of a poet or a philosopher. And this too is a platitude. . . ."

Kotikokura's eyes blinked painfully.

"Yet this, too, is a matter of mood. Love may hide from us the truth of heaven and earth. Hate, the struggle for survival, may be the sole compass of Reality, Kotikokura."

Kotikokura grinned feebly.

"But how shall a man in love think if not platitudinously, seeing that love itself is the quintessence of all platitudes? Perhaps Cartaphilus will lose his own soul, if he returns to his mate. Perhaps the Great God Ennui will prevail in the end. Perhaps, to escape from his clutches, we must migrate to another planet."

Kotikokura snored

I lit another cigarette.

The smoke that wound and unwound, like some strange and occult sculptor, shaped the face of my Love.

"All is vanity save love."

The smoke rose to the ceiling, curled about the electric bulbs, and vanished.

"Love, too, is vanity."

Kotikokura gnashed his teeth in his sleep.

"And the truth of all things is—irony."

EPILOGUE

THE DISAPPEARANCE OF ISAAC LAQUEDEM

FATHER AMBROSE, his cross swinging about his neck, a pair of shoes in one hand and in the other two telegrams, ran, out of breath, toward the wing of the monastery in which Professor Basil Bassermann and Dr. Aubrey Lowell were quartered.

It was early morning, but already several monks were working in the garden, while others were walking slowly, counting the beads of Christ.

Since the arrival of Isaac Laquedem, the monks had seen their Father Superior act strangely, and, at times, they suspected, even a little out of harmony with the rules of their sacred order. They could not rebel, however, for they were unable to specify their grievances. To see, therefore, the Holy Father run out of breath, a pair of shoes in one hand and telegrams in the other, seemed only one more strange episode in a long chain of extravagant happenings.

They stopped in their work or in their prayers, looked at one another, shrugged their shoulders, and muttered mainly to themselves: "Since those foreigners came here, everything is topsy-turvy."—"The Lord Jesus will punish us, I am sure."—"Everything is going to the dogs."—"I never used to lose one count of my rosaries. Nowadays I must go over them five times before I do the right number—and then I am not sure!"

Father Ambrose had meanwhile reached the door of Professor Bassermann's room. He placed the shoes upon the floor and rapped nervously. The Professor, already dressed, opened.

"Ah, Father Ambrose, good morning."

"The Lord be with you, my son."

"What makes you so matinal, Father? As for me, I could not sleep the whole night through. There was something restless in the air. I finally dressed and was about to go out for a walk in your beautiful gardens."

Father Ambrose stared at him. "I too found it impossible to sleep

494

and when, at last, I did fall asleep for a half hour or so, I had the wildest dreams."

"Our experiments are very fatiguing, Father. We should take ? rest for a few days."

"We shall take a much longer rest than that, Professor." Father Ambrose pointed to the shoes.

The door of Aubrey's room opened and the young scientist appeared.

"Good morning, gentlemen. Up so early too? I could not sleep and thought of taking a walk."

Father Ambrose crossed himself. "What a fool man is, gentlemen, and how little he understands the hidden meaning of things! During the last half hour of my restless sleep, I dreamt continually of wings flapping and enormous gates opening and closing. It was a warning."

"A warning of what?" questioned Aubrey.

Father Ambrose pointed to the shoes. "Isaac Laquedem and his valet Kotikokura are gone!"

Professor Bassermann smiled sarcastically.

"Impossible!" exclaimed Aubrey, "his story is still unfinished. There are loose ends and contradictions that will plague us forever, unless he gives the key. Have you looked everywhere?"

"Everywhere, my son. Everywhere. The only things he left us are this pair of shoes and these two telegrams which, in my excitement, I have not even read. It's incredible!"

All three bent over, their brows knit.

"These are not so easy to decipher, gentlemen," Bassermann said. "Let us sit down and analyze each one, for I am certain that the secret of Isaac Laquedem is disclosed in these missives."

"What can this mean?" Father Ambrose said. "It looks like a diagram, not a message. There are two lines——"

"Why!" Aubrey exclaimed, "the two parallel lines have met, without awaiting infinity. . . ."

"Yes, yes!" Father Ambrose remarked.

Professor Bassermann laughed. "How credulous both of you are, my friends! A bit of trickery characteristic of Isaac Laquedem. This is no telegraph blank. Where does it come from? What stamp does it bear?"

The others looked closely. Everything was erased except in the corner a water mark that looked like a tortoise.

"Why do you think it is a piece of trickery, Professor?" Aubrey asked.

"It is not an ordinary telegram," Father Ambrose admitted. "But how could the message have reached him?"

"Some more hocus-pocus," Professor Bassermann snorted.

"What makes you say so?"

"Because I think this other telegram is a real one which he did not mean to leave behind him. It is signed Nicolai Lenin. It was sent from Moscow. The language is a corruption of Sanskrit."

"What does it say?"

Professor Bassermann's eyes glued themselves upon the message. "It is susceptible of several interpretations. If I read aright it says:

" 'All is ready. Come. The Red Dawn is rising.'

"I was right all along. Isaac Lequedem is a Russian revolutionist! This is the Lenin to whom he referred last night."

"And the shoes?" Father Ambrose asked.

"A clownish trick!"

"Do you mean to say, Professor, that our analysis was absolutely futile, that he only made believe— —"

"No, no, Aubrey. He revealed himself in his analysis when he told us his dreams and his day dreams. Even our lies are a self-revelation. The more deliberate the lie the more damning the confession! He retold the history of the world as it reflects itself in one man's mind. His story is an erotic interpretation of history. There is nothing in his recital that any educated man could not distill from his reading. His memory is nothing to brag of. It cannot compare with that of the servant girl who remembered whole speeches in Greek to which her subconscious mind had listened while she was dusting the bookshelves in the house of one of my colleagues. Isaac Laquedem is undoubtedly a thinker and a remarkably well-read man, but he is also a charlatan and an adventurer."

"I do not think," Father Ambrose insisted, "that you can explain Isaac Laquedem in terms of the laboratory or of empiric psychology. Too many occult events are associated with both his coming and with his going. How do you explain the strange unrest that kept us awake last night?"

"Our sleeplessness may be the aftermath of our exciting labors. Or it may be induced by the influence of atmospheric conditions," Bassermann replied.

"What of my dream, professor?" Father Ambrose asked.

"Your dream was due to the noise of the gate as Laquedem opened it. Your room is near it, is it not?"

"But the watchmen saw no one go out, professor," the priest insisted.

"Watchmen," Bassermann laughed ironically, "are sleepy-heads. If you wish a house to be robbed, employ a watchman."

Suddenly the whir of an aeroplane overhead startled the three scientists. They rushed out. Over the crest of Mount Athos an aeroplane glided for a few moments, then disappeared in the clouds like a fantastic bird.

"It was he! I could wager my life on it!" Professor Bassermann exclaimed. "Isaac Laquedem would not relinquish the sensation of flying above the monastery on his way to Russia. He knows that we are watching him now and are speaking about him."

The monks knelt and prayed, their heads raised towards the spot where the aeroplane had been. They rose, glared at the three men, and grumbled.

"I think we have outstayed our welcome. It is time we left this retreat, Father Ambrose," Bassermann whispered.

"Your passports arrived with the visa this morning. In my excitement I kept the documents in my pocket." He extricated from his cassock two passports, adorned fantastically with many seals.

"I welcome the long delay," he added. "Who knows whether we shall meet again this side of Paradise? But let us elucidate, if we can, before your departure, the mystery of our guest."

"I," Aubrey remarked, "am convinced that Isaac Laquedem has lived nearly two thousand years, and that, except for obvious lapses and exaggerations, his story is true."

"How can you reconcile that supposition with your scientific conscience?" Professor Bassermann derisively asked.

"Like Laquedem, I reject the occult interpretation of his extraordinary experience. He himself supplies the clue to the mystery," replied Aubrey Lowell. "Isaac Laquedem suffered a severe psychological shock on his way to the crucifixion of Jesus. The shock mysteriously disarrayed the mechanism of his metabolism. It overstimulated his glands to such an extent that they were able to eliminate completely the byproduct of life, the waste which, accumulating in the channels of our body, produces old age and death. Death, I am convinced, is not a biological necessity. The experiments of Carrel have established that tissue may renew itself indefinitely."

"He has," Professor Bassermann growled, "established only the immortality of the chicken heart!"

"The immortality of Isaac Laquedem rests on an analogeus process. Carrel keeps the tissue young by constantly purging it of all impurities. Isaac Laquedem's system in some way which I cannot explain, performs for him naturally the functions which Carrel's test tubes and chemical reagents perform for his tissue. Nature, anticipating Steinach, accelerated the internal at the expense of the external secretions of his glands. She made him a great lover but denied him progeny. The internal secretions stimulate his metabolism enormously. Every tissue of Laquedem's body, including his brain, is uncannily alive. We have barely touched the accumulations of his memory . . ."

"But how," Professor Bassermann asked, "do you explain the longevity of Kotikokura, who was exposed to no such psychic shock."

"Laquedem transferred to Kotikukura certain hormones with his blood. Kotikokura's body offered a favorable soil to these hormones; they accentuated the activity of his glands in the same manner in which they quickened the vital processes of his master. For some mysterious physiological reason Laquedem's blood thrived in the missing link, but was fatal to Damis. It is a hypothesis by no means to be rejected that the venom of the snake bite may have acted as an antidote to certain toxins in Laquedem's blood. Perhaps Kotikokura's robust constitution was sufficient in itself to neutralize the poisonous substance."

"Very ingenious!" Bassermann exclaimed. "But how do you explain the inaccuracies and anachronisms with which Laquedem's tale abounds? He confuses historical characters and juggles with time. I doubt if he could pass successfully a college entrance examination in history!"

"Probably not," Aubrey remarked. "Laquedem is as human as we are. His brain is subject to the same errors as ours. His recollections are colored by his own personality. It takes two years to perform an ordinary analysis. It would take fifty years to analyze Laquedem in such a way as to unravel all the complexes which constitute his personality and to eliminate from his recollections the factor of human error. Incidentally," Aubrey laughed, "the joke is on us."

"How so?" Bassermann asked.

"We wished to discover whether the memory of the race can be reached through the subconscious. Unfortunately, of all beings in the world, we selected for our experiments the one man whose memory extends over two thousand years! We reached the end of his conscious life, but have hardly opened the portals of his sub-conscious."

"Then," Father Ambrose remarked, "you would say the experiment failed."

"No. Like Columbus we set out to discover one thing and discovered another. What is your opinion of our experiment, Father?"

"I agree with you that Isaac Laquedem told the truth. He is indeed the Wandering Jew. I cannot tell how God wrought the miracle, but it is a miracle. By every sign and token he, Isaac Laquedem, is Ahasuerus."

"Nonsense," Bassermann exclaimed irritably, "he is a Russian conspirator."

"Have you forgotten the sudden storm on his arrival? Do you recall the seven plovers and the broken bell? Don't you remember how the wounds of the Crucified reopened when he entered the room? He is unquestionably the Wandering Jew."

"Fiddlesticks," Bassermann thundered. "He is a Russian spy!"

"I am inclined to agree with Father Ambrose," Aubrey replied, "without accepting his supernatural implications. But if we are right, if he is the Wandering Jew, do you know what we have done———?"

"Well?" Bassermann snapped.

"We have killed him. We have condemned him to death."

"Killed him?" the other two added.

"Having traced the shock—the trauma of the psychologists—to its origin, we have broken the spell. The long chain snaps. The glands are restored to their normal function. The hypnotic command is dissolved. The curse, if it be a curse, is lifted. Henceforth Isaac Laquedem is like other mortals. His glands will function like ours. We have cured the patient. If our cure is effective, the patient will die. . ."

"No, my son, he will live on until Jesus returns. 'Tarry thou till I come.' Isaac Laquedem can find no peace until the Saviour returns to judge the quick and the dead."

Father Ambrose made the sign of the cross.

"Whatever our final judgment may be," Aubrey said, "we have conducted together a phenomenal investigation."

"That is no doubt true," Bassermann said. "Laquedem's analysis constitutes a complete mental chart of civilized man."

"The world will be startled when we print our notes."

"Startled and probably angered," Bassermann added, rubbing his hands.

"Laquedem's story," Aubrey added, "sheds a new and colorful light on history, religion, sex, morality, occultism, rejuvenation, reincarnation, recurrence of type. There is in Laquedem something of Don Juan and Casanova, and something of Faust. He is Faustian in that he attempts to face the problem of human life in its entirety."

"Many writers have attempted to tell the story of Ahasuerus," Bassermann remarked.

"Yes, but they confined themselves to one incident, or like Goethe, contented themselves with a fragment. This is the first time the story is told in his own words, and is told as a whole. Technically, especially in view of the manner in which we probed his memory by psychoanalysis, the recital of his tale presents almost insurmountable difficulties. . . ."

"The story," Bassermann remarked, "must be told backwards, or rather, it must be unfolded from the beginning. Isaac Laquedem told his life from maturity to youth. Such a procedure would be abstruse and difficult to follow. It is like reading through a mirror. We must begin with his youth and carry his life forward from its beginning to where it ends."

"If it ends," softly remarked Father Ambrose.

"Perhaps you are right," Aubrey said. "His story can never end. The life of Isaac Laquedem is the history of human passion."

"Will the Censor permit you to tell his story?" Father Ambrose remarked. "I hear that policemen in Boston and the chief of the lettercarriers in Washington are the arbiters of literature and morals in the United States."

"We cannot destroy this most remarkable record in the history of psychology in deference to vulgar prudery," Aubrey replied. "However bizarre Isaac Laquedem's adventures may be, however curious the bypaths of his sensations, however exotic the labyrinths of his passion, there is nothing in his story that does not lurk somewhere in the subconscious of everyone of us. His experiences are purely human. *Nihil humanum* . . . nothing human is alien to him."

"I am less afraid," Professor Bassermann remarked, "of the moralists than of religious zealots who may consider the confessions of Isaac Laquedem an attack upon all religion."

"Only," Father Ambrose interjected gravely, "if they do not read his confessions in their entirety. Every phase in his development is but a link in a chain. It may be the chain between man and God. Both mystic and rationalist will find in Laquedem's confession the confirmation of their convictions."

The conversation was interrupted by the arrival of three monks, pale and tottering.

"These are the watchmen," Father Ambrose remarked. "Now we shall hear how Isaac Laquedem escaped."

The monks seemed to be unable to speak articulately.

Professor Bassermann looked into their eyes and examined their pulse.

"These men are hypnotized," he exclaimed. "It was thus that the Russian spy managed to get away."

"This proves my contention. He is the Wandering Jew," Father Ambrose asserted heatedly. "No one but a person with extraordinary psychic powers can hypnotize three men simultaneously. He has repeated for us the feat which freed him from the claws of the Inquisition. The Lord has given him supernatural powers to extricate himself from his predicaments that he may continue his pilgrimage unhindered."

The three scientists remained silent for a while, watching the monks recovering slowly from a state bordering closely on catalepsy.

"You will take your notes with you, gentlemen," Father Ambrose said sadly. "May I keep the shoes and the telegrams?"

"Of course," the two answered.

"It will not be easy to step into those shoes," Aubrey Lowell said softly.

"You exaggerate the size of his feet," Professor Bassermann laughed. "These shoes are by no means enormous. It seems to me that they are his evening slippers. . . ."

"Come, gentlemen," Father Ambrose remarked, reminding himself of his duties as a host, "breakfast is waiting."

The three men walked slowly toward the monastery. Their shadows mingled as if the three great divisions of human thought, absolute faith, absolute denial and pragmatic acceptance, were at last reconciled.

The aeroplane had left the skies unruffled, but in its trail seven plovers disappeared in the distance.

The sun, rising from the Ægean, hurled spears of fire at the golden cross gleaming undimmed and undaunted on the marble peak of Mount Athos.

THE END

Lightning Source UK Ltd.
Milton Keynes UK
UKHW052044240221
379317UK00015B/118